ALSO BY JUNO RUSHDAN

Final Hour
Every Last Breath
Nothing to Fear

Turn the Tide romantic suspense anthology

NOTHING
TO
FEAR

JUNO
RUSHDAN

sourcebooks
casablanca

Published by Sourcebooks Casablanca, an imprint of Sourcebooks
P.O. Box 4410, Naperville, Illinois 60567-4410
(630) 961-3900
sourcebooks.com

Printed and bound in Canada.
MBP 10 9 8 7 6 5 4 3 2 1

GRAY BOX HEADQUARTERS, NORTHERN VIRGINIA
SATURDAY, JUNE 29, 9:58 P.M. EDT

CODE NAME: COBALT

The man locked in the interrogation room had to die tonight, or he'd ruin everything.

Most sins whispered in the darkness, but murder was a bullhorn echo in broad daylight. Under different circumstances, eliminating an assassin—a terrorist—would be hailed as just. But the avalanche of lies Cobalt had been telling—wearing two faces for so long neither were real, the depth of betrayal, committing treason—could never be forgiven. Not that there had been a choice.

Dread burned in Cobalt's chest, but determination overrode it. Killing Aleksander Novak wasn't about money, ideology, or ego. This boiled down to something far more basic: survival.

Cobalt entered the mark's personal identification number into the keypad on the server room door. The analyst was so trusting and never hid her PIN when she used it. If the entry log was checked later, *and it would be*, this breadcrumb would lead down a carefully planted trail.

Inside, Cobalt found the correct button on the control

panel and shut off power in the currently unmanned observation room. The camera in Novak's adjacent holding room was still on, but the surveillance feed was now dead. Nothing would be recorded.

How long would the window of opportunity last? Minutes?

There was zero margin for error. Novak had to be silenced permanently. The Gray Box could never learn the truth about Daedalus. *Or me.*

Cobalt walked at a brisk but steady pace toward the opposite end of the sprawling subterranean facility. Heart at a cold gallop, Cobalt risked a furtive over-the-shoulder glance.

Fear was a constant stalker, a cruel companion.

Rounding the corner to the main corridor, Cobalt braced for anything. *Be empty.*

No one loitered in the hall making small talk. Everyone was exhausted from the grueling mission, writing after-action reports, storing gear, eager to go home.

Cobalt slipped into the break room and released a heavy breath, fingers tingling from adrenaline. *Don't stop moving. Not a second to spare.*

After pouring a cup of coffee, Cobalt dumped the poison in and stirred. The mushroom-colored granules dissolved and would only leave a mild aftertaste that'd be dismissed as a poor brew. Cobalt grabbed a box of doughnuts, hustled to the interrogation room, and opened the door.

Novak looked up, premature relief gleaming in his bloodshot eyes at the coffee and food he'd requested. Face bruised, chain restraints rattling, he had the nerve to flash a gloating smile.

Ignorant psychopath. Novak thought he was going to receive a get-out-of-jail-free card in the morning. Instead, he was getting an express ticket straight to hell. Cobalt set the items down, snuck a quick look into the hall—*all clear*—and chanced waiting outside.

Running into trouble here would mean game over. Thirty seconds for the poison to work, but it only took one sloppy second to get caught. Cobalt hid the rubber-band tension stretching every muscle taut, trying not to snap. Desperation set in and thickened. It was impossible to walk this tightrope forever, but right now, containing this disaster was all that mattered.

Cobalt put on latex gloves, withdrew a hotel keycard— swiped from Novak's confiscated belongings before it was inventoried—snapped it in half, and ducked back into the room.

Now the messy part. Cobalt ignored Novak's vacant stare and sawed the jagged edge of plastic across his wrists, his skin still warm. Deep vertical cuts along the radial arteries for a speedy bleed out. Blood flowed across the table, dripping on the tile floor into a pool.

The stage was set for what at first glance would appear to be a suicide. Outright murder would trigger an immediate lockdown of the facility and everyone would be detained.

Heart racing, mind clear, insides numb, Cobalt took the doughnuts and coffee for disposal.

Bruce Sanborn, director of the Gray Box, was a shrewd, careful man. The director would order an autopsy and begin counterintelligence polygraphs as soon as possible.

Both would take days, time Cobalt needed to set the

fail-safe in motion. Shocking how easy it was to form a plan on the fly after hearing about Novak's pending deal.

Then again, this wasn't the first time Cobalt had plotted and killed to survive. And before this was finished, it wouldn't be the last.

Everyone has been polygraphed," Gideon Stone said, flipping a switch to tint the conference room's glass walls opaque, "and put under surveillance."

"We still have nothing." Strain leaked into Maddox Kinkade's voice. Their team was undermanned and overwhelmed, stretched to the breaking point. "We won't win playing this long game."

Maddox was right. This approach was only working to the advantage of their mole.

Gideon sat at the touch screen table and brought up the final autopsy report, swiping through the digital pages. Conclusive results indicated homicide. A fast-acting poison that mimicked natural causes had killed Aleksander Novak, one so rare it was missed on the first toxicology panel.

Someone in his unit, someone they trusted with their lives, had murdered the one person capable of helping them discover the identity of the traitor—right under their noses here in the ultrasecure facility.

The obscene moxie that must've taken made Gideon's blood simmer.

"We need to get up close and personal with each

suspect." Maddox looked around the table. "Run this to ground as quickly as possible."

Only the six people sitting in that room had solid alibis for the estimated time of death and could be relied on without question. They were a close-knit crew and had been through the thick of it together.

"Let's deal with Dad first," Maddox said.

Slim odds that Bruce Sanborn, director of the Gray Box, was guilty of treason and murdering a suspect in custody. Dad, as they called him behind his back, cared too deeply about his people to endanger them. Still, they had to do their due diligence and investigate everyone who had access and opportunity, including the boss.

"Dad keeps secrets locked up tighter than gold in the Federal Reserve Bank," Gideon said. "And he's the best at tradecraft."

"Who has balls big enough to take him?" Maddox asked.

"I think it's safe to say I have the biggest pair." Castle Kinkade, Maddox's brother, dragged a hand across his bald brown head. Nobody laughed. He'd proven his mettle often enough in the field, putting his ex-Navy SEAL experience to use. "But to make it fair, whoever is left last without a target should get the headache of taking Sanborn."

Across the table, Alistair Allen clucked his tongue. "Nice try, Elephant Balls." His posh James Bond accent clashed with his hipster haircut and grunge attire. "As Sanborn's protégé, you're the best choice to get close enough without triggering his Spidey senses."

Steel-toe boots clubbed a vacant chair as John Reece threw his feet up into it. "I'm all for fair, but that's a valid point. I think you're stuck with the short end of the stick."

Castle folded his thick arms over his linebacker chest. "All right, the hot potato is mine."

"You can handle the heat." Maddox fiddled with her new engagement ring. The massive rock must've cost her fiancé a kidney. "Next, Sybil Parker. Her epic fail is the reason we're here."

Parker's position as insider threat monitor was protected. The ITM and her henchmen were watchdogs, blessed with unfettered access to mission details and the authority to surveil any computer system and phone line to prevent insider threats—to catch spies. The irony.

Complicating this shitshow, the director of national intelligence had hired the ITM three-pack, and only he could fire them, making the lot untouchable without irrefutable evidence.

"I'm up for the challenge," Reece said.

"Got a death wish?" Maddox snickered. "That praying mantis will eat you for a midday snack. It won't be easy to play Parker. She'll anticipate it."

Reece tugged down a ball cap that read *I'm Your Huckleberry*. "No worries. I got this. I'll approach her with *serious concerns*," he said, using air quotes, "about her nemesis."

"No love lost between her and Sanborn," Sean "Ares" Whitlock said. The guy had dark eyes, dark hair, and an even darker presence that'd make the average man wet himself. "That's catnip Parker won't be able to resist. Guess you're not an insult to our profession after all."

Reece grinned and flipped him off. "And I'll try to dig deeper into her minions."

Stand-up guy taking one for the team. Gideon gave him a two-finger salute.

"Maddox," Ares said, his voice full of grit and gravel, "you should take Doc."

No secret the man had a thing for their resident CDC scientist, Emily "Doc" Duvall, but she avoided Ares as if he had a communicable disease. Ares obviously didn't intend to let the hound dogs he worked with sniff around the one lady he wanted and couldn't have.

"Doc is dying to be BFFs." Maddox winced. "But it gives me the perfect in. Okay."

No one would deny Ares a favor. Going along was sure as heck easier than opposing him.

"At the top of the list after Parker," Maddox said, "is Willow Harper."

Gideon's pulse spiked, his insides doing a one-eighty just hearing her name.

"A sharp cryptologist. Talented programmer. Skilled hacker." Maddox rubbed her brow. "I don't get a malicious read from Harper, but she's a loner. A textbook red flag. And she made critical mistakes during the last op that can't be ignored. She was also the one who redesigned our firewalls." Knowing gazes were exchanged. "She could dig into our network without leaving a trace."

All true, but Gideon's intuition—or whatever he had relied on to stay alive in this brutal job for ten years—protested. Willow Harper was no mole. Or a murderer.

There was an awkwardness about her that he found genuine. Refreshing. Her modest charm hid a loneliness he recognized. But he kept his distance. She was refined and had a gift for creating elegant programs. He was rough around the edges and had a knack for terminating threats. They were different breeds.

"I can try reeling her in with my charm and repartee," Alistair said. "If a friendly approach doesn't work, I can always use a bit of pressure to crack her odd shell."

Gideon choked on the chewing gum slipping down his throat. *What the—*

"I should have a go at her," Ares said. "I'm the one who's been surveilling her."

A snowball's chance in hell either would succeed. Ares was a bull in a china shop, and his atomic intimidation factor would render her mute. Alistair's crass tongue and droll facade wouldn't scratch her shell. The team couldn't squander time on the speed bumps of their failures.

"Applying pressure is my specialty." Gideon's voice was low and cool. He *was* the only one in the group trained in interrogation. The cruel kind at CIA black sites. "I'll take Willow."

The room flatlined. Everyone's attention snapped to him, wary looks surfacing.

"*Willow?*" Ares chortled. Even his grim laugh could scare someone shitless.

Gideon could count on one hand the times he'd spoken to her beyond a passing salutation. On the rare occasions he had mentioned her, it'd been by surname. How he thought of her was a different story. Letting that slip was unlike him.

Gideon shrugged. "Getting on a first-name basis is logical. I'll need to get close." *Willow* had rolled off his tongue smoother and sweeter than soft-serve ice cream. Something about her inspired whimsical thoughts and deranged hope for a drop of goodness in his life.

Maddox's insightful green-eyed gaze pinned him. His best friend saw through people, picked up on the things others sought to hide, and she knew him better than anyone. He wanted to squirm under the dissection of her scalpel-sharp scrutiny but merely flexed his jaw.

"If Harper *isn't* the leak, she doesn't deserve you on her tail." Maddox shook her head. "I've seen how you look at her. I know how you'll handle this."

Really? He didn't. Arching a brow, he waited.

"The lover angle," she said. "It's the wrong play. We don't know enough about her—whether she's into girls or guys or no one at all. And if you're her type and she's *not* our traitor, heaven help her."

He knew what she was saying. One-night stands and no attachments suited him. No one got burned. No one got a chance to see the truth about him—not since his late wife, and she'd been terrified.

"Give me some credit. I'll feel her out and determine how to play it, but the reality is *lovers* fosters intimacy faster than other methods. Yields more reliable results too."

Not that he'd ever worked a honey trap before, and sleeping with Willow hadn't been on his agenda. Walking into the conference room, he hadn't even planned on getting within two feet of her, never mind taking her as a target. But after observing her the last three years—her unfaltering work ethic, how she interacted with others, avoided office politics—he had an advantage the others didn't. He knew Willow's character.

Maddox drew her dark curls into a ponytail, accentuating the striking features of her golden-brown face. "I have a hunch Harper is innocent. If she's cleared, she still has to work with you. The situation could get messy. Ugly. I don't like it."

Gideon shared her concern. There was something wholesome yet complex about Willow. He wanted to protect her, not hurt her. Out of their other choices for the job, he was the best one.

"We're at war," Castle said. "We were supposed to be impenetrable, but the enemy is embedded, has been fooling *us* for years. If this isn't resolved ASAP, heads are going to roll."

A mole inside the CIA or FBI would be bad, but this was worse. Their off-the-books unit operated beyond the black-and-white lines of other agencies and at times beyond the law. They were sanctioned for direct action on foreign and domestic soil with access to the most classified data. A traitor selling secrets meant getting burned in the field, being spoon-fed false intel, and ultimately threat of exposure. Nasty possibilities piled up fast. This was a political nightmare that could end careers, starting at the very top.

"We don't have the luxury of indulging a hunch," Alistair said. "Sometimes we do bad things for good reasons."

"This isn't really your forte, Gideon," Maddox said, pausing as if waiting for him to agree, but he held her gaze and his tongue. "Flirting and finesse," she finally added.

Gideon was good at many things and some of those began with the letter *F*, but only his best friend knew he couldn't flirt *or* finesse his way out of a paper bag.

To keep the others off Willow, however, he'd be willing to try.

"Are you kidding? If anyone can quickly get that

analyst to lower her guard, whether it's inside or outside the bedroom"—Castle hiked a thumb at him—"it's our Golden Boy."

The nickname prickled Gideon's nerves, poking fun at his college days as a quarterback as well as fair looks that had always been more of a curse than a blessing.

The guys thought Gideon was an expert pickup artist based on his appearance. In truth, he was a magnet for flirtatious bombshells and let *them* pick him up instead. He was good at asking questions, not at having bullshit conversations.

"I'm capable of getting close and finding answers without…complications," Gideon said.

"Capable, maybe, but not without complications. I'll take her instead of handling Doc."

"Our leak divulged classified mission details, compromised you and nearly cost your life." Ares stabbed the air at Maddox. "Harper's at the top of the list of suspects, and we're worried about her feelings? Lives are on the line, national security is at risk, and the clock's ticking. We find the mole, no matter the cost."

An uncomfortable silence settled around the room.

"Gideon takes Harper," Ares said. "You'll keep Doc."

Maddox raised both palms. "Fine." She slid her hand in her pocket and dumped a pile of memory sticks in a clatter on the glass table.

Flash drives loaded with a cloning program. The small device plugged into the USB port of a personal computer and would copy the hard drive. Those were courtesy of Maddox's fiancé, who worked at a private security company that specialized in corporate intelligence gathering.

"Anything I should know about her?" Gideon asked Ares as he swiped a flash drive.

Everyone would assume *anything not in the surveillance report* that Gideon should've read by now, but snooping on Willow's personal life was a temptation he'd resisted.

"She wrote in a notebook two nights ago. Keeps it in her bedside table. I haven't had a chance to break in and look at it with that old bulldog on patrol. And she has insomnia."

Something they had in common.

"You don't need me for the rest." Gideon threw on his jacket, covering his holstered Maxim 9, and shoved through the door before bickering kicked up over the remaining targets.

The sooner he proved Willow's innocence, whittling down the list of suspects, the better.

Muted blue partitions, beige walls, and pale-gray carpet gave the interior offices a serene atmosphere. News chatter flowed from nine large-screen TVs lining the main wall of Intel. Gideon glimpsed a report on a tropical depression over the Bahamas as he skirted the periphery of the open layout, bypassing small talk with the others. Only Willow was on his radar.

He spotted her nestled in a remote corner, facing the wall. She was typing on her dual-monitor workstation, automatic-fire keystrokes. A sleek, chocolate-brown bun with never a hair out of place showcased her slender neck and sophisticated string of pearls. But the vulnerability of her position—her six exposed and earbuds in—grated on his operational wiring.

Worst of all, the angle at which she sat deprived him of seeing her face as he approached.

Whenever he set eyes on her, he smiled, even if he didn't show it on the outside.

He hesitated behind her, within arm's reach. Her long, unpainted fingernails clicked keys in a blur. Lines of source code materialized. Interrupting her would be like disturbing Picasso.

In the screen's reflection, her gaze darted up to his. She swiveled, giving him her profile, and yanked out an earbud. A lithe leg extended from her pencil skirt.

She wasn't a classic knockout, but her haunting beauty knocked him on his heels.

"Yes?" Her surprised look read pure professional. "Did you need something?"

Now to turn on the charm. Too bad he didn't have any. "Hey, I was wondering, would you maybe like to get a drink with me after work?"

"No, thank you."

Ouch. He blinked like a dumbstruck idiot. Willow had little reason to be interested in him. She was demure, brainy, better than he deserved, and most of all, she knew what he really was, but he hadn't expected such a rapid shootdown.

He stuffed his hands in his jeans pockets, regrouping. "I was impressed with your work on the last op, hacking the cell phone. You helped us find Maddox. Means a lot. Can I buy you dinner as thanks? Or a cup of coffee? I know a cozy café. Good music. Great espressos."

She stared at him with those enigmatic hazel eyes, the barest flush to her porcelain skin, looking sweet enough to eat. "No need to thank me. I was doing my job. That's why I get paid."

Damn, she intrigued him. The sensation was unfamiliar. But at this rate, he'd have better luck playing Russian roulette than finessing his way past her defenses.

03

Willow sat at her desk, stunned. Gideon Stone was talking to her and not about a mission.

Sometimes she overheard people call him pretty, but she didn't understand why. There was a brutality to everything about him. From his black ops call sign—*Reaper*—down to his ferocious good looks: a lean face, sharp angles, bold features, and a tumble of hair the color of sunshine glinting off ice. Even his eyes were a severe blue—the palest shade, so arresting she never dared look too long for fear of staring.

Not staring was a rule she'd learned not to break, since it made people uncomfortable.

The bridge of his once-broken nose was millimeters flatter than it should've been. A slight crook hinted at the violence in his life, but the flaw added character to his face.

Humanized him.

Whenever she ventured close to Gideon, caution drummed inside her. The kind smart people heeded, and she had a genius-level IQ. She was likely to say the wrong thing, while he never seemed to want to say anything to her at all.

"No drinks. No dinner. No coffee," he said, his brows drawing together in a look of concentration.

What was wrong with him? Nothing ever rattled his iceberg composure.

She was the one with social issues.

Perhaps she shouldn't have said *no*, but she didn't drink alcohol, didn't exceed four cups of coffee a day unless working overtime, and it was absurd to thank her for doing her job. Right?

Did he really want to have dinner with her? Why? She'd smiled at him once, after taking a class on how to make friends, and a scowl had darkened his face in return.

"What are you listening to?" He pointed to her earbuds.

She pulled the other one out, tossing them on her desk. "Nothing." The always-on TVs and chatter from her colleagues clogged her thoughts. The high-fidelity earplugs lowered the decibels of the environment to a natural sound—clean and clear—allowing her to focus.

Gideon traded his typical grimace for a feral sort of grin. At least, she hoped it was a grin. His mouth curved up, lifting his incredible cheekbones, but the rest of his face had a strained expression disturbingly similar to the one her dad got when constipated.

"What type of code are you working on?" He gestured with his chin at her computer.

"Something new." Eager to discuss anything that wouldn't trip her up, she turned, pointing at one monitor. Source code was safe.

Whenever she talked too long, it was evident the motherboard of her brain was wired differently. People called her odd, peculiar. Her sisters preferred the term *dweeb*.

"I call it the Pandora Program. It'll detect and flag any internal security vulnerabilities in our operations, so I can mitigate the possibility of us being compromised from the inside."

He stepped up behind her, resting a hand on the back of her chair. The unexpected heat from his body tickled her spine. He always looked too removed to touch, glacier-cold, but the warmth radiating from him now was undeniable.

Clenching her thighs, she was tempted to brush against his arm for the barest contact but scooted to the edge of her seat instead. "I'm about forty-six working hours from testing it."

"Wow. The program will be ready in a week?"

"Less. Three point two-eight days. I've been putting in extra hours." It still wasn't enough. They had a traitor in the unit, as everyone knew after the debacle with the dead guy. The program needed to be ready yesterday.

"You're amazing," Gideon said.

"It's just a program." Her computer alarm beeped. *Six thirty already?* "I have to go."

She silenced the chime, saved her work, and logged off, removing her ID badge from the card reader. As she slipped on her heels, she spun the miniature globe designed out of binary digits that sat on her desk—the last thing she always did in her routine.

If only the world were as simple as the two-symbol coding system.

Snagging her purse, she stood and turned around.

Gideon's expression went slack, his eyes growing wide. "What happened to your face?" He closed in, swallowing her comfort zone like a black hole.

She staggered back, bumping into her desk, and touched the cut on her cheek near her left ear. "It's just a nick. He threw a dish and the broken pieces went flying. It was an accident."

"Who?" Gideon reached for her cheek, and she sidestepped him. "Your boyfriend?"

Boyfriend? She'd only have one of those in her dreams. Unfortunately, she never dreamed.

"I-I'm going to be late." She scrambled into the aisle, avoiding him. "I have to go."

He strolled alongside her for some unfathomable reason. His strong physique and weightless stride—propelled by athletic grace—projected his lethal ability to handle anything.

"I'll walk you out to your car." A declaration, not a question.

Her stomach somersaulted. "What? Why?"

It took nine minutes to get from her desk to the parking lot, depending on the wait for the elevator. An extra two to her car since she parked on the far end. That meant for eleven minutes, she'd have to talk. *With him.* Concentrate on the rules to seem nice. She wasn't unfriendly, but things got lost in translation.

Her rib cage tightened, making it hard to breathe. "There's no need to walk me out."

"I'm leaving anyway. It's no trouble." Gideon peered down at her and the intense look in his piercing blue eyes sent butterflies dancing in her belly.

She stared at him, trying to recall why it was a bad idea, and tripped over her feet. *Gah!*

Tearing her gaze away, she focused on what was going on around her, determined to pull it together and not fall flat on her face.

Holding center stage in the middle of Intel as she passed around a platter of fudge was Janet Price, the director's assistant. She was a Rubenesque woman who had an effortless way of bringing people together over her homemade dishes.

Gideon stopped and joined the gaggle. Willow considered hurrying to the elevator, but she needed to work on being socially acceptable in the office. So she stayed, following etiquette about mingling for a minute or two to avoid coming across as antisocial.

Laughter floated in the air over the background noise of the news. Doc and Janet giggled, practically arm-in-arm and breathless over one of Daniel Cutter's Marine Force Recon stories.

On and on Daniel went. His stories always sounded the same, not at all funny to Willow. She never got their humor.

Voracious hands shoveled chocolate into eager mouths. Chatter flowed easy as a breeze.

Willow swallowed past the tightening in her throat. Sometimes she longed to be a sail riding that breeze but usually found herself a feather adrift in it. Social codes and cues she couldn't decipher layered their conversations. There was a wall between Willow and everyone else. She didn't know how to break it down, and trying was overwhelming.

Gideon swiped a couple pieces of fudge, and a slow-burning smile spread across his face. An odd tingle gathered in Willow's chest, making her toes bunch in her shoes.

"Janet," Gideon said, "your fudge is the best."

Everyone else chimed in with a chorus of compliments.

Willow's obligated two minutes of office mingling were up. This was the perfect moment to skedaddle to the elevator. Alone.

She pivoted and nearly bumped into Amanda Woodrow, the lead analyst.

"Willow," Amanda said, smiling. "I'm glad I caught you. I wanted to talk to you."

"Not now. I need to leave." Willow rolled her pearls between her fingers, hoping her honesty didn't sound rude. Amanda was a lovely supervisor, never giving her a hard time about special accommodations like the setup of her workstation. Willow didn't want to offend her.

"It'll just take a sec. You're doing a great job. I'm really impressed with the counterintelligence program you're developing."

As Amanda kept praising her, taking far longer than a second, Willow got a queasy ache in her stomach. She had to end this conversation. In a book she'd read, one technique was to change the subject with unexpected flattery followed by a direct farewell. But what to say? Her gaze roamed over Amanda's desk, past colorful crayon drawings and to the photo of her five-year-old son, finally with a full head of hair since his leukemia had gone into remission.

"I like your son's curls," Willow said, cutting off Amanda. "They're really pretty."

"Uh." Amanda's brow furrowed. "Thank you."

"See you tomorrow."

Before Willow took ten steps, Gideon stalked off from his friends, waving goodbye. He was at her side again, stirring unease in her and, at the same time, a shocking sense of comfort.

What in *The Twilight Zone* was happening?

Gideon popped the chocolate in his mouth, moaning *mmmm*, an intense look on his face, fingers curling as he savored it. Oh, she'd love to melt in his mouth like that. *Mmmm*, indeed.

But even if she managed to get through a conversation without babbling or blowing it by being herself, she'd heard through office gossip about the way he picked up women at Rocky's Bar. For one night only. Reminded her of a Broadway musical song her mom had loved.

"*One night only*," she sang under her breath, "*come on, baby.*"

"What'd you say?" Gideon licked the remnants of chocolate from his fingers.

"Oh, nothing." Her cheeks burned. *Shut. Up.*

"Why didn't you take any fudge? Don't like chocolate?"

"I love chocolate, but I don't eat homemade stuff other people bring in."

"Why not?"

"I don't know if their kitchen is clean, if they have cats or wash their hands before cooking. Amanda told me her son, Jackson, sneezed in cake batter once, and she still baked it."

Willow's skin crawled with the heebie-jeebies.

"Don't you have a dog?"

"Cats and dogs are different. Cats climb all over everything. But no, I don't have a dog."

Gideon nodded with another constipated expression. She bit her lip, quickening her step.

In the central hall, they passed Director Sanborn talking to two forensic accountants who'd been ordered to report here even though it was a holiday. The chief wanted to follow the money to find the mole by auditing everyone. The pressure on him was immense. Surely, the director of national intelligence and the president, the only two people Sanborn answered to, were looking at this situation under a microscope.

The chief was a good man and always looked out for her. She didn't want to let him down. Hopefully, her new program would help catch the traitor.

Gideon tapped the button for the elevator and stood behind her, where she'd have to look over her shoulder to see him. Glancing at the carpet, she slipped her purse strap across her body and peeked back to glimpse his boots. He had big feet to match the rest of him.

"Sorry I held you up at your desk." His warm breath brushed the nape of her neck, and her skin tingled.

"It's okay." She fought the dangerous impulse to look back.

"Are you hurrying off to an appointment?"

"Sort of." After the last around-the-clock mission, she'd made a promise to be home for dinner every night this week and make fresh-cooked meals.

The ten-inch reinforced-steel elevator doors opened. She stepped inside with a shaky exhale and slunk to the far corner, needing a little distance between herself and him.

Gideon strode into the car. The heavy doors slid shut with a soft thud. He leaned against the side of the elevator and crossed his arms. Light danced off his hair, forming a halo, but his hard body and smooth swagger spelled unabashed sinner rather than saint.

His gaze homed in on hers. A shiver chased through her down to her thighs.

"You never told me what happened to your face," he said.

"Yes, I did." Her voice was the barest thread of sound.

"You neglected to mention who's responsible."

"It's none of your business."

He pressed his lips together and lowered his head for a second. "You're right. I don't mean to pry. I'm concerned, that's all." He pushed off the wall and moved toward her. The stark power of his impossible-to-ignore masculinity drove her feet backward.

"There's nothing to be concerned about," she said.

"Then what happened? A guy threw something at you?"

"Not at me." Her nerves drummed. "It's personal. I don't discuss my private life with coworkers." The steel wall at her spine stopped her retreat. "And we're not friends."

He halted shy of breaching her personal space, a good foot between them, and stared down at her for so long with his brows scrunched, she wondered what he'd say next, if anything.

Then he gave her a sexy, lopsided grin.

A zing speared her belly. She clutched her purse against her stomach to steady herself.

"You don't have many friends here, do you?" His tone was soft as velvet.

"No. Not many." Zero friends, at work or otherwise. Her dad didn't count.

"Sounds lonely. Might be nice to let someone get to know you, spend time with you."

His warm smile spread, lighting up his face, thawing

his icy eyes. Her mouth went dry, and she licked her lips. If he'd been within tongue's reach, she would've licked *him*.

"I'd like to be that someone."

Her mind pinwheeled. "Huh?" She'd heard him, but he might as well have spoken Greek.

His perfect smile dimmed. "I'm saying that I'd like for us to be friends."

She managed a swallow, loud enough to punctuate the thickening tension.

Gideon's gaze fell to where she was clutching her purse like a lifeline and back up to her face. "Do I scare you?"

"Sometimes." Big. Fat. Lie. He scared the heck out of her all the time.

She'd involuntarily memorized his personnel file. Information had a way of wallpapering itself to her mind. Age: thirty-two. Height: six-three. Weight: two-ten. Trained by the CIA. Sole Gray Box helicopter pilot. The specifics of all his assignments. She'd even hacked into the sealed parts of his record and devoured every nugget that'd been redacted. Savage details, extreme things he'd done out of duty and in self-defense. How he'd killed with his bare hands and once ripped a man's carotid out with his teeth.

She was as frightened by him as she was attracted to him. What did that say about her?

He backed away at her admission.

Frowning, he tugged at his shirt collar as if it'd gotten too tight and raked back his unruly forelock. She wanted to erase the uncharacteristic red dots of color surfacing on his cheeks.

"You don't need to be afraid of me." That was the first

time she'd heard his voice sound so low and shaky. "I'd never hurt you, Willow."

Another hard swallow. He'd said her first name. She didn't think he knew it. "I didn't mean it like that. I know you wouldn't hurt me."

"Is it okay to walk you to your car? I can hang back in the lobby if it's not."

Who wouldn't want a hot guy walking them to their car? It just didn't make an iota of sense why he wanted to. "It's okay."

The elevator opened onto the same floor. They hadn't moved. She hadn't pressed the button for the lobby and neither had Gideon. She was going to be late.

Castle, a hardnosed operative built like a howitzer, entered and hit the button for the lobby. He jerked his chin up, and Gideon did likewise.

The elevator cage crowded in, and she wanted to run off. Gripping her purse strap, she watched the floor numbers illuminate as they ascended from the secure sixth sublevel. She'd rather look at Gideon but couldn't pry her gaze from the elevator's display until the doors opened. It was one of many things she couldn't explain to others about her spectrum disorder.

The elevator dinged and the doors slid open. Castle strode out first. Gideon stepped off at her side. Her kitten heels clicked across the smooth sea of concrete polished to a mirror finish. The sharp sound echoed in the austere, high-ceilinged lobby.

Castle swiped his ID card along one of the electronic turnstiles that sandwiched the metal detector and strolled outside. Gideon waved to the armed plainclothes guards seated behind the ivory marble desk, addressing both by their first names.

Maybe it meant nothing that he knew hers as well. Something inside her deflated.

A sign embossed with *Helios Importing & Exporting* in elegant gold script hung on the wall. The business front provided a plausible explanation for the specialized vehicles on the compound and the helicopter in the warehouse behind the main building and a credible cover story to family members for operatives traveling at a moment's notice.

She swiped her ID card. The plexiglass flaps of the turnstile retracted, and she walked through. Gideon hurried ahead and pushed the door open for her, standing on the threshold. She brushed the steel frame on the way out to avoid physical contact that might be too personal at work—yet another rule.

The slap of broiling heat and unforgiving humidity had her blouse sticking to her dampening skin before they reached the tree-shaded parking lot.

"Where are you headed for your appointment?" he asked.

"Wolf Trap."

"Where's home?"

"Wolf Trap."

She rushed to her car. Her pulse had a wild, skittering beat. He asked a lot of questions—twenty since he'd come to her desk. It was kind of nice. Answering questions was easier than racking her brain for something interesting to say. But his tone on the elevator had delved deeper toward *want to take your clothes off* than *want to grab a latte*, if she hadn't misread things—as she often did. Now he stayed two feet away as if he were the one afraid—to get too close to her.

Maybe she shouldn't have admitted that he scared her, but she wasn't worried about her physical safety with him. She probably messed up the entire conversation, acted the wrong way, said the wrong thing. *As usual.* What if he never talked to her again?

Regret burned her face. She pressed a palm to her forehead. "Tomorrow, if you need me to do research for you, I don't mind."

He nodded, his expression unreadable, those blue eyes deadly serious. "Sure."

"No need to be my friend. It's my job." *Idiot. Such a poor choice of words, although true.* It might be *really* nice to have him for a friend. She unlocked her car door. "I mean, I'm happy to help you."

"Everyone needs an ally, Willow."

Ally? What a strange way of putting it.

She hopped into her older yellow VW bug and brought the engine to life with a sputtering rumble. She cranked the air-conditioning and fastened her seat belt over her purse strap.

With her hands at the ten and two o'clock positions, she pulled off. She glimpsed Gideon in the rearview mirror, watching her drive out of the lot. He pivoted as if to step away but then lowered his head. Staring at the ground, he knelt and touched the asphalt.

She turned onto the single lane dotted with twelve-inch diameter silver disks. Headed to the front gate, she noted the sign that warned against exceeding thirty-five miles per hour. Higher speeds would activate the retractable pneumatic bollards—electrohydraulic stainless-steel pillars—that'd pop up from the ground. One of many security features of their lockdown protocol, also intended to prevent hostile intrusion.

Huge shade trees lined the road up to the six-foot rebar-reinforced concrete barriers that edged the first few hundred yards of the entrance. The automatic armored gate slid open.

The traffic light changed from green to yellow. She punched the gas, zipping by the small manned gatehouse, and cleared the light as she sped down the access road to hit the highway.

The George Washington Parkway ran along the Potomac River northwest to Langley, where it bled into I-495. Blowing past the fifty-miles-per-hour sign on the GWP, she eased off the gas. A slight incline slowed the car to sixty. She merged onto the two-lane highway. With the holiday, traffic would either flow smoothly or cramp in a blink. Hoping for the former, she switched on cruise control for fuel efficiency. Every nickel saved added up.

Drawing in a breath, she prepped for sensory triggers. She had difficulty processing certain sounds. Sirens overloaded her synapses, and the unbearable noise of metal on metal was crippling. Growing up, if an emergency services vehicle passed with sirens blaring, lights flashing, her sensory meltdowns in front of other kids had infuriated her sisters.

Her father never wanted her to drive, but she had no choice if she wanted to work at the NSA. In time, her excellent driving record had lessened his qualms.

The parkway merged into I-495, looping the urban

fringes of Virginia and Maryland, encircling DC. The southbound strip of highway construction wasn't hampering her commute, but she hated the claustrophobic effect of the concrete barricades funneling four streams of traffic into three and blocking the shoulder. Barring any jams, she wouldn't be too late.

Her car zipped up on a white minivan. She sighed, glancing at the adjacent lane to see if she could maneuver over. No such luck. She tapped the brake, but her car didn't slow. The cruise control should've deactivated, but the light stayed on and the speedometer didn't budge as her car devoured the pavement, getting closer to the van. *This can't be happening.* She'd taken the car for routine service last month, and everything had been fine this morning.

She jabbed the button and pumped the brake again. The ABS light blinked on. The distance to the minivan closed at a staggering rate. She stomped her foot, and something in the brake assembly shifted this time, the spongy response giving way to no resistance.

The brakes are gone. Her heart pounded in a dizzying rush, and fear overrode disbelief.

A glimmer of light bounced inside the van. Cartoons played on two flip-down screens. Kids were inside, and she was rushing toward them with no brakes and nowhere to pull over.

Panic buzzed in her skull. What was she going to do?

An opening appeared. She darted behind a truck, despite the position drawing her further from the exit lane. Blocked on all sides, the speedometer snagged on sixty, and her options dwindled to nil. Her car barreled toward the back of the eighteen-wheeler. Horror flooded her.

She jammed down on the brake, the pedal to the floor, and prayed for a miracle. Honking, she signaled to change lanes, first trying to the left, then right, but no one let her in on either side.

The distance between her and the back of the truck's high steel wall shrank. Two hundred feet dropped to a hundred. Eighty. Forty. Blood roared in her ears. Her stomach knotted.

If no one would let her change lanes, she'd have to force her way in.

A hairsbreadth from impact, she laid on the horn and swerved into the HOV lane.

04

NORTHERN VIRGINIA
THURSDAY, JULY 4, 6:50 P.M. EDT

The slick puddle on Willow's parking spot, oily with a slight brown tint, was brake fluid. Gideon estimated almost a quart had leaked onto the ground.

He zoomed down the G. W. Parkway in his Jeep Wrangler, weaving through traffic, headed toward Wolf Trap. Gideon had spotted Willow taking the turnoff to the Beltway, I-495, bearing south—a treacherous roadway with random pockets of congestion. If she stayed on 495 too long, she'd hit a choked patch and risk hurting herself or someone else.

A cold pit split open in his gut. Accelerating off the southbound ramp, he scoured the condensed three lanes for her car.

Come on. Where are you?

A blip of yellow in the raging current of steel hooked his gaze but disappeared in front of a SUV before he identified the make. He swore, slapping the steering wheel.

The car on his left sped up, and he zipped over. Hazard lights flashed on a yellow Beetle trapped in a tight rush of traffic.

Willow.

Her bug passed a semi and cut across into the centerline

of the roadway, riding the edge of the right lane, honking. The other car held firm, not letting her in.

Stuck in the middle of the two lanes, her vehicle rammed a black sedan. Horns wailed. Her VW bumped the car again. The sedan accelerated, and she slipped into the slow lane but just missed an exit.

A chill peppered the nape of his neck. She must be frantic with terror.

His wife's last moments, helpless as his truck lost control and tumbled over the side of an embankment, must've been horrifying. He hadn't been in the vehicle with Kelli, but the accident had nevertheless been his fault.

Despite their laundry list of marital problems, Kelli hadn't deserved to go out that way. No one did, but especially not Willow. The only thing Willow was guilty of was being afraid of his advances. She'd shrunk away from his touch, stark fear in her face, but something else, too, had glimmered in her eyes, brought a flush to her cheeks. If he hadn't been thrown for a double loop by her reaction, he would've realized what the fluid on the ground was sooner.

He slammed a fist on the dash.

As he rolled down the window, exhaust fumes hit him. He stuck his arm out, waving the car with the smoky transmission to move over while he laid on the horn until the vehicle changed lanes.

Up ahead on the parkway, traffic pinched into a grinding halt, dotted with steady red brake lights. The gridlock would stop her car, but the number of injuries and possible fatalities would be high.

Another exit sign appeared on the right. This was

Willow's last chance to get off before the jam. She swerved, taking the ramp. The yellow car raked the guardrail, screeching around the bend.

He signaled and beat on his horn, slashing in between cars to follow her.

Whipping around the curved off-ramp, the tail end of his Jeep swung out. Tires squealed, burning rubber. He wrestled the wheel and straightened out of the power slide.

He had to reach her. Help her somehow. Maybe it was his pent-up guilt over Kelli, all the things he'd done wrong that led to her accident. Or maybe it was simply how he was wired.

Not once in his life had he sat on the sideline when he should've been in the game. Never left a battle brother or sister hanging—not under fire, not under duress, not under any circumstances. He'd do everything possible to prevent anything bad from happening to Willow.

Aluminum scraped against steel as Willow's car grated the guardrail. Sparks flared. The agonizing cry of metal clashing together stabbed her eardrums, and spiky pain bloomed in her head.

She squeezed her eyes shut and let go of the wheel, pressing her palms to her ears.

The metallic shriek drilled into Willow's skull, jarring her senses. Her muscles hurt, paralyzed, like her body was caught in a steel-jaw trap. Her thoughts garbled in a wave of static.

Then a sudden, abrupt silence fell. Blessed peace pried her eyes open.

Blinding light cleared to a cloudy world as her car nosedived down a long slope. The ramp had straightened, mouthing open to three lanes. Vehicles lining the two on the left were stopped at a red light. She grabbed the wheel and veered toward the empty right lane.

The disorienting fog of agony lifted. Relief flashed through her, but as quickly as it came, it was gone. Her car was on a collision course with a major intersection of traffic.

Pressure welled in her chest.

Figures. She'd just had the most highly charged experience in her short life with a guy she was crazy attracted to, and now she was going to die. After living a neutral—

Neutral. She shifted from drive to neutral and dragged the tires against the concrete curb. The friction would shave off some speed but not enough. Not while pitched downhill on a trajectory sending her right into traffic with the cruise control jammed at sixty.

She had to avoid causing a domino effect of collisions in the intersection. Cranking the wheel, she plowed over the curb, scraping the undercarriage, and climbed the grassy berm over uneven terrain. Her gaze flickered up to the rearview mirror and a red Jeep speeding up behind her.

A concrete barricade ahead stole her attention and her breath. She spun the wheel, turning into the main street traffic. Cars squealed, braking. Another skidded and rear-ended a truck.

The Jeep bulldozed up beside her in the left lane, horn honking.

What was she supposed to do? What could she do?

The four-wheel-drive vehicle nosed past her bumper and crashed into her car, forcing her to make a hard right—straight into the parking lot of a grocery store.

A woman yapping on her cell phone while rooting in her purse crossed in front of them. Willow's chest turned to a block of ice.

The Jeep that had run up beside her tapped her car to the right, engaging her focus.

She steered away from the woman to the side of the building and a vacant part of the lot.

"Willow!"

The sound of her name penetrated her shroud of fear. She looked over through the Jeep's open passenger-side window.

Gideon.

He signaled to her, punching his hand down and yanking his fist up toward his shoulder. She glanced to her side.

Gear selector? *No.*

Emergency brake. He wanted her to pull up on the emergency brake.

She gripped the handle and wrenched up. The car whipped into a wild spin. She gasped. Light swirled into a haze of gray. Nausea flooded her in a violent wave. Her body shivered like it wanted to splinter into a hundred pieces.

Pressing her head against the seat, she released the wheel and crossed her arms, hands to her shoulders. The tail of the car crashed into something, shattering the back window. The vehicle rocked, jostling her forward.

Phfowmph!

A dense pillow punched her, throttling her back. A white cloud engulfed everything. The airbag sucked up the space around her. A scream strangled in her throat and died.

Dust and white powder clogged her nose and esophagus. She choked on the remnants of terror.

Her car door swung open. "Willow! You okay?"

A loud pop echoed. Her airbag deflated with a hiss, as if it'd been cut. She drew in a shuddering breath and waved to clear the congesting dust from her face.

Gideon whipped a double-handled knife closed and reached for her.

A whimper slipped from her lips as she cringed, raising her arm. It was all too much—losing the brakes, the sound of metal grating, hitting vehicles. Almost dying. She needed to breathe, gain her bearings, before he touched her.

"I want to help you from the car and make sure you're okay. I won't hurt you." He reached for her slowly. "Okay?"

Shutting her eyes, she clutched the strap of her purse still draped over her and nodded.

He unfastened her seatbelt. One strong arm slipped under her legs, the other curled around her shoulders. He lifted her out the car, tucking her against his large frame.

Particles clung to her nostrils, burned her throat, and filled her lungs. She coughed and raked in a glorious breath of fresh air.

Gideon's long legs stretched quickly, carrying her to his car. In his powerful arms, warm and solid, a blanket of calm covered her, dampening her chaotic thoughts save one.

She was safe with him.

He opened the passenger's door and set her inside, but she didn't want him to let go. Not yet.

"Are you okay?" he asked.

Everything had unraveled in minutes. Trying to slow the car, the parking lot. Gideon helping. She still couldn't make sense of it.

Gideon crouched in front of Willow and examined her, smoothing his big hands over her face and her hair. He tilted her chin up. "Did you hit your head? You might have a concussion."

Staring into his wide eyes, now darkened to the blue-gray of a stormy sky in this light, her breathing slowed and her bunched muscles uncoiled. He looked shaken, off beat from his normal steady cadence.

"Willow? Are you all right?"

I'm okay. How bizarre since she'd almost died. "Everything is fuzzy, but I didn't hit my head. I don't think I have a concussion."

"You can get it from whiplash. A doctor should check you."

Before she voiced objections, a sheriff's car pulled into the lot, lights flashing, siren muted. Gideon patted her knee and left her side. He spoke to the officer, pointing to her car, waving his hands in the air as if explaining everything that'd happened.

What exactly *had* happened?

This morning, nothing was wrong with her brakes. She'd had the car checked recently, never pushed the service due date. Yet she'd nearly been killed.

The officer approached, pad and pen in hand. His stern face looked hard enough to crack stone. His narrowing gaze scrutinized her from head to toe. She tensed, gaze falling to the asphalt, and roped an arm around her stomach to steady herself.

"Ma'am, I'm Deputy Martin. Your boyfriend was telling me what happened."

She glanced at Gideon. Why didn't he correct him? She looked up at the cop but avoided his probing eyes, choosing to stare at his cleft chin. "Gideon isn't my boyfriend. He's a coworker."

"Oh, not the impression I got." He scribbled on his pad. "Ma'am, I need to see your driver's license."

Scanning for her purse, she noticed she was tapping her fingers on the seat. The habit soothed her whenever she was tense or overly tired, but it tended to make others uncomfortable. She clenched her hand a moment and fished her wallet from the purse draped around her.

She took out her license, and the white Asperger Network card she kept in case of emergencies such as this slipped onto the ground.

Her jaw dropped. The words rising in her throat clumped together. The card was designed to help ease communication with first responders, but she didn't want Gideon to see it.

The deputy bypassed the license trembling in her hand, bent down, and picked up the card. He went to hand it to her but glanced a little too long. The words *To Law Enforcement and First Responders* written on the front must've captured his attention because he pulled the card back. That side only gave personal details like her name, date of birth, and emergency contacts—her dad and sister Laurel. Willow would've preferred never to list Laurel as any sort of contact, but her other sister, Ivy, lived abroad.

The officer turned the card over. Gideon glanced at it from the side.

She held her breath. *No, no. Please don't read it.* Her skin grew tight as shrink-wrap.

Gideon would never look at her the same. Today was the first day he'd even bothered to look at all. Now each word he read incinerated any chance she might've had to ashes.

Because of my Autism Spectrum Disorder, I may:
- Panic if yelled at and lash out if touched or physically restrained.
- Misinterpret things you tell me or ask me to do.
- Not be able to answer your questions.
- Tend to interpret statements literally.
- Appear rude or say things that sound tactless, especially when anxious or confused.
- Have difficulty making eye contact.

There was more, but she didn't want to think about the words Gideon read as she peered at his face, searching for a reaction. His expression was a mask she couldn't decipher. The ASD label was probably already redefining her in his head from *normal* to *treat with caution*.

The deputy took the license from her hand, swapping it carefully with the card, using his fingertips like her disorder was contagious.

"Ma'am, do you need medical attention?" His tone turned, riding the cusp of loud, the words drawn out and emphasizing each syllable, kicking her heartbeat into a sprint.

Cringing, she shoved the card into her wallet, regretting the decision to carry it.

When her father had suggested keeping the card in her purse, it sounded logical, practical even, since she'd need a little assistance communicating with a stranger in situations of high or traumatic stress. But now she wanted to dissolve. Simply disappear.

"Deputy, she doesn't have a hearing disability." Gideon moved toward her and turned in front of the deputy, shielding her with his body. "There's no need to raise your voice."

Deputy Martin peered around Gideon. "Are you like Rain Man?"

She aimed for his eyes, but her gaze only reached his sharp beak of a nose. "What's a rain man?"

"A movie." Gideon stepped forward, and the deputy backed away.

Putting a hand on a hip, Deputy Martin used his knuckle to tap up the front of his stiff, wide-brimmed hat. "I'm going to need her to take a breathalyzer."

"That won't be necessary. I don't drink." She'd tried on several occasions but never tasted anything she liked.

Peering around Gideon as if afraid to cross the invisible boundary line he'd created, the deputy looked at her. "Still need you to take one, ma'am."

Gideon glanced at her over his shoulder and waited. For what? Her permission? The man was an officer of the law. How could she refuse?

She nodded. "Of course."

An ambulance pulled into the lot. Thankfully, the siren was off.

"Let me help you," Gideon said, as if he could see the shock of everything curtaining her.

She took his extended hand.

His long, thick fingers closed around hers, and his palm rested on her lower back as he helped her down from the vehicle. The step had been high for her five-foot-four frame.

When he let go of her, she swayed, and he clutched her arm.

She had no idea what had happened to her balance. She wasn't dizzy, but as Gideon's hands had left her body, she floated like a kite let loose in a breeze.

He helped her up into the ambulance, holding her at the waist. The EMT steered her to sit on a gurney, asked her questions, and pointed a small flashlight in her eyes. The tow truck arrived, and Gideon talked to the driver at length. The man in overalls kept writing for several minutes. She had no idea what Gideon said, beyond explaining the brakes had failed.

As the officer approached her again, Gideon broke away from the tow truck driver and hurried to her side.

"Ma'am, please take a deep breath and blow until I tell you to stop. Okay?" Although the officer spoke to her, he stared at Gideon, who'd recovered his usual unflappable demeanor and stared back at the deputy.

Sitting on the end of the gurney in the ambulance, Willow leaned forward, took a deep breath, and blew into a white tube. When the deputy raised his hand, she stopped.

He looked at the small device in his hand. "Okay, ma'am. You're free to go."

Gideon reached up for her with both hands but met her gaze before touching her. She nodded, and he grasped her at the waist, lifting her down from the ambulance.

More sheriff's deputies had arrived on the scene. Officers were managing the traffic and other accidents she'd caused. Gideon roped an arm around her midsection, bringing her close to his body, anchoring her with the strength of his grip as they headed to his vehicle.

He opened the car door and hoisted her up onto the seat.

"I'm having the tow truck driver take your car to a mechanic I know, if that's okay."

The local garage she'd used had overlooked a problem, and she'd almost died as a result. "That's fine."

"I'll finish with the driver and take you home." He shut the door and hurried off.

Her skin was warm around her waist and on her arm where he'd touched her. She was surprised how a man capable of brutal but necessary things could also be so tender and kind.

She glanced around the Jeep. The inside further contradicted her expectations.

A faceted crystal ball, a beautiful prism of light, hung from the rearview mirror. Custom covers wrapped the console lid, steering wheel, and front seats in a striped mosaic fabric of blues, purple, and pink. The touch was feminine and the car tidier than hers, which was saying a lot, since she vacuumed her VW and wiped everything down every Saturday morning.

Even her glove box only held the essentials—a car manual, tire gauge, packet of tissues, and mini first aid kit. She opened his to see if it was similar.

A large manila envelope fell out. A rectangular label from a law firm was in the top left corner in bold red letters, and it was addressed to Kelli Stone, his wife, who had died in a car accident a year after Willow transferred to the Gray Box.

Sanborn had come across Willow at an NSA briefing, pulled her to the side, and asked her a bunch of questions. Next thing she knew, he'd added her to his Gray Box collection. That was what Sanborn did—collected those with special talents from across the board: NSA, CIA, Special Forces, DEA, even MI6, the British foreign intelligence service.

The driver's-side door opened.

"What are you doing?" The harshness in Gideon's voice made her jump.

Heart racing, she licked her lips. "Looking in your glove box."

Gideon climbed in and snatched the envelope from her hand. He stuffed it into the glove compartment and slapped the door shut. "Were you going through my things?"

"Yes."

He flinched as if the honesty had stung him like a bee. "Did you open it?"

"No." In the chaos of the accident and the comfort Gideon offered, her guard had slipped, and she'd overstepped. If she'd been thinking, she would've remembered the rules she needed to follow to keep others relaxed. "Are you angry at me?"

His jaw tightened. "I don't like people going through my stuff." His head dipped, and he rubbed the back of his neck. "I need to take you home. Where do you live?"

"I could put it in the GPS."

With a nod, he started the car. She punched in her address, glancing at him.

"Sorry I went through your things." Willow waited for a response to guide her in what to say and do, but silence reigned.

As her dizziness subsided, the time to reach her house on the GPS display counted down. She was used to the awkwardness at the beginning of the end. Not that they had ever begun.

Boys were chatty at first until they discovered she was different. Then they were quiet. Except for two. Michael Dutton in college, who had been in a rush to touch her as if autistic meant easy. She'd been overwhelmed and frightened by his groping and hit him, giving him a black eye. Afterward, *autistic* meant *dangerous*.

And there was Simon Peterson at the NSA. He had been nice and as nervous as her. The second he got her in his bedroom, everything popped off at lightning speed. Including him.

"I owe you an apology," Gideon said, his fingers tightening and loosening on the wheel.

"Apology for what?"

"I was concerned about the cut on your face and tried to touch you at the office without thinking. It upset you. The card in your wallet said to avoid touching you."

"No, the card is for the police. You can touch me." *Touch is good.* It happened so infrequently since her mother died, she wasn't used to it anymore and needed warning. There'd been a time when her parents had showered her in affection and she'd loved it.

She pulled on an uneasy smile, but he didn't look at her or smile back.

Her heart sank. "I didn't expect it at the office. I wasn't prepared." Tapping her purse, she lowered her head. *I may be a bit sensitive, but I'm still a woman who likes to be touched.*

Heat rose, flaming in her face, and she wrung her hands.

"You did good slowing your car by dragging the tires against the curb. Nice job not losing your head. How did you know what to do?"

"Sanborn makes all the analysts go through a watered-down version of the defensive driving course the field officers go through. Once my head cleared from the sensory overload, some training came back." She retained lots of details that an analyst should never have to use, like how to lose a tail if you were being followed or how to fire a gun.

He pulled to a stop, and she looked up at the quaint three-bedroom house she called home. Four-bedroom since her father had converted the basement into a mini apartment for her.

"Thanks for the ride. For helping me." She let out a heavy sigh, grasping the door handle. "I appreciate it."

"Do you mind if I come in for a glass of water?"

The heaviness in her chest lifted. "Yes, please." Grinning, she struggled to open the door. The handle was nothing like the one in her VW.

By the time she gave up fiddling with the door, Gideon was standing on her side and opened it for her. She jumped out, dropping several inches to the ground. At least he wasn't running for the hills. She didn't know what Gideon wanted from her, if anything besides extra help at work, but she wanted to find out.

Turning, she faced the house. The white curtain in the front window drew back, and the most cantankerous man alive appeared, watching them.

05

A wheelchair ramp led from the front door to the drive-way, where a van with a handicap sticker was parked. The curtains in the bay window drew apart, and an old man peered out at them.

"Who is that?" Gideon asked.

"My dad." Her voice turned brittle.

The mark on her cheek, the way she'd evaded answering his questions at work, the man in the window—it all connected. Painful memories clawed up through him, and he stiffened under a flare of protectiveness. "Is he the reason you have a cut on your face?"

She wrapped her arms around herself. "It was an accident. He didn't mean to hurt me."

All too common for a child to defend an abusive parent. He'd seen it before, had once lived and breathed the agony of it. "Do you have many accidents?"

Her gaze snapped to his. "Of course not. He's been sick and hasn't been himself. This last recurrence of Hodgkin's hit him hard. His temperament seesaws between that of a petulant child to being depressed." The compassion in her tone touched him, inclined him to relax.

Gideon had never seen cuts or bruises on her before

today. Not that it wasn't possible to hide marks. Maddox did it all the time thanks to her job in the field, but he believed Willow.

"Your father lives with you?"

Surprise flitted across her face. "No one ever framed it like that. People usually ask if *I* live with my dad, like there's something wrong with me." She pressed her lips in a grim line. "But I do live with him. There's nothing wrong with me. It just sort of worked out that way. I take care of him, without help from my sisters. They're too busy, and they hate me."

"I'm sure your sisters don't hate you."

"How can you say that?" Her nose wrinkled. "You've never met them."

"No, but I know you."

"You know I'm a good analyst. That people call me the *Factinator* behind my back, like I'm a machine instead of a person. Aside from that, you don't know me."

"You're the sharpest analyst I've met, yet humble." He wanted to caress her cheek or shoulder and erase the lonesome look on her face. "You speak frankly, but you're never mean."

She kept that air of sweetness and quiet strength even under pressure. The harder she tried to fade into the background at work, the more he noticed little things about her. Every day, she brought a chicken salad for lunch. She always wore those classy pearls and the same blouse and skirt but in different colors. At first, he'd thought she randomly rotated, but he'd figured out her system was based on calendar dates. On the fourth—like today—it was a dove-gray blouse and navy skirt. Besides being beautiful and the best kind of quirky, she was brilliant, but the most telling thing about her was that whenever she made a mistake, she owned it and apologized without hesitation. That spoke volumes, considering one of the tenets of their profession was CYA—cover your ass.

He wasn't a closet sleazebag or a stalker. She just piqued his curiosity, and there was still so much about her he longed to puzzle out.

"You're doing the tough work of taking care of your dad by yourself. I don't see how anyone could hate you, especially a sister."

A pink flush crept up her face. She smiled, pure and unrestrained, holding his gaze with a glimmer in her eyes. Training and a complement of experience had taught him to compartmentalize emotion, to be the storm that devastated and washed things clean, but in that moment, he wanted to think less and feel more.

For a few seconds anyway.

She didn't deserve to be accused of treason and definitely didn't deserve to have her life invaded by him—a professional liar and bloody butcher by trade.

Their traitor was skilled at subterfuge and manipulation. On the off chance Willow was an Oscar-worthy actress, pretenses faltered under strain. Like in the high-stress situation she'd just been through. She wasn't the mole, but he needed to prove her innocence beyond a doubt.

And then he'd stay far away from her.

The old man banged on the window. "Willow! I'm starving!" He disappeared, the curtains falling back into place.

She hustled up the walkway to the front stoop, Gideon staying a stride behind her.

As she fumbled with her key, the door swung open. Her father sat in a wheelchair, blocking the entryway, his liver-spotted face pinched in a grimace.

"You're almost two hours late and you didn't call. I have to take my medicine. Where's your car? And who's this?" He scowled at Gideon.

Willow shooed her father back with both hands. The house was a moderate twenty degrees cooler than the oven-baked temp outside.

"Sorry I'm late, Dad. I had a car accident and I didn't think to call."

"You hurt? Got whiplash? Concussion?" Withered from age and sickness, the gray-haired man rolled to the kitchen. He wore a bathrobe and cotton pajamas. An IV bag hung from the back of the wheelchair. "I keep telling you, women are lousy drivers."

She tossed her purse on the tile countertop and washed her hands. Gideon hovered in the natural divide between the eat-in kitchen and the living room.

"My car was towed." Willow dried her hands. "But I'm fine, thanks to Gideon."

And luck. The situation could've played out much differently, where she didn't walk away. After he'd deflated the airbag, seeing her swamped with fear and shock had twisted something inside him. He'd wanted to gather her in his arms and make sure she wasn't hurt.

"Nice to meet you, Mr. Harper. I'm Gideon Stone." He proffered his hand. "The accident wasn't her fault. Your daughter handled the situation remarkably well."

Her dad stared at Gideon's extended hand, then cut his eyes back to Willow. "Why didn't you bring me a double bacon cheeseburger and fries if you were going to be late?"

Gideon dropped his hand, taking in the understated furnishings situated to accommodate a wheelchair. The homey living room was spotless, devoid of clutter, like the kitchen.

"It's bad for your heart." She sighed. "Why didn't you microwave a frozen meal?"

"You promised to cook for me every night this week. And you have chicken à la king labeled for Thursdays in the freezer. Last time I took a meal out of order, you got all squirrelly."

"It's tuna, not chicken."

His mouth twisted, nose scrunching. "Tastes like à la friggin' ass. I won't eat it. I want a damn burger." He pounded a wrinkled fist on a round yellow Formica table the seventies rejected. "I'm dying. I can have a burger once a month. I've earned it."

"I'm only doing what's best for you, following the doctor's advice."

Gideon preferred to make things easier for her after the hell she'd been through earlier, but he had a job to do. "A burger or pizza sounds great. I'm starved. May I have a cup of water?"

Her shoulders bunched. "Glasses are there." She pointed as she dug into the freezer.

He ventured into the kitchen, ignoring her father's flagging glower, and opened a cabinet. Spices and seasoning were arranged in alphabetical order. Organization taken to the nth degree. He grabbed a glass from the next cabinet, filled it with tap water, and took a sip.

"Even *what's his name* is in favor of a burger. Or pizza. Sounds so good."

"How about a Friday meal, Dad? Tortellini surprise. I bet you'd like that one."

Her sweet optimism—despite Mr. Harper barking complaints and Gideon's deliberately inciteful suggestion—was another reason he admired her. She had fortitude.

"I like good surprises," said her father. "The kind that make me happy. Not the ones you keep frozen in those Tupperware containers."

With the distraction in full swing, Gideon asked, "Willow, where's the bathroom?"

The father wheeled back, eyeing him as if his presence was an invasion of his territory.

"Down the hall." Willow put a meal in the microwave. "Second door on the left."

"Don't nuke that," Mr. Harper said. "Order a pizza. Or make waffles. I'll eat those."

"Breakfast for dinner again?" Her voice dipped low and turned pleading. "Not while I have company. Please, eat the tortellini."

"I'll eat it without a fuss if you give me some whiskey to wash down the unpleasantness."

As Willow fought with her father, holding her own against the ornery old bulldog, Gideon headed down the hall. He poked his head into two bedrooms, both outfitted with the basics of spare rooms. Bypassing the bathroom, he ducked into what appeared to be the master. Pill bottles lined the low dresser and an oxygen tank sat in the corner. Her father's room.

He eavesdropped on the chatter in the kitchen. Willow mentioned putting a movie on for her father. Gideon had a little time, but not much. He darted down the stairs into the basement.

Hopper windows partially illuminated the space. The walls were a warm white with a touch of beige. It had a bright, refurbished look of a modern apartment. He hesitated to walk on the plush cream carpet with his boots, but he didn't have seconds to spare removing them.

He trod lightly to the desk at the opposite side of the large room. Three computer monitors sat side by side. Papers piled in untidy heaps were the first sign of any mess in the house. She probably had some order in the apparent chaos. He tapped a button on the keyboard.

A prompt on the middle screen awaited a password. He inserted the cloning flash drive and hit the Enter button, activating it. A red light blinked. The download was in progress.

He fingered through a stack of magazines. *Clean Eating, Simple and Delicious, Cooking Light*. He shifted his attention to the loose sheets of paper. Programming code, algorithms, grocery lists, questions to ask doctors about her dad's health.

A file cabinet drawer was closed but unlocked. Noise from upstairs sounded as if she'd turned on a television. He flipped through folders of recipes, medical information about her father, and hospital bills. Her world revolved around work and her dad—innocent enough, even heartwarming—but she had a mountain of debt. Money

was a classic motive. Opportunity for her to access classified data without detection had already been established.

But Willow wasn't a murderer. No way she'd killed
Novak.

A green light popped up on the USB drive. He ejected
it, shoving it into his pocket. Turning, he noticed a full-
sized bed made neater than a pin in the next room. He
palmed the door open wider. Her tight bedroom only had
extra space for a dresser and nightstand.

He went in, opened the bedside table drawer, and
found a leather-bound book.

Diaries always led to trouble. Any secret worth keeping
shouldn't be written down, not even shared with a trusted
friend. People were fallible and could be compromised.

He leafed through the pages. Doodles. Algorithms. A
circular pattern of intricate lines repeated—a maze with a
bull's head drawn in the center. Words on one page stayed
his hand.

Briarwood
Bridge of Sighs
Symphony
The Ghost

Names of previous ops over the last three years that'd
had hiccups. All due to their mole?

The Ghost, Aleksander Novak, had confirmed the
leak. In exchange for immunity, Novak had agreed to give
details about an information broker who bartered secrets
using a global network of spies. One name—the deadly
spider controlling a funnel-web of traitors. But they'd
failed to keep Novak alive long enough to talk.

Their team had pored over previous ops, looking for

a link to their insider, any indication other missions had been tampered with. But they had no idea how far back to look. No clue how long they'd had a traitor among them. Gideon turned the page and his breath stalled.

More mazes drawn around a single word. *Babel.* A code name for the operation to kill Daedalus, one of Gideon's solo missions. He'd volunteered for it to get distance from the problems smothering his marriage. Less than twenty-four hours after he'd returned, Kelli had been killed in a car accident. Guilt still weighed on him.

A keen analyst would connect the dots between compromised ops, searching for a pattern, a common thread tied to the leak. But this list of classified missions in an unsecured place violated Protocol 101. It could also be notes of someone looking to wrap up loose ends. That's how Ares or Alistair would see it if either of them got their hands on it.

Except evidence left in a notebook in a bedside table would be sloppy, too careless for a traitor who had, thus far, been pathological about covering their tracks.

Why had she written *Babel*? Nothing had gone wrong on his op to terminate Daedalus.

"It's only fair for you to go through my stuff after I looked through your glove box." The angelic lilt of her voice made his pulse spike.

He didn't turn at once, taking a beat to decide on his approach, and looked at her. She sauntered toward him with a guileless smile. There was nothing flirtatious about it. She moved divested of the surety of purpose she carried in the office, now seeming uncertain and unguarded.

Willow eased into the narrow space beside him with her back to the wall.

A gentleman would've moved away, not taken advantage of her raw emotions in the wake of the car crash, but he was no gentleman. And she was a job.

She'd listed classified operations, and he needed to know why.

He faced her, almost bringing their bodies flush. His physical awareness of her was so palpable, desire was a live wire crackling through him. But after reading the ASD card, he was reluctant to lay a finger on her. Better to let her initiate contact in the same manner he'd let her determine their proximity.

"I don't want you to have the wrong impression about me from my emergency responder card." She wrung her hands but met his eyes. "I don't want you to think you can't touch me. You can. I want you to, if you want to. I-I know you wouldn't hurt me."

She put a palm flat on his sternum. Her slender fingers feathered across his chest, stroking him like he was a piece of fragile glass that might break.

The gentleness was startling. With a target, he stayed numb. Impervious. But when she touched him, a tenderness he didn't know he possessed—and couldn't afford to keep—bloomed.

This was just a means to an end, nothing more. He couldn't forget that.

"In your journal," he said, keeping his tone curious rather than accusatory, as gentle as he knew how, "why do you have missions written down?"

The color bled from her face. She lowered her head, curling her fingers against her chest. If only he had a playlist of moves to loosen her up. Maybe he needed to act naturally but take everything down from a ten to a two. He brushed his knuckles up her arms, forcing himself to go slowly, and looked for the subtlest indication that his advance was unwanted.

She relaxed in degrees—her clenched hand opened, and lowered, fingertips skimming his thighs, and she looked up at him. "There were whispers Novak's death wasn't suicide. A couple of nights ago, I started thinking about other missions where something had gone wrong."

"Why all the drawings?" he asked.

"I have trouble sleeping." Her voice was a whisper. "Doodling relaxes me."

Inching higher, he caressed her shoulders. Her genuine warmth and vibrancy reeled him in, daring him to act on baser impulses. "But why a maze with the head of a bull at the center?"

"It's from the Greek myth about Daedalus and the Minotaur. The king of Crete had Daedalus, a brilliant architect, construct a labyrinth the Minotaur—a violent monster, half bull, half human—could never escape. Those missions are pieces of a puzzle, like working your way out of a labyrinth. Only I'm missing a clue."

What if with enough time and resources, she could find the mole?

He reached up and hesitated, giving her a chance to retreat, and when she didn't, he cupped her face. The silkiness of her skin sent a jolt through him.

She gave a shy smile and shivered with an enticing vulnerability that made him ache. Made every muscle in his body tighten with an appetite that was both familiar and foreign.

Ah, hell. He needed to rein things in, not take this too far, so he dropped his hand and propped his forearms on the wall above her head. She ran a palm up his torso, angling her face toward his shoulder and—with a long, deep inhalation—smelled him.

06

WOLF TRAP, VIRGINIA
THURSDAY, JULY 4, 8:40 P.M. EDT

With Gideon standing close, his arms resting on the wall above her head, the urge to smell him was overwhelming. Before she could stop herself, Willow drew her nose to the crook of his shoulder and inhaled.

God, he smelled good, warm and lemony. Not a sharp citrus, but closer to the mellow freshness of the *citronnelle* soap Ivy and her wife had brought on their last visit, and there was a manly hint of musk that made her toes curl. There should be dryer sheets that smelled like him.

Her cheeks burned hot with shame. Whenever she stood too close to someone, she had that mortifying compulsion. Crammed elevators were the worst. She avoided them at all costs.

"Did you enjoy that?" Gideon asked.

Squeezing her eyes shut, she couldn't bear to look at him and see ridicule, or worse, pity. "Smelling you? Or the way you smelled?"

"Both." His breath licked her face, sending a rush of tingles through her.

She wanted to absorb the air, taste him on her tongue. Pressing her lips together, she risked looking up at him. A bright smile spread across his mouth. Lightness filled her like helium in a balloon, and she laughed, comforted he wasn't staring as if she were a weirdo.

"I'm sorry," she said. "I can't help it when I'm in very close proximity to someone."

He lowered his arms. "So it's not just an effect I have on you. I'm a little disappointed."

"Don't be. You affect me." Oh boy, did he ever.

His gaze dipped to her mouth. "I liked it. The way you smelled me. Indulge any time."

Relief bloomed in her chest, and the pull toward him intensified.

"I thought you had to use the bathroom. What are you doing down here in my room?"

"I was curious. About you."

Her fingers slid over the sculpted muscle of his arm. She was not only still touching him but had groped her way to his bicep. She dropped her hand, grazing his. Long fingers stroked hers in a feathery caress, drawing her belly tight, and she ached for more.

Now primed, she could handle lots more. She clutched his hand, not wanting this to end, and met his gaze. His eyes were mesmerizing, pale yet vivid in color at the same time.

She was staring but couldn't stop. He leaned in, bringing his mouth close.

Panic bubbled up inside her. Affection was welcomed, but the last time a guy had kissed her, it'd felt like an angry eel had been unleashed in her mouth.

"A ten-second French kiss transfers eighty million germs."

That gross fact had stopped any other guys from

attempting to swap spit. Not that there had been many who'd tried. With her long work hours and sick father, she didn't get out much.

Gideon looked amused. She hoped he wasn't laughing at her.

He caressed her lip with his thumb, and something inside her loosened while other things tightened. "I'll take my chances," he said. "You're worth the risk."

There went that little tug to him again. "The study also showed that the more partners kissed, the higher the likelihood of them having a similar profile colonizing their tongues."

"So you're saying if you like the way I kiss, I should do it a lot."

Is that what she was saying?

His calloused fingertips stroked the hollow of her throat with titillating lightness, and butterflies collided in her belly.

"Are you afraid of me now?" he asked.

"No." She liked this side of Gideon. Liked it a lot.

"Do you want me to stop?" His voice was gruff and low.

"No." An overwhelming need for more, of him and from him, rushed over her.

He lifted her chin and brushed his lips across hers—a sweet, devastating tease that drew her closer with anticipation—and his tongue slipped inside her mouth.

She stiffened, but the unhurried press of his lips, the gentle caress of his tongue, the firmness of his hands had her melting. The mash of mouths and unsettling amount of saliva she'd experienced in the past couldn't compare to this sensual onslaught. She'd taken Gideon for a man who tore into things rather than savoring them, but she couldn't have been more wrong.

His fingers trailed down and caressed her breast through her clothes, his mouth growing hungrier, feeding her own appetite for him. Everything inside her was turned on, lit brighter than a one-hundred-watt LED bulb.

A groan rumbled in his throat, and with startling abruptness, he broke off the kiss. She shuddered a breath out and rested her head back on the wall, uncertain what to do, hoping the moment wouldn't end there.

"Are we going to have sex?" Whenever she'd been alone with a man in a bedroom, he kissed her and endeavored to have sex with her. But this was different. Gideon was different.

He drew back slightly. "Do you want to?"

"I'm not sure." She swallowed thickly. Did she want to be a notch on his bedpost, become a *for one night only* girl? "I tried it once, and it wasn't pleasant. He just shoved it in, grunted on top of me for a few minutes, and then it was over."

Simon had smelled like oatmeal. It should've been the first indicator sex would be equally as horrid. His eel-tongued kisses should've been the second.

Gideon's brows drew together. "You've only been with one guy?"

"Yes."

Gideon pulled away, dropping his hands from her, but she wasn't ready to let him go. When she moved forward, he stepped back toward the door.

"What's wrong?"

A loud banging erupted from the top of the stairs. "Willow! No boys in your room!"

The one time she managed to get a guy she wanted in her room, her father was spoiling it.

"Willow! What are you two doing down there?"

Sighing, she adjusted her clothes. "Gideon wanted to see my room. We'll be right up!"

"I bet he wanted to see your room. Get up here. Now!" Harsh knocking resounded.

Her father must be slamming his baseball bat on the floor.

"I'm twenty-five," she said to Gideon. "You'd think he'd stop treating me like a child."

"Why did you write *Babel*, my mission to get Daedalus?" His cold eyes shot to her book.

The warmth in him had evaporated, replaced with a lethal edge of menace. He'd reverted to the hard, killing machine who stalked the halls of the Gray Box. What happened?

"Nothing went wrong on that op," he said. "I completed the mission."

She smoothed her hair with a trembling hand. "You eliminated the target, Daedalus, which was your primary objective, but you failed to retrieve data he had on a jump drive."

Rocking back on his heels, he crossed his arms, gaze pinned to the floor.

"You never completed your debriefing because…" His wife had been killed. The shock had thrown everyone off, and the detail had been overlooked by Daniel, the analyst assigned.

"Willow!" Hammering resonated through the wood floor above.

She wished she'd given her father the glass of whiskey.

07

The Daedalus mission had fallen through the cracks.

Young operatives didn't lose spouses to death. Divorce took them. Most black ops agents screwed up their marriages with secrecy, disappearing on missions for unspecified periods of time. It was tough on partners and incomprehensible to regular civilians such as in-laws.

The car accident, Kelli's death, had shaken everyone. What no one else at the Gray Box knew was that his wife hadn't been in the vehicle alone. The cop on-site had told Gideon the cause of the accident was a combination of rainy road conditions and distraction while driving.

At first, he hadn't understood, but the cop painted the picture for him. His wife in the passenger's seat, no seatbelt on. Male driver, also deceased, with his privates exposed.

Gideon had later stumbled on the divorce papers inside her Jeep's glove box and had paid her best friend a visit, demanding the truth. The affair had gone on for two years.

The guy had also been married with kids but had decided to leave his wife for Kelli.

Gideon had just gotten back from the Daedalus mission and hadn't seen her in weeks. When he suggested that they both take time off to spend together, she'd shot him down with excuses. One of many was that her Jeep needed an oil change and tune-up, and she insisted he handle it and had taken his truck.

After learning Kelli had died while giving her lover a blow job, he hadn't bothered reading the police report. Maybe it was time he did.

"Willow! Come upstairs!" Her father banged something hard on the floor.

She hung her head and wrapped her arms around her waist, hugging herself. Gideon ached to finish what he'd started but stuffed his hands in his pockets, retreating to the doorway.

The usual disconnect wasn't there. When he looked at her, he didn't see a target or a mission. Only an exquisite woman, tender and sweet, ready to open herself. She was giving him the precious gift of her trust—a miracle and a mistake inextricably tangled.

He was a bad man, who did bad things for a living.

Screwing to get off was easy, but he wouldn't screw over Willow. He was capable of gruesome, cold-blooded stuff, but there was a line he wouldn't cross. Not with her. He respected her too much. Where in the hell had his sudden pang of conscience come from?

Tomorrow, he'd swap targets with Maddox and contend with Ares.

"We should go upstairs," Willow said, not looking at him.

"I'm sorry." He wanted to say more but lacked the right words. "Your father sounds anxious." Gideon understood and wouldn't want his daughter in a basement with a guy like him either. Stepping out of the bedroom, he extended an arm for her to walk ahead, and she did.

At the top of the landing, her dad had a baseball bat on his lap. "No boys in your room."

Willow hurried up the stairs, her movement graceful, not making a sound. She slid around her dad and wheeled his chair down the hall.

Gideon came up behind them, hovering between the kitchen and living room, while she settled her father in front of a dining tray, facing a forty-inch television.

"There are rules for a reason. You'll respect them," her dad said. "No boys downstairs."

"Gideon isn't a boy." She handed him a fork, her face flushed and lips a deep pink from kissing. "He's a coworker, Dad."

"Bullshit. If that boy can whip out nerd code, I can shit gold." Her father took the fork.

"I'm not an analyst, sir. I manage problems of a physical nature."

"Physical, huh?" Her father eyed him hard. "Any good at it?"

"He has thirteen commendations," Willow said.

Gideon schooled his features, not letting his unease show. *Thirteen* included his time at the CIA. Was his entire personnel file logged in her head? He hoped she didn't try to hack into the sealed parts, if she hadn't already. The idea of her reading the redacted sections made him squirm on the inside. Willow caught him staring at her.

"I'm not a stalker," she said. "I remember facts, figures, dates."

Her dad nodded. "Do yourself a favor and stay away

from this one. Everything gets locked up in that steel trap upstairs. It'll come back to bite your ass in the middle of the night. Her mother had the same thing, woke me up at all hours. Steel trap." He stuffed a forkful of food in his mouth and gagged. "Don't misunderstand. You shouldn't be sleeping with my daughter."

Willow smoothed down her skirt. "Dad, stop. He isn't interested in sleeping with me."

Mr. Harper threw his fork on the plate. "I don't want you sleeping with my daughter, but why aren't you interested? Think you're too good for her?"

"No, sir. She's beautiful and brilliant and has a big heart. She's too good for me."

Willow's wide eyes met his. The urge to touch her, to taste those lips again, rushed up like a riptide, but he eased himself toward the door.

"I like this kid. He's got good answers." Her dad smiled. "You drink whiskey?"

"Yes, sir, but not tonight." Gideon put his hand on the doorknob, fighting the desire to stay. "I need to get going."

"You're welcome back to have a drink with me. The ole warden"—he hiked a thumb at Willow—"won't deny me, if I have company."

"Dad." Willow waved a hand at him. "You're giving him the wrong impression, making our home sound like jail."

"Sorry." The old guy cleared his throat. "Let me clarify. I hate ambiguity. Visiting hours here in the slammer are anytime you bring a bottle of whiskey."

Gideon chuckled. "Willow, what time should I pick you up tomorrow?"

"No need. I can drive my dad's van." She lowered her

head. Chocolate-brown wisps of hair stroked her cheeks. He itched to sweep them from her face and smooth them into place.

"Nobody drives Betty but me." Her father ate another painful bite of food.

"I've been leaving at five to work on the program." Still, she wouldn't meet his eyes.

Gideon wanted to slug himself for messing with her emotions. The cause was just, the method proven to produce results, yet he felt lower than pond scum. And not the stuff that floated at the top but the sludge at the bottom.

He opened the door. "Can we make it eight?" The garage where her car had been taken opened at six. He wanted to be sure the inspection was thorough.

"Okay." She finally looked up, her gaze crashing into his. The unguarded look on her face, the beautiful honesty in her expression, took hold of him like a prisoner.

His judgment was clouded, and his presence was only doing damage. He needed to get out of there, away from her. Gideon stepped across the threshold.

"Good night." He closed the door, took long strides to his car, and peeled off.

Hurrying away after reeling her in rubbed him all kinds of wrong. Guilt and self-loathing knotted in his chest. Tomorrow, he'd talk to her and at the very least give a better apology.

He drove to the storage unit he'd opened while Kelli was alive and believed he still worked for the CIA, since the existence of the Gray Box was classified. Whenever he'd come home with injuries, she'd ask questions and search his things. His heavily filtered answers pushed their marriage from troubled to terminal—although the demise was probably inevitable the moment he'd agreed to marry Kelli. With her dogged determination, it was only a matter of time before she'd find his go bag hidden in the house, so he'd moved it to the storage unit.

Every operative had a go bag with international passports in different names and cash in a variety of currencies. Sometimes missions kicked off with no notice, and one had to be ready.

After Kelli's death, he let her parents take what they wanted of hers, and Maddox had helped him sort through the rest of Kelli's things. But he'd kept her Jeep exactly as she'd left it. Guilt plagued him for not giving her the life she'd expected. She never wanted to live in the Beltway with the oppressive traffic, hitched to a civil servant. Never even wanted the Jeep.

He parked in front of the climate-controlled storage facility. Musty air circulated inside the dim corridors. His unit sat at the intersection of two rows in the middle of the building, giving him two routes to access it.

Motion-activated lights flickered on as he passed. He punched in the code to the lock, opened his unit, and slid the metal door closed behind him.

He hadn't been here in months. Since her death, each visit stung a little less. He rifled through reams of folders in boxes until he found the right one and fished out the police report.

Willow's accident nagged at him. One way or another, he was going to get to the bottom of it. With the file in hand, he locked up and drove home.

Inside his townhouse, he pulled off his boots and

grabbed a German beer from the wide assortment lined up in the fridge. Most nights since Kelli died, he needed an Ambien to sleep. One pill equaled three hours, four if he also knocked back a couple of beers.

His job never kept him up at night; compartmentalization was the key. But seeing how much Kelli had despised what he stood for, how far she'd gone to disrespect him, and knowing if he'd only let her go—or never married her—she'd still be alive…that denied him peace of mind.

Crossing into the living room, he eyed the metronome sitting dead center on the bookshelf. A memento of his past, keeping him rooted in purpose.

Taking a swig of ice-cold hefeweizen, he plopped on the sofa and opened the police file. No Ambien tonight. He needed to be up early, and before hitting the sack, he wanted to get through this and research the autism spectrum disorder to learn more.

Gritty details and graphic pictures in the file chipped away at old wounds, making his gut burn. Kelli and her lover's blood alcohol count indicated they'd had drinks but weren't inebriated. His truck's antilock braking system light and brake warning lights had both engaged, but the vehicle had never been examined for a mechanical malfunction. At the time, the initial ugly facts had spelled out what'd happened, and he'd been shredded by the news. But if he'd scanned the report, maybe he would've had the vehicle inspected and discovered something far more nefarious. Now there was no way to know.

If someone had tampered with his vehicle after the Daedalus op, the same person might've sabotaged Willow's.

He was overlooking a vital detail about that mission, something bigger than a flash drive he'd failed to recover. Once he figured out what it was, things might make more sense.

08

Willow sat on the front stoop, waiting for Gideon, too restless to enjoy the tepid breeze. Anxiety ticked through her over the hours wasted when she should've been working.

Gray Box field officers lazed in around nine and drifted out no later than three when not on an assignment. During missions, they worked as long and hard as necessary, sometimes around the clock. It was an unspoken rule that'd taken her a while to learn.

Understanding the rules, particularly social ones, and remembering them was a hundred times harder than learning how to write code. Ivy had assured her after high school, everything would get easier. But it'd only gotten more challenging.

By sixteen, she'd tested out of high school early, and at Princeton, it'd taken her two months to have a conversation that lasted longer than two minutes with her roommate, Hayley. She'd been nice, did most of the chatting, and Willow didn't mind doing her math assignments. Hayley dragged her to parties, where the music had always been too loud and Willow lurked in the corner, examining gestures, dissecting what others talked about so she didn't do or say the wrong thing. It had been exhausting.

The first time she'd pretended she was like the other girls at a frat party, Michael Dutton had noticed her. He'd lured her into a bedroom. She'd managed to get him off her, but he'd left bruises. The kind of bruises people saw on her body. The kind she carried deep inside years later.

She told her father everything over Christmas break. He thought it best if she transferred to Georgetown and lived at home. The suggestion had been a great relief.

Willow opened her eyes. The breeze brushed her skin, and she imagined it was Gideon touching her, making sensation flare. The kiss replayed on a loop, as it had the better part of the night. His hands spanning her hips, pressing her against the wall with his heavy, delicious weight. His mouth hot and sure on hers, the intimate tangle of their tongues…obscene and addictive and nothing eel-like about it. She'd remember it until the day she died.

But she'd done or said something wrong, missed some rule, a behavioral cue. If she fixed the problem, maybe he'd want to see her room again. Better yet, he might show her his place.

She fiddled with her fingers, longing to know what had thrown things off.

Gideon pulled up, and her heart fluttered. She stood, grabbing the chicken salad packed in her insulated bag and the Tupperware container of scones she'd baked earlier. Stomach tightening, she opened the door and hoisted herself into the Jeep, determined to get answers.

"Good morning." Gideon extended a hand.

She put her palm on his, letting him help her inside. "Thank you. I appreciate the ride." She shut the door, and he pulled off.

"I hope you weren't waiting long."

After he'd stirred so many different sensations in her, she hadn't fallen asleep until two in the morning. Her eyes opened at four before her alarm went off, body vibrating with anticipation. She'd made her dad a huge breakfast, baked scones for Gideon, and waited.

"Two and a half hours." Smiling, she wondered if she should ease into the discussion. Her sisters hated when she blurted stuff out, but she didn't know how to talk around things.

"Coffee?" He handed her a paper cup with a plastic lid. "Splash of cream, two sugars."

Taken aback, she accepted the cup. "How do you know how I take my coffee?"

"I paid attention during our ops whenever you made a cup in the conference room."

Warm flutters stroked her insides, like she'd swallowed a swarm of sun-soaked butterflies. "Gideon, I enjoyed the way you touched me in my room yesterday."

His head snapped forward, his body stiffening ramrod straight.

"I'm sorry if I said or did something wrong," she said.

His face was a blank slate as he sipped his coffee.

"I'd like to be friends." She put her hand on his thigh, and his muscles tensed. "I want to have sex with you."

Gideon choked, spewing coffee on the steering wheel as the car swerved. He went to set his cup in the beverage holder without looking and fumbled. Hot liquid splashed on the console.

"Shit." The car swerved again.

She reeled her hand away from his thigh and back into her lap.

"It's not a good idea for us to be friends. I crossed the line yesterday. I shouldn't have touched you like that. I'm sorry."

"Why? I enjoyed it. I thought you did too." There was no mistaking he'd been aroused.

"It's not you, Willow. It's me. I'm not the right type of guy for you."

A weight settled in her chest along with the true meaning of his words. *She* wasn't the right type of girl for *him*. He could have anyone. A gorgeous woman with beauty queen potential who'd mastered the sexual techniques those magazines outlined.

Willow was simple, nothing fancy, nothing stunning. She struggled through briefings, with her stomach twisting into knots. What would she be like on a date?

Gideon probably socialized a lot. He was always at Rocky's bar with the rest of Black Ops and wouldn't want an awkward misfit hiding in the corner, or worse, embarrassing him. He wouldn't waste his time on her, but why had he initiated anything in the first place?

A dull ache swelled inside. Misinterpreting things said, misreading cues, led her to make mistakes that ballooned into shame. This was the type of humiliation she was desperate to avoid.

Safer and easier to keep to herself.

Gideon cleared his throat. "Your car was inspected. I swung by the auto garage this morning. My mechanic said your cruise control cable was stuck, and the linkage in the manifold vacuum from the servo to the throttle was sticky.

Which can happen in an older car, short-circuiting the cruise control. But he's never seen a brake line shredded and rusted like yours. He couldn't be certain, due the age of your car, but something about the corrosion and tears seemed off to him. It's possible someone tampered with your brakes."

"Why would someone mess with my car?"

"I don't know. Maybe it's the new program you're creating. Pandora. Maybe the mole thinks your program will expose him."

The information rattled her mind. She stroked her pearls, willing her off-beat pulse to steady. Someone wanted to kill her? Over a computer program? Sounded like a plotline from one of the TV shows her dad watched. What if they tried again? Was the Gray Box safe?

But she had to go to work. Her job and her new program just became more important, if someone wanted to kill her because of it. Her stomach soured, and bile coated her tongue.

"What am I supposed to do?"

"Finish the program while we work to find the mole. I'll ask Maddox to give you a ride home after work, if that's okay."

Someone trying to kill her was the only thing that mattered in her head, but she cringed at the idea of Gideon pawning her off onto Maddox. If she earned a bigger paycheck, she would've insisted on taking a taxi. But a thirty-minute cab ride in the Beltway would cost a fortune.

Who was she kidding anyway? Willow being with a guy like him was as statistically likely as hitting the lottery. She was the quiet girl no one noticed, who lived with her daddy.

At least she didn't have cats.

"Please, let Maddox know I'd appreciate a ride."

09

GRAY BOX HEADQUARTERS, NORTHERN VIRGINIA
FRIDAY, JULY 5, 8:35 A.M. EDT

Quiet settled in the car like a rancid smell in the air. Gideon turned on the radio, but music didn't ease the strained silence. Willow's blunt words, declaring what she wanted, had shocked the shit out of him. Nothing about her was disingenuous, making her even more appealing. He admired her chutzpah and wished things were different.

Wished he was different.

He parked in the closest spot, relieved to be at work. They hopped out of the Jeep and walked to the building without exchanging a word. He held the door open for Willow, letting her walk ahead, and waved hello to Stewart and Peter, the armed plainclothes security guards on duty behind the solid marble desk. There was an additional sniper positioned on the top landing, overlooking the entire main floor. Gideon always looked but never found him.

Avoiding the elevator ride with Willow by striking up small talk with the guards would've been easy but a chickenshit play. Besides, he enjoyed looking at her, talking to her, listening to her gentle voice.

Being near her sparked a strange desire for a simple connection, an insane longing for something he couldn't explain, and it was testing him in a way he hadn't imagined possible.

After a retinal scan, the elevator doors opened. They stepped in. Green lasers scanned them for unregistered devices that transmitted a signal, such as bugs or cell phones. Ridiculous how movies and TV shows had operatives in classified facilities with freaking personal cell phones. Nothing would ever stay classified if that was the real world. The green lights died and the elevator engaged, descending to the sixth sublevel.

The awkward tension in the confined space was worse, heavy and thick, static electricity a breath away from igniting the molecules between them. She stared at the illuminated numbers, making no attempt at idle chitchat. He hated when people spoke without purpose or a point.

With a chime, the elevator doors opened, and they strode off together.

"Thank you." Willow stared at the floor as if she couldn't bear the sight of him. "For yesterday. For everything."

Finally, her gaze lifted and settled on his face. The hurt and disappointment reflected in her eyes plowed through the defenses he'd spent the elevator ride building.

Willow was exposing his emotional soft spots better left locked in his vault. The woman was…whatever you'd call the opposite of the apple in the Garden of Eden. Instead of tempting him to sin, she made him long to be a better man.

For a moment, he couldn't tell the difference between what he was fighting for and defending against. "You're welcome. My pleasure to help."

"These are for you." She handed him a Tupperware

container, and he took it. "They're blueberry scones with a lemon glaze. My mother's recipe."

She turned, hurrying to the Intelligence section before he could thank her. A foreign sensation erupted in his chest, dark and brutal. He couldn't shake the sense he was losing something important. He fucking hated losing.

Daniel Cutter—a real fast-burner who used others for fuel—intercepted her. "You're late." He cut in front of Willow, bringing her to a jerky halt. "I need your status on the Pandora program for the weekly situation report to send to the chief."

Built like a boxer, Cutter had a stellar reputation with the Marine Force Recon before joining the Gray Box, but his busy nose was in almost every mission.

"The program will be finished in less than three days." Willow sidestepped him, clutching her purse and pressing forward.

The douchebag maneuvered into her path, walking backward, peering into her face as if trying to force eye contact. "Once the program is done, I should check it before Sanborn sees it. Ensure there are no bugs."

Recoiling, Willow skirted around him. "I'll check for flaws before I send it to the chief."

"Another set of eyes would be better to catch hiccups. Just want to help."

Daniel Cutter MO 101. He offered to help with legwork no one else wanted to do, provide an extra set of eyes, anything to weasel his way in and ride the coattails of others.

"Danny," Amanda said, stepping into the hall, "let Willow settle in and catch her breath before you start harassing her. We have plenty of time to send the report."

Amanda had softened after she became a mother, cutting everyone slack, including herself, and Gideon noted this wasn't the first time she'd looked out for Willow.

"It took months to convince you to finally let me handle some extra duties, and I want to make sure the PowerPoint slides are perfect," Cutter said. "I'm not going to blow it because she's late." He circled Willow like a damn vulture and had the gumption to block her again.

Something protective and predatory stirred inside Gideon. He was ready to knock Cutter out of her way, but Willow stopped and raised a hand, steering the guy out of her personal space.

"Daniel, is there anything else you need?" Her voice was firm, and her chin was high.

Amanda came up alongside her in either a show of solidarity or as backup.

Pinching his lips, Cutter shook his head *no*.

"Then I need to get to work." Willow walked off as Amanda laid into Cutter about toning down his enthusiasm.

Gideon smiled with pride at how Willow had handled Cutter. She was tougher than he'd expected.

He strode down the main walkway and pulled off the lid of the container she'd given him. A heavenly aroma greeted him. He bit into a scone, and the crumbly biscuit melted in his mouth. Sweetness from ripe blueberries mixed with the tartness of lemon, creating a medley of flavors. There was good, and then there was culinary greatness. This was perfection.

He crammed a second one into his mouth like a starving caveman and licked his fingers.

"Good morning," Janet said. "They're gathered in the conference room."

"What's up?"

"Big meeting with the forensic accountants. They've already gotten started."

Quickening his stride, Gideon ate another scone, imagining how it'd taste warm.

The conference room door opened, and Parker sashayed out. Sanborn followed, looking sharp and tireless in a fresh suit despite the fact that the guy lived at the office.

Gideon checked the clocks on the wall, a row of different time zones from Washington, DC, to Tokyo. 8:50. The original plan had been to convene at 9:30, but with the tension radiating from their rigid bodies and frosty gazes, he gathered he'd missed something important.

Sanborn shut the door and faced Parker. "Sybil, stay the fuck out of my conference room."

Gideon had *never* heard the chief curse. If something had gotten under Sanborn's skin enough to make him sully his tongue with profanity, Gideon damn sure wanted to know what the hell it was.

10

Sanborn glimpsed Gideon "Reaper" Stone duck out of sight fifteen feet away but sensed the man lingering within earshot. *Wonderful.*

His first choice wasn't to hash things out with Sybil in front of his subordinates. There was no dignity in the leadership airing their dirty laundry. So he'd stepped into the hall to talk, but this couldn't wait until they were behind the closed door of his office.

A smug-ass expression swept across Sybil's face. She put a fist on her hip and pointed a French manicured talon at his face. "Let me remind you, the director of national intelligence, *our boss*, asked me to provide oversight due to your glaring incompetence."

One, the DNI was a liaison acting on behalf of the White House, and the president was Sanborn's boss. Two, he had things under control until the DNI anointed this backstabbing viper with enough power to do serious damage. The Gray Box might very well get crushed as a result.

"Follow protocol," she said, jabbing her talon at him again. If she stuck that finger in his face one more time, there was no guarantee he wouldn't bite it off. "You can't dismiss the evidence."

Evidence he didn't trust. Twenty-seven years of operational experience told him protocol, in this instance, would make matters worse. "It's within my discretion to handle this as I see fit. Overstep your bounds, and you'll regret the day you ventured into my lane."

"If you don't get this clusterfuck cleaned up, the DNI will *whitewash this house*."

They'd both been in the business long enough for the meaning to ring clear without elaboration. Funny how the threat hadn't been mentioned to him last time he spoke to Lee.

"Do your damn job." She spat the words. "If you don't, I intend to salvage what I can of my division."

Her section wouldn't survive. Nothing survived a whitewash.

As much as he hated to admit it, a breach of this magnitude warranted a purge if he couldn't clean his house. This operation had gone from finding a traitor to literally saving his people and the Gray Box—after he'd risked everything to secure its future.

Sanborn tamped down his rage to keep his voice smooth as cold steel and stepped forward, not stopping until Sybil lowered her finger and reeled back. "Don't presume to tell me how to do my job. In this situation, your reach exceeds your grasp. You have no clue what it takes to run Operations. The only reason Lee gave you *oversight* is because you have your head shoved so far up his butt, he can't think straight with his prostate throbbing in his throat."

"Watch yourself." Sybil shifted her weight from one hip to the other, balancing on her killer three-inch heels. Contempt set her brown eyes ablaze. "I will go balls to the wall with you. We may have once had a relationship, but I will do everything I can to see you prosecuted if you fail to follow procedure and lock up the traitor."

Au contraire. She wanted him to burn precisely *because* they'd had a brief thing and he hadn't fallen for the Machiavellian maneuvers behind her seduction. A damn shame she'd tried to manipulate him. She was fierce and cunning and would've made a formidable ally. Instead, she'd foolishly declared herself his enemy.

As if he'd ever let her win this war.

It was one thing to prosecute a mole for treason, another entirely to prosecute the director of the Gray Box, an organization that wasn't supposed to exist. Sybil was dancing with the devil, and they were all going to fry because she had a vendetta.

He needed the viper out of his hair. "We never had a relationship. We screwed around to pass the time." He let his tone dip to the ugly bowels of condescension, the only way to send her scurrying off and keep her out of the conference room. "I'm sorry if our brief and forgettable time meant more to you."

Her pale cheeks flamed to match the crimson dress that fitted her like a second skin. "Don't flatter yourself." She swiped long platinum layers from her eye. "Now I'm going to be sweet, give you a break from my company while I call the DNI and give him an update about the new evidence. Maybe I'll even pay him a visit and tell him about all this face-to-face."

"Don't do me any favors, Sybil. And be sure to wipe your mouth and brush your teeth when you're done with Lee."

"Well, you do know how to clean up after a good rim job, Bruce. Thanks for the tip."

Sybil spun on her heel, flipping her shock-white hair, and strutted off. His blood pressure lowered, but the repugnance left a vile aftertaste in his mouth.

Hard to believe he'd ever slept with her, even if it had been years ago.

Turning to go back into the conference room, he caught sight of Emily "Doc" Duvall, their resident CDC scientist. Her gaze met his and her face lit up bright as sunshine. He couldn't help but wonder what she saw in him to spark joy.

"Any leads on where the bioweapon came from?" he asked.

Their last op to prevent the sale of a super strain of smallpox left them with this proverbial ticking time bomb of a traitor. Doc was doing what she could to find the origins of the biological weapon.

"I keep getting the runaround, hitting brick walls." The warmth in her voice wrapped around him like the first sip of single malt scotch at the end of a hard day. "It's only strengthening my resolve to knock them down. I won't stop until I find out who created it. My job is usually pretty boring, but this is the perfect challenge."

Since she'd been at the Gray Box, Doc had been exposed to horrors most civilians didn't have the backbone to handle, and yet she never lost her optimism and always saw the silver lining.

"Keep me posted on your progress. Is there anything else?"

"I heard there was a meeting." She strode up to him

and stood close, testing the bounds of professional propriety. Teasing him with the scent of her hair, strawberries and cream. "Came to see if you needed me."

After his divorce, he'd made certain never to need any woman again, but part of him wanted to see if she tasted as sweet as she smelled.

Sanborn shook his head. "No, you're not needed."

"Maybe I can be of assistance in another way. I overheard your conversation. Sounds like you're having a rough morning."

Oh, crap. He didn't want Doc to know he'd slept with that hell-raiser Sybil.

"If you need a nonjudgmental ear to listen," she said, "or want to go for a run to blow off steam or something, let me know."

Confiding in others was a firm no-go, and he always ran alone to clear his head. "A generous offer. Thank you."

She was radiant, full of life, and he couldn't help but stare. He swore he could read her emotions in the bright blue depths of her eyes, as if she didn't want to hide any part of herself.

An inclination he'd never understand.

"I'm sure you've been under a lot of stress lately," she said. "You should take a break."

"Breaks are for slackers." But he needed one from the relentless high-ops tempo, and he wanted time to know Doc better. "Even if I took one, I wouldn't be able to unwind."

"Melatonin would help you relax. Or exercise for the release of endorphins." She tousled her hair, a languid gesture, kicking up that sweet scent. "Any vigorous exercise would do. Sex works too." She laughed nervously as though embarrassed, dropping her gaze for a heartbeat, then looked at him again, throwing an inviting smile his way. "I'm always up to lend a friendly ear over dinner or"—she shrugged—"for some exercise."

He was tempted. What sane man wouldn't be? And thankfully, Doc was only a liaison, and the CDC director of the Washington office was her boss, so she wasn't off-limits as a subordinate. But her timing was piss-poor. Too much at stake. He'd never let anyone close while hunting a mole. Not even his protégé, Castle, who'd started hovering over Sanborn like a scavenging grizzly— part of the job to weed out the traitor.

"I might give melatonin a try," Reaper said behind him.

Hell's bells. The man had the stealth of a wraith. Good for this line of work, but bad for Sanborn this morning. As soon as he saw Doc, he'd forgotten about Reaper lurking behind the cubicle divider.

"You can get it at any health food store," she said.

Sanborn cleared his throat.

"I should get inside," Reaper said, picking up the cue. "Lots of great *tips* this morning." He went into the conference room before Sanborn gave in to the urge to throw him the evil eye.

Sanborn refocused his attention on the beautiful young woman in front of him. "Doc—"

"Emily. Please."

"I appreciate your thoughtfulness, but—"

"I get it. It's unlike me to be so forward. I'm not the put-yourself-out-there type of girl." She eased back, running a hand through her copper-blond hair. "When I'm around you, I find myself saying whatever pops into my head. I can't shut my mouth—like right now. I should really stop talking. Let you get back to work." She spun as if ready to bolt.

"Wait." He hated the noticeable edge in his voice and erased it. She tossed a glance at him over her shoulder. "Once this situation is done, let's talk."

She smiled, rousing something long forgotten inside him. "I'd like that."

———————   ———————

Inside the conference room, Gideon cursed the lingering smell of Sybil Parker. Her overpowering perfume infested the air, expensive and fussy with a dizzying mix of scents. Trapped in a room with any fragrance, especially one so potent, would give him a headache before too long.

Setting the container of scones on the table, he sat beside Maddox, grateful she knew him well enough not to wear any perfume, much less something that horrendous.

From the conversation he'd overheard in the hall, they'd caught a break in finding the mole, but for some reason, the chief was locking horns with Parker over the new evidence. It was rare to hear the term *whitewash* used, and even more rare for such an order to be issued. He only knew what it meant in such excruciating detail because people with his training were the ones who did the cleansing.

Tension hung in the conference room like a noose. Ares sat across the table eyeing him, arms folded. Reece sighed and tipped the bill of his "Beaver Lover" cap down.

Castle and Alistair swiped through pages on their touch-screens, reading something with furrowed brows while the forensic accountants whispered among themselves.

"What's up?" he asked Maddox.

"See for yourself." She tapped the built-in screen in front of him and brought up a forensic report.

The chief strode into the room and sat at the head of the table. To his right and left were the forensic accountants. Brainiacs in brown and black suits respectively, who lived and breathed to cull data and follow monetary trails.

"I still find this hard to believe," Sanborn said.

Gideon scanned the digital documents. An offshore account. Grand Cayman Island, Nova World Bank. One-million-dollar balance.

Account holder: Willow Harper.

He went dead still, eyes locked on her name.

"We have enough for you to hold her for interrogation," the heavier-set accountant in the brown suit said. "This type of account had to be opened in person. We'll request copies of all supporting documentation, but these banks are notorious for not cooperating. We can't wait for additional proof that may never turn up."

Sanborn ran his fingers through his salt-and-pepper hair. "Let's start with verifying the date the account was opened and cross-check her whereabouts. If she was here at work, that's reasonable doubt, and we can take a step back."

"Not necessarily," the lanky accountant in black said. "If she was out from work anytime within the month prior to the account being opened, that would be enough. Account holders can submit documentation at least thirty days in advance and specify a future date for activation. With the short flight time, she'd only need to be out one day. And if she planned it correctly, flying in the night before, theoretically she could've made it back early enough, only missing half a day."

Gideon's teeth ached for a piece of gum, but he held a neutral expression as he read the rest of the information. Dates. Amounts of deposits.

The account had been opened with a four-hundred-thousand-dollar initial deposit right after Kelli died. A fist of ice punched his heart.

Sanborn had given everyone the day off when they received news about the accident, and all personnel had been excused from work for the funeral. Ample time for anyone to have flown out, opened the account, and returned without missing an unexcused work day, but the documentation painted a flaming bull's-eye on Willow.

This was bad. His pulse hammered at his temples and he fought to stay focused, to think, for Willow's sake.

Gideon never went against protocol, never acted against evidence, but his gut was churning with certainty that this was a setup. Someone had gone to tremendous effort and trouble to frame Willow.

"I'll check the TSA data logs for a specific date," Maddox said. "Her passport would've been scanned departing and reentering the country. But I'm with you, this doesn't feel right."

"According to ITM Parker, Ms. Harper didn't pass the polygraph last week." The lanky accountant looked at Sanborn, his gaze stern.

Every muscle in Gideon's body tightened. Willow was

the worst at deception. When he'd asked about the cut on her face, she'd gotten choked up, but she hadn't lied.

"The first was inconclusive." Sanborn leaned back in his chair. "Harper has a condition the examiner didn't understand. Nothing that prevents her from doing her job, but it skewed the results. She passed the second polygraph without any doubt."

The information Gideon had read last night on ASD substantiated the fact that Willow might have difficulty passing a high-stress examination administered by a stranger. For someone with her extraordinary talent and verifiable condition, a covert agency such as theirs would allow accommodations. They'd given her multiple opportunities to pass, but it also made her the perfect choice to take the fall for someone else. During an interrogation under pressure, her answers could be read as evasive, sealing her supposed guilt.

"Are you okay?" Maddox whispered to Gideon.

He met her gaze, raking his mind over what had given away his concern. "I ate something bad last night." He grimaced and held his stomach. "Probably the sushi."

Nodding, Maddox refocused on the main discussion.

Willow was no mole. Gideon would stake his career on it. But things might get even worse. More falsified evidence incriminating her could surface. And if she was held in custody while they tried to prove her innocence, the real traitor would find a way to get to her like they had gotten to Novak. Whoever was setting her up must be confident that either the evidence would crucify her, or they could kill her.

"You should pull her clearance. Begin interrogation,"

the guy in the brown suit said. "Even ITM Parker agrees with that course of action."

Gideon repeated the offshore account number in his mind, memorizing it. "The last person to enter our holding cell was murdered."

"I presume you have a safe house somewhere in the city. You could hold her there," the black suit suggested.

Sure, they had a safe house but wouldn't disclose the location. Not to the suits or even the director of national intelligence.

"We have to entertain the possibility," Castle said, "that someone could reach out and touch her there. We don't know how deep this problem goes."

The traitor worked for a mysterious information broker. They knew that much. Novak, the psychopath who had been murdered under their noses, insisted the broker had spies all over the damn place, from government agencies to high-value corporations.

"We should turn her over to a different agency," Gideon said deadpan, feigning ignorance that he'd just pulled the pin from a live grenade with the suggestion.

Sanborn's jaw tightened, a vein in his temple bulging. The brown suit nodded, bright-eyed with enthusiasm. The black suit launched into a list of pros and cons.

The idea would never leave the room. The Gray Box couldn't call attention to itself. Besides, no agency wanted to admit they had an in-house problem they couldn't handle. Not to mention that red tape required time. And Parker had the authority to take this over Sanborn's head to the DNI and all the way up to the president if Willow wasn't detained today.

Protocol dictated that Sanborn interrogate her and hold her in custody. She had an inconclusive polygraph and supposedly one million dollars sitting in a bank on Grand Cayman Island. Sanborn wasn't in a position to refuse.

Gideon stood, holding his stomach. "Excuse me. Bad sushi last night. I'm going to see if Doc has anything to help."

Sanborn waved at him to leave as if relieved to be rid of him, but Maddox stared at Gideon with her hawk-eyed gaze. He strolled out of the room and headed to his cubicle, a rough plan full of holes forming in his mind.

If he miscalculated in the slightest in the next five minutes, he could end up with a bullet in his head, and Willow would be left to whatever fate the mole had in store for her.

He hustled to his desk. The gut-reaction idea forming in his head was insane. It was madness to go against the evidence and behind Sanborn's back no less, but there wasn't any other way to keep her safe. He had to get Willow out of the Gray Box now.

Yesterday, someone possibly tampered with her brake line. Today, there was an offshore account in her name. What would happen tomorrow? The traitor had managed to kill Aleksander Novak, an experienced assassin with combat training. Taking out someone like Willow would be easy if given the opportunity.

This investigation would drag on, the team's attention divided between protecting Willow in custody while trying to prove her innocence. Opportunities would be plentiful, and the mole was clever.

Opening a drawer, he spotted the lightweight bullet-proof vest he'd acquired while working with the special operations unit of the Mossad—the Israeli intelligence service. True badasses. The Israeli-designed vest hugged the body like a glove, the best he'd ever seen. He stuffed it inside the empty rucksack he kept for weighted jogs—a training routine he'd picked up from Reece—then scribbled a note telling Maddox to have Willow's car inspected by someone in forensics she trusted, along with the address of the garage. He put it on her desk, where only she'd see it. Telling the chief what'd happened to Willow's car wouldn't clear her. The mechanic's assessment proved nothing, but maybe Maddox could dig up something concrete the chief could use.

Walking as quickly as possible without drawing attention, he took the long way to Intelligence to pass by the break room. As he darted in, a woman from Parker's department, Nicole Tully, threw him a high-beam smile.

He flashed a superficial grin in return.

Once Nicole left with a cup of coffee, he unhooked the ABC fire extinguisher from the wall and threw it into the rucksack. Duct tape on the counter caught his eye, and he swiped the roll. Fastening the bag loosely, he pressed on to find Willow.

There wasn't a minute to spare. The second the shit hit the fan, Willow *and* Gideon would both be in the crosshairs of his own team.

11

GRAY BOX HEADQUARTERS, NORTHERN VIRGINIA
FRIDAY, JULY 5, 9:25 A.M. EDT

Willow glimpsed Gideon's imposing frame stalking up behind her in the reflection of her computer monitor. Her breath hitched in her throat, and her insides squeezed. Hadn't he humiliated her enough?

He wanted nothing to do with her, message received. No need to repeat it.

Sweeping up beside her, he snatched her purse.

"What are you doing?" She yanked out her earbuds, gawking up at him.

"Don't ask questions. You're in danger. Get up and walk with me."

"Wh-what?"

"Now, Willow." His low tone had a deadly edge, driving her to spring to her feet.

She reached for her identification card stuck in the log-in unit connected to her computer.

"Leave it." The harshness of the order made her flinch. His body, tone, eyes—all of it was hard and cold as an iceberg about to capsize her world. "Walk with me."

Her heart started racing, but her legs were frozen in place.

"Please, Willow. There's no time. Walk with me."

She nodded. The slight movement fired the rest of her body into action. She slipped on her shoes, spun the binary globe on her desk and hurried alongside him.

"I'm sure you're flagged." His voice sounded so calm, it was eerie. "Someone in ITM is probably monitoring your computer activity. If you log off, they'll ask security to stop you."

"Why would I be flagged?" She scanned the Intel section to see if anyone noticed them.

"Don't glance around like you're scared. Look straight ahead. Trust me, *please*."

Straightening, she trained her gaze on their path. The hallway was clear. Trotting to keep pace with him, she couldn't process everything, like her brain was short-circuiting.

They rounded the corner. The elevator was within sight.

Panic started creeping in. Why did she have to leave the building? Why would the ITM department have security stop her? "What's going on?"

"Hit the button for the elevator." He darted down the hallway without waiting for her to acknowledge him and unhooked a fire extinguisher from the wall.

She did as he asked, her breath backing up in her lungs.

Coming up beside her, he stuffed the red cylinder inside a huge tan backpack.

"What are we doing?" she asked, trying to keep from spiraling into a tizzy.

The heavy doors opened, and they dashed inside.

He slapped L for the lobby and tossed her his car keys and her purse. "If security stops us, use me as cover. Stay behind me. Run to the car."

Her queasy belly pitched and rolled. She fastened her

gaze to the lit numbers on the elevator display. "What are you talking about? Cover from what?"

Out the corner of her eye, she saw him pull off his shirt and strap on a bulletproof vest. The realization was a slap in the face. A bulletproof vest meant he expected gunfire.

Did she need a vest? "Who's going to shoot at us?"

He threw his shirt back on. "The sniper hidden in the lobby. Possibly."

Oh my God. Oh my God. She'd heard rumors about the last-resort security measure but hadn't believed it. Sometimes people said things to mess with her, but this was no joke.

Her gaze fixed to the illuminated five on the elevator panel. "How possible? What are the odds we'll get shot at?"

"Sixty-forty. In our favor."

"Forty percent chance of getting shot at by snipers?" Was he serious?

The unmistakable harsh click of a gun chambering a round echoed inside the elevator and Willow's chest. The situation was getting worse by the second, and Gideon hadn't explained anything.

"What's happening?" she asked, watching the numbers on the display change from four to three. Bile burned up her throat.

He pulled two fire extinguishers from his pack and shoved both into her arms. "They think you're the mole."

She gasped, recoiling from the ludicrous idea. Ludicrous and horrifying.

"They found an offshore account with a million bucks. Had your name on it."

It was like the floor dropped from under her. She

shook her head, fingers tightening around the steel canisters. *Impossible*. There had to be a mistake.

Two lit up on the panel. Her saliva dried up completely and she couldn't swallow.

Wrapping duct tape around both red cylinders, binding them together, he said, "I know you're innocent. No time to discuss it. We need to get out of the building. When those doors open, go to the car. Do. Not. Stop."

They passed the first sublevel. He stuffed the extinguishers into the deep bag, leaving the flap on top open, then took the strap of her purse and slipped it over her head across her body.

L illuminated and the elevator pinged. The steel doors slid open. Nausea rippled through her, and she feared she'd puke.

He ushered her into the lobby, his bag on his shoulder. "If we get separated, don't go home. Stay away from family, anything familiar."

Separated. Where was she supposed to go? Familiarity and family were the glue holding together her carefully orchestrated life.

She floated through the lobby, unable to process how her legs were moving. Nothing seemed real. Not Gideon at her side, not his locked and loaded weapon, not the allegation she was the mole. And certainly not a sniper hidden in the lobby. The ballooning lump in her throat threatened to choke her.

Her heart drummed, her whole body growing weaker with each step. Gripping the car keys in a fist, metal digging into her palms, the fingers of her other hand tapped wildly on her purse as she strained to focus on breathing and walking.

The phone at the security desk rang. One of the guards picked up the receiver. "Topside."

"Hurry," Gideon whispered. "Our odds just dropped. Thirty-seventy. Against us."

She quickened her step. Her heels clicked in a machine-gun staccato matching her pulse. They closed in on the turnstile as the guard's gaze flickered up to them, and she realized she didn't have her badge to swipe through.

"Officer Stone, Officer Harper," the guard said. "I need you two to stop."

"Run through the metal detectors." Gideon stopped, hands raised, providing cover for her with his body.

She bolted through the steel frame of the sensor. The clacking of her heels flattened in her ears. Sprinting, she ran so fast, her feet barely touched the concrete floor.

The outer front steps loomed. A few more feet. Not far, but the space stretched in her mind, escape receding from her grasp. Her heart pounded under the rush of adrenaline. She reached for the door, and the security alarm blared.

The deafening noise pierced her eardrums, and dizzying bursts of white light flashed in the lobby. Willow covered her ears, her senses shredded, and dropped to her knees.

12

GRAY BOX HEADQUARTERS, NORTHERN VIRGINIA
FRIDAY, JULY 5, 9:32 A.M. EDT

The harsh wail of the security alarm blared in the lobby. Gideon stared down at the red laser dot painted center mass on his chest.

He knew every guy in security, made it his personal mission to make sure they also knew him. Whenever he spotted one at Rocky's Bar, he always bought them a round of drinks. It was a lot harder to put down a buddy than a nameless target. Although he didn't know which topside guard in the sniper's nest had Gideon in the cross-hairs, it was someone he'd interacted with.

That rapport might buy him a few precious seconds of hesitation on the sniper's part.

Glancing over his shoulder, he spotted Willow on her knees, holding her ears, rocking. She'd been so close. So damn close to making it. At least she was positioned directly in front of the door, preventing the guards from engaging a full lockdown.

If they did, a mechanized, reinforced steel gate would slam down and block the door. Similar shutters would seal the windows, all from the inside. It prevented forced entry and stopped unwanted egress. But if they lowered it now, the steel gate would crush her body.

As long as they appeared to cooperate, the guards wouldn't initiate a lockdown.

"Officer Stone." Stewart, one of the guards at the desk, kept it formal, using a title and last name.

Not good. Even worse, both Stewart and the other guard, Peter, held Glocks pointed at Gideon.

"We're going to need you to drop the bag and disarm," Stewart continued.

Gideon scanned the top landing, assessing the location of the sniper.

Slowly, he removed his weapon from behind his back, finger on the trigger but barrel pointed skyward. He raised the rucksack with his other hand in the same manner of non-aggressive compliance.

He gripped the back of the rucksack with the open flap toward the security desk and pitched it with a jerk, momentum propelling the duct-taped extinguishers out of the bag. The cylinders struck the marble floor in front of the security desk with a strident metallic ring that clamored over the alarm, drawing the gazes of the guards.

Gideon fired, hitting one of the extinguishers. The canister exploded in a loud pop, a white billowy cloud flared, and at the same time, the sniper shot off two rounds.

The bullets slammed into Gideon's chest with the jarring impact of a sledgehammer, knocking him to the floor.

He'd been hit hard, right over his heart, but his grip on the Maxim 9 hadn't faltered, as if the pistol was an extension of his hand. Gasping for air, down on his side, he aimed for the second extinguisher and squeezed the trigger.

Another cloud of dry chemical powder mushroomed, providing cover.

Training and ruthless survival instincts kicked in. He ignored the aftershocks of pain rippling through his body, his brain focused entirely on doing whatever was necessary to get out of there alive with Willow. He rolled toward the door, away from the incoming volley he expected. Automatic fire peppered the ground where he had just been.

A buzzing, bell-like sound blasted in rapid succession. Red lights began flashing in concert with the bright white bursts. Lockdown protocol initiated.

The reinforced steel gate started to roll down. Ten seconds before it slammed closed.

Gideon shuffled to his feet. Raw agony exploded in his chest, bringing him to his knees.

Gears rattled overhead, drawing the thick sheet of steel toward the floor. In seconds, the armored security gate would crush Willow.

His mind unplugged from the pain, and adrenaline took over. He leapt into a crouched position, grabbed her, and steamrolled through the front doors.

A heavy clunk boomed behind them as the solid gate sealed shut. They hit the rough concrete outside.

Gideon winced from taking the full force of the impact and Willow's weight on his torso. Clutching her against his body, his primal awareness surged, distracting him for a heartbeat.

In five minutes, the guards would reset the system, lifting the gate, and a quick response force would be on their asses.

God, his chest hurt, but they had to keep moving. He lumbered to his feet, hauling in an agonizing breath, and kept a solid grip on Willow. The steel shutter door dampened the alarm, but the noise still must've been too loud outside, since she kept her hands plastered over her ears and her eyes closed.

They staggered down the front steps, him doing his best to help her along. His vision wavered. He slipped, nearly dropping to a knee. *Shit.* Those bullets hurt like a son of a bitch, making Willow's small frame against him feel heavier than it should. He gritted his teeth, refusing to let the tidal wave of pain swamp him.

As they drew toward the car, she came back to herself, opening her eyes. She hooked an arm around his torso, slipping under his shoulder, propping him upright.

She hit the key fob, unlocking the doors.

He hustled to the driver's side, started the car, and helped her up into the seat. Before she'd shut the door, he jerked the car in gear and peeled out of the parking lot. The tires screamed against the hot asphalt. He wheeled around the corner toward the road leading to the front gate and slammed on the brakes.

Security lockdown triggered the bollards to pop up—a series of stainless-steel pillars, four feet high, six inches in diameter. No vehicle could get through those. Not even a Mack truck. And even if they found a way, the gate at the entrance would be sealed tight.

He punched the Jeep in reverse and railed the wheel, whipping the car in a tight one-eighty J-turn. Then he shifted to forward gear and stamped the gas. He took the road toward the back side of the compound.

Cutting a hard right, he narrowly avoided plowing into a bollard and shot up onto the grass berm. The car bumped and rocked from the change in terrain. Willow shot him an anxious glance, her hands flinging out to brace against the dash and door.

Barreling over the grassy median, he headed behind the main building to the warehouse, where they stored mission vehicles and the AVX high-speed helicopter. Sanborn had persuaded the head of the Senate Select Intelligence Committee to let the Gray Box have a military prototype rather than shipping the sleek, low-drag aircraft to a museum to sit idle.

He wove past a huge oak and swerved to avoid plowing into a sycamore. Bypassing the small patch of concrete for parking, he sped to the door. "Let's go." He jerked the car into park.

Without waiting for Willow, Gideon jumped out and ran to the warehouse door, hissing through the agony in his body. He stabbed the code on the digital lock. Seven digits. He was one of four to receive the weekly changes in the updated codes, since he could pilot the chopper.

A red light blinked and the lock beeped. Crap.

The door didn't open. Security lockdown wasn't linked to the warehouse door. It should've opened.

He cleared his mind, concentrated on the last set of numbers and tried again.

Green light. The lock clinked. He yanked the door open as Willow ran up behind him.

"See those hangar doors?" He pointed to the massive steel doors, wide enough to get a semi through. "There's a big black button on the side wall that opens them. Hit it and meet me in the helicopter. I'll get it started."

Her face was pale, hazel eyes glassy, and her body trembled. He wanted to haul her into his arms, reassure her they'd get through this if they kept moving. Hesitation could get them killed.

Something fired through her. Resolve. Purpose. Maybe good ol' grit. She straightened before he said anything else, expression hardening, and took off running toward the hangar doors.

Gideon raced past a black fleet of bulletproof SUVS to the AVX. Hopping inside, he settled into the leather seat with the long cyclic control stick between his legs. He'd learned to fly at a CIA black site in Tangier before Sanborn recruited him. Flight startup procedures came to him like muscle memory. He switched on the master fuel and flipped the hydraulics up. Scanning the console overhead, he ensured all fuses were in and toggled the battery on.

The hangar doors clattered open. He checked his watch. Lockdown would end any second, and then topside security and his team would be bearing down on them, guns hot.

Time was an enemy. He adjusted the throttle, gauges zeroed.

His gaze locked on Willow as she cut in front of the helicopter and climbed into the seat. "Can you handle the sound of the chopper?"

"I don't know. I think so."

"Check your side for a headset. It'll reduce the noise."

She snatched a headset and put it on. He grabbed the lever of the collective control mounted on the left side of his seat and pressed the red start button. The engine wound up with a keening sound.

While they waited for the throttle to reach one hundred percent rpm, he helped her with the multiple

buckles of the seatbelt and strapped himself in. He threw
on a headset in case she needed to talk to him.

One hundred percent rpm. Finally.

He pulled up on the collective to lift off. The wheels
cleared, and he pushed the cyclic stick between his thighs,
cruising out of the hangar. He steered the chopper up,
climbing altitude.

Five figures sprinted from the main building below.
Sharp pings echoed from the bullets ricocheting off the
helicopter. The tail of the helo swung violently from side
to side.

Lucky a bullet didn't hit the fuel tank or a rotor.

He tightened his grip on the control handles to steady
the copter and pitched to clear the compound. Good to
know how far his friends might go, but getting shot down
by one of his own wasn't part of his half-baked plan.

Using the tail rotor pedals, Gideon rolled the helicopter in a hard left over the freeway.

"They can disable the chopper while we're in the air,"
Willow said.

Stunned, he threw her a wary glance. "I had no idea
that could be done."

"Most don't. You have to hack into the AVX system
and input override control codes."

"Who in the Gray Box can do that?"

"Sanborn knows it can be done. Daniel Cutter is
capable of executing it."

"Damn it to hell." Falling from the sky in a disabled
helo and crashing into the freeway wasn't on his top ten
list of ways to go.

The Tysons Corner Center mall had a parking garage

and wasn't far. They could land on the uncovered top level. This time of day, it'd be vacant.

On the way, he shared everything he knew. Details of the offshore account, timing of when it was opened, the not-so-coincidental correlation to his late wife's accident, Willow's failed polygraph, the heat Sanborn was under. The possibility of a whitewash.

When he'd finished taking a wrecking ball to her life, she looked dazed, face ashen, arms clenched around herself. He set the chopper down on the top level of the multistory garage. It was empty as he'd expected. He unbuckled her harness to help her hurry along, but she stared straight ahead, unblinking.

If she went into shock, they were screwed.

"Willow." He caressed her cheek, aching to erase the sudden insanity engulfing her life.

An unnamed longing beat at his chest—the primal need for something deeper than physical pleasure with this woman, something greater than the instinct to protect her. The inclination was undeniably dangerous.

"Willow," he said again, more firmly.

She blinked, snapping out of her trance. Her hazel eyes found him.

"You with me?"

Grasping her pearls like a lifeline, she nodded.

"We've got to move." He wished there was time to comfort her, but it wouldn't take the Gray Box long to track them.

They hopped out, meeting in front of the helicopter. While scoping out the location of security cameras, he offered his hand. Her delicate fingers wrapped around his, and his body tightened at the shocking warmth, the innocent way she blindly trusted him.

He couldn't fail her.

They hustled down four flights of stairs. The mall's doors opened before the stores at seven thirty for walkers. College kids flocked to the Starbucks with its early hours and free Wi-Fi, and they tended to drive cheap beaters prime for stealing.

He prowled for a car easy to hotwire.

Isolated at the end of a row, an old Ford looked good. They made a beeline for it. Empty coffee cups and brown fast-food napkins littered the back seat. The front passenger window was cracked low enough for a small hand to get through.

"Stick your arm through the window and pull up the little black knob."

"We're stealing someone's car?"

"Borrowing."

Brow furrowed, she stuck her arm through the crack in the window. Even on her tiptoes, she couldn't reach the knob.

"I'm going to lift you, okay?" He scanned the parking garage. Still alone.

Once she nodded, he put his hands on her hips and lifted. A vicious twinge ripped into his chest from where the bullets had struck the vest. She grasped the knob and pulled, unlocking the door. She scooted inside to the driver's seat, unlocked the other door, and climbed back to the passenger's side as Gideon hustled around the car.

He jumped in and removed the panel of the steering column. Glancing around, he felt for the right wires, stripped the tips, and tried them until he sparked the engine and the beater started.

"Where are we going?" she asked.

"We have to make a couple of stops. Then we're going to see a friend about passports."

She clutched her purse, face riddled with worry.

"I'll keep you safe and we'll figure out who's framing you. Everything will be okay."

He left out the part about how things would get a hell of a lot worse before they got better.

13

Chaotic chatter filled the halls. Every cubicle buzzed. Black Ops was a flurry of activity in the wake of one of their own violating protocol and breaching the lockdown.

Cobalt had waited and waited, but daring to delay a minute longer was suicide. Rushing from the facility immediately after the lockdown ended would've drawn attention and raised dangerous questions, but the phone call had to be made. Now.

Everyone was focused on Stone and Harper. No one noticed Cobalt slip into the elevator.

None of the horrible, ugly things Cobalt had done had been easy to pull off or stomach. Most orders involved passing along information, and following those instructions was habit at this point—an ingrained routine. No thought, just action.

Other orders, such as sabotaging Harper's brake line, had left Cobalt's mouth dry and heart palpitating in a wild streak like a train about to derail. Endless hours spent wide awake at night, replaying deeds stained in blood… but that was good. Caring meant one still had a soul.

A soul that was going to burn in hell.

Buck up!

The elevator doors opened on the ground level. Cobalt strode off as if the world wasn't in a tailspin with everything about to crash and burn. White dust blanketed the concrete floor and marble security desk. A choking odor of ammonia permeated the lobby.

Stone had no clue he'd been spotted taking the fire extinguisher off the wall and ducking into the elevator with Harper. *If I'd called security sooner, this disaster could've been averted and the two of them detained.* The plan was falling apart, collapsing in on itself.

Harper had been chosen with time and care. The perfect patsy.

After reality sank in that there was no way out of working for Daedalus—besides in a body bag—a scapegoat had to be found for a rainy day. Boy oh boy, it was pouring now.

If Harper had died in her car yesterday, everything would be as it should today.

In the event the analyst survived, measures were in place to eliminate her while she was held for interrogation. Except Cobalt had no contingency plan for Harper escaping.

Damn it! Every minute ticking by with Harper and Stone on the run was one minute closer to Cobalt getting a bullet in the back of the head.

Stone's interference couldn't have been anticipated. No link between him and the girl existed, much less anything that would drive him to make such a risky move to help her.

Daedalus won't care to hear about circumstances beyond my control.

But he *would* care that Gideon Stone had meddled.

The security guards were so wrapped up cursing and kicking themselves for letting Harper and Stone escape that they paid no attention as Cobalt left the building. Cobalt strolled to the car, hopped inside, and took the burner phone from the glove compartment.

What if he wouldn't help? What if he wanted to eliminate all loose ends instead?

I'm not a loose end. Not yet. I still have value. He'll help me.

Cobalt dialed the number, letting calm reason prevail over panic. The phone rang.

"Yes." Daedalus's voice carried a chilling current of power.

"Willow Harper survived the car accident. They found the offshore account and were about to hold her, but a field officer helped her escape from the facility before I could get the guards to initiate a lockdown. Gideon Stone."

"Stone? How do I know the name?"

"He was the one sent to terminate you."

Two years ago, the Gray Box had received a tip from one of their CIs—confidential informant—who was a major government contractor. A device that could compromise certain government security measures was going to be sold to a man known as Daedalus—an information broker dealing in counterintelligence and corporate espionage.

A man who stayed so well hidden, he was more myth than reality.

Daedalus had already been on the Gray Box radar. They'd wanted to bag him for years but had no idea what he looked like or how to find him.

Cobalt had managed to alter enough mission details to lead Stone to kill the man Daedalus met for the exchange. Still, Stone had unknowingly seen the real Daedalus, making the operative a loose end. Cobalt had followed the subsequent instructions down to the finest detail, tampering with Stone's brake line and seat belt. But his wife had ruined everything by taking his truck. A second attempt on Stone's life would've raised red flags.

"Ah, yes. Agent Gideon Stone." Daedalus sighed, deep, long. Feral. "The man was like a ghost that day. Never even sensed his presence. He's a problem."

The simple thing would've been to let Stone do his job and eliminate Daedalus.

Simple, but a colossal mistake. If Daedalus was arrested or met an untimely death, he'd taken precautions to ensure everyone connected to him went down. He called it *insurance*.

"Too bad you weren't able to take care of Stone when you had the chance." The disgust in his tone struck a match of outrage in Cobalt.

Daedalus was safe, his identity and his empire protected even though the Gray Box had gotten close enough to destroy him. Not once had he expressed the slightest appreciation.

"You're alive today because of me." Cobalt stopped short of saying anything else, already regretting the anger fueling the words.

"Careful. Goad my temper at your own peril." The threat was issued with cool aplomb. "Your next words will determine the nature of the help I deign to give. I suggest you consider your current position as you choose them wisely."

Desperation swelled inside. Desperation and enough anxiety to give a person a heart attack. The expectation was clear. If not met, the best Cobalt could hope for was a quick death. "I apologize. I misspoke."

Stark silence fell. And dragged.

Every nerve pinged. This fiasco would only end in one way—death. But it needed to be Harper's and Stone's. Whatever needed to be said, whatever needed to be done to survive. Even beg. "Forgive me, Daedalus. Please."

A bone-chilling laugh resounded. "Of course I forgive you. After all, aren't we friends?"

Said the devil to the worm wriggling on the hook. "Yes."

"You're one of the most valuable assets I've ever had," Daedalus said. "It's imperative you stay in place. Lose you, and no guarantee I'd get another asset inside the Gray Box."

Cobalt drew in a shuddering breath of relief.

"I'll send a small team," he continued. "They can be there within three hours. In the meantime, activate the tracking device."

Daedalus's empire spread far and deep, giving him access to the black market, politicians, hitmen, classified information, and cutting-edge technology the government didn't know about. Like the tracker planted on Harper. When in stealth mode, it was undetectable to any scanner, including the one with a six-figure price tag inside the Gray Box.

Once activated, the microchip would emit a signal so powerful, Harper wouldn't be able to hide underground. The small team being deployed would be able to monitor her movements with a real-time video feed via satellite. Yep, Daedalus had access to one of those as well.

"You need to find a way to delay Harper from fleeing the area," Daedalus said.

"Why? The tracker will give us her location no matter where she runs."

"You've underestimated Stone twice. A third time

wouldn't be good for your health. He could detect the tracker once it's active. If they're in the area, we'll still have a reasonable shot at finding them. My men will make her death look like an accident or suicide, and we can finally eliminate Stone as well. Make sure they don't go far."

No pressure. "How? They're already on the run."

"Make it personal. Newsworthy. Does she have family? Anyone she cares about?"

Were there no limits, no acts too low? "Yes."

Now everything was down to hurting a sick old man confined to a wheelchair?

But that was how Daedalus got you.

First, he found your weakness and exploited it. You gave him little bits of information, which spiraled into lots as he reeled you in tighter. Before long, you were doing anything he asked. Because he had you. He *owned* you.

"Take care of it, and don't mess this up," Daedalus said. "It'd also be good to have leverage over Stone. You dug into him before. Gather everything you have on him, and give the team all the information when they arrive. I'll send the location via regular protocol."

Staying in the office meant being able to keep track of the situation, and disappearing for hours would be noticed, but there was no choice. "Okay."

"Do your part, and I'll do everything in my power to protect you."

"Thank you." Cobalt hung up, removed the phone's battery and SIM card, and started the car. If this didn't work, Daedalus's protection could flip into his order to take care of all loose ends. *Maybe it's time to get my own insurance policy.*

14

SPRINGFIELD, VIRGINIA
FRIDAY, JULY 5, 10:53 A.M. EDT

I'm a fugitive.

Willow sat in the old Ford, staring into the black backpack Gideon had thrown on her lap while he concentrated on the road.

Needing to busy her hands to calm her nerves, she sifted through the contents of the bag. A gun. Four loaded magazines. A black wand thingy. Pack of Parliament cigarettes and a lighter.

"You smoke?" A trivial question, but it beat out agonizing over her situation.

"Not since college." Everything about him, from his low tone to preternatural composure, was severe. "Traded the habit for chewing gum, but I keep a pack of smokes. Lighting up a cig on the street in plain sight is a good way to keep a low profile while taking in your surroundings."

She rifled deeper in the bag, finding a standard-issue med kit for operators. But the rest, the earpiece, small electronic scanner, and ENVGs—enhanced night vision goggles with thermal and infrared capability—were expensive, specialized equipment and not standard.

"Why do you have this stuff?"

He glanced at her with a pinning focus that made her shiver. "I like to be prepared."

She tucked the equipment in the bag and ran her fingers over bundles of major international currency. Must've been ten thousand dollars in American bills alone.

A gnawing sensation dropped through her, as if her whole world was getting sucked down a garbage disposal.

Who'd look after her father while she was on the run? The freezer was well-stocked, so he wouldn't starve, but what if he needed help or had an accident getting in and out of his chair?

One of her sisters would have to pitch in, which meant Laurel. Ivy lived in Paris. When she was working on her PhD at the Sorbonne, she'd fallen in love with a beautiful woman called Delphine and the city. Laurel lived a five-hour drive away in Connecticut with her plastic surgeon husband, twin daughters, and au pair—a young woman who cleaned, cooked, and watched the girls. Willow would rather have root canal surgery without an anesthetic before asking Laurel for help, but she had no choice.

Her gaze fell to a box of hair dye Gideon had picked up for her when he made a pit stop at a drugstore. The color was *White Chocolate*, a light blond. His wife had been blond. Must be his preference.

"Why did you pick this color?" She held up the box.

He turned into a garage beside a movie theater and parked in a spot shrouded in darkness. "We need to change the color so you look different. Lighter makes more sense. I always think of your hair as chocolate-brown, and when I saw White Chocolate, something clicked. If you want a fiery red, I grabbed one of those too, but I think a subtle shade would work better."

She glanced at the fire-engine red hair on the other box. Subtle was better.

Gideon pulled on a nondescript ball cap, handed her one, and wiped down the car with a plain white cloth—the steering wheel, dash, console, anything they'd touched. He scanned the garage and adjusted her cap, lowering the bill to cover her face.

His fingers grazed her ears, and she wanted to throw her arms around his neck and thank him for saving her twice. For having the foresight and gumption to risk his life to save hers. But he was already out of the car before she had the chance.

He moved quickly around the front, in that predatory way of his, and opened her door. She slipped on the backpack and hopped out. He did a sweep on her side with the cloth.

"Keep your head down in case we pass any surveillance cameras," he said.

The Gray Box would be searching for them, using the upgraded facial recognition program she'd designed. If she'd had any idea her program would be used against her one day, she might've been less thorough.

Resting a hand on the small of her back, he set a quick pace through the garage. She trotted to keep up, but it was the firm weight of his palm pressed to her spine, not the exercise, that threw off the rhythm of her heartbeat.

The physical contact, like in the car, hadn't shocked her. Some part of her had probably reached maximum freak-out capacity. Maybe she even expected the grounding feel of his hands at this point, keeping her moving and focused.

They strolled four blocks through an area of northern Virginia she didn't recognize. Based on the signs they'd passed on the freeway, she suspected they were close to Springfield. Apartment buildings, small businesses, shops, and restaurants dominated the urban area.

Stopping at a doughnut shop, he opened the door. The most delicious aroma hit her. "I thought we were going to see a friend. Why are we getting doughnuts?"

"I'm starving. Aren't you?" Without waiting for an answer, he squired her inside.

Customers occupied three small tables. The rest of the shop was empty other than a couple of employees. They strode to the counter, passing a conveyor belt and deep fryer, where doughnuts were made fresh on the other side of plexiglass.

A young Asian woman stood behind the register. She smiled at Gideon, her eyes lighting up the way Ivy's did whenever she came home for a visit, but he gave no indication of knowing her. The woman's gaze swung to Willow, and her smile fell.

"What would you like?" The woman glanced between them.

"A half dozen," Gideon said. "Ken's Special."

The woman hesitated, holding his gaze. "For here or to go?"

"For here."

Willow glanced at the overhead board. There was one type of doughnut, with an array of glazes and extras to choose from, but she didn't see any Ken's Special.

The young woman stared at Willow, then looked back at him. "A name for the order?"

"Gideon Stone."

Willow flinched so hard, she nearly jumped out of her skin. They were fugitives, and he'd given his real name. In a doughnut shop?

Gideon ushered Willow to the side of the shop where the doughnuts were made.

"What's going on?" she asked.

The woman behind the register picked up the phone and made a call, staring at them.

Willow tensed. Their names hadn't been released to the public yet. Unlikely the woman was dialing the police, but the call was definitely about them.

"Patience." Gideon pointed to the doughnut-making process. White bundles of dough fell into a vat of hot oil. A teenage boy fished them out once they turned golden and dunked them in various glazes. "These are the best doughnuts you'll ever have."

How could he act relaxed? Nonchalant?

They'd escaped from the Gray Box and had almost been shot. Actually, he *had* been shot. Twice. And they'd left Director Sanborn in a precarious position.

"What happens in a whitewash?" On the helicopter ride, she'd been too shell-shocked to ask specifics.

"It's a twofold process." His voice was low, smooth. "All paper trails verifying the deep black ops team, division, or agency are erased. Cleaners are sent in. Personnel who have knowledge that poses a threat are eliminated. The rest are disavowed. No government work history, no pension— but they have their lives."

An icy tingle ran down her spine. "They can't do that. Not to American citizens."

"Who is *they*?"

She was at a loss for an answer.

"A whitewash only happens to an organization or unit that isn't supposed to exist. One that can't see the light of day or subvert its purpose of safeguarding national security. *They* can and will, if deemed necessary."

Her breath hitched in her throat. It was all too startling and grim to be real.

The teenager approached them and proffered the box of doughnuts.

Gideon took it and strolled to the register. "How much?"

"It's on the house." The young woman winked.

"Thanks, Mariko."

The woman didn't wear a nametag. Gideon knew her.

"Why the ruse?" Willow asked.

"In the event I'm being coerced, I could warn them without anyone being the wiser."

He put a hand to her lower back in the comforting manner that was growing on her. His masculine heat teased her skin, anchoring her in a way that took the edge off the pervasive dread.

They passed an *Employees Only* sign and stopped at an unmarked door. He looked up at a security camera. After a soft buzz, Gideon opened the door to a staircase.

He bounded up the steps two at a time, agile power rippling through him. She jogged up behind him until they reached a metal door. A series of deadbolts unlocked, a heavy latch slid on the other side, and the door swung open to the outside.

A guy who looked like a male version of Mariko—midtwenties, long, glossy black hair—gave Gideon a one-armed hug. "I take it this isn't a social visit."

"Afraid not."

The guy waved them inside.

The lavish upstairs apartment had an inviting open-concept layout. A high-end sofa and club chairs comprised a cozy living room. Concrete countertops graced the eat-in kitchen, where a steel table was adorned with laptop and shotgun. The dining-area-turned-makeshift-office had a table with a lightbox on top, and a black photo background hung on the wall.

A red beacon light was mounted high above the doorframe.

"Ken, this is Willow," Gideon said. "Willow, Ken. I helped him out of a hairy situation once."

She didn't recall any *Ken* from Gideon's case files.

"Hairy?" Ken scoffed, closing the door. "You saved my life. I owe you big time."

"I need to collect on the favor," Gideon said.

"What do you need?"

"Passports and a place to crash until they're ready."

"Done," Ken said. "Take the third bedroom at the far end. It's got an en suite. Should take about three hours. Four, tops."

There was a hall off either end of the main living area. Toward the kitchen, Willow spotted one door. On the other side, where Ken had indicated, were two more doors.

"Willow needs to dye her hair first."

"If I know the color, I can digitally alter the picture to match. While I'm working on the passports, she can dye her hair. It'll save time." Ken glanced at Willow. "What's the color?"

She pulled out the light blond dye box.

"Oh, sweetie," Ken said, grimacing, "that'll make you look like a fried pumpkin if you don't bleach carefully first. You've got great hair. Don't ruin it." He reached out and felt the strands that'd fallen loose from her bun.

She stiffened and jerked away. "Don't touch me." Based on their expressions—she'd seen them many times on others—her reaction made them uncomfortable, even though she'd been the one touched without consent. "I'm sorry."

"My bad. I'm too friendly for my own good." Ken smiled. "Any other options?"

She showed him the ghastly red.

"Perfect. That'll turn you from brunette into a bright auburn and make my bathroom look like a crime scene, but I'm willing to sacrifice for Gideon. And since you're a friend, I'll hook you up with the best conditioner for silky smooth locks. Let's get cracking."

15

Cobalt parked down the street from Willow Harper's home.

The Gray Box quick response force had surely hit the airports and Stone's place by now, in the hopes he'd try to retrieve his go bag. Personnel could be here any minute.

Cobalt switched on the portable multiband jammer and slipped it inside the messenger bag. There was no way to be certain, but it was safe to assume the black ops team had wireless surveillance in every suspect's home. The Wi-Fi jammer would block all signals, video and audio, within a seventy-meter radius.

After pulling on clear vinyl gloves, Cobalt ensured the syringe—filled with a mixture of methyl iodide and sodium chloride—was within quick reach in the bag, then got out of the car.

Six months after recruitment, Daedalus arranged for Cobalt to spend a week in Montana. The cover story had been a romantic trip with a significant other, fishing and horseback riding.

Turned out to be a week-long course in learning how to do evil shit. Detonating and disarming explosive devices. How to administer various poisons and what easy-to-get materials to use in a pinch. The essentials of beating a polygraph. Tampering with a car to make it look like an accident.

The job on Stone's truck had been precise, the brake line set to trickle slowly, requiring the brakes to be pumped numerous times before complete failure.

Rigging Harper's car at the Gray Box had been rushed, spurred on by the arrival of the forensic accountants. Cobalt hadn't expected them so quickly and especially not to pop up on a holiday. It was tidier for Harper to have an accident before the offshore account was discovered.

Fear of getting caught red-handed sabotaging Harper's car had kept Cobalt on edge. A good thing too, since someone had come out into the parking lot.

A detail Daedalus didn't need to know. Not if Cobalt wanted to keep breathing.

Cobalt rang the bell with a heavy heart. A moment later, the front door opened.

"Yes." Mr. Harper rolled to the side in his wheelchair, repositioning his chair inside the doorway. An IV bag dangled from a metal pole attached to the chair. This would be easier than expected. Distract the old man and inject the solution into the IV.

This composition should put him in a coma, based on an approximation of his weight. Then things needed to be taken to the next level to ensure this hit the news, where Willow Harper would see it and feel compelled to rush to her father's side.

Once the team took her out, Cobalt would take care of her dad, tying up the loose end.

"Hello, sir," Cobalt said, keeping gloved hands out of sight. "I work with your daughter. There's been a troubling incident. Do you mind if I come in? It's urgent I speak with you."

16

In the third room at the far end of the hall, Gideon set down the clippers he'd borrowed from Ken on the bed next to a trash bag and roll of paper towels. The rustle of plastic drew his attention to the bathroom. The door was cracked open. Based on the moving shadow, Willow was hunched over the tub, probably working dye into her hair.

He'd rubbed petroleum jelly that Ken had given him over the tub before Willow got started to make clean up as painless as possible. Every inch of him hurt during the small task. He slipped out of his holster, peeled off his shirt, and unstrapped the bulletproof vest. His muscles screamed, his torso aching like he'd been hit by a pile driver. Two bright red spots from the impact of the bullets, each about the size of an orange, would turn purple by tomorrow.

Stretching through the pain, he stood and traipsed to the window. He scanned the back alley running along the rear of the stores and lined with dumpsters and focused on the next step.

To find out who was framing Willow, they had to follow the money. The offshore account had been opened in person, and there would be a picture on file. With luck, the mole was a woman and had used her own photo along with Willow's name to establish the account. If the traitor was a man, good odds he'd use a woman close to him, someone he could control.

Either way, it was their one shot in the dark. Flying to Grand Cayman wasn't an option. Safe bet the Gray Box was monitoring airports using Willow's facial recognition program. He needed to figure out an alternate form of transportation and to know the Gray Box's next move.

Grabbing the clippers, Gideon rapped a knuckle on the bathroom door. "Mind if I cut my hair?" Ken had been generous enough to give them one room to use. He wouldn't impose by dirtying a second bathroom. "It'll take two minutes."

Two, and he'd get to work on creating an exit plan out of the city.

Water ran in the tub. "Come in."

He ducked inside with his head lowered, but he still caught her rise to her knees, clad in only her bra and underwear, and dunk her head under the faucet. His thoughts careened. The sight of her creamy pale skin, narrow waist dipping to the small of her back, and heart-shaped ass tipped in the air lit up his central nervous system like a football stadium on game night.

Fastening his gaze in the opposite direction, he hustled four strides to the sink. The snapshot of Willow, her curves and every movement, had imprinted on his brain, filling in the missing pieces in his mind for a complete picture he could visit whenever he closed his eyes. For the first time, his memory was a liability instead of an advantage.

Might've been smarter to wait for her to finish. Gideon redirected the trajectory of his misfiring mind. He opened a trash bag over the sink to collect the hair and set the timer on his watch, determined to stick to two minutes and not a second longer.

Changing his appearance with a shave and haircut wouldn't thwart a facial recognition program. But adding a pair of sunglasses and ball cap would make him less recognizable in a crowd, give him a slight advantage in person.

He flipped on the cordless clippers. First, he shaved under his chin, up and over his jaw, above his upper lip. Quick, methodical swipes to get the job done. Nothing fancy. He did the same with his hair, running the clippers from the nape of his neck to the front, his head hanging over the trash bag. The goal was simple—keep it neat, clean, even.

When he was done, he looked like a younger version of himself. One less cynical and guarded, a man who had naively believed he was capable of having a successful relationship. He no longer recognized that version of himself staring back.

The water stopped running in the tub. He wiped the sink and collected the trash bag. In the mirror, he watched Willow wrap her hair in a towel. His gaze slid over her sensual figure. Looking at her without being able to touch her was pure hell.

His alarm chirped. Perfect timing. He bolted from the room before she made it to her feet.

Before he could pat himself on the back, a sharp gasp came from the bathroom. Willow started crying. The pit of his stomach tightened.

Those weren't crocodile tears. From extensive experience with his ex's episodes of bawling on demand, he could detect fake tears at the first sniffle.

The pained sounds from Willow were real and had the inside of his chest twisting.

He hated how her life had been turned upside down. Over the last few hours, he'd asked a lot of her—high-pressure, high-risk things. She'd handled all of it with grit and trusted him with little explanation. It bumped his admiration of her several notches higher.

The absolute last thing he should do was go back in there, but her crying turned to sobbing, and he didn't need her falling apart.

He threw his T-shirt on, set a five-minute timer—estimating it'd take longer than two to console her but not giving himself enough time to succumb to temptation—and stepped into the bathroom. Sanguine dye smeared the edge of the white tub on his right, making it look like a bloodbath. Plastic gloves lay on the floor.

Leaving the door ajar, he pivoted left. Willow stood trembling in front of the sink and mirror. Weeping, she faced him.

Water dripped from her dark-red hair in rivulets down her delicate body. Her flimsy gossamer underwear was see-through. Blindsided, he stiffened.

He pinned his gaze on her face, refusing to veer for a second below her neck.

"I don't look like me." Tears spilled from her eyes.

Unable to stop his feet from moving closer, he went to touch her but thought better of it and drew his hands back to his sides.

"I-I hate this hair." She burst into a series of hiccupping sobs. "None of this is me. Running. Dodging bullets. Stealing cars. Being a fugitive."

Her raw vulnerability gutted him. He had to say or do something—only a heartless asshole wouldn't comfort her—but he was frozen in place. "Please, don't cry."

She reached for him. He couldn't avoid the collision of contact as she fell against his chest and pressed a trembling palm to her mouth. Or perhaps he didn't want to.

He wrapped his arms around her shivering body and held her, cradling her head against his sore sternum. She was warm, so warm and soft. Her fear was palpable, tearing him up on the inside. She really started sobbing as if she'd been holding back a moment ago.

Tightening his embrace, he shushed her and stroked her hair.

"Gideon, I can't do this. I don't know how. I need things to go back to being normal. I need normal."

"You can do this. Your hair changed, not who you are. I see you, Willow."

She blinked up at him. He wiped the tears still streaming with his fingertips while keeping an arm around her.

"Same hazel eyes that can't decide if they want to be brown or green." He brushed his knuckles across her cheek, a whisper of touch, and she leaned into his caress. "Same kind spirit."

Her sobs slowed, her breathing steadied, her body growing calmer.

"Same brilliant mind. You're a survivor. *I see you.*"

He skimmed her lower lip with the pad of his thumb, heat burning his face. She stilled, like she was holding her breath the same as him. He'd been attracted to scores of women…and then there was *this*.

Not mere attraction but a draw far stronger and more intense.

Kissing her would be a catastrophic mistake. An epic disaster. But only a blind monk would have the willpower to resist.

Her hands flew to his cheeks as she rose on her tiptoes and yanked his mouth down to hers. Their lips locked—his ability to think rationally shut down on impact—and their tongues tangled in a sweet, filthy slide of a kiss.

His heart kicked into a frantic pounding like machine gunfire against his breastbone.

On a sharp, mingled breath, it turned deeper, hot and hard and hungry.

Her supple body pressed tight to his, her leg hooking on his hip like she wanted to climb him. All her soft warmth ground against the growing bulge in his pants. Every single point of connection sparked more heat.

He had to stop this, stop her, stop himself somehow.

Then she slid her hand along his torso, down to his erection. He nearly burst from his skin. Gripping the nape of her neck and her hip with his other hand, he jerked her closer. The hard suction of her mouth, the way she licked and laved, tied him up in knots.

Shuffling her back against the wall, he palmed her ass and caressed her breasts, flicking a thumb hard over her nipple.

It registered on some distant level when the thin mesh of her bra tore in his rough hands that he was being too aggressive. But her moans grew throaty and her hips rocked against his.

The absolute last thing he'd do was take her in a rush,

in a bathroom, without condoms, when he needed to protect this scared, trusting woman from *any* danger. And that included him.

His alarm beeped like a time bomb, and the fantasy detonated. This wasn't make-believe with no consequences to actions, and this wasn't a mission where the fallout didn't matter.

In an act of sheer will, he ended the kiss. Their breaths came in ragged pants. There was too much space between their lips and at the same time not nearly enough.

She had the most beautiful mouth, lush and pink. Every atom of his being longed to hold her, taste her in a way that would erase necessary boundaries, but he had better sense.

"I'm sorry for taking advantage of you." He'd underestimated his weakness and overestimated how far out of control things could spin in five minutes.

"No, you're not taking advantage." She drew her mouth dangerously close to his, leaning into him, and he was in misery.

Torn.

"I am. You're upset, vulnerable. You needed comfort, not canoodling." What kind of lowlife was he? With a hot stab in his gut, he dropped his arms and staggered away. "That was a mistake. It shouldn't have happened."

He cut his eyes from the hurt, confused look on her face and left, slamming the door shut behind him. His conscience was lead-heavy, and that sensation he was losing rushed up again. He wished he could push a button, turn ice-cold and disconnect, but his usual self-distancing techniques were failing. He holstered his Maxim, grabbed the extra 9mm from his go bag, and got the hell out of the bedroom.

Willow leaned against the wall. The ghost of Gideon's kiss haunted her lips, the taste of him plaguing her tongue. Fingers shaking, she traced her wet mouth. A cruel echo of sensation throbbed between her legs. She closed her eyes, still feeling his arms bandaged around her, his hot hands on her bare skin. His fingers tight across her nape, running along her spine, clutching her bottom, kneading her breasts, pinching her nipple—causing a pain that hurt so good, her whimper poured down his throat.

In those few heated moments, she'd forgotten the fear, the dread, her sick father home alone, the uncertainty of the future, her utter lack of control in this uncontrollable nightmare.

Gideon had filled her up with something intoxicating and intense, the most intimate experience she'd ever had. Nothing else had existed besides the desire running liquid through her.

And for some reason, he still walked away.

Her stomach twisted, her heart beating heavily.

Lowering her head, she stared at her bra, stained with dye and torn. Ruined.

She hated underwear. The only reason she wore any was her father's insistence it was inappropriate if she didn't.

After the NSA hired her, her dad explained in nauseating detail the importance of dressing professionally to fit in. Her biggest issue was the uncomfortable textures of some fabrics on her skin. Cotton, silk, and cashmere were her go-to materials. In college, she lived in T-shirts and sweatpants. For the job, she'd Googled "best store for women business attire," and Banana Republic came up first. At their outlet in Leesburg, she had found a comfortable seasonless skirt and classic button-down blouse. A saleswoman had recommended kitten heels, since she had little experience wearing pumps.

She bought the outfit, two in every color, and made a detailed chart on what dates she'd wear certain combinations, adding cardigans during the winter. No one seemed to notice, and Amanda complimented her often that she was always very well put-together.

Willow chucked the bra and bikini briefs in the trash. They were a matching set—she couldn't wear one without the other—and she was glad to be rid of both.

She looked at herself in the mirror.

The hair looked awful—unnatural—but this time, she concentrated on her flushed face and not the floppy reddish-brown mane. Ken had armed her with a blow dryer and arsenal of hair products, everything from a pleasant-smelling leave-in conditioner to hair spray. No wonder the guy had gorgeous locks.

She threw on her top and slipped into her skirt in the bedroom. Gideon's voice was muffled through the wall of the room next door. Padding barefoot into the hall, she spotted Ken hunched over the lightbox on the table. She reached for the handle of the adjacent bedroom, but Gideon's sharp tone and the clipped edge in his voice pricked her nerves, staying her hand.

"Listen to me, Maddox. It was a judgment call. Willow is my target, and this is like any other assignment," he said on the other side of the door.

Willow cringed, bracing a hand on the wall.

"This is the only way to find the real mole. Trust me, this isn't personal. This is business. Let me do my job."

Her heart lurched, the beats bleeding together. She spun, rushing back to the bedroom. Shaking, she closed the door and locked it.

Willow is my target.

This isn't personal. This is business.

Humiliation burned inside her, followed by a sickening realization. Everything finally made sense. His sudden interest in her, a plain Jane misfit, when he was obviously into drop-dead gorgeous women. His deceased wife had looked like a Victoria's Secret model.

No surprise the only reason he cozied up to her, came into her house, snooped through her room, distracted her with a kiss, was for an investigation.

She slid down the door, her lungs squeezing. She was his assignment. She was business.

Business!

Hope that anything romantic with him might've been possible ruptured like a burst water pipe. She slapped the wall, wanting to slap Gideon. He didn't care about her. He was only using her to find the mole.

She'd trusted him on the most intimate level, knowing he'd never take anything from her that she didn't willingly give. No, he'd never hurt her physically, but she'd been short-sighted. She hadn't considered her heart.

17

L isten to me, Maddox." Gideon paced in the room, chewing on a piece of gum. "It was a judgment call. Willow is my target, and this is like any other assignment."

"This isn't the way," Maddox said over the phone. "You've lost your objectivity."

No shit. He'd made the mistake of touching her, and the contact had robbed him of all common sense.

"This is the only way to find the real mole. Trust me, this isn't personal." He doubted Maddox was buying the bullshit he no longer sold to himself. Things had gone from professional straight to *intimate.* "This is business. Let me do my job."

Glancing at his watch, he checked the time. He'd bet his left nut Maddox wasn't tracing the call, but he liked his balls as a set and wasn't willing to risk being wrong.

At the forty-five second mark, he'd hang up.

"For what it's worth," Maddox said, "I think she's innocent. Forensics is checking her brake line now, and I think Sanborn is doing what he can to impede the hunt. I get the feeling he doesn't want Harper in a holding cell or interrogated any more than you or I do, but Parker is hitting him hard. The DNI is going to force his hand soon under orders from the president."

"I'm asking a lot, but I need you to buy me time. And someone should check on Willow's dad. The guy's in a wheelchair and may need some help."

"I know what you're going to do next because it's what I'd do. Don't fly." She hung up, ending the call before he did. Her way of reassuring him she was on his side.

Good to know Sanborn believed in Willow. But unless the chief had evidence that she was innocent, he could vouch for her until his lungs burned and it wouldn't matter.

If Maddox knew they were going to the Cayman Islands, so did Sanborn. Gideon just needed the hunt steered away from the bank long enough for him to get proof.

Parker and those pencil-pushing accountants wouldn't expect this move, since they assumed Willow was guilty. In their minds, if the account was hers, she'd wire the money out rather than go there in person. He had to get Willow to the Cayman Islands by the time the bank opened on Monday.

How was he supposed to look her in the eye for two days after overstepping boundaries?

Being near her, he felt human, hungry for a connection. But humanity came hand in hand with weakness, opening the door to mistakes. Maybe that posed the biggest threat to their survival.

He punched the air with his fist. The soreness in his chest from where the bullets bruised him bloomed into pain, peppered with a throbbing ache. He slogged out to Ken's office where his old friend worked on the passports. Willow needed two. One with her real name to access the offshore account at the bank and one with an alias for travel. Ken was busting his butt to complete a job he could charge fifteen grand for, as quickly as possible, for free.

Gideon disabled the burner phone Ken had loaned him in the same manner he'd already disabled his own cell, pulling the SIM card and battery. "I need to hop on the internet."

Ken pointed to a laptop in the kitchen beside the shotgun. An action movie played on the television with the volume low. Gideon turned to the news out of habit.

The weather forecast showed a tropical storm projected to head up the western coast of Florida into the Gulf of Mexico and inland over Alabama. Maybe this was a sign of good luck—at least it was one less thing he'd have to worry about.

Bringing up a web browser, he searched for local homes for sale on the water. Once he pinpointed a nongated community, he brought up maps with satellite images, looking for homes with boats docked. The commercial satellite imagery for Google was updated regularly and would give him a solid idea of where to find an available boat to steal.

A long street backing onto the Occoquan River showed fifteen boats. With some on-site recon, he'd be able to pick the most vulnerable one to snatch. First, he needed to load up on supplies. Depending on the speed of the boat he found, they'd be on the water until early Monday morning. Stocking up was essential to avoid stops.

Two days alone with Willow on the open sea in tight quarters. No way around it, but he needed to get his head on straight.

He pinched the bridge of his nose, his thoughts bunching over what to say to her. How in the hell to explain to Willow the problem was he wanted her too damned much? He'd never met a woman like her, who stirred his blood with longing, knotted his brain with crazy ideas of normalcy. Not even Kelli had come close to having this effect on him.

Gideon cleared his search history. "I've got to head out. Tell Willow I went to get supplies. I'll be back soon."

"No problem." Ken didn't look up from the table, wearing a respirator mask to protect against the fumes of the dangerous chemicals he used.

Gideon should ask Willow if she needed him to pick up anything specific, but he couldn't afford to get sidetracked behind closed doors with her.

Head lowered, he strolled out of the doughnut shop to the parking garage. He'd never been with a woman so refreshingly raw in her sexuality. She took him from zero to a hundred, making him quake. Her sincerity and vulnerability were sexy as hell, and the body she hid under her clothes was killer.

He'd had his share of forward ladies, had seen a lot of dirty things—done a lot too. But Willow had a way of blindsiding him.

And he loved it.

He entered the garage, scanning for a different car to swipe in case the other had been reported stolen.

Two middle-aged guys turned into a parking spot and hopped out of a blue sedan.

The driver speed-walked, leaving the other behind. "Hurry up. This is the last time I see a movie with you on opening day. You know I hate to miss the previews."

The passenger groaned and caught up. "Settle down." He took the other guy's hand and gave him a quick kiss. "I'll wait in the concessions line while you grab the seats. We've got time. You won't miss anything."

Once they rounded the corner out of sight, Gideon checked the doors of their car. Open. He slipped in and popped off the cover of the steering wheel column to see if he could hotwire this one. A spark brought the engine to life in a rumble.

A mega store, one of those hypermarkets that was a discount department store rolled up with a grocery store, took up almost half a city block about two miles down the road. He pulled out of the garage and drove to it. There'd be lots of cameras but also lots of people. The facial recognition program couldn't tap into every surveillance camera in every city. They were twenty miles from the Gray Box. Chances were good they hadn't accessed any cameras this far south and focused more around the airports, but precaution was his best friend.

Head down, he snagged a shopping cart and a couple of cheap thermal bags to keep perishables cool. Checking to see if Willow had any allergies would've been smart, but he'd seen her eat poultry and dairy.

Steak, veggies, fruit, and sliced turkey made the cart. He avoided anything with nuts, strawberries, or shellfish to be on the safe side. In the camping gear area, he picked up a portable propane stove and instant ice packs that used a chemical reaction to generate cold.

In the clothing section, he grabbed extra T-shirts, a button-up shirt to conceal his weapon once they docked, and a pair of pants. For Willow, he estimated her size and tossed in a couple of wrinkle-resistant sundresses. He'd never seen her wear any patterns, always solid colors, and she'd never had a crease. He wasn't sure if they bothered her, but no sense chancing it.

Heels weren't practical, but gauging shoe size was harder. Kelli had worn an eight, but Willow had smaller feet. He threw a box of size seven Keds in the cart.

On his way to get toothpaste, he passed an aisle with condoms and stopped.

Shaking his head, he pressed on and picked up tooth-brushes. He rounded the corner, waltzed down the aisle, and found himself in front of the display of condoms again.

Just in case. They were going to be stuck together in a confined space for two days. Safety first. He grabbed the value pack. But the only way to be sure he did the right thing and showed Willow the respect she deserved was *not* to get the condoms. Right?

He put the rubbers back.

Or he could get them in case things got out of hand. He knocked a box from the shelf into the cart. Having them didn't mean he'd use them.

The situation could get messy. Ugly. Maddox's words rattled in his head.

Willow needed a nice straitlaced gentleman who did sweet things and made her feel special every day. Besides, Gideon didn't do sex *tender* and *gentle* and *slow*, the way a lady like her would want. His type was someone cut from the same cloth as him—another damaged, train wreck of a soul who enjoyed sex no-holds-barred dirty.

That wasn't Willow. They made no sense together, and the last thing he wanted was to put her in a position where she felt trapped with him on a boat or beholden because he was helping her. Only a pig would do that to her.

He threw the box of condoms back on the shelf and hustled out of the aisle.

For once, he needed to be a better man.

18

Traffic crossing the freeway overhead rumbled low. Sweat beaded Cobalt's brow. The muggy air was ten degrees hotter under the overpass along the rarely used service road. A slight breeze brought welcome relief from the godforsaken heat wave pounding the city, but the foul stench of death and desperation lingered.

Daedalus's tactical unit was inbound. Once those animals were unleashed, they couldn't be bought off, and they wouldn't stop. No matter how much blood flowed in the streets, no matter how many cops, agents, women, or children they had to kill or maim to get the job done.

They weren't mindless dogs. Oh no. They were merciless, organized, well-trained.

A shiny black SUV, windows tinted dark, turned onto the road, followed by two motorcycles polished to such a high-gloss finish, it looked as if they'd taken the time to roll through a car wash on their way over. Well, it wasn't their necks on the chopping block if this went south.

The roar of the bikes thundered in the oven-like space under the freeway. The three vehicles pulled to a stop, and the SUV's driver emerged. A familiar face, Ray-Bans hiding eyes of ice. Omega, Daedalus's second-in-command. He was known for producing results. Rumor had it he once crippled a kid to get information from the boy's father, then terminated them both.

Cobalt had first met Omega in Montana and was forced to watch his handiwork up close. Betray your country, you got life in prison. Betray Daedalus, you spent days in a tiny, dark hole, naked. Then Omega carried out the real punishment, the nature of which depended on his mood. Peeled off your skin if he was inclined toward benevolence. Diced you up if he wasn't, starting with your tongue, ending with severing your ribs from your vertebral column.

Either way, you ended up back in the tiny, dark hole.

After Montana, Cobalt rarely saw Daedalus, but it didn't limit his control. Distance only magnified it. He had fashioned himself into a god, and faith in his power didn't necessitate his presence. For anything hands-on, Omega stepped in.

Wiping a hand over his square, clean-shaven jaw, Omega approached, radiating the lethality of a python on the hunt. Skintight black tee over a powerhouse torso. Dark pants highlighted the cruel ability caged within his muscular frame. The sound of thick-soled, heavy boots striking the pavement echoed in Cobalt's chest. Omega circled Cobalt, the way a serpent would an injured mongoose, then finally stopped and held out his palm.

Gaze fixed on the jagged white scar on Omega's bottom lip, Cobalt put a manila envelope in his hand. A sheet inside contained detailed information to help them find Harper and Stone in the event the electronic tracker was lost.

"Her father is in ICU at Saint Margaret's. The address

is inside. He's her closest relative. She seems devoted to him. I believe she'll go there."

A smirk laced with strychnine spread across Omega's face. "We'll have coverage on the hospital, and we'll close in on the tracking device signal." He strutted toward the car. "For your sake, we better get the girl."

Panic sliced through Cobalt like a hot blade. But bleeding out, entrails in hand, wasn't an option. The only recourse was to fight, tooth and nail, by any means fucking possible.

"I took out insurance." A neighbor held a sealed envelope containing enough information to bury Daedalus. If Cobalt didn't retrieve the envelope in person in one week, it would be mailed to someone who wouldn't rest until the scales were balanced. "I burn, Daedalus burns."

Omega halted. Didn't turn. Didn't move. Didn't speak. Cobalt almost shit standing right there. Maybe it wasn't too late to take it back and pretend it was a sick joke.

Once time resumed, Omega looked over his shoulder at Cobalt. "Sure you want me to deliver that message?" His tone was venomous.

No matter the response, the message would be delivered. Better to reinforce the threat with a show of confidence than let fear dilute the only possible play. "Positive."

"You've got some volleyball-sized nuts. I'll give you that." A vicious cackle boomed under the overpass, but it was hollow, devoid of humor.

Omega got in the car, slamming the door. Engines revved. The SUV streaked past with the roaring entourage in tow, leaving a bitter chill in their wake.

19

The room Gideon had been in earlier was empty when Willow emerged. She had accepted the truth: Gideon's interest in her was only professional, a means to get the mole.

She wasn't sure which was worse, her anger over being so gullible, the overwhelming sense of disappointment, or the sting behind his actions.

Despite everything, she needed him. Escaping danger of this magnitude by herself was impossible. She hated this state of helplessness and dependency on others.

Ken still worked on her passports. She glanced at the four closed-circuit TV screens mounted on the wall beside Ken, rotating between real-time images of the doughnut shop, the stairwell, and various points around the building.

"Where's Gideon?"

"Supply run." The respirator mask he wore muffled his voice. "He'll be back soon."

Pungent chemicals stung her nose, making her back away. "I need to make a phone call."

Ken's gaze snapped up to her as he stopped working. "Who are you going to call, sweetheart?"

Tapping her fingers on the side of her leg, she focused

on Ken's shiny raven hair instead of meeting his eyes. "My sister. My dad is sick at home on his own. Without me, he needs help."

He peeled off his gloves, opened a drawer on the side of the desk, and fiddled with a cell phone, putting in components. "Keep the call under forty-five seconds. I'm sure you're running from something that you don't want to catch you, and I don't want to get burned in the process."

"Okay."

He held onto the phone, eyeing her. "Forty-five seconds, sweetheart. No matter what."

"I won't do anything to jeopardize your operation. I understand."

He tossed her the phone. She wandered into the kitchen, trying to formulate the right words. If there were any, they didn't come to her. She dialed Laurel. The line rang twice.

"Hello." Laurel sounded light and lilting as wind chimes.

"It's Willow. I'm in trouble."

An exasperated sigh. "Angels don't get into trouble unless they fall from grace."

Gritting her teeth, Willow swallowed her immediate frustration. "This is serious, Laurel."

"I'm driving the girls to their piano lesson right now. Can it wait?"

"No! I have to leave town for a few days. I can't explain, but Dad shouldn't be left alone that long." Anything could happen to him on his own.

"Are you pregnant?" Amusement raised the pitch of Laurel's voice. "Are you going off with a guy? Some decoder from work?"

"You mean coder. Not *decoder*."

"Look, I'm the first to throw a party that you've got a life, and as much as I'd *love* to help, I can't drop everything to—"

"I've never asked you for anything." Willow sat at the kitchen table, rubbing her knee. "Not even after Mom died and I needed a lot of help. And what I am asking now isn't for me. It's for Dad, who has done a lot for you."

Laurel groaned. "Fine. I'll send Simone."

"Simone?" *The au pair?*

Dad had met her the one time they'd been invited to Connecticut for Thanksgiving and hated her instantly. He'd warned Laurel that her husband was sleeping with the vivacious lady and should get rid of her.

"My au pair. She cleans and cooks. She'll do great."

"You'll come." Willow sprang to her feet, slapping the table. "Not your au pair, who Dad won't tolerate. Say you understand, you narcissistic, selfish—"

"Okay, you brat. I'll come. But don't you ever run another guilt trip on me."

"Thank you." Willow disconnected the call, taking deep breaths to calm down. Her sister better go. She didn't know what she'd do if Laurel didn't keep her word, but Willow would think of something.

She handed Ken the phone.

"Good job, sweetheart. You cut it close but packed a lot in forty-two seconds."

Smiling, she drifted toward the door. The aromatic smell of sugary delight was strongest in this part of the apartment, cutting through the stench of chemicals around Ken's desk. Her stomach grumbled. She went back into the kitchen to see if there were any doughnuts left.

Her gaze flickered up to the television, catching a cutaway from an update on a tropical storm upgrading to a hurricane in the Atlantic to a breaking news headline. An aerial shot of a house on fire popped up. The neighborhood looked familiar. The bright green house next door to the one burning almost looked like Mr. Thompson's but...

The horrifying realization solidified hard and cold as a rock in the pit of her stomach.

My house is on fire—with my father inside.

Willow staggered closer to the television and turned up the volume.

"An elderly man was found in the house," the female reporter said. "He was rushed to Saint Margaret's Hospital and is currently in a coma in intensive care. Authorities suspect arson and are looking to question the man's daughter, Willow Harper." Her picture came up on the television. "If anyone has seen this woman or knows her current whereabouts, they should contact authorities immediately."

Her head spun like her brain was caught in a centrifuge. The room began to tilt, and she slumped into a chair.

Could smoke inhalation cause a coma? How did the fire even start? Did her dad have an accident trying to cook? He'd almost set a fire once at the stove, and afterward, she always made certain the freezer was stocked with food he only had to microwave.

Oh God. Daddy. She couldn't leave town, not with her dad in a coma and her house burning down. She glanced at the screen.

A blazing inferno shot up the back of the house. Plumes of thick black smoke billowed into the air. The fire was destroying every single possession: her bedroom, computer, her carefully assembled wardrobe, her dad's rare vinyl collection, stacks of photo albums—generations' worth of memories. Her entire life was being rendered to ash.

Her mother had loved that house. Willow had been born there.

She shut her eyes, blocking out the sight and holding back tears.

What if her dad never woke up? What if he died and she never said goodbye?

Exhaling a shuddering breath, she lurched to her feet and groped her pearls. "I have to go to the hospital. I-I-I need a cab. Can you call a cab?"

"Whoa, sweetheart." Ken rose, holding up both gloved hands. "I don't think Gideon wants you to leave. He wanted you to stay here, to keep you safe."

"Gideon doesn't care about me, and he doesn't care about my father. I'm just a mission to him. My dad is in a coma. My house is on fire!" Hearing the words solidified them, made them terribly real. She beat back nausea and struggled to get a hold on her emotions, the only thing in the world she could control right now.

Ken removed the mask. "Calm down, sugar. We'll talk this through."

"There's no time to talk. I have to go to Saint Margaret's Hospital. Now."

Willow stormed to the back bedroom. She knew the hospital layout from the last time her father had been admitted after his cancer had recurred. She had to get there and find a way to sneak in. There was always a way.

If she could access the in-house laundry room, maybe steal a dirty lab coat, she could pretend to be a doctor.

With her changed hair, it was possible no one would recognize her.

Ken rushed into the room behind her.

She grabbed the black backpack and rifled through it to find money. Exasperation tore through her fraying patience. She dumped the entire bag out onto the bed, plucked three one hundred-dollar bills from a bundle of American cash, and slung the strap of her purse across her body.

"Will you help me, or do I need to find a payphone to call a cab?"

Payphones were disappearing relics. They hadn't passed a single one on the way to the doughnut shop. If he didn't help, she'd have to order an Uber through his computer under false pretenses, a digital trail she'd prefer not to leave.

Narrowing his dark eyes, Ken placed a fist on a hip and scratched his smooth chin. Deliberation was better than a flat *no*. "Passports are almost done, and Gideon will be back soon. Hang on an hour. Your dad will still be there."

"What if Gideon won't let me go?" He'd turn his bulldozer force of will on her, and she wouldn't stand a chance. "I have to see my father and find out if he's going to be okay."

She had to leave before Gideon returned. Her dad wasn't just her parent. He was her best friend, the only person who'd never lied to her, hurt her, or used her for anything. She wouldn't abandon him when he needed her the most.

"Please, help me. Or I'll find a cab by myself. But I'm leaving." She balled the money in her fist and straightened.

"This shit just goes to show, never underestimate the dynamite hidden inside a pretty little package." Ken sighed. "If I help, you know Gideon's going to kill me, right?"

20

With supplies stashed in the back of the stolen car, Gideon parked in the alley on the side of the building, out of view of any video surveillance. He strode through the doughnut shop, nodded at Mariko, and bounded up the stairs to Ken's apartment.

At the top of the landing, his buddy stood in the doorway, features grim. "You're earning your guardian angel wings today. Talk about cutting things close." Ken's hushed voice was strained. "Your girl is about to bolt."

"What?" Gideon's protective instincts fired hot. "Why would she want to leave?"

He should've spoken to her before taking off, made sure she was okay after the way he'd left her in the bathroom, but his self-control had been threadbare. One minute longer behind closed doors with her, he would've come loose at the seams.

"Something happened to her dad. He's in a coma at Saint Margaret's. And her house burned down. Half of it is in ashes. It's on every news station."

Dread slushed through Gideon, but he hardened against it. This was crazier than Willow being accused of treason. For it to happen within hours of them getting out of the Gray Box wasn't coincidence.

"Where is she?" Gideon headed for the threshold.

"Kitchen." Ken held up a palm, stopping him. "She probably thinks you're Mariko bringing a set of car keys. I told my sister to stall while I tried to calm your girl down, but she keeps spiraling. Tight, man." He twirled his index fingers in a circle. "Corkscrew tight. I was about to let her go before she explodes."

Gideon pushed past Ken, rushing into the apartment. His gaze fixed on Willow, and a crushing weight lifted from his lungs. She sat in a chair with the strap of her purse draped across her body, elbows on the table, wringing her hands.

She caught sight of him. Her eyes slammed shut, shoulders rolling inward as she held her head in her hands. Gideon stilled, his relief curdling. She reacted as though seeing him was the last thing she wanted.

"You called him?" she asked Ken in a hushed voice that was nonetheless sharp with panic. "You swore it was your sister on the phone. You said Mariko was bringing the keys. You promised you'd help me."

Ken crept into his eye line, brows raised. He lifted both forefingers, repeating the spinning up motion as he mouthed *corkscrew tight*.

Taking a breath, Gideon kept a grip on his composure. "He didn't call me." His tone sounded rough, so he dialed it down. "He had every intention of keeping his word."

Her head snapped up, her gaze flying to him. The look in her eyes was unguarded and unglued. The raw suffering in her face was a fist to the gut. His first instinct was to go to her, but he didn't move. Didn't dare presume she'd accept comfort from him. Didn't dare imagine he was equipped to make things better.

He knew his own limitations well. This trick bag of emotional flash grenades was beyond his expertise.

"You expect me to believe you happen to show up just as I was leaving?" Her tone was scathing. "You really do take me for the biggest, most gullible fool."

Jeez, that pain-wrecked face of hers. He'd never been so helpless, but this sudden, hair-trigger rift between them left him confused.

"Yes, I expect you to believe me." He took a cautious step forward. "Because it's the truth. Ken told me about your father—"

"I have to go to the hospital." She drummed her fingers on her leg, almost mindlessly, uncontrollably.

"No." He shook his head. "Whoever set you up did this. They hurt your father and burned down your house to flush you out. The hospital is a trap. You can't go."

"Can't?" She sprang to her feet. Wildfire incinerated sadness. "I'm not your prisoner. I can do whatever I please."

This emotional reflex was natural, Willow freaking out about her dad, but going to the hospital was a bad move. Fighting him on it was worse.

"I won't let you go. It's suicide."

She couldn't outmuscle him, but given the proper motivation and chance, she could outsmart him. She was motivated in spades, so he couldn't give her the opportunity. Even if he had to zip-tie her to a chair. The hospital was a bad call. He wouldn't let her make the play.

Lowering her head, she pressed a hand to her mouth.

Reason must be sinking in. They had enough to handle without fighting over something that made no sense.

He ate up the gap between them and reached for her.

"It's not suicide if you're with me, Gideon."

He reeled back, dumbstruck by her redirection.

"The firewalls of hospitals aren't as robust as most people think," she said. "I can hack into the surveillance system to give us eyes. Your comms equipment gives us ears."

Determination blazing in her face, Willow closed in on him. The strength radiating from her entirely defied her lean frame as she challenged him. It took everything in him to stand fast and not give her one inch.

"I know your file inside and out," she said in a low voice. "Every detail. Even the redacted parts."

He squirmed on the inside but didn't flinch. Willow came toe-to-toe with him, drawing the air from his lungs, sucking up the space around him until only she existed. She damn near bowled him over, her imposing will turned on full blast.

"You've pulled off dangerous jobs. You know how to evade other agents, disappear in the shadows. You even wiped out an entire paramilitary group single-handedly."

True, but it'd been in the jungle. He'd used the terrain as a weapon. "Willow—"

"You're good at this sort thing. One of the best. Use your expertise to help me."

"I already am."

"If the real traitor was waiting at the hospital to kill me or turn me in, you'd stop them. It'd give you an opportunity to catch them and bring them in. You've done this sort of thing for Sanborn plenty of times. Now, I'm asking you to do it for me."

Breathless. She left him utterly breathless. Listening to her, you'd think he had the power to move heaven and earth, to redirect the orbit of the sun.

For a moment, he believed her. Almost considered how to pull off the impossible and get her out alive. She made him want to be that man. A better man, one capable of all she claimed.

She was dangerous, planting insidious ideas that were sure to get them both killed. Couldn't she see the truth? He was no savior. Just a man who was good at killing.

"No telling what's waiting for us at the hospital," he said. Baiting her by using her father was a smart move. "Gray Box operatives could be lurking in an ambush. Circumventing our own is possible." He knew what to anticipate from them and had an advantage with comms. "But the X factor might be in play. That'd be worse. We've no idea who or what we're up against. Going to the hospital is reckless. Your father is in a coma. There's nothing you can do for him."

Her lip curled in disgust or disappointment—he couldn't be sure. Both were bad. "I expected you'd say that."

Ken winced at her harsh words and slunk away to the makeshift office in the dining area, but moving ten feet didn't give them privacy. Gideon's gut burned.

"You'd never jeopardize a mission," she said. "Even if it was the right thing to do."

"The right thing is to protect you." He was risking everything for her, and she was acting as if he were the enemy. "If anything happened to you, I…"

He clenched his jaw at the flare-up of weakness and beat down the thought of losing her. Nothing was going to happen to Willow. Not while he was breathing.

"If anything happened to me, it'd ruin your chances to catch the traitor." She wrapped her arms around herself as if she were cold and glanced at the television. The flames consuming her house dominated the screen, while a ticker about an elderly man in a coma scrolled across the bottom. "Finding the mole is all you care about. Not me. Not my father."

"They're one and the same." To help her and keep her safe, they had to find the mole. Were they even talking about the same thing? "Whoever is framing you is capable of anything. Nothing is off-limits. You can't help your father. The risk of going to the hospital isn't worth it."

"My dad has always been there for me, no matter how difficult it was at times." Her tone softened, but pain packed her voice with enough power to grip him by the jugular.

Rubbing her arms, she paced in the kitchen.

"He's never let me down. He's taken on ignorant parents, battled principals who wanted to stick me in classes where the IQ was 75 instead of 145. Had a public showdown with the president of Bettie's Brownies because they said I wasn't the right fit. Took out a second mortgage on *that* house so I graduated college without debt. He's all I have. Don't you dare tell me he's not worth the risk!"

Gideon went to put a gentle hand on her shoulder to stop her from prowling in circles, but their eyes locked, pinning him in place.

"Have you ever felt that way about anyone?" Her voice was a whisper of cool steel.

His father had run off when Gideon was too young to remember him. His mother had been so desperate for the affection of any man—even alcoholics and druggies who'd preferred to communicate with fists—that he'd endured bruises, broken bones, and countless sleepless nights with pain as his best friend.

The only person in the world he'd ever truly had, who'd never let him down, was himself.

"Then how could you possibly understand?" she asked in the wake of his silence.

He couldn't. Might never.

When he buried Kelli, he'd laid to rest hope for something more. Some people were meant to have love and kids and puppies. Happily-ever-after shit.

He was meant to be hard, detached. To clean up the trash, eliminate threats, do whatever dirty work was necessary to make the world a better, safer place. Even if he'd never enjoy the luxury of the happiness he safeguarded.

"I know your father wants you to stay alive." He curled his fingers around her arms and drew her close, hoping she'd soften at the nearness. "Not risk getting hurt to see him when he's laid up in a coma."

Her body stayed taut, muscles tense. "I can't abandon him."

Smoothing her hair from her face, he stared into her glassy eyes, longing to make this all better. One step at a time. He might, if she let him. But first they had to clear her name.

"Uh, guys." Ken stared at the four monitors mounted on the wall. "We've got company."

The red beacon light flashed above the door.

"Cops?" Gideon asked, turning toward him.

"Oh no." Ken's voice dropped, and his body went

rigid. "Mariko…" Raking both hands through his hair, he straightened. "Not cops."

Gideon went to look at the screen. "How many?"

"Four. Five. Maybe."

"Where are they?" Gideon peered over Ken's shoulder at the monitors.

"Everywhere."

21

SPRINGFIELD, VIRGINIA
FRIDAY, JULY 5, 3:02 P.M. EDT

Gideon glanced at the screens. Three dead bodies in the doughnut shop. A customer, the teenage kid who worked there and…Mariko. His heart sank, but he couldn't afford to feel.

There'd been no sound of gunfire. Silencers.

Two men wearing serious tactical gear and armed with assault weapons, black balaclavas covering their faces, circled the back and side of the building. A hulking bruiser sized up the heavy metal door of the apartment, which swung out to prevent forced entry with a battering ram.

Another two nosed around on the roof.

They moved in controlled, coordinated bursts. Vigilant surveillance of their six. Highly skilled. Technical. Even the way they held their weapons pointed to paramilitary training. They were either no-bullshit operators from a special black ops unit or had come from one and served anyone willing to pay enough. Mercs.

But how in the hell did they find Willow and Gideon?

"Is it the Gray Box?" Willow came up beside him.

"No. Mercenaries."

The metronome ticking in his head set the controlled beat he'd learned to operate under. Not at the Farm, where the CIA had formally trained him. Not at the Gray Box, where he had refined his skills to a new level. Much earlier, when his path had first been forged and he'd been taught to follow through—*all the way*.

Gideon glanced at Ken. Guilt rolled through him. Mariko wouldn't be lying in a pool of blood if they hadn't come here. "I'm sorry about your sister, but we need to leave."

His friend stared at the rotating images on the screen as if in a trance.

"Pull it together." Gideon sharpened his voice to flint. "Is there another exit?"

Ken blinked, coming back online. "Uh, yeah."

"Grab our stuff while I make sure the exit is safe," Gideon said to Willow as he followed Ken toward the master bedroom on the other side of the kitchen.

"I dumped everything out of the bag. I need a minute to gather it up."

"Thirty seconds."

She took off for the third bedroom, and he hustled into the master. Ken pointed at the metal ladder flush against the wall that led to a steel hatch in the ceiling for rooftop access.

One problem. Tangos were already up there. And he couldn't jump from a second-story window with Willow. "Other options?"

The locked hatch door rattled. *Ping. Ping.* Bullets struck metal. Steady gunfire would rain down until those guys got in.

Drawing his Maxim 9, Gideon motioned Ken away from the hatch with a nod. Instinctively, Gideon's hand went to his pocket, checking for extra clips. The rest of the ammo was in the backpack. He patted the extra 9mm pressed against his kidney under his shirt.

Ken dropped to a knee, grabbing a bag from under his bed, and flew to his feet, backing toward the door. They exchanged a knowing glance.

Digging in and fighting was the only way out. They hurried to the living room.

Ken scooped up passports from the table and tossed them to Gideon. "I didn't get to finish the one with her fake name."

Shit. They'd have to evade customs going into the Cayman Islands and figure out how to get back into the United States later. Problems were mounting.

First things first—kill every baddie gunning for them.

More bullets struck the hatch door. Gideon lunged to check the cameras again. The two on the ground were gone. No sign of them on the other screens. *Damn.*

The fifth guy outside the apartment door unzipped a pouch, removing a wad of plastic explosives. The dude was going to blow the door. The ones on the roof just breached the hatch.

Splendid. Shit kept getting better. "Willow, hurry."

"Almost finished," she called from the third bedroom.

Gideon shoved the sofa to the side to provide cover as Ken grabbed the shotgun, situating himself in the kitchen. Locked and loaded to stop anyone coming down the hall from the master bedroom.

Glass shattered from the second bedroom. A thud— something hitting carpet. Footfalls crunched glass. Heavy. Quick. They were inside.

Willow. Gideon surged up and forward.

A hot spray of bullets from behind him riddled the wall and furniture, forcing him to drop to the ground. The mercs from the hatch door had a prime position in the hall off the kitchen. Under the fusillade of shots, bits of drywall, glass, and sofa padding kicked into the air.

Pinned, his back to the sofa, Gideon's options shrank. The blanket of suppressive fire was buying the enemy time to strategize and maneuver. Precious seconds evaporated.

In the doorway of the second bedroom, next to Willow's, an operator peeped into sight. He wore an H-harness. Bastard had rappelled in.

The guy ducked out of full view but raised a fist. Universal hand signal to halt. Sure enough, the hail of gunfire stopped. Debris and hot brass littered the floor. The merc peeked back around the doorframe, getting the lay of the apartment, not exposing much of his body.

Let that head slip another inch, for two seconds, and Gideon would nail him.

Come on. One inch.

Willow peered out of the adjacent room at the end of the hall. The timing. The luck. All bad. Murphy's fucking law bad.

The merc in the next room caught a glimpse of her. Gideon squeezed off rounds. The guy ducked back into the room, taking cover.

Willow's eyes widened, meeting his for a nanosecond before she disappeared into the bedroom, slamming the door. The lock clicked into place.

Bullets popped from the hall off the kitchen, battering what was left of the sofa.

If he didn't force the game to change, they were screwed. "Ken, on my mark."

"I'm with you."

Gideon rolled out from behind the sofa, his body flat and low to the ground, aimed and shot each man in the ankle. Gunfire lashed up to the ceiling as one roared in pain. The other hit the floor, and Gideon put a hot slug in his brainpan.

Ken stepped out and pulled the hammer of the shotgun, pumping four shells into the injured guy still standing. "That's for my sister."

"Get out of here," Gideon said to Ken.

"Good luck, man." Ken dashed to the master suite.

Boom! The front door blew off, ripping out the reinforced frame along with it. Steel smacked the stairs in a resounding clank and went clattering down the steps.

Smoke and dust punched into the apartment, filling Gideon's throat with chalky residue and obstructing his vision.

Whack! Wood cracked behind him as the merc from the adjacent bedroom kicked in Willow's door.

Gideon sprang up from the floor, sprinted through the living room to help her, and barreled into yet another merc who'd gotten in.

Grabbing the fucker's gun arm, Gideon slammed his wrist against the doorjamb and knocked the weapon from his hand. The gun clattered to the floor out of sight. He whipped his elbow up into the merc's jaw. The man stumbled, his head thrown back, then he drew a blade and lunged faster than expected.

A searing slash ripped across Gideon's side.

Willow searched through the cabinet under the bathroom sink for a possible weapon. Toilet paper. Plunger. Disinfectant wipes. Plastic caddy of hair products.

What was she going to do, mousse the guy to death?

Gideon had taken both the 9mm and tactical blade from the go bag earlier, but she wasn't comfortable using either anyway. Her weapons were computers and source code. She ripped open the backpack, pushing aside the purse that she'd stuffed inside, and rifled through the contents.

The cold stainless steel of the cigarette lighter passed through her fingers, and she clenched it in her palm. If she could find something flammable, she might stand a chance.

Her gaze flickered to the bathroom door. The lock wouldn't hold him off for long.

Delving back in the cabinet, she scanned the contents for anything she could use. Blood pounded in her ears as she searched the tackle box. Conditioner. Hair spray.

Yes. That was flammable. Her gaze flickered back to the door. She grabbed the aerosol can and shook it.

The bedroom door smashed open as if kicked in, wood smacking against drywall. Her throat closed around a knot of panic, and she broke out in a sweat.

Footsteps pounded across the carpet.

Jumping into position by the wall, she pressed her thumb on the spark wheel of the lighter. The bathroom door handle rattled, sending her heart fluttering like a hummingbird's wings.

With her left hand, she held out the hair spray. The can, her arm, her whole body shook as if she might shatter. She flicked the lighter, and her damp thumb slipped across the metal wheel.

Nothing. Not even a spark. *Oh crap!*

Bile flooded her mouth.

Whack! The door burst in, the frame splintering. She sucked in a startled breath, her gaze glued to the doorway. A man in all black swooped into the bathroom. Cold, black eyes pinned her.

Stark fear cramped in her chest, but if she froze, she was as good as dead. She flipped the serrated wheel, hard enough to bruise her thumb, hitting the ignition button as he raised the automatic weapon.

A flame burst from the lighter, and she pressed the nozzle of the aerosol can.

A raging stream of fire sprayed his face, and the balaclava went up in a blaze. He roared, swinging out violently, trying to smother the flames. Smoke and the stench of burnt hair and charred flesh tainted the air. Frantic and whirling, the man tripped into the tub.

Willow dashed across the threshold and through the bedroom. Trembling, she pushed into the hall. She had to find Gideon.

Smoke clouded the living room, but through the gray haze, she made out Gideon fighting another man.

He knocked a knife away from his black-clad attacker, and then a violent dance ensued. Strikes and blocks, fists and kicks flew back and forth in a dizzying blur as they hammered each other with martial arts moves she'd only seen in movies and when black ops personnel sparred in the gym. The man landed a boot heel to Gideon's ribs, propelling him back.

She winced, her body squeezing tight as she imagined the force of the blow he'd taken.

Gideon clutched his side but didn't hesitate. With a growl, he charged and tackled the guy, slamming him to the floor. He smashed his elbow across the man's jaw.

The sickening sound of flesh striking flesh stung her ears, chilling her spine. Gideon slipped a knife from his waistband holster and plunged the blade into the man's throat. With astounding dexterity, Gideon hopped back on his feet, barely winded.

He glanced over his shoulder at her, still holding the bloody knife. "Are you okay?"

She rushed to him. "Fine." A simple word that underrated everything. "Are you hurt? Did he break a rib?" She went to check his side, but he brushed her away.

"Nothing's broken." His voice was steady and cold. No hint of pain.

Blood poured from the dead man's throat, pooling on the dark wood floor. Two more black-clad men lay in the hall on the other side of the kitchen.

"Who are they? How did they find us?" She scanned the apartment. "Where's Ken?"

Gideon's head whipped right, and Willow's gaze followed.

A man shaped like a powerlifter, shrouded in black, crept up to the spot where the front door used to be. Gideon grabbed her by the shoulders and took her down hard to the ground with him. Scooping up his gun, he rolled.

Before she blinked, Gideon was on his feet again. He fired at the man—a series of soft pops. The built-in silencer swallowed the sound.

Willow's heart pounded like it wanted to beat its way out of her chest. She scooted back on her heels and palms and passed a dead body. Her gaze trained on the empty eyes of the corpse, and she heaved. She scurried away on her butt, avoiding the puddle of blood, into the hall near the bedrooms, and used the wall for cover.

The black-clad powerlifter stayed in the stairwell while shooting off a thunderous volley of hot rounds. She jumped at each unexpected boom of gunfire. The sound of regular bullets being discharged she could handle, but this was like a cannon going off. Those were something super high caliber, punching holes the size of bread plates into the walls.

Squeezing her eyes shut, she clamped her hands over her ears, wishing it would all stop.

What if something happened to Gideon while her eyes were closed? Keeping her hands over her ears, she peeked back at the carnage to see if he was okay.

Everything happened so quickly, only seconds, and in a dreadful sluggish way at the same time—a nightmare in slow motion.

Gideon pumped bullets at the doorway, forcing the man deeper into the stairwell. Using the break of incoming fire, Gideon snagged a weapon off the shoulder of the man whose throat he'd slit. It was big and single-barreled like a shotgun, but shorter and fatter. He plucked thick shells off the corpse's vest and loaded it.

Rushing the door, Gideon squeezed off shots with his

handgun. His Maxim 9 clicked out of ammo before he reached the threshold. The dead clack was deafening, stilling her.

The man leapt into the doorway and fired. Gideon hit the hardwood in a slide. With both feet, he kicked the guy in the knees and blasted two shells from the other weapon at the man's chest. The powerlifter fell backward out of sight.

Two thunderous bangs echoed, and bright flashes of light came from the stairwell, shaking the building like an earthquake even as a fist snatched Willow by the hair and dragged her backward across the floor. Terror knocked the breath out of her, clogging her throat.

"Want to burn me!" A string of curses flowed. "I'll show you pain." He yanked her head viciously, ripping strands from her scalp.

Fighting wildly, she kicked the air, the wall, clawed at his arm to gain purchase. He was going to hurt her, really hurt her before he killed her.

Hot tears flooded her eyes, and everything dissolved into a watery hell.

The distinct clack of a clip sliding into a gun resounded. Her heart clutched.

Oh God. Oh God. She choked on a sob, scratching and punching at the arm locked onto her. Blinking away tears, her vision cleared.

She saw Gideon.

Then a whisper of a shot. Blood splattered the wall. The man's fist in her hair loosened, and he hit the floor with a nauseating thud behind her.

It took a dazed second to process everything. Her pulse

raced. Willow rolled to her knees, desperate to get away from the body and smell of burnt flesh, but her muscles locked. She sputtered for breath and fought the need to retch.

Gideon's hand closed on her arm, lifting her from the floor to her feet. In the thick of the fray, he was all cool control and grim readiness, steadying her like an anchor.

A tidal wave of relief crashed over her, and she gulped back convulsive tears of gratitude. There was no time to feel anything besides the need to keep moving.

Gideon crouched beside the dead guy with partially missing skull, keeping his knees out of the bloody brain matter on the floor. After unfastening the man's nylon belt, he yanked it off. Snagging a carabiner from the harness, his gaze stayed glued to the front doorway where smoke still poured in.

Throwing on the backpack, Willow strung together the remaining threads of her faculties. Gideon hauled her to the bedroom, wrapped the dead man's belt around her waist and tied it in a tight knot.

Ushering her to the busted window, he hooked the carabiner on the belt. "Are you afraid of heights?"

"I'm more afraid of dying."

His mouth cocked in a half smile, and he brushed the tears from her eyes. The exquisite sight of him ensnared her for a split second.

He grabbed the rope dangling outside, gave it a firm tug, and looped it through the carabiner. "I'm going to help you out the window and lower you to the ground."

Swallowing a spike of alarm, she nodded. What other choice did she have?

22

Gideon wrapped the rope around his forearm and lifted Willow's legs over the jagged pieces of glass protruding from the tattered window frame, supporting her back with his other arm. Pain shredded his side where he'd been cut and his chest ached. He beat back a wince.

He was walking and talking, and Willow was alive. That was all that mattered. He'd come so close to losing her, stark fear had burned a hole through him. God, he wanted to hold her, see what kind of damage that animal had done, but they didn't have a second to spare.

The big guy would be back. Sooner rather than later.

Instinct, training, years of experience prodded him to hunt that motherfucker down and end him, but getting Willow out safely was top priority. The merc could still get the drop on him.

She held the rope as he lowered her gradually. If she was terrified of heights, she didn't let it show. This ordeal would've been enough to shell-shock anyone not used to the field, but she was resilient and stronger than he ever imagined. She was sensational.

With his leg braced against the wall below the windowsill, he let a few inches of rope glide through his palms, easing her toward the side of a dumpster. Agony ripped through his abdomen, but he gritted his teeth through the groan rising in his throat.

Once she cleared the second story, he trained his gaze on the doorway again.

Any second, the bruiser would emerge. The concussion grenades would've only slowed him down. The merc was big as a linebacker and quiet. Deadly quiet.

It'd been a calculated risk to stay in one location, but they'd had little choice. The passports were necessary. But a tactical team had been formed and dispatched within hours of breaking her out of the Gray Box, which meant someone had been prepared to deploy these mercs at a moment's notice. Someone who knew exactly where to find them.

Gideon glanced out the window. Willow was less than five feet off the ground. Her light frame was an advantage, not taxing him much. The hole in his gut was enough strain.

A shadow moved out of the corner of his eye. Whipping his head, he glimpsed the merc scanning the room while crossing to the other side of the doorway. Gideon freed his right hand of the rope and pulled his gun, aiming for the opening.

The static rope shot through his left hand, burning his palm and the leather of his jacket around his forearm. Jamming his hip against the windowsill, Gideon rounded the cord in his fist to keep Willow from slamming to the pavement.

Her weight jerked to a stop, and he hissed at the sharp pang wrenching through him.

The wide-mouth barrel of a grenade launcher poked into the room. Specialized shells came in an assorted range: concussion, fragmentation, incendiary. He wasn't sticking around to find out which was coming his way. Letting the rope go, Gideon jumped out the window.

He crashed onto the closed lid of the dumpster below. Blinding pain burst in his side, the ache in his chest flaring. Rolling off the top, he landed in a crouch and stumbled as Willow climbed to her feet from the ground.

A blast of fire exploded in the second-story bedroom. Flames spewed from the window, lashing the air, and black plumes snaked up into the sky.

Adrenaline keyed him up tight. Applying pressure to his side, he leapt toward Willow and cupped her arm. They ran through the alley to the car he'd parked at the corner, but he kept a vigilant eye on their six.

"Gideon, are you okay?"

Without answering, he jumped in behind the wheel and connected the dangling wires, firing up the engine while she got in the other side.

The bruiser dashed into the alley from the opposite end. Fucker was too damn fast.

"Get down." Shifting into reverse, Gideon smashed the gas pedal.

Willow ducked low in her seat as they sped backward out of the alley. The merc opened fire, knocking the driver's-side mirror clean off. Gideon hooked a hard ninety-degree turn into the side street, whipping the car around. He jerked into drive and slammed through an intersection, narrowly avoiding a collision.

"In the backpack, find the countersurveillance signal detector." Pressing a hand to his side to slow the bleeding, he checked the rearview mirror for a tail. Nothing.

"What signal detector?"

"Looks like a black stick with a small paddle on the end." To be sure they weren't being followed, he took a right and immediate left, hitting Manchester Boulevard.

No tail. But if his hunch was correct, those guys didn't need to follow them overtly.

Willow rifled through the bag and pulled out the counter-surveillance detector. If there was a bug or GPS locator anywhere on her, the device would pick up an active signal.

He careened right, taking the Springfield Parkway. Less than a mile down, he pulled off and roared into the parking garage for the Franconia–Springfield Metro station. On the third floor, he found a spot in a corner. Holding his side, he climbed out and hurried to the passenger's door.

"Oh God, Gideon." Willow flew out of her seat and peeled his jacket to the side. "You're bleeding."

"It can wait."

"No, it can't. There's so much blood." Fear colored her face. "We have to stop the bleeding."

"The gash isn't too deep. The knife didn't hit a major organ." He took the detector from her hand and clicked the button at the bottom, switching it on. "We need to know if there's a tracking device planted on you. They could be on their way here."

He swept the detector across the pearls around her throat. No chirp sounded to alert him of a transmitting signal. The necklace was clean.

"Wouldn't any bugs have been picked up by the countersurveillance detector at the Gray Box?" Her wide doe eyes scanned his face, searching for an answer in his expression.

"They should've. That's why I didn't think to check you sooner." Gideon waved the detector over her blood-speckled shirt, arms, down her torso and smudged legs to her pumps.

No alarm pealed.

Couldn't be. A planted locator was the only explanation for how they'd been found. He hadn't been sloppy near any CCTV cameras, had only used cash in the stores.

Think. There's an answer.

He swept her again, making sure to run the wand along her back and up in between her legs. She flushed, eyes rolling up to the ceiling. He hated that she had to go through this. Wanted to tear the flesh from the bones of the men after her.

Still no indication of a planted bug. Gideon shook his head. He was missing something, an item she had to carry with her every day. Looking her over, he asked, "Where's your purse?"

It was the only thing not on her.

As she ducked into the car and grabbed the backpack, he checked his wound. The blood flow *was* cause for concern. He needed to clean and suture the wound. Sooner rather than later.

Holding up her handbag, she spun around to face him. He unzipped the bag and stuck the black wand inside.

A high-pitched chirp bleeped.

"How?" she breathed.

He yanked out her wallet and dropped the bag. The chirps grew louder in a rising crescendo.

Damn it. He should have swept her at the mall before they'd nabbed a vehicle. He never made mistakes like this, always saw every angle. Closed every loophole. Every mission completed.

This was his fault they'd found her, even though the question of how pricked his mind. "I don't know *how* this made it past our security protocol."

He chucked the wallet over the balcony toward the outdoor platform for the Metro trains.

Willow's eyes grew wide as she gasped. "No."

He steered her into the car.

"My pictures," she breathed.

"Pictures?" He sped down the exit ramp, tires screeching on every sharp turn.

"Of my parents, in my wallet." She squeezed her eyes shut.

Grimacing at his lack of sensitivity, he tore out of the parking garage. "I'm sorry. There was no time. I wasn't thinking about—"

"Don't apologize. You did what was best." She wrung her hands, opening her eyes. "There's R&D on stealth surveillance. Expensive, next-gen tech that's not on the market. Designed to avoid detection unless activated."

Gideon swore under his breath in four languages. Even if he had swept her at the mall, the bug might not have been active then. "We'll worry about the tech later. For now, we need to get the hell out of Dodge."

"Why do people use that phrase? What's wrong with Dodge that people always want to leave it?"

"It's from *Gunsmoke*, an old show." Reruns used to play on TV when he was little. "It was set in Dodge City, Kansas, during the settlement of the American West. Nothing was wrong with Dodge—the opposite, in fact.

The sheriff always warned the villain to get out of town, to protect the city."

"Seems odd for you to use it in this context."

Perhaps it did. He'd said it without thinking.

He made a beeline for I-95. The interstate was a straight shot southbound to the Occoquan River neighborhood he'd scoped out online. His exit strategy from Virginia was still solid.

Willow opened the med kit, grabbing an all-in-one adhesive gauze pad, the perfect solution to get him through until he could properly tend to his wound. The pads were pretreated with a microdispersed oxidized cellulose called Celox—a blood-clotting agent to temporarily stop the bleeding. He should've thought of it. Basic Survival 101. And he would've too, if his brain wasn't misfiring.

What in the hell was wrong with him?

Rookie mistakes like these put operatives in body bags.

She ripped open a packet of Sani-Hands wipes and cleaned her hands. Leaning over, she tucked his jacket to the side and peeled his shirt gingerly away from the gummy blood with her fingers. It didn't seem to make her squeamish.

The more he learned about her, the more he admired her. She kept her head in life-or-death situations, sharp-witted enough to patch him up, and she was a fighter.

She'd apparently set a merc on fire from the looks of his torched face. A quick-thinking, ballsy move. And when that fucker had grabbed her, she'd clawed like a rabid alley cat scrapping for all nine lives. He never would've guessed, before all this went down, that such a fierce spirit lurked beneath her shy veneer.

She dabbed away blood from around the wound and put the pad on with a tender touch, patting the edges to seal it.

"You've lost a lot of blood. Are you light-headed?"

His gaze bounced from the road to the rearview mirror every twenty seconds. He needed to be sure those blood-hounds weren't tracking them. No one followed.

"I'm good." He glanced at the red speckles on her face. "You'll need to clean up before we get out of the car. We're almost there."

"Where exactly is *there*?" She fished through the glove box and nabbed tissues.

"We need to steal a boat. We're sailing to the Cayman Islands."

Her gaze fell to her lap and she fiddled with her pearls.

He would've killed to have a clear read on her. "What's wrong? Can't swim? Hydrophobic?"

"My dad. Going to the hospital is out of the question, but…"

"Try not to worry. He's worth more to them alive. If you're running, he stands a chance." The anxiety in her eyes twisted his insides. He opened his hand to her. Without hesitation, she pressed her palm to his, interlacing their fingers.

"I'll help you through this, Willow. I swear. Not for the sake of the Gray Box but for you." He'd do anything to keep her safe.

She gave him a brave face, letting his hand go, but her muscles stayed rigid and her body was shaking. "Did you ever suspect me of being the mole? Or was it always your plan to use me somehow to figure out who the leak is?"

What had given her that idea? "God, no. To both."

"The only reason you asked me out and came to my house was to investigate me. Right?"

"You were on the list of suspects due to circumstances, but investigating you was a waste of time and resources. I only wanted to prove your innocence. Then false evidence turned up, and I knew I had to get you out of the Gray Box and keep you safe."

Seeming appeased with his answers, she looked in the mirror on the visor and scrubbed the blood off her face.

He applied pressure to his wound to slow the bleeding. "Did that animal hurt you?" The way the guy had grabbed her by the hair and dragged her had been vicious.

She lowered her head, closing the visor. "We're alive. That's all that matters."

Damn. One of those bastards not only put his hands on her but hurt her in the process. Fury burned his veins. "I never should've let him get close enough to—"

"Gideon." She slid her hand over his thigh, and the heat in him shifted from a kill-everything blaze to a gentler warmth that softened him, derailing his thoughts.

This was the last thing he needed. He had to be on point, stay sharper and harder than the bloodthirsty animals gunning for her. But the idea of pushing her away in that moment hurt worse than the gash in his gut.

"You saved my life. Again." She gave his leg a little squeeze, and his heart jerked hard. "I'm sorry you're hurt because of me. You could've been killed."

"This isn't your fault. Whoever the mole is, they're playing the long game. They've put in a great deal of effort and resources to frame you. To plant a next-gen locator, covering their bases in case you ran. To send a hit squad."

And not just any hit squad but one unlike any he'd encountered. Brutal and precise. He recognized his own kind. She didn't stand a chance alone.

"Or whoever the mole works for is doing all this," Willow said, clutching his leg.

Made sense. The leak had to have a powerful employer, one who wanted to ensure the traitor stayed embedded in the Gray Box. Otherwise, a smart mole would've punched out by now.

"That's the million-dollar question. Who is the wizard behind the curtain?"

———————

After a twenty-minute drive, Gideon turned onto Poplar Lane and drove past the million-dollar homes along the Occoquan River. On an initial pass scanning for anything exploitable, he spotted newspapers—at least five of them sleeved in plastic—stacked in the walkway leading to the door of one house. A prime sign. That or overflowing mail was the best indicator a homeowner was on vacation. Easy enough to put that stuff on hold, but it was a common oversight made by many.

Some fools even advertised their actual status on social media. Once you found a house that might be unoccupied, it took one minute to run an address through a county property records search engine to get the owner's name. Another five minutes stalking them on Facebook to see what exotic locale they'd chosen to frolic and play in. But he needed to see a boat firsthand.

He parked two doors from the vacant home and dug out the flathead screwdriver and hammer he'd purchased from the superstore. "Wait here."

Their eyes caught. The anxiety exuding from her caused a weird drop in his stomach. There was little he could do to comfort her. They had to press on and get to safety on the water.

He tightened his grip on the tools and slipped out of the car. "I won't be long."

Zipping his jacket to hide his blood-soaked shirt, he stuffed the tools in his back pocket. He tipped his cap down and strode past manicured front lawns, up the driveway to the back of the vacant palatial house.

A large, white cruiser sat docked. Sabre model, forty-footer with a housed, raised cockpit, deck, and outdoor seating. The small motor yacht looked made for entertaining. *Pay dirt.* Assuming he could get her started.

He scanned the open row of sprawling backyards, left and right. Empty, and the water was calm. He strode down the dock, head up as if he belonged there, and hopped onto the boat. Bypassing an outdoor dining set, he headed for the double glass doors leading to the cockpit.

Locked.

No deadbolt. A simple mortise latch. He wouldn't have to break the glass.

He jimmied the screwdriver between the doors, angling toward the latch. Two taps with the hammer, and he was in.

Hotwiring a boat for a long trip was dicey, always the chance of getting stranded on the water. And they weren't in a position to radio for help. He'd risk hotwiring it if he had to, but the owner already demonstrated a gross lack of caution. No alarm. Advertising that they'd left the house vacant by not stopping the newspapers. No deadbolt on the boat.

High odds in their favor the keys were somewhere onboard.

He waltzed inside past an L-shaped settee and bolted-down table to check the ignition first. No luck. The owner was a moron but not brain-dead. He glanced around the captain's chair and spotted the cockpit locker. Unlocked. He thumbed it open.

A smile edged his lips. Inside were maps, boat manuals, a fire extinguisher, one life jacket, safety certificate. Keys. *Ding, ding.* His grin widened.

He peeked at the certificate. "Thanks, Matt Trumball. Will try not to damage her."

Ducking a few steps into the lower part of the cabin, he crossed a tiny galley with its compact fridge and two-burner stove. To the right, a rudimentary bathroom had a shower. He poked his head in the bedroom straight ahead. Tight quarters, but a full-size bed and closet.

The forty-footer was more than adequate. Plenty of room to stretch his legs between the cabin and the deck, and Willow would be able to rest on the bed.

Since they had the means to cook, he wouldn't need the tabletop butane stove he'd purchased. He fired up the boat to ensure no engine problems and noted a full gas tank. Gideon liked this Matt Trumball more and more.

He strode back to the car to find Willow fiddling with her pearls. The world must be moving at a breakneck pace for her. Everything that transpired in the last eight hours would've left any normal person in need of a Xanax, Valium—something prescription-strength for sure.

The grind and hustle and blood were his norm. For him, it was the downtime, the mundanities of everyday life where others thrived but he struggled.

He opened her door. Startled, she jumped, gaping up at him.

She'd been through so much, he'd do whatever possible to make it easier from here.

Squatting beside her, he rested his hand on her jiggling knee until she settled. "We should go." He brushed her cheek with his knuckles.

She nodded, and a resigned calm fell over her.

He gathered the bags from the backseat. The slight weight made his side throb. Willow closed the door and took a couple from his hands. Under normal circumstances, he wouldn't have let her carry anything, but today broke all the rules.

Speckled blood stained the front of her shirt. Her right cheek and throat were pink from the ordeal. Once they were underway, she'd be able to clean up.

Ushering Willow with his arm, they hurried to the boat. As they cut across the backyard, headed for the dock, a neighbor playing with her ivory toy poodle spotted them. The middle-aged woman narrowed her eyes and picked up the small fluffy furball, which began barking at them. Clutching the dog to her chest like it was a baby she was trying to soothe, her laser-like scrutiny intensified.

Gideon scooted Willow to his right side, keeping his arm low over the hole in his jacket, and waved with his left.

"Hi. I'm John." He plastered on his perfected

quarterback smile. Sometimes charm and flashing his pearly whites were the best weapons for a situation. "Matt was kind enough to let us take her out for a couple of days while he's away."

"Oh, okay." The woman returned the smile and waved. "Have fun. The weather is supposed to be gorgeous this weekend."

"Thanks. Enjoy your evening."

The older woman set the dog on the grass and tossed her pooch a toy. Gideon let out a tense breath. Good thing that hadn't blown up in their faces.

They hustled onto the boat. He pulled away from the dock and steered down the Occoquan River. Immaculate yards and tricked-out patios with huge decks and outdoor kitchens stretched along the bank.

Once they hit the intersection with the larger Potomac River, he let his lungs relax, took a deep breath, and settled into the captain's chair. "Can you hand me the med kit?"

Willow set the backpack on the floor to grab the kit. He slipped out of his jacket and grunted, peeling off his T-shirt, careful not to smear any blood. Plenty already on his abdomen. He didn't need more in other places.

When he looked up, he found her staring at him, her gaze touring his torso. An odd look swam in her glazed eyes, as if she vacillated between curiosity and pity.

Pity was the worst. He never wanted anyone feeling sorry for him, and he'd rather scoop out his eyes with a rusty spoon than see it in anyone else's. Not since he was eight, when one of his mom's boyfriends busted his jaw. It'd taken two plates, twelve screws, and six weeks to heal.

He held out his hand for the kit, willing to trade a kidney to know her thoughts.

She glanced at his abdomen and set the med case in his palm. "The gauze is soaked."

"You should go out on deck. Get some air while I take care of this."

"Take care of it?" Incredulity washed across her face. "You're going to clean the wound and stitch yourself up while driving the boat?"

"Yep." Wouldn't be easy, but he'd done it before. More than once. Well, not while driving anything. "I'll put the boat on autopilot. If you could keep an eye out for obstacles, that'd be good."

Her eyebrows ratcheted up and her jaw unhinged. "That's crazy. You're going to stop the boat, and I'm going to help you."

"It'll be messy. Not just the blood. The sight of soft tissue can be too much for some." And he'd rather not put her through that.

She snatched the kit from him. "Tell me what to do and I'll do it. You're not alone."

23

The last time he let a woman take care of him in any capacity—Maddox not included—it had ended up being one of the biggest regrets of his life.

Gideon shook his head. "I've stitched up others and myself so many times, I should be an honorary medic."

"You're hurt because of me. Let me help you." The unadulterated look of entreaty on her face sent the strangest sensation rolling through the pit of his stomach. "Please, Gideon."

Her eyes shone with a resolve that wouldn't take *no* for a response. Not many people would be willing to do what she proposed, and fewer still could stomach it. Her offer meant more than he'd care to admit. Against his better judgment, he nodded.

"Tell me what to do," she said.

"Put this in the squeeze bottle." He gave her a packet of salt. "Fill it with water to flush out the wound." A saline solution was better than alcohol or hydrogen peroxide, which could damage the skin and delay healing. "And I need an extra four ounces of plain water."

While she scrubbed her hands at the sink, he shut the engine and laid out everything from the med kit. Damn it, he was out of gloves and thread for stitches, which meant they'd have to use the skin stapler.

She hurried to him with the other supplies. He stared at her, looking past her stained blouse, the loose red hair flowing around her shoulders, soiled legs, scuffed shoes. Past her haunting beauty that had hooked him and wouldn't let go. She exuded such an alluring warmth.

Tension shivered through him, rippling deep to that cold pit in his gut.

The ugliness that was his job drained him, sucked the soul dry, leaving him a wretched husk on a good day. But the way she made him feel—the fact that she made him feel anything at all—was nothing short of a miracle.

"Maybe asking you to do something that'll give you nightmares isn't a good idea." With this shitstorm she had to contend with, he didn't want to add to her troubles. "It's okay if you want to reconsider." No way he'd blame her. "Besides, I don't have gloves."

Which was reason enough not to embroil her in the horrible nitty-gritty bits of this job analysts never had to see. Bits he never wanted *her* to see. Much less touch without gloves.

"You didn't ask. I offered. And I don't dream, so no danger of nightmares." She set everything on the dinette table. "I'll work better without gloves. Latex irritates my skin."

Suddenly, not having condoms was a positive.

As quickly as the errant thought had sprouted, he hacked it away. He was bleeding from his gut. This wasn't the time to think about the wild, dirty sex he wasn't going to have with her.

"Let's get started." She gave him an expectant look. "Take off your pants and lie down on the bed."

The words tangled in his head, curling like strangling vines. "What?"

"With the irrigation, you should remove your jeans. The blood will ruin them."

"Yeah. Sure. Okay." *Hell no.* Trapped in a confined space with Willow and no pants on added up to *bad idea. Far from okay.*

"Gideon." A question danced in her eyes. "Your pants?"

Holy mother. He was scared, a big yellow-bellied coward, and *nothing* scared him. Nada. Zilch. Not deep-cover missions, hunting terrorists, hit squads, the prospect of dying—none of it elevated his pulse past eighty. Yet this sexy half-pint had his pulse in a flat-out sprint over the idea of taking off his stupid pants.

Willow snagged a finger through a belt loop and tugged him closer. His mutinous feet moved forward, and the next thing he knew, she lowered his zipper.

He swatted her hand away. "I've got it."

If his pants were coming off—and they had to, as clothes were limited and blood on his jeans wouldn't be inconspicuous in the Caymans—then he'd be the one to remove them.

"Don't snap at me when I'm only trying to help," she said, letting her steely backbone show. "I don't appreciate it."

He admired a woman who wasn't afraid to put him in his place. "Got it. Sorry." Kicking off his boots, he slid his pants down, revealing his boxer briefs, and shoved them aside.

Her gaze dipped past his waist. She wet her bottom

lip and snagged it between her teeth. "You'd be more comfortable lying down. Let's go to the bed."

Yeah, that was *not* going to happen. "We'll do it out here." He sat on the L-shaped bench.

"Fine." She sank to her knees between his legs and draped a towel across his hip below the wound. Her knuckles skimmed his inner thigh, stirring a tingle across every nerve ending. The hot and hungry kiss they'd shared came roaring back to him, her curves filling his palms, her eager tongue licking up into his mouth and luring him deeper.

Stiffening, he beat his monstrous libido unconscious, threw it in a trunk along with the memory of that kiss, and locked both away.

He popped a couple of pain-reliever tablets and snagged a packet of ceftriaxone. The one-dose antibiotic came as a crystalline powder. He mixed it with water, filled a sterile syringe, and injected it in a vein in his arm.

Peeling off the gauze, Willow inspected his injury. Then she looked up at him with those sparkling eyes. His skin turned tight as a vacuum-sealed pack with the need for something ineffable, and for a split second, he forgot the pain.

Ice-cold saline shot into the wound. Shards of agony bloomed and splintered through his body.

"Jeez!" He clenched his jaw and turned his hands into fists, breathing through his nose. "It's freezing. A little warning next time."

"Warm water sits in a hot water tank where sediment and sludge accumulate. I thought it was better to use cold water to flush the wound."

In theory, it sounded smart. In reality, it gave him the

startling equivalent of a much-needed cold shower. He'd take a lot of those in the next two days.

Blood leaked from the gaping flesh onto the towel. She dabbed at his abdomen with gauze. He watched for any signs she was about to toss her cookies, but her gaze didn't waver, and her fingers stayed steady. Impressive.

She grabbed a new dressing treated with the blood-clotting agent and pressed it to the slit. "You'll have to talk me through stitches. The more specifics, the better. In college, I could wing anything, except social stuff. I've always sucked at that."

Her openness was astonishing, took his breath away, and left him in awe.

"No stitches. You'll have to use this." He handed her the skin stapler. "Hold the wound closed and line up the arrow with the center of the cut. Then press down hard with the device and deploy a staple about every centimeter."

He pulled away the gauze. The blood-clotting agent had worked, giving him a clear view. All in all, the wound wasn't too bad. Barring infection, it would heal, but with a nasty scar.

"This is going to hurt, isn't it? A lot."

He nodded. It was going to hurt like a son of a bitch, but there was no way around it. "Have at it. Has to be done." He gripped the edge of the table and braced himself.

She held the two sides of the wound together and, following his instructions, pressed the first of ten staples in.

A sharp pang arced through him and he gritted his teeth. If he were the one wielding the stapler, he'd focus on the internal ticking in his head until he was done. But with Willow touching him, the one sound in the world he longed to hear was her voice.

"Talk to me. How is it that you're not squeamish about this?"

"During my checkups, I have to watch as they draw blood. Not seeing the needle sink into a vein is unbearable. When I was little, I had trouble with some types of physical sensations."

He recalled reading about that in his research. "Sensory processing disorder?"

Her gaze flickered up to his, her mouth agape for an instant in surprise. "Uh, yeah."

She lowered her eyes and pushed another staple in. He groaned through the pain.

"Touching certain things would make my skin crawl. My parents had me work with a therapist who put me through loads of tactile exercises like putting my hand in a box filled with sand or grains of rice and groping around for as long as possible." Drawing in a deep breath, she shuddered. "I'd last a whopping thirty seconds. And it felt an eternity, screaming on the inside, wanting to rip off my skin."

He stayed focused on her voice as she manipulated his gaping flesh. She worked quickly but with precision, and he gripped the table, refusing to flinch or make the slightest sound of weakness.

"Then the therapist had me accomplish something specific such as fishing out ten marbles from funny foam. Shifting the focus from time to completing a task changed everything. This daunting world crammed with insurmountable obstacles became something manageable."

She depressed the last staple, and he hissed with relief.

"Attagirl. You showed no mercy." *Downright ruthless.* Kind of twisted, but he liked that about her. A lot.

"It had to be done. Besides, I knew you could take it."

Hot. Damn. He didn't know if it was her smile, the way she'd bucked up to help him without getting jittery and squeamish, or how she didn't apologize for torturing him, but what she'd said was so damn hot.

He ached to do the one thing he absolutely couldn't.

Kiss her.

Willow was thankful Gideon had accepted her help.

Tough didn't skim the surface of what he was. She'd wondered how he'd survived some of his missions, the ordeals he'd endured. Must be his high threshold for pain, combined with a rare quality most people lacked—mettle.

She finished cleaning around the wound, pressed a fresh dressing on, and used the last antiseptic wipe on her hands. His gaze landed on hers. Their eyes locked, and her belly fluttered, but she couldn't tell whether he wanted to haul her closer or push her away.

"I would've guessed you had a delicate disposition, but your intestinal fortitude is a surprise." He licked his lips, and she clenched her thighs. "I wish…things were different."

Things was such a vague word. He meant more than this on-the-run-for-her-life situation, but she had no clue what.

"Thank you for doing the staples."

"You're welcome."

Sitting back on her heels, she took him in. Really took him in. This was the first time she'd seen him practically naked. Two hundred and ten pounds of pure shredded muscle, with eight-pack abs—apparently that was a real thing.

After everything they'd just survived, what she needed most was to curl up against his warm, broad chest and sink into the security of his strong arms wrapped around her. To take comfort in his skin on hers and bask in his smell.

Oh, the smell of him.

She placed her hand on his knee and stroked his thigh. He snapped ramrod straight, nostrils flaring.

"Gideon—"

"We should get underway. We need to make it to the Atlantic." His brusque tone had her sitting back on her heels away from him. "It's not good to sit out in the open. We're in a vulnerable position."

"Of course." What was she thinking?

She scrambled to her feet, gathered the gauze, and reached to take the towel across his lap.

He blocked her hand. "I need it."

Nodding, she went to chuck the blood-soaked materials in the bathroom trash. Her cheeks burned, flames fanning down her chest. She looked in the mirror. Her face was berry-red.

"You idiot," she whispered. "You're a mission. An assignment."

Don't confuse his kindness for something more. No foolish, trumped-up fantasy is going to happen. You're still you, and he's still amazing. And working.

Drawing a deep breath, she left the bathroom. Gideon

sat in the captain's chair, pants on but glorious chest on full display, steering the boat.

If she could call it a boat. You wouldn't call a Maserati or Lamborghini just a car.

When he mentioned they'd travel by boat to the Cayman Islands, she'd pictured a little dinghy or a canoe with a motor. Silly in hindsight, considering they had to travel to the Caribbean Sea, but she wouldn't have imagined something quite so spacious.

In movies, fugitives on the run slept in cars and hid out in seedy motels. He'd managed to steal a high-speed vessel outfitted with a cabin. But this was his job. Outmaneuvering. Improvising. Using his wits to survive.

"Look in the cockpit locker," he said to her, pointing to a compartment by his leg. "Get the manual for the boat and find out the top speed. I bought maps. They should be in one of the bags. Calculate how long it'll take us to reach Grand Cayman Island."

Reaper was back, barking orders like she was a robot instead of a person. She was used to this side of him, the composed operative who never got rattled and rarely smiled.

The beautiful man cloaked in mystery she'd longed to know.

Today was the first time, though, she'd seen the killing machine up close. Steel and ice, too sharp to hesitate, too cold to feel. Necessary, of course. Someone wanted to nail her as a traitor. He was all that stood between her and death.

But with her life hacked into ones and zeros that no longer added up, she needed the gentleness he hid so well. Needed *him*, regardless of his motives. She could handle long work hours and a high-ops tempo. Caring for her sick father was taxing, but she'd do anything for him. Solitude recharged her batteries, and she enjoyed her alone time. More or less.

Around Gideon, it was definitely less.

She'd gone a long time without being touched, almost stopped missing the physical warmth. Almost forgot the healing power of an embrace.

Almost.

Then he'd kissed her, his hands running all over her body, gentle and full of heat, and her universe changed gears. Like that moment in *The Wizard of Oz* when Dorothy was ripped from a black-and-white Kansas and crashed into a Technicolor world—vibrant energy and singing and dancing.

His affection was a salve. She could use a simple hug in this tornado of chaos. Something to let her forget the horrors wrecking her life for a few seconds. Her house had burned down. Her poor father was helpless in a coma. And it was her fault.

Her lack of friends, her isolated lifestyle, her difficulty passing a polygraph—something had painted her as the perfect person to frame, making her sick to her stomach.

"Willow." The sharpness of Gideon's voice brought her back to the task at hand.

Following his orders, she dug out the manual and maps from the locker and did the calculations. Although Grand Cayman Island was a short flight away, the number of nautical miles they had to cross was staggering.

She'd never ventured more than a five-hour drive from home. Breaking from her routine and doing it by herself was too unnerving. Every possible deviation from the safety net of structure unraveled a thread that held her life together.

Now everything was gone, and she was free-falling. She drew in a deep breath.

"If you run the boat at top speed, with no sleep, we could be there in thirty-two hours."

He raked a hand over his close-cropped hair. "Eventually, I'm going to need sleep." His tone and countenance were glacial. "I didn't get any last night. The bank closes at two on Saturday afternoon, and we won't make it in time. I planned supplies for two days on the water, so we'll shoot for Sunday evening. It'll give me time to scope out the bank and limit our exposure on the island before it opens on Monday morning."

Glancing around, Willow looked for something useful to do. She unpacked the shopping bags and put away the groceries. The fridge already had butter, eggs, bacon, beer, and water. The owner must use the boat regularly. Gideon had bought a variety of foods, ensuring no threat of going hungry.

After rooting through the cabinets, she wiped out the cupboards, washed the dishes, and reorganized everything to stay busy—any out-of-band patch for a semblance of normalcy.

Whenever Gideon's gaze fell to her, she sensed it—a trickle of heat running down her spine like warm syrup— but she never managed to catch him looking. Only the turn of his head while he radiated *assassin on a mission*.

By the time she finished alphabetizing the spices, her jitters were gone.

"Try not to worry," he said. "I'll do everything I can to help you."

Gideon was an army of one. *Everything* for a man like him would be nothing short of World War III. She stared at the bruises on his chest and the wound on his abdomen. "I couldn't do this without you, but you've already done too much. If anything happened to you because of me, if you—"

"I'm hard to kill. Nothing's going to happen to me. I'm going to keep breathing, because I won't let anything happen to you. Okay?"

She nodded, although she wanted to do the exact opposite.

"Get some rest. Once the adrenaline fades, you'll need it."

Her body was fatigued, but her mind was still restless. She trudged to the bathroom and flipped on the light. Her gaze raked the compact facility, bouncing from one spot of grime to the next. Most people wouldn't label the bathroom filthy, but the dirt nettled her.

She scrubbed every inch until it gleamed and the scent of orange oil tickled her nose.

A hot shower loosened her muscles, and she was relieved to scour off remaining traces of blood. She wrapped a towel around herself and traipsed to the bedroom two feet away.

She took the clothes Gideon purchased to the closet. Inside, she found an extra life jacket, a folded blanket, a windbreaker, and a feminine sweater. She hung Gideon's clothes and ran her hands over two dresses from the same bag. Both smelled of plastic and were the same mix of fabrics. The polyester blend chafed her fingers, and without looking at the tag, she could tell they were a size too small.

The good news was he'd chosen solid colors and the material wouldn't wrinkle, but she wouldn't be able to sleep in either dress, much less wear one for hours.

Tomorrow was supposed to be navy skirt and baby-blue blouse day.

She'd double-checked the bags. No pajamas. She didn't wear any at home, but with Gideon vacillating between consuming her in a rush of sweet fire and freezing her out, the situation warranted jammies.

She ran her fingers over the thin cream-colored cardigan in the closet, baby-soft cashmere smelling like fabric softener. It was long enough to act as a robe but didn't have buttons to close the front. If she also threw on one of Gideon's T-shirts, the makeshift PJs would do. She adjusted the towel wrapped around her and padded around to the foot of the bed.

A beam of golden light fractured the darkness in the kitchen.

Gideon was crouched in front of the open mini fridge. His gaze collided with hers. Electric awareness arced between them in the charged silence.

She quivered at the tingle licking her spine, the erotic tease of possibility.

He rose, holding a beer, and kicked the refrigerator door shut, ensconcing him in darkness. She couldn't see his eyes but felt his stare caress her bare skin. Her breath stilled. A languid ache snaked through her, twisting in her belly.

They were safe on the water, out of danger. He didn't have to be Reaper anymore, just Gideon. It stung he didn't want her in the same way she wanted him, but she did want him. The one-sided desire embarrassed her. Heat whipped over her face, trailing down her body. If only she could make it go away and be numb.

He sauntered toward her, his steps measured. A quiver shot straight between her thighs, and her toes curled against the smooth hardwood floor.

His darkening eyes burned, lips parted in a ragged exhale. The bottle of beer shook in his hand. Stopping in the threshold, he grasped the door handle. His gaze wandered along the length of her body in a slow perusal.

"You should rest." The husky gravel in his voice stirred butterflies in her chest, but the words deflated her silly drop of hope. "I'll sleep out here later." He shuttered his eyes and closed the door.

Her heart hurt as if he'd dragged it across sandpaper. She was lost on how to fake her way through this. How was she going to bear two days on the boat with him?

Her fingers throbbed with restlessness and her mind spun. She pulled on a T-shirt and the sumptuous sweater. Climbing on the bed, she hugged her knees to her chest and rocked, wanting to shrink into herself. Being trapped in this box of a room for hours would drive her stir-crazy. If only she had her computer and the internet—an electronic lifeline to cling to.

With nothing familiar to buoy her, she had to figure out how to stay afloat and not drown.

24

Sanborn strode into Rocky's, gritting his teeth at being reduced to skulking around in a bar because his multimillion-dollar, state-of-the-art Gray Box facility had been compromised.

Not just by the mole conspiring in their midst. He suspected the walls had eyes and ears. Sybil Parker was gunning for Willow by any means necessary, including trying to twist any conversation or correspondence into a way to save her own hide. Not even the conference room was safe after the stunt Gideon had pulled.

Sanborn nodded his thanks to Rocky for arranging to shut down the bar under the guise of *training* to give him the place for a clandestine powwow with his tactical team. She waved and locked the door on her way out, leaving them alone. As the sister-in-law of a black ops member, Jagger—currently deployed to the sandbox—Rocky was family and could be trusted.

The team looked out for her and patronized her bar so frequently, they should have stools engraved with their names.

Sanborn's divorce had been finalized shortly after he stood up the Gray Box. His wife of twenty-three years closed that chapter on his life, putting an end to the dinner parties and barbecues they used to hold for his team at their lavish home when he was with the Agency.

Now, he preferred to keep a little distance, except for his second-in-command, Knox, who already knew him far too well and was also deployed. Sanborn guided and protected all his people, would sacrifice for them if necessary, but he couldn't let them *in* as he once had. Still, every now and again, he needed to bring them together in a social setting. Remind them that they were more than coworkers, tight as family, and the team would be stronger for it. And when he held one of his gatherings, he did it at Rocky's.

Today, however, he'd brought them here for a darker reason.

"Is everyone *clean*?" he asked.

Heads nodded around the table.

Cell phones should've been turned off in the parking lot of the Gray Box, so it'd show as their last known location. Removing the battery prevented them from being tracked. Cutting the power supply was the only way to temporarily disable a roving bug or any other potential malware on their phones capable of spoofing an authentic shutdown while keeping the phone very much on, traceable, and vulnerable to eavesdropping. Then they were to run a surveillance detection route to the bar, ensuring they weren't followed.

Sanborn sat at the head of the table. "The evidence on Willow Harper is convenient and tidy. It reeks. I don't believe she's guilty." He'd plucked that brilliant ingenue as an NSA newbie, and in all the time he'd known her, she'd never been one who'd prevaricate. "I suspect neither does Reaper. If anyone here isn't on the same page, you should leave now."

Heads bobbed in agreement and butts stayed planted.

"Has Reaper contacted anyone?" Sanborn asked the group but stared at Maddox.

If Reaper had reached out to anyone, it would've been her. The two were close. Very close. Sanborn had once worried something romantic might've started between them after Gideon's wife died and the grieving widower started sleeping at Maddox's place. Office hookups that went badly inevitably spelled trouble, as he'd learned from experience.

But *office romances* that took a wrong turn careened into disasters.

Fortunately, Reaper had only crashed at her place for a few weeks. Eventually, he had started making his rounds at Rocky's, and Maddox hadn't seemed to care.

Maddox sat silent, holding Sanborn's gaze. The deliberation in her eyes was subtle, but the fact that it was there at all stuck in his craw.

"He called me," she said finally.

"I'm happy to see you're being forthright and no longer consider me a possible suspect."

"Whoever the leak is wants Harper dead. If you were the mole, she already would be."

"Thank you." Maddox didn't mean it as a compliment, but he'd take it as such.

"Gideon thinks her brakes were sabotaged," she said. "Forensics is examining her car."

Sanborn shrugged. "Even if her brakes were tampered with, it doesn't prove anything. There's damning circumstantial evidence against her. What's Reaper's plan?"

"Follow the money."

"Good." It had to be done with boots on the ground, since the bank couldn't be hacked into from the outside.

"He's too smart to fly," Alistair said, "but going by boat will be dicey."

"Why?" Sanborn asked.

Alistair took a long pull on his tap beer. "The tropical storm in the Atlantic was upgraded to a hurricane. It's been erratic, fast-moving, and was supposed to swing up the Gulf. But it just turned toward the Eastern Seaboard, putting itself smack-dab in their path."

Wonderful. Reaper better have been resourceful enough to get more than a gosh-darned dinghy, or those two were going to be fish food. "Is there a protective detail on Willow's father?"

"You bet," said Reece. "Local law enforcement's there around the clock. In the first 911 call that came in about the fire, someone mentioned that they saw Willow arguing with her father and overheard her threaten to kill him. Our surveillance of the house was jammed at the time the fire was set."

This tumbleweed kept rolling and growing uglier by the minute. "Get a copy of the call. Whoever made it is our mole."

"Problem," Castle said. "Willow is our best hacker and the only one in that department we can trust."

"We have another option." Ares looked around the table like he was reluctant to share it.

From the corner of his eye, Sanborn glimpsed Castle shake his head.

"Spill it," Sanborn said. "I don't have energy to waste ripping anyone a new one over a transgression."

"Well then, bless us, father, for we have sinned." Ares cracked a dark smile. The look was downright menacing. "A private security and risk management firm has been helping us go through the electronic data we've been gathering on all the suspects."

The artery throbbing in Sanborn's temple nearly burst as his blood pressure spiked through the roof. Were they trying to give him a stroke?

He folded his hands on the table. "You served civilians the personal data of the director of the most covert unit in the country on a silver platter? *My* personal data?"

Ares's eyebrows rose. "Well, not *your* data, sir. You haven't had any transmissions from your apartment for us to intercept since this mess started."

Relief feathered through him, ever so lightly. He'd only been home long enough to pick up fresh suits and workout gear. "So instead, you handed civilians the identities of the support personnel for the most covert unit in the country?"

"When you phrase it like that, sir, you make it sound far worse. Eyes and ears on the information have been limited. It was a calculated risk, yes, but our backs are against the wall on this one."

They had no idea. It wasn't their backs against the wall but rather their heads on the chopping block, with a *whitewash* as a possibility.

"It's the company where Cole works," Maddox said, referring to her fiancé. "His boss, Donovan Carmichael, said based on your history and our situation, you'd agree he was the best option."

Donovan was prior Agency, knew the ropes, knew

Sanborn, and was the epitome of discretion. "Better than turning to someone in the NSA or CIA." Unfortunate, but true. "Going to Donovan was a smart move. See if he can get us the 911 call."

25

The cruiser slashed through the choppy blue waves. Gideon had pushed the throttle hard all night, foregoing sleep. Thanks to the impressive pickup of the twin engines—he estimated three hundred horsepower—they topped out at thirty knots.

They were far enough out in the ocean not to see land. A cool, salty breeze blew in from the open doors to the rear.

He checked the time.

Willow had stopped moving around in the bedroom shortly after sunrise and was finally resting. Every minute without her dragged. Giddy anticipation wound him up, and he itched to see her, talk to her. At the same damn time, he dreaded being physically near her, wanting her in a way that would only lead to disaster.

The toilet flushed in the bathroom and water ran. He white-knuckled the wheel. Damn, he hadn't even seen her yet and he was grinning like a fool on the inside.

She sauntered into the kitchen, wearing his T-shirt and her dirty skirt.

"Good morning. How are you feeling?" he asked.

"Fine."

"Why didn't you put on one of the dresses I bought?"

"The synthetic material will irritate me, but I'll put it on when we get to Grand Cayman so I don't draw attention."

He'd considered numerous factors, except that one. "I'm sorry I got the wrong thing."

"You couldn't have known." She turned toward him. Her eyes normally sparkled every fleck of brown, green, and gold in the light, but they were dim and swollen as if she'd spent most of the night crying. She looked drained and her face was drawn. "I'm starving. How about I make breakfast?"

"Sounds great, if you don't mind." Something in his chest dipped at giving her the cold shoulder last night, when she probably needed a little comfort.

He hadn't been equipped to handle it with her wrapped in a towel, but he'd make more of an effort today.

She arranged food in an orderly line on the tiny counter, whipped out pans, and got to work, throwing slabs of bacon in a sizzling skillet, cracking eggs, and chopping fruit. A sense of peace settled over him as he watched her.

Strange. Quiet mundanity usually keyed him up, setting him so much on edge, it was impossible to enjoy it. As if he should be prepping in some way—his body with a workout, guarding his mind against a question he needed to evade, cleaning his weapons, steeling his soul for some new horrific task.

But right now, there was only Willow and the smell of bacon.

"Food is ready." She carried two plates up the steps past him to the L-shaped dining unit.

He killed the engine and joined her.

They each took a side of the L-shaped settee. He

dug into the scrambled eggs. Perfectly cooked, light and creamy. The bacon was crisp with a hint of chewy texture, the way he preferred. She'd even made a fruit salad and toast smeared with smashed avocado and a sprinkle of salt.

"This is a kick-ass breakfast."

She nibbled a piece of bacon and bit into the toast. "Breakfast is my specialty. Before my mom died, we would cook breakfast together from scratch. Waffles, pancakes, frittatas, buttermilk biscuits with gravy. And I make a mean hollandaise sauce."

The mouthwatering rundown had him anxious to have her whip up more food, pronto.

"Those scones you made were amazing." He wiped crumbs from the corner of her mouth with his thumb, thinking about her dad's reaction to her frozen meals. "You never helped your mother with dinner?"

"My dad always made dinner." Her gaze drifted, a shadow of sadness falling over her. "He said cooking alone, listening to music, relaxed him. He'd play Frank Sinatra or Coltrane."

When she didn't go back to eating, he took her hand in his.

"His Hodgkin's got bad three years ago. The fatigue and pain have been hard on him, and my cooking hasn't helped." She gave a woeful look. "He always wants me to make breakfast for dinner—waffles, home fries with sausage and eggs—but the doctor said to watch his diet. Low cholesterol. Low sodium. Low fat. I've tried seasoning things with broth and herbs, but he's not happy."

The closeness and bond of affection she shared with her father was beautiful. Special. They were lucky to have that.

"What happened to your mom?"

"Breast cancer. She died when I was eleven." Her voice was solemn, like someone reading an obituary out loud.

To lose her mother at that age must've been tough. He wanted to scoot closer and comfort her in his arms, but asking these types of personal questions already erased and redrew the professional chalk line closer to the point of no return.

"Did your sisters take over around the house?"

She tucked hair behind her ears. "Laurel is ten years older than me, and Ivy's eight. When my mom passed, they were at college, busy in their own lives. Ivy checked on me, took me shopping, got me fitted for my first bra." She shrugged. "That sort of thing. Until she moved to Paris."

As an only child, Gideon was used to fending for himself. After his dad left, it was like his mother had resented being a parent. It used to eat away at him. He'd been desperate for her to want him, to have the normalcy other kids took for granted.

Then someone had come along who reformed how he saw the world, changing him forever.

"I hope my dad is going to be okay." She stroked her bare throat. No pearls.

Before he could stop himself, he took her hand from her neck into his. "I'm sure the doctors are going to do everything they can to help him."

The Gray Box would know about her dad by now. Hopefully, they'd connected the dots and assigned a protective detail to watch over him. Whoever hurt her father to bait Willow to come out of hiding would want to tie up any loose ends eventually.

"Try to focus on something else. Any distraction is good."

She nodded with a brave smile, and he let her hand go.

While they ate, she told him stories about her childhood. Little things she missed about her mom, embarrassing slipups with boys, how hard it had been to make friends in school. She was like a spout turned on, pouring herself out to him. No filters. No shyness.

He took it in, not stopping her. It wasn't as though they could spend two days together in confined quarters and not speak at all. Idle chatter usually grated on him, but her openness was surprisingly relaxing.

She picked up their empty plates when they were done and went to the galley.

In the kitchen, she turned on the radio. An upbeat pop song filled the cabin. Finishing his black coffee, he strode to the helm. She washed dishes, bobbing her head at first and slowly working up to shimmying her hips to the beat of the music, drawing a smile to his face.

Talking must've helped her. He admired how free and open she could be in some circumstances. The vulnerability to put yourself out there the way she did took great courage and strength. She was far braver and stronger than him in that regard.

She wiped her hands on a dish towel and sauntered closer, hips swaying to the beat of the music, a slight jiggle to her breasts. Her lightness was infectious. He was almost weightless, like he'd swallowed a balloon, but he couldn't let his common sense drift away as well.

She was on the run and under immense pressure to clear her name. He couldn't take advantage of her. They had to talk about boundaries, for both their sakes.

"Dance with me," she said.

"I don't dance." And he didn't, which was a good thing. Where Willow was concerned, he was a weak man. A little cha-cha could easily lead to the horizontal mambo.

"Come on." She tried to tug him from his seat to no avail. "It'll keep me from thinking. You said any distraction is good."

"I never dance." He sharpened his tone, needing some emotional and physical distance from her. "Besides, I'm steering the boat. I need to keep us on track." *In more ways than one.*

Willow looked deflated, that renewed spot of light in her eyes going back out.

Guilt ate away at him. He was the most conflicted bastard on the planet at that moment. Comforting her and not getting sucked down the emotional rabbit hole were two needs at war.

She retreated outside to the deck with the notebook and box of drawing pencils he'd picked up for her from the store.

He kept his back turned to her, smothering the desire to stare at her. She was so beautiful.

Proximity and physical contact had always been occupational hazards as a government assassin. Now it seemed they had become personal ones too.

26

The air in the parking garage was thick with unrelenting heat and sticky humidity.

Omega sat in the passenger's side of the van with the window lowered, sucking down a disgusting wheatgrass protein smoothie. His taste buds revolted with every gag-worthy swallow.

The protein was essential for him, and the wheatgrass was a treat for Daedalus.

Seven years ago, Daedalus had remarked how the nutrient-rich sprout enhanced Omega's essence, making the taste addictive. What lover wouldn't endure the putrid flavor of liquefied lawn clippings after receiving such an endorsement? He'd been slinging back the sickening green stuff ever since. Now that was love, or some twisted version of it.

But he was going to sever the spinal cord of the next motherfucker who got his order wrong and had the wheatgrass added to his smoothie instead of getting a double shot on the side.

The elevator doors opened. Keys jangled, and heels clickety-clacked across concrete.

"Richard, both of our girls can't be mistaken about

seeing Simone kiss you," said the woman, her voice booming off the walls. "They're six, not stupid. And I'm not being paranoid."

The suburban snowflake prattled on ad nauseum as she passed the van without a glance in their direction. Omega nodded. Epsilon put the van in drive, trailing her.

She strolled toward the far end of the garage, blabbing on her cell phone, oblivious to the dark force bearing down on her. The pampered princess was insufferable, with her whiny complaints and complete lack of situational awareness. Her head was buried so deep in the sand, it was a wonder she hadn't suffocated to death already.

"You have no idea the stress I'm under. After I finish a five-hour drive, I find out my father's in a coma, the house burned down, and the cops are saying Willow did it! That brat ran off with some *guy*, leaving me to clean up her mess. I can't handle any *misunderstandings* right now, Richard. I've been thinking, the girls are so big, we don't need an au pair anymore."

Lights flashed on a Jaguar as she hit the key fob. The elitist snob had parked in an isolated position, far from other vehicles, probably out of fear of an accidental scratch or ding.

Omega gave the hand signal to advance. Epsilon drove past the Jag into a position parallel to her vehicle with one empty spot between them. Her cloying perfume tainted the air, mixing with the earthy taste of his wretched smoothie.

She dropped her keys and bent to grab them. "I'm not overreacting or jumping the gun," she snapped. "Yes, I know, but—" Rolling her eyes, she shook her head. "No, *we* don't want you to be late for tee time." She sighed. "I love you too. I'll be home as soon as I can. Bye."

After she disconnected, she swore in mommy-speak, "Fudging fiddlesticks." She tossed her cell into the designer purse slung over her forearm.

That hothouse flower didn't stand a chance. Omega gave the go sign, draining the last of his repugnant drink with a slurp. The side door of the van slid open. *One second.*

His men hopped out from the back. *Two.*

She gave a long, slow blink before their presence registered and she gasped.

Three.

Duct tape was slapped on her mouth, flex-cuffs around her wrists, a hood thrown over her head, and she was tossed into the van.

It took four seconds to bag her. *Pathetic.*

27

ATLANTIC OCEAN
SATURDAY, JULY 6, 11:20 P.M. EDT

Gideon stirred, lying on the bench near the glass doors. The haze of sleep shrouding his brain cleared. Rain pelting the boat sounded like gunfire.

He longed to stretch his cramped legs and opened his eyes.

A bolt of lightning cracked the night. Choppy waves rocked the boat, almost sending him sliding out of the booth if not for the table in the way.

A loud thud came from the bedroom. He assumed it was Willow hitting the floor.

He sat up and pushed out from the seat. The rain hammered the vessel, and the wind had picked up.

"We must have sailed into a storm," she said, coming out into the cabin, wearing one of his T-shirts and a long sweater.

It had started raining before he dozed off, but nothing more than a drizzle. "I think it's worse than a storm. Wait here." Gideon went out onto the deck.

Ominous clouds rolled across an angry, dark sky. Lightning flickered, and thunder roared on cue. Conditions had flipped from rainy to perilous while he slept. The tropical storm must've changed course and grown into a full-blown hurricane.

Willow slid the deck door open and came out into the rain.

"Go back below," he said. "You shouldn't be out here."

"Neither should you."

"This isn't good." He wasn't an experienced helmsman or sailor or whatever the heck you called a boating expert, but he'd driven Knox's houseboat a few times and picked up tips.

They were close to the shore of some barrier islands on the leeward side of the boat, which was dangerous. The gale could drive them onto land and wreck them. They had to get out of the teeth of the storm and needed sea room—a safe distance from anything they might crash into like the coastline. First, he needed to turn the bow into the waves to keep a swell from striking the side of the hull and capsizing the boat.

He steered Willow inside the cabin and handed her the life jacket from the locker. "Put it on."

While she donned the yellow vest, he started the engine, cranked the wheel over to point the bow in the correct direction, and shifted into forward.

The boat jerked violently against the waves, the stern fishtailing. He throttled up, accelerating, but the vessel only pitched, refusing to move, as if the hull was caught on something.

Earlier, they'd been far enough out to sea that it would've been pointless to drop anchor since it wouldn't have landed on the bottom. He had no clue why they weren't moving.

"Do you smell that?" she asked.

Taking in a deep lungful, he detected the faintest scent of smoke and burnt oil. She had a very sensitive nose.

He killed the motor. "It's the engine. I need to see what we're hung up on." He met her wide, panicked eyes. "Stay here."

He slid the door open, bracing to go back out into the deluge. Driving rain whipped him. Grasping the handrail, he pulled himself toward the bow, checking over the side along the way. Strong gusts dragged at him, and he fought to keep his balance on the slick deck.

At the front of the cruiser, he checked the anchor. The chain stopper had broken off, unlocking the anchor. The storm had carried them close enough to shore for it to hook into the bottom. He pressed the button to reel in the anchor and waited for the distinct grumbling sound that never came. The boat dipped and rose with the waves.

A clinking sliced through the roar of the wind. The anchor was stuck.

He'd have to cut the nylon line to free the boat.

As he made his way back to the rear to get his bowie knife, the yacht did a wicked roll, going from thirty degrees heeled over one side to swing thirty degrees the other way within seconds.

He rounded the corner onto the back deck and ran into Willow.

"I was worried. You were gone so long." Clutching the railing, she handed him another life jacket. "I found it in the closet. You shouldn't be out here without one."

The wind snapped with a sudden ferocity, turning the deck more treacherous. The yacht rose on the crest of a great swell, and they both braced. The tremendous wave broke, foaming over the handrail, and the boat came crashing down.

Gideon's feet slid, but he held tight to the rail and reached for her. Willow lost her footing in the gush of water washing across the deck and slipped through his fingers.

A violent wave broadsided the cruiser, and she toppled over the railing into the darkness.

Gideon's heart stopped; the whole world seemed to shift into a slower gear.

One moment she'd been right beside him, and the next she was gone. As if the wind and darkness and raging ocean had conspired to pluck her from the air.

Adrenaline kicked in, his pulse cranking up to a hammering beat. Training had hard-wired him never to panic, but alarm tore out of his vault and straight through his chest. He rushed to the aft railing and scanned the water.

There was nothing. Only thrashing waves and foamy white caps.

"Willow!" he called into the brutal storm, his chest constricting.

Rain pelted him as the wind buffeted the boat. Every second it took to find her, the sea would put more distance between them.

He dashed inside the cabin and fished out a white flare from the locker. Hustling into the rain, he pulled off the cap. He lit it the same way one would a match, rubbing the end of the flare against the striking surface of the cap.

Ignited molten material sprayed like an angry tongue, casting a bright white light. Hoisting the flare high, he scanned one hundred eighty degrees.

There! A spot of yellow and flash of the vest's white reflective strip.

An arm popped out of the turbulent water. She flailed at the surface, trying to keep her head up. Then a wave slapped her under a swell.

Gideon grabbed the life ring that was tethered to the boat and tossed it out like a Frisbee to the spot where he'd seen her. He launched himself from the stern into the savage sea.

The shock of hitting the chilled, pounding water snatched his breath. Frothing waves dragged at him, trying to suck him down into the water's black heart, but he fought against them. He arrowed through the water in the direction of the life buoy, desperately searching for her.

The fierce current pulled on him, slowing him down. The metallic taste of fear mixed with brine in his mouth as the watery bowels contracted around him, jostling him like a toy trapped inside a humongous washing machine.

A ghostlike arm snaked hold of the orange ring. Willow hauled herself up, clinging to the flotation device.

Gusting winds sloshed water in his face, preventing him from catching a full breath. Spray stung his eyes. She was twenty feet away, the distance stretching in the turbulence as though it were a hundred.

He grabbed onto the line and pulled her closer. She reached for him. Their fingertips grazed. Jealous waves buffeted them, tearing them apart in an exhausting tease.

With fickle quickness, the sea swept them back together. This time, he caught hold of the buoy and helped Willow get a better grip.

She gagged, sputtering out water while the ocean force-fed her more. He got her higher onto the ring where she could get a breath. Keeping the flotation device between them, he started swimming, angling back toward the boat. She kicked, doing her best to assist him, with her arms looped over the ring.

Panic receded now that he had her. He kept his head up like a polo player, chin above water, sights trained on the bobbing yacht, struggling against the unrelenting current.

Wildfire burned in his side—he was in agony from his wound.

His arms and legs were growing heavier, but he gave each kick, each stroke everything he had, tugging the buoy along with him. He refused to lose.

Gritting his teeth, he pumped even harder for the last few feet, battling the ocean, the storm, Mother Nature herself, to get Willow to safety. He hooked his free hand onto the ladder and hauled her to his side. Straining, he heaved Willow up to the rail.

His gut screamed, and he grunted in anguish, but he didn't let go of her until she made it to the deck.

A watery fist gripped him with impossible strength, trying to drag him under. Holding steadfast to the ladder, he had to go all the way, not permitting an ounce of weakness.

The metronome ticked in time with his heartbeat.

He wrestled the snarling swell and stretched for the higher rung on the ladder. Raking in a ragged breath, he climbed out, putting one foot above the other, the last of his strength leaching from him.

With his right hand on the rail and his left arm around Willow, he trudged carefully toward the cabin, ensuring they weren't catapulted overboard by another surprise attack.

He slid the glass door open, ushering her inside, and shoved it closed behind him.

Breathless, they collapsed on the floor, half drowned. Trembling and clinging to one another, relief to be alive resonated in the tightness of their grips.

He still had to cut the line and free the boat, but he needed a moment to recover.

The storm raged around them, rain smacking the doors and windows loud as marbles thrown against glass. Only one thing mattered. Staying alive.

28

ATLANTIC OCEAN
SUNDAY, JULY 7, 4:37 A.M. EDT

Gideon had cut the anchor and navigated them safely out of the storm.

It was still raining, but they were in calm waters.

Willow had been freezing and shaking uncontrollably even after drying off, putting on another of his T-shirts, and lying under the covers, curled in a tight knot.

He'd climbed into the bed alongside her, clothed. His only thought was to rid the chill from her with his body heat and ease her shock from nearly drowning. He didn't know how long they stayed like that, spooning, her clutching his forearm, glued to one another.

Once his own skin and blood and bones had warmed, she stopped trembling. That was his cue to leave, but he couldn't move. His limbs were heavy. He was utterly spent, and having her in his arms was one of the simplest yet greatest pleasures of his life.

She was nuzzled against him. The top of her head under his chin, her scent invading his senses. Lounging on fresh sheets warm from the dryer on a rainy Sunday morning. A clean breeze blowing from a garden. She smelled like heaven.

Made him want to die.

She lifted his arm, brushing her cheek over his bicep, and grazed his thumb and the rest of his fingers in turn, lingering on the ones with odd nails. He'd lost three fingernails, ripped from his right hand during a mission in Syria that had hiccups. He got bagged, and the torture had escalated before Reece and Maddox found him. It had taken seven months for the nails to grow back, and they'd never looked the same.

Women didn't notice the funny shape and distorted color during a one-nighter.

But Willow kissed each fingernail, slowly, gently.

Her compassion seared through him. Pressing his face into her hair, he hugged her tight. He was tormented and confused, aching to be closer to her in the one way he knew how but not wanting to ruin things by being himself.

She rolled over in his arms, meeting his gaze with a soft, sensuous look, and stroked his hair. The air between them turned flammable as methane gas. His body hummed with arousal. The power she had, to have him unraveling with a look.

"You have such beautiful eyes. Does my staring make you uncomfortable?"

Not one little bit. "No."

"You've saved my life multiple times. If I wasn't your assignment, I'd be dead." The dark whisper clawed through him. "I know I'm just a job for you and that you're not interested in me sexually, but thank you. I really needed this, to be close to someone. To you."

She took his stance as rejection? Why didn't she see his impressive self-control as noble?

"Willow, I do want you." Like a dying man *wanted*

CPR. "I'm so attracted to you that it hurts. But emotions have been running high, and the tension and stress of the situation are distorting things."

She was eight years younger—might as well round up to a decade—was so full of light and had so much to offer. Under different circumstances, she wouldn't want this. Not with him, a man she feared on some level.

Gideon was a damaged piece of meat, scarred more on the inside than out. He didn't have clean hands or a clean conscience, and one day, his demons would catch up with him. And when that happened, he didn't want her near him, regretting anything they'd shared together.

"You don't know what I'm capable of," he said, "what this job requires of me. It brings out a darkness and feeds something terrible inside."

He often purged that same energy during sex.

She stroked his cheek with the warmest, lightest touch, making the fine hairs on his body tingle. "You have a tough job, an ugly job most couldn't handle. You help stop darkness and death and chaos from spreading, and I admire the fortitude it must take. Just because you've done monstrous things to protect our country doesn't mean you're a monster. You're a good man."

For the first time in a long time, he wanted to believe that was true.

Buttery-soft lips grazed his, but he held back. She kissed him and her tongue slipped inside his mouth, searching for his. In this intimate bubble they'd somehow created, it seemed cruel not to give her the response they both craved. He wrapped his arm around her, his tongue finding hers, and consumed her with a slow hunger.

It's just a kiss, but with giving in, there was this unexpected, intense relief. His heart bucked liked a horse against his rib cage, his pulse racing while the rest of him relaxed. As though a weight lifted and his entire body sighed with happiness.

He gripped her tighter, yearning for more in the tangle of dark wanting. The sweet heat from her was enough to melt the ice in his soul and fill up the dead spaces with warmth.

But when his hands roamed over her bare skin—up her smooth thigh and cupped the sensuous curve of her backside—the kiss was no longer just a kiss, and he stopped.

Longing broke over her face, and something equally forceful spilled through him.

"I don't want you to stop," she whispered. "Make love to me."

Temptation was a steel cable tightening through him. "I want to, but…" No one had ever expected him to *make love*.

He was in way over his head. Sex, or rather fucking, was something he did well, but this thing with Willow left him so far out of his depth. At almost twice Willow's weight, he needed self-control and a gentle approach to give her what she deserved without hurting her. But in some things, he simply wasn't capable.

"We don't have condoms. It's for the best." A dirty list of other things they could do flashed in his head, but he shook off the devilish thought.

"You had your last physical May 21. Your blood work was clean. Unless you've had unprotected sex with someone since, what's the problem?"

Okay, she really knew a heck of a lot about him and was doing too fine a job painting him into a corner. "Do you hack into everyone's records, or am I lucky?" His tone was rougher than he intended.

She reeled back, her features pinching. "I'm sorry. I was curious—"

He crushed his mouth to hers, silencing her with a kiss, and held her close. The breach of his privacy should've felt like a gross violation, but it was an excavation, freeing him. He'd spent years in a loveless marriage, hiding who he was because everything was classified, because he'd been taught too well never to share. The marathon of lies and omissions exhausted him and kept him at a distance from everyone else.

It was a relief for someone to know the truth, see the real him. And still want him.

"I haven't been with anyone since my physical, but we can't risk you getting pregnant."

Her face brightened. "Ivy got me an IUD when I was seventeen after Michael Dutton tried to force himself on me. I get it replaced every five years. I'm not due again until next year."

His heart clenched, and he wanted to pulverize a dude named Michael. "What? Did he hurt you?" Once they cleared her name, he'd pay this Dutton a visit. Gideon had never killed a civilian or enjoyed torturing others, but there was a first time for everything.

"Yes, but…" She shook her head. "It was in college. He was a lot older and got really rough. I gave him a black eye, and he left me alone."

Lucky for Michael Dutton.

"I want to be with someone I'm crazy-attracted to. Someone who makes my body come alive, who makes me feel safe. That's you, Gideon."

She moved her thigh, inadvertently brushing his groin. He nearly shot out of his skin. There was no angle at which he could shift now to keep his erection from pressing against her.

With the staples in his side and sheer exhaustion, maybe he could be gentle. Maybe it was possible to have her and maintain a grip on the situation, if there were firm rules.

Or maybe he was being foolish and reckless.

One thing he knew for certain—the woman made him a reckless fool.

"We need to establish rules first."

"I love rules. They keep me from making mistakes."

"If we do this, it has to be like Vegas. What happens on the boat stays on the boat. I can't promise anything more. And don't confuse lust with another four-letter word."

There he went, turning yellow-bellied, couldn't even say it. *Love.* As if to utter the single syllable meant one or both of them might catch it like a disease.

"Is that all?"

He was probably forgetting something important, but how was he expected to think straight in this position? "Yes."

Willow kissed him with a startling urgency that was a shock to his nerve endings. Her ravenous tongue and the sweet taste of her mouth unhinged him. No one had ever kissed him like this, with impatient need and desperate satisfaction, with the kind of undeniable hunger that matched his own.

She tugged his shirt over his head, and he lifted his arms in sublime submission. That was what this slip of a woman did, backed him into corners from which he had no desire to escape.

He yanked the oversized tee off her in return, revealing soft skin and feminine lines. Her curves molded to him as though the pair of them were two pieces of a puzzle yearning to form a complete picture.

The subtle scent of her arousal permeated the air and desire shuddered through him. She slid her bare, centerfold-perfect body up close against him, leveling the last vestiges of his defenses, and something inside him snapped.

29

Gideon kissed her unrestrained, and Willow gloried in it. His mouth was wet and hot and so demanding that it made her woozy, but she met his tongue with deep, hungry strokes of her own.

They groped and caressed, wrapping themselves around each other, wild as caged animals unloosed. Heat throbbed between her legs, liquid need rushing through her.

He didn't have to care for her in the same way she did him. He protected her, and he desired her. And that was everything.

Rolling onto his back, making a sound that was half growl and half groan, he brought her on top of him. He grabbed her hips and, as he broke their kiss, arranged her so she straddled him.

On *his face*.

The stubble of his cheeks scraped her inner thighs. Butterflies overtook her stomach and her insides trembled with anticipation. Then his mouth was on her in a full-fledged French kiss.

Gideon Stone—the sexiest man she'd ever seen, the only one she'd fantasized about—was French kissing her *there*. She never thought so much tongue could feel so good.

"Oh God." She pressed her knees into the mattress, her whole body growing weak at the charged rush of sensation.

The next deep drag of his tongue over her folds sent a thrill shooting through her. And when he slid a finger into her, Willow's vision blurred and she clawed at the wall like a feral cat. She gritted her teeth against the staggering pleasure, but failed to silence the embarrassing noises rising in her throat.

This was ten times better than what those *Cosmopolitan* articles described.

He kept doing things with his tongue and fingers, obscene things, his touch skilled and gentle, and she never wanted him to stop. Her arousal built until she couldn't control herself, her body taut as an overwound watch, aching for release.

"Willow, you taste so good." He took her into his mouth again with such ravening intensity, tightness coiled inside her to the brink of pain.

"More. I need more." Words failed her.

It was intense and incredible. She undulated on him, chasing the deep, feverish ache.

A sharp release cracked through her like a thousand twigs snapping all at once, and her stomach muscles clenched into her diaphragm, stealing her breath.

But he didn't stop. He kept feeding on her with a relentless rhythm. His mouth sucked harder, his tongue licked faster, his fingers plunged deeper.

Another wave of wonder seized her in hard, wrenching spasms. She shattered into tiny pieces, so scattered and submerged in sensation, nothing would put her back together again.

Gideon eased out from underneath her. She melted down onto the bed, exhilarated and disappointed. Guys were usually interested in taking, but Gideon had given her so much. The pleasure had been all hers. This was supposed to be about sharing.

"We should've started with something mutually beneficial. You didn't get anything out of that."

His laugh was husky. "I got plenty out of that." He unzipped his jeans and kicked them off. "I enjoyed it, and now I'm so turned on, I can't wait to be inside you."

That was good to know.

Kissing her thighs, he prowled up her body, his pale-blue eyes on fire. She ran her hands over his chest that was solid with muscle, loving the strength of him. His hands closed over her breasts, the tip of his tongue teasing a peaked nipple before he drew it into his mouth and suckled.

A shiver of anticipation of what was to come went through her.

"You're trembling. Are you scared?" Bracing over her on his elbows, his powerful body gleamed in the light of the breaking dawn.

Her gaze darted to his erection, prodding at her sex. Perfection, like the rest of him.

She gulped and clenched with nerves.

He was experienced, had been with lots of women who knew exactly what to do and how to satisfy him. She didn't want to do the wrong thing and be memorable only for having been utterly disappointing.

"I won't be any good at this. Sorry. But I'm a fast learner. You just have to teach me."

His mouth closed on hers. She welcomed his tongue and the taste of her passion mixed with his need. He nudged the blunt tip inside her, stretching her. She arched, her throat thick with longing.

On the second press into her, he swore something indecipherable, the tension in her muscles mirrored on his face. She gasped at the enormous pressure, digging her heels into the mattress.

"Relax. Don't tense." He kissed her, softly, sweetly, his tongue coaxing her to soften. "You're so tight. Let me ease in." His voice strained with an edge like he was in pain as he drove inch by inch into the clasp of her body, withdrew and slid deeper. "I need to have you more than I need to breathe. But if it hurts too much, I'll stop. Even if it kills me."

And knowing that he would soothed and excited her.

She didn't want to run from him. She wanted to crash into what she craved.

"Don't stop. Unless you're in too much pain."

"I'm fine. Taking it easy."

He pushed into her harder and held still for a suspended moment of delicious agony. She hovered on the brink, rocking her hips, desperate for motion.

Taking her face in his hands, he licked her lips and then kissed her, deep and tender and sensuous, stealing her heart, and she was lost.

Each slow thrust had her inner muscles loosening and becoming more slippery. She clenched around him, relishing the intense friction, the torturous pleasure.

"Touch me." His ragged words were low, rough. "I love the way you touch me."

His voice filled her ears, his hard flesh filled her most intimate place, and her heart was full too. She let go of the bedspread tangled in her fists. Clumsy with desire, she ran her hands along his sleek, honed body. His mouth seized hers again, and the rest of their bottled-up need overflowed in frenzied kisses.

They found a rhythm, an escalating tempo toward something fierce and breathless. An excruciating push and an aching pull.

Making love with him exceeded her wildest hopes, but not in the manner she'd expected.

This was the first time that sex had been intimate. He peered down at her with an intense look she'd never seen from him before. The tide of emotion rising in her chest and swelling between them was overwhelming.

Unbearable tension spooled low in her belly. Arousal and desire were like wire threads gathering and knotting in her core. Holding her gaze, he quickened his strokes, driving the thick breadth of him impossibly deep, to the center of her soul.

It was as if she was dissolving in sweet sensation. White-hot ecstasy stormed through her, pounding harder and faster than the rainfall beating the boat. Her body squeezed and twisted, but she surrendered to the awe-inspiring wave of pleasure that swept her away.

With a guttural roar, he jerked into her one last time. He kissed the hollow of her throat and caressed her as though she were something precious. Emotion clogged her throat, rendering her unable to speak or think straight.

He rolled to the side, retreating from the bed, and left the room.

She reeled at the striking emptiness. Shutting her eyes, she tried to hang on to the fleeting sensations, wanting to memorize them.

The mattress sank as Gideon returned, sitting beside her. The heat from his body encouraged her to open her eyes. She was groggy from the high, her heartbeat still a wild flutter.

"Are you okay? Was I too rough?" He wiped the junction of her thighs with a washcloth.

"Don't. I love the feel of you inside me." *So erotic.*

"Too late."

She sighed, missing the slippery warmth of him. "I guess we'll have to do it again."

"We can do whatever you want, as many times as you want. While we're on the boat."

She pressed her fingers to his lips. "Vegas."

No promises of anything more. At least she wasn't a for-one-night-only girl, and she planned to make the most of the little time they'd have together.

He got back into the bed and held her. Wrapped in Gideon Stone's arms, her body was languorous and replete. Satisfied. Closing her eyes, she drifted to sleep with a man for the very first time.

30

GRAY BOX HEADQUARTERS, NORTHERN VIRGINIA
SUNDAY, JULY 7, 12:31 P.M. EDT

The hall was quiet as Sanborn strode to his office, keen to ditch his suit. His body ached for exercise, craving the surge of endorphins.

The compounded stress of hunting for the mole while trying to protect Willow and Gideon was getting to him. Restless energy thrummed in his veins, and his joints were tight.

Rounding the corner, he stopped short and then ducked behind the wall.

Janet stood in the next corridor, embroiled in a heated argument with Sybil Parker's right-hand man, Ricky Olsen. He was tall and leggy, equally as dogged and territorial as Janet.

What was he doing sniffing around outside Sanborn's office?

She had her hands planted on her full hips, jaw clenched, head held high. The two snapped back and forth at each other, neither backing down. Ricky shook his head and stepped around her to walk away, but she caught his arm and spun him around, not letting him skulk off.

Janet wasn't simply Sanborn's gatekeeper. She was his

freaking stormtrooper. No one set foot inside his office without her permission.

Pride spread across his face in a smile and fell just as quickly. Ricky pressed his palm to Janet's cheek, her body instantly, visibly, softening in response.

A chill ran through Sanborn, like someone had walked over his grave.

Ricky leaned in as if to kiss her, but Sanborn strode around the corner into plain view. The two shot apart with deadpan expressions. Not a hint of surprise or guilt on either face.

Whatever was going on between those two, it had been happening for a while. They had grown accustomed to hiding, pretending, coming so close to being caught that their reactions were well-practiced.

Ricky hurried past Sanborn with his eyes lowered.

Janet handed him a stack of phone messages without batting a lash, sparking anger inside him. "The top two should be returned while you're on the treadmill or out for a run."

He glanced at the papers. The director of national intelligence and the aide to the president. POTUS must've gotten wind of this fiasco and wanted to ensure this mess wouldn't blow back on him.

"Not in your office," she added. "I found Olsen nosing around when I got back."

Now the walls officially had eyes and ears. Sanborn had given Sybil too much credit, assuming she'd already bugged his office in the same manner he had hers. He'd used a set of her own threat monitor equipment that been cleared by the director of national intelligence to use in the facility.

"Where were you?"

"Doing what you asked."

Stalling Ms. Sybil Parker away from her office by any means necessary. Only three computers in the Gray Box had active USB ports for uploading external data: his, Willow's, and Sybil's. Sanborn used the distraction to copy Sybil's computer on the flash drive that was burning a hole in his pocket. But if Parker's techie had been in Sanborn's office at the same time, exactly who had been the one stalling whom?

Didn't matter. With the cloned drive, he'd ascertain what Sybil was up to. It was a violation of ethics, not to mention the law, to spy on the insider threat monitor, but the only way Sanborn fought was dirty.

"Care to explain about you and Ricky Olsen?" he asked, his fury over their charade rising.

She tensed. "I told you. I caught him in your office and read him the riot act."

He lifted a brow and waited.

A flush crept into her cheeks as she started fast talking. "I never told you because it's embarrassing. The whole May-December thing. I'm much too old for him, by fifteen years."

That was what embarrassed her? Sanborn was no ageist and no hypocrite. The age gap was bigger between him and Doc. But some desires simply couldn't be indulged if it made you a liability.

And now he had to examine under a microscope of suspicion someone outside black ops he had trusted implicitly, who'd been with him since his Agency days—Janet.

He'd all but ruled out his own people as the traitor.

He knew the fiber of their characters, what made them tick. They would never betray him for money, ideology, or out of arrogance. But after what he'd witnessed in the hall, he was painfully aware that it was possible someone had gotten close to one of his people, inside or outside the office, and had found a way to compromise and coerce them. Fear was a powerful motivator for the weak and would prevent someone from coming to him for help.

But the fact remained that Sybil would do anything to cover her ass. Perhaps she'd go so far as to lead the witch hunt on Willow while protecting a leak in her own department.

What he wouldn't give to have Knox by his side at such a time, but his second-in-command was deployed for a good reason, and recalling him wasn't an option.

Doc, Amanda, and Daniel came down the hall, Castle following close behind.

Scratch his workout time. What bomb was going to drop next?

"You and I need to have a chat," he said to Janet before the others were within earshot.

Her eyes grew wide, and she nodded.

Entering his office, he removed his suit jacket. Janet swiped it from his hand, throwing it on a hanger and hook in the corner. She insisted the bespoke Savile Row garment shouldn't be slung on the back of his chair. After his divorce, it mattered little to him where he hung the handmade suits his silver-spoon ex-wife had purchased.

The smell of strawberries and cream wafted into the room along with Doc, giving him a jolt of energy. With her beatnik, flower child charisma, he always expected her to smell like patchouli.

Thankfully, she didn't.

"Coffee?" Janet asked him.

He shook his head and sat.

Doc's gaze met his as she claimed a chair in front of his desk with a smile. Her bright baby-blues reeled him in, her coppery-blond hair falling in soft curls. She was some kind of beautiful.

He forced his thoughts to realign, reminding himself— everyone's motives were suspect.

"What's up?"

"Time for the situational report," Amanda said. "I'm still trying to help Doc run down the origin of our small-pox weapon." With Amanda's DEA background, she was an expert at picking up trails and tracking things down. "Whoever modified and weaponized the strain had to get an original sample from somewhere. So far, I've hit lots of dead ends."

"I'm flying to Atlanta today," Doc said. "To follow up on a possible lead."

CDC headquarters on a Sunday. "Why can't you handle it over the phone?"

"A contact at headquarters might know something, but he's scared. Won't talk over the phone."

"If you think it might be dangerous, I can send someone with you. Maybe Ares?"

No secret Ares was sweet on Doc. Once the mole problem was resolved and Doc was no longer under suspicion, Sanborn would take her up on her offer of dinner and *exercise*. As long as he wasn't stepping on toes. Lady's choice, of course.

She usually went out of her way to avoid Ares like the

man was a walking bad rash, but it made Sanborn wonder whether she hated Ares or had a thing for him.

"No, please don't send him."

Halle-freaking-lujah.

"I don't need backup, and if I did, Maddox would be a better choice. She's warmer than I expected. There's a real girl's girl hidden beneath her tough exterior."

Maddox, a warm girl's girl?

He smothered a chuckle. Maddox was fishing for the mole, and Doc must be her target.

"Okay. No backup. Keep me posted and hurry back."

"We're monitoring airports, bus and rail stations," Amanda continued. "Danny is digging into Reaper's and Willow's personnel files."

"I'm looking into their known associates," the kid said, munching on one of Janet's cookies. "Maybe there's someone local they'd turn to for help. I'm also diving deeper into Willow's financials, since the accountants aren't doing anything further until the requisitioned records come in from the bank in Grand Cayman."

Reaper wouldn't have gone to anyone who could be traced back to his records, but anything Daniel found on Willow would be more planted evidence and a waste of time. With his office bugged, he couldn't tell the kid to flat out drop it.

"The forensic accountants are the experts. We'll let them do what they do best. I don't think looking into Willow's financials is the right use of your time."

The gung ho *I'm-a-dog-with-a-bone* gleam in Daniel's eyes told Sanborn the kid wasn't going to back down. Hard to tell if an ulterior motive ran beneath his tenacity.

"But, sir, I—"

"One," Sanborn said, "never question me. Two, keep the facial recognition program searching for them. Is that all from Analysis?"

Amanda nodded, and the kid wiped crumbs from his face, his head lowered. Then she, Doc, and Daniel left.

While the door was open, he heard Janet firing up the Nespresso machine.

Once Daniel shut the door behind him, Sanborn looked at Castle, who leaned against a wall with his thick arms crossed. "Did you get it?" he asked, referring to the copy of the 911 call.

Castle nodded. "Dead end. A digital voice modulator was used."

Not only did they not have the identity of the caller, they still didn't know the gender.

Sanborn expelled a breath. "Go through this with a fine-toothed comb." He handed Castle the flash drive containing a copy of Parker's computer.

With a nod, Castle took it and left.

Janet walked in with a tentative expression and set an espresso on his desk.

He gave a nod of appreciation for the hot hit of caffeine. "Shut the door and take a seat."

31

CARIBBEAN SEA
SUNDAY, JULY 7, 5:30 P.M. EDT

Out on the water, temporarily safe in the middle of nowhere, time became an ecstatic blur. Willow had lots of questions about sex, and Gideon had lots of answers, with both words and actions.

Their first time together had nearly split him down the middle. His lungs had shuddered, eyes rolled into the back of his head, and he'd entirely forgotten about the pain in his side. He'd lost himself in her warmth, in the exquisite sensation that was more than primal.

Afterward, she'd explored his body in a fascinated, studied fashion. Her slim fingers found every knife scar and bullet wound. The fact that she already knew how he'd gotten each one had been a staggering comfort. She didn't have to ask, and he didn't have to lie.

With each conversation, she delved deeper. How many lovers had he had? How many at once? Not a barrage as if in interrogation or for leverage to use against him. She just seemed curious about him. None of his answers, no matter how startling he'd assumed they'd be, had been met with judgment. She soaked in everything he said as though bathing in sunlight.

People assumed he had panache, loved to party, knew

how to command, all based on his looks and history as a quarterback. When they discovered he was terse, the last to arrive and first to leave a gathering, and his interest in shepherding a team was sorely lacking, they were disappointed and found it weird. They found *him* weird for being a contradiction to their expectations.

The brutal honesty he shared with Willow—her vision of him as something heroic rather than monstrous, where he was enough instead of a letdown—was more than he'd ever had.

A greedy, selfish part of him never wanted to let that go. But she deserved more. Happily-ever-after was bullshit for guys like him anyway, but he'd take happy-for-right-now. *With her.*

"When you were married," she asked, washing the dishes from the dinner he'd fixed, "did your wife do all the cooking? Or did you pitch in like my dad?"

His mouth turned as dry as burned toast. Her questions rolled out with such casual ease, as if there were no boundaries. Answering her so far hadn't felt like he was pulling his own teeth out with pliers as it had with Kelli, but this was the first time she'd asked about his dead wife. He was wired to disengage, but for some reason, with Willow, all he wanted was to connect.

She already knew the ugliest things in his personnel file. Seemed silly to hide the rest.

"I believe in carrying my weight. I helped with laundry, cooking, cleaning."

"I saw her picture. She was gorgeous. She looked like a supermodel." Her voice took on an edge that made his chest tighten. "You two made the perfect couple."

That was what everyone had thought, and in pictures, they had. Not in any way that had mattered. "We made the worst couple," he said, and she looked at him over her shoulder with a hint of surprise. "I was gone a lot. We led separate lives, where I paid the bills. Win-win for her unless I was in town. It only lasted as long as it did because I hate to lose."

If only he had let her go…

"You sound like your marriage was a game, and not a fun one."

Yeah, the Thunderdome where they'd dueled gladiator-style.

She faced him, wiping her hands on a towel. "Why did you get married?"

He heaved a breath, ashamed of his reasons. "I met her when I was playing football, right before a bad injury." He'd taken a nasty hit junior year. The doctor didn't know if he'd play again. "She took care of me. Cooked. Cleaned. Drove me to physical therapy."

He shrugged, but his gut burned. Kelli had slipped close by taking care of things he could've paid someone to do. He'd assigned great value to it because he didn't know what that type of attention was worth.

"Anyway, I healed, came back stronger senior year. When she suggested we go to the courthouse and get married, I said yes." Mistook lust for love. "My buddies said she wanted to nab a guy who'd play pro." What a fool he'd been. "She swore it didn't matter if I went pro or not. I'd never had someone of my own. Stupid and crazy, but I wanted to try it."

He looked out at the calm waves.

"Before I graduated, the Agency recruited me. It felt right." Like it was what he was meant to do. "I turned down a multimillion-dollar football deal and joined the CIA instead."

Furrowing her brow, she tilted her head. "The CIA doesn't recruit out of the blue."

She was right. They didn't.

"How did they lure you away from the fame and money of professional football? Why would they approach you in the first place? When they look for undergraduates, they covet linguists and those who score off the charts on particular aptitude tests."

Nothing slipped past Willow.

Gideon spoke Farsi, Arabic, and German, but he hadn't learned those in college. Sometimes the CIA disguised decryption challenges and potential field agent profiling as extra-credit questionnaires and psychological experiments. They loved former military with highly specialized skills, but they didn't recruit all-star athletes.

"Ask me another time." Discussing his failed marriage was one thing. Explaining how he had become the man he was today, well, that was a different story. "Mind grabbing me a beer?"

He pushed the throttle, increasing the boat's speed.

She handed him a cold longneck and pressed her palm to his chest. "Did your marriage not work because you both missed being with other people? Or was it a personality thing?"

"I didn't give Kelli the life she lied about wanting. She wasn't happy. With my choices or with me. She cheated, more than once." The first time, he'd found out by reading her diary. She'd claimed it had been a mistake bred out of loneliness and swore it wouldn't happen again.

"Did you ever cheat?"

He'd been miserable with a capital M, but he wasn't a shitbag who'd break a sacred vow. For better or worse, and he'd meant it. Gideon was a lot of things, many of which weren't good, but a cheat with a wandering eye wasn't one of them.

"No."

"Why didn't she just leave you, if she wasn't happy?"

"I think she was looking for my replacement. Someone else who'd pay the bills and take care of her. When she found him, she'd planned to divorce me. The paperwork is still sitting in her glove compartment."

Unloading all of that hadn't stung the way he'd expected. Instead, a great weight lifted, but he braced for the inevitable look of pity from Willow and the obligatory *I'm sorry*.

"You're smart, honest, strong enough to do scary things that'd make most people lose sleep or their lunch. You can cook and you're a fantastic kisser. An even better lover. I can't imagine why any woman would cheat on you." She gave him that look again that made him feel like he was a superhero who could leap tall buildings in a single bound. His ego could get used to the adoration in her eyes, if it wasn't such a problem.

"Throwing steaks in a pan isn't cooking," he said, "and I could be a shitty lover, since I'm only the second one you've had."

"Guess when our time together is up, if I'm still alive and not in prison, I'll have to find a new lover for the sake of comparison."

Stone-cold jealousy smacked him senseless. It came out of nowhere, like a brass-knuckle sucker punch. Insane since he had no claims on her and didn't want any. Everything she needed was the opposite of him.

He shuttered the reckless emotion. When this thing between them had run out of steam and she was cleared, she should find someone else. In the meantime, he'd focus on setting the right standard in the bedroom, raise the bar so high some nice guy couldn't live up to it.

"You should indulge and experiment with a few lovers." He sounded remarkably nonchalant, despite the wrenching twist in the pit of his stomach. "Before you settle on one guy."

The hurt expression that tightened across her face gave him the distinct impression he'd been tested and had failed. What shocked him was the instant desire to do anything to wipe that look off her face.

Willow patted his chest, something in her receding, and strutted away to the bathroom. A minute later, the shower started. The relief he'd expected—at no subsequent deep conversation or flaming circus hoops for him to jump through to fix whatever he'd done wrong—didn't come.

Instead, the urge to check on her niggled at him.

I can't imagine why any woman would cheat on you.

He scrubbed a hand over his jaw, doing more than imagining why Kelli had cheated. The bitterness of his own limitations alongside the memory of their last argument hacksawed through him. Tamping it down, he took a long pull on the beer.

Humming from the bathroom rose above the beating

sound of the shower. He smiled at the sweet melody, drumming his fingers on the wheel to the tune.

The water shut off. Her humming flowed into pitch-perfect singing. She waltzed through the kitchen naked, drying her hair with a towel.

Willow was sexy as hell, a constant temptation, and he'd never tire of looking at her.

She ascended the steps, graceful, the most sensual woman he'd ever seen, no trying required. He roped an arm around her slender waist and hauled her onto his lap. She fell against him. Cool wet tendrils of her hair clung to his cheek and chest. A damp sheen covered her skin the way he wanted his mouth and fingers to. Suddenly, he was jealous of the shower.

"What's that song?" Faintly familiar, the name danced on his tongue.

Resting her head on his shoulder, she gazed at him. Fading sunlight twinkled in her soulful eyes. She curled her arm around his neck and kissed him. Those petal-smooth lips subjugated him with a frightening softness.

"'I Love You, Baby.'" The whisper roared through him like thunder.

It'd been four high-stress, high-octane-fueled days, amplified by adrenaline, but one thing was certain. He wanted to know what loving her and being loved by her would be like.

For the first time in his life, he was drawn to a woman without wanting to own her. Kelli had been a possession more than a partner. It'd taken him a long time to reconcile to that horrible fact.

With Willow, he cared so deeply about her happiness,

he wanted her to be free of him to find someone better. As crazy as it sounded, it was the sanest thing in his life.

"That's the name of the song. Actually, 'Can't Take My Eyes Off You.' By Frankie Valli. Released May 1967. My parents' song. Dad always sang the *I love you, baby* part to my mom."

A wistful smile rose on her lips, but sadness swam in her eyes. She caressed the stubble on his face, kissed him lightly, and drifted onto the back deck.

He swiveled around in the chair, his gaze drawn to follow. Wind whipped through her hair, the incandescent light of the early evening framing her in a golden glow. With no clothes, no makeup, hair caught in a soft breeze, she was a striking beauty. He'd always remember how she looked right now.

Not once did she glance back at him, but the sense she needed him chafed inside his chest. He lowered the throttle and cut the engine.

Strolling outside, he said, "What are you thinking, starling?"

She stilled, and her radiant eyes found his. "Why did you call me that?"

"You remind me of one of those wild songbirds with glossy, dark feathers."

"But I'm a redhead now."

"Not forever." He eased up beside her.

Sunlight bounced off the shimmering, crystalline water. There were no other boats around and the sea was gentle.

She looked out over the water. A cool distance yawned between them. She seemed far away even though she was next to him.

His throat tightened around an unbearable lump. "Where are your pearls?"

"In the backpack. If they fell in the water or anything happened to them, I'd be devastated." She gazed at the sky. "They were my mom's. Those pearls have been in my family for three generations. They're all I have left of her."

Exhaustion would only compound all the negatives, making her anxiety worse. "You should sleep."

"I tried. I can't. If I had my computer, I'd be fine, but it's in ashes, with my clothes, mementos, pictures of my mom I never saved to the cloud, my house. My mom loved that house. I was born there."

This was the most grueling thing she'd ever endured, losing every material possession, her career at stake, life at risk, and her father, who she cherished, was in a coma. Gideon was blown away by her quiet strength. Most people would've unraveled, wallowed in tears. Not his starling. She was titanium at the core.

"I appreciate you risking everything to help me." She sighed. "I know it's your job to find the mole and I'm nothing more to you than a mission, but you don't have to babysit me."

"You started out as a target." Not even that was true. He'd picked her because he wanted to know her, to get close, and not for a job. "But you're not just a mission. You're…" *Everything I didn't know I wanted but that I don't deserve.*

She gazed up at him, waiting, a bright look of expectation dancing across her face.

"You're important. To the Gray Box." *To me.* He rubbed the back of his neck, anxious to make her understand what he was still figuring out. "I'm sorry this forced us together."

Her gaze fell, and her shoulders slumped as if something inside her had deflated.

Fuck, it wasn't coming out right. "I'm here for you." He white-knuckled the railing. "I'll do whatever I can to ease the strain of this on you."

"I'm not a baby you need to coddle." Her voice was a little too sharp, too defensive.

He fought the urge to pull her into a fierce hug. "Then it's good the only thing I know how to coddle is an egg." Eyes on the water, he roped an arm around her shoulders.

After a few minutes, her tense body melted pliantly against him, and she rested her head on his chest. They stood there, not talking, the silence an easy comfort. She let out a heavy breath as if surrendering and turned in to him, wrapping herself in his arms.

A strange sensation soaked through him, both comforting and disturbing. He held her, giving the hug she must've needed. She'd lost so much and was hurting. He wanted to give her anything and everything, gift wrap the world for her if it'd make her feel better.

This woman had ambushed his heart with the little sneak attacks of an insurgent. She owned him now, from skin to viscera to bone.

32

GRAND CAYMAN ISLAND
SUNDAY, JULY 7, 7:35 P.M. EST/8:35 P.M. EDT

G ideon had slept a total of eight hours in the last forty-seven. With twin 550 horsepower engines and a tank capacity of 525 gallons, they'd only made two pit stops at small fuel docks that wouldn't have surveillance cameras linked to a real-time facial recognition system and then pressed on wide-open throttle.

Docking at Grand Cayman Island was a sobering dose of reality. The journey had been a reprieve Willow needed, and the languid interludes of honesty and sharing in a manner that was foreign to him had been... nice.

But the vacay vibe dulled his edge. He needed to be wired, sharp, and hard. No room for softness.

He'd steered clear of customs, avoiding the harbors packed with cruise ships, and picked a smaller one for locals. Stealing a car would've been simple. A plethora of older models lined the streets. It'd been a while since he'd driven on the left side of the road—though like riding a bike, he'd pick it up again—but no need to draw unnecessary attention to themselves. The British territory provided conveniences such as a public bus system, and a sign indicated a stop a short walk from the residential harbor. He slung the backpack over his shoulder and helped Willow off the boat onto the dock.

The pink sundress clung to her, draping her curves and showing off her legs. He must've gotten the size wrong, too small. The fabric looked airbrushed on.

At the bus stop, they caught the shuttle, a glorified van with seats for twelve. He steered Willow to a rear seat by a window and sat next to her, settling the backpack on his lap. Angled to leap into action at a nanosecond of notice, he gave everyone who boarded the once-over.

There were no security cameras on the van and no CCTV on the roads. If the Gray Box or whoever else was after Willow tried to tap into any surveillance feeds here, the coverage would be limited and easy to evade on the streets.

The bank was a wild card. A thirty-minute drive away, considering the island's sluggish speed limit of twenty-five miles per hour, the bank wouldn't open for another thirteen hours, but he wanted to scope out the exits and windows before they walked in. They needed the passport with Willow's real name to access the account, but he'd have to devise an exit strategy and get her a passport with a fake name to leave later.

Willow gazed out the window, fiddling with the hem of her dress and balling her fingers into knots. If the situation were different, not overcast with danger, he would've taken her hand in his. They'd enjoy the long drive down the coast, gazing at the sparkling sea, her warm body nuzzled against him. She'd let her inner starling out, snap pictures of the clusters of houses that adorned the landscape in a vivid palette of color. He'd offer to take her parasailing or snorkeling, or if she preferred, they'd simply laze around.

He shoved the quiet longing into the darkness. Time for indulging in fantasies was done.

In the heart of bustling George Town, they passed the Nova World Bank, a two-story building on a busy corner. Gideon didn't see any traffic cams and no security camera above the front entrance. He still needed to do a walk-by.

He signaled Willow, and they hopped off at the next stop on the long drag of Church Street adjacent to the beach. The bank was two blocks back to the north on the main strip. Shops, restaurants, and hotels dotted the road in splashes of color, prodding his spirit to lift, but he tuned it out. He needed detachment to stay focused.

She pointed out an electronics store and he followed her inside. Back on the boat, he'd explained his rough plan, but she'd had a better one. He didn't understand the technical jargon, but she needed a laptop, thumb drive, and had to create something called a rootkit to pull it off.

While she collected the items in the store, he blocked her profile from the security cameras. They paid in cash and ventured outside. With his hand pressed to the small of her back, they meandered south through a stream of pedestrians, past a side street lined with stores and restaurants.

The first accommodation they came upon was a behemoth resort on the busy corner of the shopping row. Too much activity. Low-key was better.

They crossed the congested street to a modest four-story

hotel on the beach. Nothing flashy. A good place to hole up until morning.

"What are we doing here?" she asked. "I thought we were staying on the boat tonight."

He held the door open for her. "Docked in the harbor, someone might nose around. Better to be close to the bank, and I could use a shower where I'm not cramped."

Strolling across the polished floor of the lobby, he scanned for surveillance cameras. He noted elevators, stairwells, an exit to the beach, sign for a restaurant, and two bellboys.

At the reception desk, he turned, facing Willow. His back to one camera, limited profile to the other, he screened her partially from both.

"Good evening," said a middle-aged man with inky curls. "How may I help you?"

"Checking in. No reservation. One room. One night. Top floor, if you have it available. Something with easy access to the elevators and stairs, but away from ice or vending machines."

More than one egress point was essential, and those machines made too much noise. More important, they provided a plausible reason for someone to loiter.

"Ocean or pool view, sir?"

"Doesn't matter."

Willow took his hand, drawing his gaze, stirring his blood. "I'd like the ocean view."

The honed instinct to break free of the physical contact wrestled with the impulse to tug her closer. He'd never worn two hats in mission mode before, and he didn't know how to label the second hat. Playing a role for an op was natural, but his ability to compartmentalize with Willow had malfunctioned.

Straddling the chasm was a tricky spot. The gateway to mistakes.

She was as dangerous to him as he was bad for her. He couldn't risk alienating her or ratcheting up her nerves to a precarious high. Keeping her calm, close, and safe mattered most.

He curled his fingers around hers. "Ocean view it is."

_____

The seaside hotel sat on the beach, their room facing the water. As Gideon showered, Willow opened every window, drawing the balcony doors wide. A warm cross-flow breeze whipped the white gossamer curtains into the air. Waves broke on the sandy beach below.

She peeled off the scratchy, plastered-on dress, tossing it to the bed. Briny air danced across her skin like brushed silk, and the smell of sea salt curled around her until she tasted it.

The bathroom door flew open, and she turned. Gideon hovered in the threshold, dressed, steam snaking out from behind him. His golden hair shone like a halo, his pale-blue gaze hard as bulletproof glass. She stilled.

He stalked across the room and slammed all the windows shut. Reaper was back.

The tender man who'd made love to her and cooked for her on the boat was gone. This other side of him she respected, even admired, but she didn't like it one on one.

She'd never get over how easily he shifted from giving off so much heat he could melt the polar ice caps when he touched her to being agent-on-duty, radiating an arctic chill.

"I'm going to scope out the bank." He locked the last window, drawing the curtains. "When I get back, I'll grab food from the restaurant. We'll eat in the room. While I'm gone, windows and balcony doors stay shut, babe." The biting tone he used when barking out orders was worse than fingernails scraping chalkboard.

Lobbing in a *babe* didn't do a smidge to soften it.

"What's wrong with fresh air? We're on the top floor. There's no fire escape for someone to climb up, and no one knows we're here. We're safe. Aren't we?"

In two long strides, he crossed the distance separating them, snatching the oxygen from her lungs. "It's easy to jump from one balcony to another."

There were too many factors throwing off her equilibrium, wreaking havoc on her brain waves, while he circumnavigated everything fearlessly.

"The windows stay locked, curtains closed while I'm out." His tone was caustic.

"I know you're trying to keep me safe, and I can follow orders. I take them from the chief all the time. But I won't be *ordered about*. There's a difference." She rubbed her arms, glancing around the small room, not much larger than the quarters on the boat. "I want to eat in the restaurant. Not cooped up in here."

Eyeing her, he went motionless, growing so rigid that she had to look away from the unearthliness of him.

"Please." She stared at her feet, suddenly self-conscious

about her nudity. "I need it. My life is in pieces. I have no idea what's going to happen. I had to leave my father, everything familiar behind, with nothing certain. I was confined on the boat, then the ride in the little van, now this room." Anxiety spiraled inside her, her mind racing. The walls were closing in. "I need a long walk, but I know it's too risky. Please, let's eat in the restaurant."

Heavy silence followed—a gaping hole where the conversation should've continued. A shiver ran through her. You could hear a pin drop. She pulled at the skin on the back of her hand, taking comfort in the slight pain from the pinch.

"Dangerous." His voice was low, harsh.

Her gaze flickered to him. He looked like a terrifying, beautiful god ready to smite a wayward mortal.

"The restaurant's dangerous?"

"No." The icy word pierced the air, and she was lost as to what he was talking about. "We'll eat in the restaurant." He pulled out the gun tucked against the small of his back. A sci-fi looking 9mm with built-in silencer. "Do you remember how to fire one?"

Her eyes went wide, pulse skipping a beat. "Uh. Remove the safety. Aim. Breathe. Exhale, put my finger on the trigger. Second exhale, fire."

He thumbed off the safety and chambered a round. The sharp sound made her flinch.

"Keep your eyes open no matter what. Aim for the head or chest. Don't hesitate."

She took the gun, disliking the weight of the steel in her hands and the bitter taste filling her mouth. "You might need this out there."

"I'll be fine." He took the hammer from the bag he'd packed, slipped it through a belt loop, and shoved the screwdriver into his pocket, then concealed the tools with a long-sleeved shirt. "I won't be long."

She walked toward him, the gun shaking in her hand. At the door, he looked down at her, his eyes fixed on her mouth. She hoped he was going to kiss her, and her lips tingled at the thought.

"Lock it behind me." He gave her a peck on the forehead and shut the door.

Beating back disappointment, she turned the deadbolt and exhaled the breath she'd been holding.

"Chain," he said from the other side of the door.

She threw the chain on and set the gun on the night-stand. In four days, her entire world had been pulverized to so many unrecognizable bits, nothing left was tangible.

Finally, everything was hitting her at once. She might go to prison for something she didn't do. Assassins were hunting her, and her father...

Willow sat on the bed and stared at the new laptop. She needed to get her life back, starting by taking care of her end of the plan.

In the electronic store they'd stopped at, she had bought a pair of high-fidelity earplugs designed for concert goers, but they should filter sound the same. She was so used to the comforting feel of the earbuds while working at the office that she used them at home as well.

She set up the laptop, logged into the hotel Wi-Fi, and downloaded Tor—the onion router. The program allowed her to surf the darknet. In *Onionland*, as it was also known, people traded in Bitcoin, bought hacking services, and hired contract killers, and she'd even discovered a nasty bioweapon for sale.

Which was precisely how all this trouble started less than a month ago, when she stumbled upon the auction of weaponized smallpox that had led the Gray Box to Aleksander "the Ghost" Novak. In a roundabout way, she was responsible for putting herself dead center in the mole's crosshairs and for jeopardizing Gideon's life. She had to do everything in her power to save herself and give him any possible assistance.

Surfing the layers of the dark web, she nosed around in one of her peer-to-peer networks. She wasn't friends or colleagues with anyone on here—at least she didn't think so. Everyone hid their identity. She fished through the available files and found the illegal kernel-mode rootkit.

The clandestine software wasn't malware on its own but had the stealth capability to make the malicious payload bundled with it undetectable. The program was complex, highly sophisticated. It would run as part of the operating system itself on the targeted computer, opening a back door and giving her carte blanche security access.

Willow embedded the program in a link in an email, which wouldn't be flagged by IT, unlike some attachments, and sent it to every offshore-accounts manager at the bank. She and Gideon would sit with one of those managers in the morning, and as a million-dollar client, she could ensure that they not only opened the email but also clicked the link.

Tomorrow, they just had to distract the account manager outside the office long enough for her to get onto their computer and copy the relevant files. To pull this off, every detail had to be perfectly synchronized.

Willow rubbed her eyes and glanced at the clock. Her sister should've made it to Virginia. Hopefully, she wasn't in any danger and their father was recovering.

She needed to call, but it wasn't safe to do so from a landline that would give away her location instantly if Laurel's phone was being monitored. A voice-over-IP call through the computer, on the other hand, would be difficult to trace.

Laurel had the Viber app on her cell phone, same as Willow, allowing them to speak to Ivy overseas for free. The app also enabled VoIP-to-mobile calls.

She installed the necessary plug-ins on the computer for Viber along with a virtual private network software that'd hide her real IP address and assign a fake one tied to a country of her choosing.

Casablanca, Morocco, seemed plausible. Lots of flights in and out, large enough city to disappear, and the country had no formal extradition treaty with the United States.

Once everything was set up, she placed the call. The line rang and rang. Finally, her sister answered.

"Hello. Willow?" Laurel's voice was brittle, sending a flicker of fear through her.

She prayed their father's condition hadn't worsened. "It's me. Are you with Dad? How is he?"

33

NEAR THE POTOMAC RIVER, VIRGINIA
SUNDAY, JULY 7, 10:10 P.M. EDT

Omega nodded, prompting the woman to continue.

"Dad is in a coma," the bound woman said into the cell phone on speaker that one of his men held in front of her mouth. "They're not sure what's causing it. Where are you?"

"I can't tell you," Willow Harper said. "Thanks for driving out. I wouldn't have asked if it wasn't important. I'm in trouble. Some bad people are after me. I think they hurt Dad, burned down the house. If you see anything suspicious, go to hospital security and call the police."

Dead silence as the sister shut her eyes and pressed her lips in a grim line.

"Laurel? Are you okay?"

Omega had prepped the woman for this very call. Rho, his second in charge and topnotch techie, was ready to track it. Omega pressed the muzzle of his gun to the woman's temple.

"Willow, I'm worried about Dad. He might not recover. I don't want you to miss a chance to say goodbye. Where are you? When are you coming back?"

He looked to his tech guru. Rho shook his head. Omega went to him, out of range of the phone.

"What's the hold up?" he mouthed.

"She's calling over the Internet and masking her IP," Rho whispered. "I need time."

"I'm not sure when I'll be back," Willow said. "I can't stay on the phone much longer."

Omega gestured with his gun to keep the conversation going.

"Wait. Wait…I love you. I'm sorry for giving you a hard time when we were younger. I was pretty mean sometimes, and now I have kids…" The sister sobbed into the phone. "My sweet girls…I miss my girls. And Daddy might die. I'm counting on you to come home soon."

Omega could tell Rho was close—the dude's face was twisted in an intense expression like he was jerking off and about to blow a load as his fingers flew across the keyboard.

"I'm trying, Laurel. Thank you for—"

"What happened to the house? And to Dad? The cops are saying you did it. But you wouldn't, would you? Mom loved that house. You were born there. And you're Dad's favorite—you wouldn't hurt him. Would you?"

Rho threw his head back with an ecstatic look, raising his hands from the laptop. Omega would swear Rho enjoyed hacking more than fucking.

"I didn't do it, Laurel. I have to go. Give Dad a kiss from me. I love you."

The line went dead.

"You got it?" Omega asked.

Rho nodded, grinning like the cat who swallowed the canary. "There's a new security flaw in Web Real-Time Communication. The vulnerability is browser-based in Chrome, Firefox, Internet Explorer, and Opera. She was on one of them. I had to use JavaScript to send a STUN request through WebRTC to the third-party network server on the other side of NAT. It returned her real IP address."

Yada, yada, nerd speak—whatever. "Where are they?"

"A hotel on Grand Cayman Island," Rho said.

"They're going after the money." Drawing in a breath, Omega did a rough flight-time calculation. Eight to nine hours by helicopter. A commercial flight was exponentially faster, but they'd be hard-pressed to get a flight this late, and they'd have to contend with securing weapons on the island. Taking the helo gave them the ability to travel anonymously and carry all their gear and the flexibility to touch down as close to the bank as possible. Hell, if he wanted, he could land on the beach.

"Is Epsilon going?" Rho asked.

Omega quirked a brow. "I was taking you."

Not true. Rho had sharper leadership skills than E and was better suited to hold things down here with the girl and take point on security once Daedalus arrived. But Omega needed to make sure Rho was up for anything.

"Stone took out Beta, Delta, Kappa, *and* Sigma by himself," Rho said, making it sound as though Stone had obliterated a row of fraternities.

The codenames made him think of a Quentin Tarantino film, but Daedalus had insisted. Omega rarely opposed him. Reserving a hard stance for when it was absolutely necessary kept Daedalus more inclined to agree on those rare occasions. Not easy to bend such a man's ear or his will to do anything he didn't want to do.

"What do we know about Gideon Stone?" Rho asked.

"No military record. Agency issue."

They were the worst. With a military guy, you knew what to prepare for, understood how they thought. They were predictable. But those Agency-bred beasts were unique.

"Where do we stand on getting leverage on Stone?" Omega asked.

Everyone had a weakness. Omega had found Gideon Stone's in the file Cobalt had delivered. Those Gray Box Boy Scouts were hardwired to risk their lives to save innocent civilians, but making it personal, tugging at the heartstrings, was better.

Emotions always knocked someone off their game.

There was one person in Stone's life who he cared about but had kept at a distance to protect them. If he'd really wanted to keep them safe, Stone should've cut them off completely. No calls, no emails.

"The guys went to the farmhouse in Martinsburg, West Virginia, found it empty, but spoke to a neighbor. The target is on a cruise and will be back Tuesday. Hopefully, this will be resolved by then, but in the meantime, we need more men," Rho said flatly.

Omega didn't tolerate cowards, but Rho wasn't afraid. They'd fought and bled together in the meat grinder and come out the other side. This was a simple matter of common sense. Rho was right. They needed more men, but waiting for extra guns would delay them. The sooner they had boots on the ground, the easier it'd be to catch Stone off guard.

The island was small. If Omega could place men at the hotel and the bank, getting them was an inevitability. Once the chick learned they had her sister, it would be easy as pie to reel in that bleeding heart.

"Daedalus is flying in with a handful of men," Omega said.

The man was in a touchy mood after hearing about Cobalt's threat of insurance and wanted to see this finished firsthand.

"I'll wait for him to arrive and make it work with the men on hand." Omega strode around the table to the window of the warehouse and looked down at the abandoned waterfront. "No time to wait for more."

Rho straightened. "When will he arrive?"

Three hours, eleven minutes. No need to look at his watch again. "Soon."

Once Daedalus landed, Omega would switch gears and feel him out, make sure he didn't go doomsday-explosive. The man swung to extremes, and when he got bloodthirsty, he was relentless in a fashion that left even Omega breathless. Daedalus was magnificent to behold in action, but if left unchecked, he became a danger to himself.

Everything was on the line. Omega had peeled a lot of flesh and shed a lot of blood to crown Daedalus king of this empire. They'd both do anything necessary to keep this hard-earned monopoly on U.S. counterintelligence and corporate espionage.

Daedalus would never admit it, but Cobalt was a priceless asset. The Gray Box had unrestricted access to every American intelligence agency, from the CIA and NSA to every sector of the Department of Defense. The intel Cobalt provided had been a gold mine, affording them the opportunity to expand their kingdom in ways far exceeding their wildest imaginations. The continued flow of information would solidify their hold.

This bold move to safeguard Cobalt was a massive

gamble, but if they pulled it off, there'd be no stopping them. They'd already lost more men than anticipated and stuck their necks out well beyond comfortable limits, but there was no glory without sacrifice. So long as Omega kept Daedalus levelheaded and protected, he'd find a way to manage the rest. "I don't want you to go with me and the boys to the Caymans."

Rho shot to his feet. "Why not? I'm rock-steady. Ready to roll."

"I need you here with Daedalus. If anything goes wrong and Stone makes it past me—"

"What are you saying?" Rho's dark eyes narrowed.

"If something goes *wrong*, I need you to make sure Daedalus doesn't go apeshit."

No one planned for their own funeral, not in this business. And Omega wasn't about to start. He couldn't care less about dying, but he wouldn't be able to focus unless he knew Rho would cover down and keep Daedalus safe.

Omega scrubbed a hand over the back of his neck. "If you don't hear from me, Daedalus should let Cobalt burn, then cut and run while he can."

"You should be the one to tell him." Rho lowered his gaze and shook his head. "He only listens to you."

If that were true, things would be simple. "I'll tell him."

A lot needed to be said. The time for such talk was never right. Work always came first, and he'd never unload before going out on something this big. Omega would only talk about what mattered most to him in the world: keeping Daedalus safe and alive, no matter the cost.

"You'll need to remind him," Omega said. "Just in case."

"We go out, but we come back. Always, bro. Get your

head straight. Stone rattled you, threw you a curveball, but it's nothing you can't handle. When we're in a fight, we're like gods. We can tackle anything thrown our way."

Even gods fall, but now wasn't the time to remember the damn Titans. "Yeah, you're right." He threw Rho an easy smile to put his brother-in-arms at ease. "You know me. I cover all bases. Worst case, do whatever's necessary to keep him safe."

"That's the prime directive."

Daedalus wasn't just a mission and Rho knew it, but Omega didn't need to say the words.

"Oh, G-G-God," the woman whimpered.

What was her fucking name? Lauren? Laura?

"You're going to k-k-kill me. I've seen your faces. You're talking about your plans. I'm not going to see my girls again, am I? Simone is going to steal my life. I should've fired her."

Rho grabbed a roll of duct tape and unpeeled a long strip to muzzle the woman.

Omega lifted a palm, stopping him. "Listen, little momma, I hate tears and whining. If you don't pipe down, I'll have to pay your family a visit once I'm done with your sister."

He picked up her wallet from the table, plucked out her driver's license, read off her address in North Haven, Connecticut, and slipped out a photo of two blond girls from the plastic picture holder. "Twins? Six? Seven? A tough age to lose a mother. And a father. Think of your children and how you don't want them to be orphans."

The woman sucked in a shuddering sob, and then blessed silence.

"Ahhh, see? No need to waste the tape."

34

GRAND CAYMAN
SUNDAY, JULY 7 9:19 P.M. EST/10:19 P.M. EDT

After a shower, Willow blow-dried her hair, longing for a brush, elastic bands, and hair pins. Minuscule items that meant nothing separately but added up to the pieces that held her together.

On the boat, she'd been removed from the real world—her problems seemed an ocean away—and had created a new routine with Gideon.

Here, she stared at the gun on the counter, praying there'd be no reason to use it.

Gathering her damp auburn strands as if for a ponytail, she coiled her hair into a tight bun, tucking the ends, and secured it with a ballpoint pen. The twist was messier than she preferred, but she was grounded, better prepared to handle the unexpected.

She stared in the mirror. Could Gideon be with someone like her back home?

Laughable. Right?

Or might it be possible?

A knock sounded at the door. She jumped and grabbed the gun.

"It's me."

Gideon. She relaxed and hurried to let him in.

"How did the bank look?" She handed him the gun.

"Fine." With a grim face and sheen of sweat on his brow, he tossed the tools on the bed, threw on his shoulder holster, stuffed the gun inside, and covered up with the long-sleeved shirt. "Small building. Two exits. There'll probably be two guards, four max."

"You think we'll have trouble?"

"I doubt the guards expect any action. People with offshore accounts wire their money in and out once it's established. Those types of banks aren't usually held up at gunpoint, but best for us to be prepared." He caressed the wispy strands dangling around her face. "I like it. The messy bun."

His gaze softened. He grasped her chin between his thumb and forefinger and kissed her. Quick. Soft. Licking his lips, he smiled for the first time since they'd docked.

Warmth flooded her chest, chasing away the chill. She had a glimmer of real hope that their plan might work, her life would be restored, and everything would be okay.

He ushered her out of the room and down the stairs to the restaurant, which stayed opened until midnight seven days a week. His hand was on her lower back in the intimate way that whispered of protection and possession. The tension in her body eased.

They waited by the hostess's podium at the entrance of the small restaurant. Less than twenty tables were inside, and a handful lined the wraparound balcony overlooking the beach.

A U-shaped bar sat catty-corner to the kitchen, enclosed in a wall of glass allowing patrons to see the inner workings. Ebullient music wafted from the overhead speakers, sultry vocals, guitar strings, and drums skirting the line between reggae and calypso.

"Good evening," the hostess said, approaching them. "Two for dinner?"

Gideon gave a curt nod, scanning the restaurant. His head didn't swivel, but his gaze panned across everything. He was always alert and stayed in this hair-trigger state of readiness.

"Inside or outside?" the hostess asked.

Willow was eager for fresh air. "Outside."

"Inside," Gideon countered. "That table in the back." He pointed to one far from the open patio doors that were letting in a balmy breeze and away from any occupied tables.

The hostess glanced between them as if waiting for a final verdict.

A million factors to keep them safe must be going through Gideon's mind, guiding his decisions. Willow needed to follow his lead instead of worrying about fresh air, but goodness, she was dying to sit on the patio.

She shrugged one shoulder. "Inside."

They were shown to the table he requested. He sat with his back to the wall, but Willow faced the balcony. If she couldn't smell the sea or feel the wind, by golly, she'd look at the flickering torch flames on the terrace.

The hostess handed them menus. "Can I get you beverages?"

"I want a real drink." Willow put a hand on his forearm. "But I don't know what to order."

"I thought you didn't like alcohol." He glanced at her for the first time since leaving the room.

"I've tried vodka and tequila."

His brows drew together. "Straight?"

She nodded. Laurel had insisted on shots of vodka with a tequila chaser during that unforgettable Thanksgiving. The sickening experience hadn't been one she wanted to repeat. Fiddling with her pearls, she tried to ignore the rapier-sharp edge in his body and wary gaze focused on everything besides her.

"Want to try a drink on the sweeter side?" he asked.

Sweet, tart, she just didn't want it to taste horrible. "Sure."

"A buttery nipple." Gideon scanned the balcony. "Two waters and a bottle of local beer."

The woman gave a smile and left.

"That's a drink?" Such an odd name.

"I think you'll like it." His stormy-blue eyes worked the room. "Sorry we couldn't sit on the balcony. Lines of sight too restricted. I need to see everyone coming in and want a solid wall at my six. We're good in this part of the restaurant. No cameras. Steer clear of the bar and the registers in the back by the restrooms."

She swallowed the dry lump of irritation swelling in her throat and tapped her fingers against her leg.

The drinks arrived. The waiter set a tumbler in front of her containing four ounces of a milky, light brown liquid, and they ordered.

With a deep breath, she took a sip. Sweet. Strong. Decadent.

Willow licked her lips and drained the glass.

Gideon surveilled their surroundings, taking another swig from the one beer he'd been nursing. No way of knowing how many hitmen were after Willow or where they'd turn up next.

They'd avoided CCTV and were most likely safe for the night at the hotel, but he couldn't stop his vigilant perusal or shut off the need to be ready any more than a bird could refuse to fly.

Two cooks never left the kitchen, churning out plates of food onto the stainless-steel counter for the waitstaff in a well-choreographed rhythm. The chatty bartender was slow at pouring drinks but attentive to customers. Four men strolled in and camped out at the bar. None were packing, and there were no slight bulges of concealed knives. His gaze fell to their shoes, a dead giveaway of a potential threat.

Loafers equaled tourists or locals looking for fun.

His attention boomeranged back to Willow. She didn't force conversation, but her proximity was a distraction. He was struggling to keep focused on sweeping for suspicious activity. His skin was too tight, nervous energy pulsed in his veins, and his fingers ached. Not from anything gearing him on alert, but because he couldn't wait to get her back to the room.

He watched her finish a second buttery nipple. She no longer played with her pearl necklace, tore paper napkins into tiny bits, or pinched the back of her hand—all coping mechanisms. And she'd taken the pen out of her hair, letting it drape her lovely shoulders.

The music switched to an upbeat remixed sound. She swayed to the beat, lounging in her chair. Hunger for his beautiful starling pumped through him. He couldn't wait to get behind closed doors with her and enjoy the solace of being in her arms.

Tomorrow would come soon enough. Once they found the mole and her life was restored, he'd let her go. He wanted a shot at...something—hell, everything with her—but what he desired and what they both needed were far from the same.

As for romance, those sweet gestures women went gaga for made him gag. He didn't do flowers, brunch with parents, throw on a suit to go to church, plan surprise vacations, dance around like a rhythm-challenged idiot, or dip into candlelit baths. Not him. Not ever. And he was far better at giving *I'm-sorry-I-fucked-up* gifts than one for a birthday or anniversary.

Who was he kidding?

Given enough time, he'd screw things up with Willow. And if by some miracle he didn't botch it, she'd weaken him. Look at them, sitting out in the open because he didn't have the strength to deny her, when they should be upstairs, lying low.

He did better on his own, and she'd be better off without him.

The waiter returned and removed their plates. "Can I get you two anything else?"

Willow perked in her seat, face flushed. "Another buttery nipple."

"No. She's had enough." Gideon shook his head, emphasizing his point, and the waiter scuttled away.

Her stubborn chin lifted, hazel eyes flaring.

Shit. He emergency tapped religion like a heathen, praying she wouldn't fight him.

"I want another drink."

"You've had enough, babe."

"When you want to touch me, it's starling, but when you want to boss me around, it's babe?"

Valid point. He hadn't noticed. "You're not used to drinking. I don't want you to get sick." *And I'm sorry for being a dipshit control freak.*

Another thing to add to the list of what she didn't deserve.

"Dance with me." Sighing, she slid her hand along his forearm. "You've barely looked at me all night." Something about the way the words rolled from her sweet tongue and the longing in her eyes had his insides softening. "Please. A few minutes."

He snatched his arm from her grasp, tearing his gaze away before he succumbed. If she ever figured out the power she held over him, he would be fucked. "I. Don't. Dance."

He didn't dance, ever, and even if he did, dancing meant distraction.

Scooting her chair back in a screech, she was on her feet before he blinked. She strode near the doors leading to the patio—in the middle of the restaurant—and started dancing.

Fuck. All eyes zeroed in on her, destroying the low profile he'd painstakingly created, setting his teeth on edge. The one good thing was she stayed clear of the cameras.

Swaying her hips and shaking her shoulders, Willow moved to the beat of the music. Closing her eyes, she swung her hair, waving her arms and rolling her hips. She was the sexiest thing he'd seen in his life and he'd seen a lot.

Gideon clenched the arms of the chair, and the wood

groaned in his tightening grip. He would've killed for a piece of gum.

A guy from the bar hopped off his barstool, his gaze fastened on her, and swooped in.

Gideon sprang to his feet. Hands tightened to fists, he cut a hard line to Willow, sights locked on the motherfucker.

Holy hell. He was not that dude, the psycho jealous type. Being with Willow was driving him asylum-certified crazy.

The guy caught sight of Gideon approaching and raised his hands, cowering away in warranted fear. Willow met Gideon's eyes, a flush rising on her cheeks. He whisked her into his arms.

"I thought that guy might ask me to dance," she said.

"Yeah, that's why I scared him off."

"I don't understand." She pulled away. "You don't dance. You can't wait for me to take other lovers. But you have a problem if someone else dances with me?"

"Why are you pissed? I feel like you've been mad at me since the boat."

"Mad?" She shook her head. "I'm disappointed."

That King Kong–sized bombshell practically knocked him on his ass. Disappointment was bound to happen in a relationship, but they were only fucking and she was already disappointed?

"This is why I don't do relationships. The double *D*s. Discontent and drama."

She squeezed her eyes shut like she couldn't bear the sight of him. He knew the look well, but seeing it on Willow's face wrenched something inside his chest.

"It was a mistake to force you to have pity sex with me." She hurried out of the restaurant.

Pity sex? Was that what she thought this was?

Gideon dropped money on the table, leaving a generous tip, and hustled after her. She was fast and almost made it to the room before he reached their floor. He waited for her to step inside and followed behind her, not wanting to cause a scene in the hall.

———————————

Willow's heart raced in her throat. Longing for something was one thing. Suddenly getting it and knowing you'd soon lose it and would continue to crave it was a rare kind of torture.

Gideon locked the door. "You didn't force me to have sex with you. Look at me." He clasped her arms, coaxing her gaze to his. "I have not been having sex with you out of pity. Please don't think that."

"Do you even like me?" She wrapped her arms around herself, not certain if she wanted to hear the answer.

"Like you?" A furious expression twisted across his face, and he shook his head. "You're not like anyone else I've ever been with."

She winced, wanting to shrivel into nothing, not needing a reminder that she was different.

"I mean, you're special to me." He brushed her jaw with his knuckles, and the wave of anxiety receded. "You're so beautiful." The smooth heat in his voice almost made her believe him.

"I know I'm not. I'm the *ugly duckling* who never fits

in." That's what Laurel used to call her. Among other things. "You don't have to—"

He silenced her with a scorching kiss. Her toes curled, her body squeezed with yearning.

"The ugly duckling was a gorgeous swan who needed to find where she belonged. You have no idea how beautiful you are. I wouldn't say it if it wasn't true." He slipped his hands in her hair, cupping her head. "I love your sensitivity. How you're fragile yet strong."

Each sweet word stole oxygen from her lungs and only deepened the craving for him.

"I love how extraordinary you are. You have such talent others envy." His words sparked a strange delight, and for as long as she lived, she'd never forget a single one. "I love your singing." He stroked the hollow of her neck. "I love this spot. Whenever you touched your pearls in a briefing, you always drew my eye right here. Delicate. Sensual. The first part of your body I fell in love with."

She was overwhelmed and had no idea how to respond.

"I love that you don't dream. It means you can't have nightmares. So when you sleep, I know you're at peace."

Lightness tickled her chest at how he remembered the small passing details.

"I love when you relax and let go." A hot whisper against her lips. "You can be so free, you make me want to let go too. Make me want to join Control Freaks Anonymous. Hi, my name is Gideon. I'm a control freak."

She laughed. "Hi, my name is Willow. I'm a control freak too." She had to organize everything a certain way, from spices to the dishes in a dishwasher. If only there were a CFA.

The only thing keeping her from losing her mind with her rigid schedule obliterated was this new routine with him.

His lips hitched in a smile, and he kissed her. In the hot rush from his mouth, she sensed *her* Gideon, the one from the boat.

"I love touching you, being inside you, and it has nothing to do with pity. Okay?"

She nodded, her heart clenching under the upsurge of emotion. The way he caressed her and spoke to her, as if he more than liked her. As if he loved her.

He opened a window, followed by another, letting in fresh air. Her heart beat a little faster, a little harder. He started stripping, leaving a trail of clothes on the way back to her. She kicked off her shoes, marveling at the stunning sight of him. Still seemed she was lost in a fantasy. He desired her, unmistakable how she aroused him, but maybe that was how it was for a man.

"Are you like this with other women?"

Tossing his jeans to the side, he glanced at her. "Like what?"

"Interested in sex all the time? Or am I lucky?"

He sauntered closer, his eyes pale-blue flames, setting her heart on fire. Placing the gun on the nightstand, he said, "I'm the lucky one. I've never been like this with anyone."

Running her palms up his chest, she kissed the wrinkled patch near his shoulder where he'd suffered a burn. Lebanon, two years ago. A light scar from a switchblade across his lower abdomen while on assignment in Nigeria the summer she began at the Gray Box. She lowered to her knees and kissed the two bullet wounds on his thigh that he'd taken on exfiltration from Venezuela.

In every kiss, every lick of her tongue, she showered him with tenderness. Every blemish she loved because they all added up to make him this amazing man capable of extraordinary things.

He cradled her face, bringing her to her feet. Stroking her lips with the pad of his thumb, he smiled, nothing between them besides warmth and anticipation. Gideon laid her down, pressing flush against her, heavy and full between her legs. The masculine heat from him erased her worries and fears about everything.

A breeze rustled the curtains, skimming her skin. She ran her hands over the chiseled landscape of his chest while he commanded her body to soften and grow slick from his touch. He drew one of her knees up, opening her, and then she was engulfed in sensation. He stretched her, groaning, seeming to lose himself as her body yielded, giving way to his.

When he touched her, thresholds disappeared and limits ceased to exist. There was only the agonizing sweetness between ecstasy and oblivion.

"Open your eyes." The dark velvet whisper brushed her mouth.

She met his penetrating gaze, and a deep flutter winged through her.

"No one's ever looked at me the way you do." He kissed her, stealing her breath.

She trembled under the reverence of his touch. Was this love? Lust? Both? It was the most powerful force she'd ever experienced.

"Am I hurting you?" His terrified gaze probed her face, hand cupping her cheek.

She swallowed hard. "No." *Enjoy what you can while you can.*

He slid deep, rolling his hips, taking her higher. Excruciating pleasure had her spinning tighter and tighter, scattering in a burst of fireworks.

"Oh fuck." Gideon growled, jerking into her roughly.

It was all too much, too overwhelming. Tears leaked from her eyes.

"Willow?" Gideon eased out of her and brought her into his arms. "At first, sex made you happy. Now it only seems to make you sad. Are you okay?"

She didn't know how to lie, and she didn't dare tell him the truth. That after being touched by him and experiencing such fullness and heat, she would never again be okay with emptiness.

He gripped her chin, angling her face to him, and locked their mouths in an all-consuming kiss. Deep and long as if he wanted to taste her soul.

No denying it, she was in love, fallen hard and fast for this incredible man.

Earlier, she would've sworn he would've told her what she longed to hear. *I'm yours and you're mine and we belong together.*

But he hadn't.

"Tired?" He played in her hair, his arm banded around her. "Want to sleep?"

Tomorrow loomed too close. Everything hung in the balance with the greatest stakes of all at risk. Tonight, she wanted to savor this time with him.

She curled her hand to her chest, where her heart was breaking. "No, I don't want to sleep."

35

The prospect of shut-eye was nowhere on the horizon for Sanborn, but he normally functioned on four hours and could power through a week with none.

"Sir, wait!" Maddox came running down the hall as he was about to enter the conference room. "The apartment in Springfield that's been on the news, the one over a doughnut shop, belonged to a passport forger. Reece and I followed a hunch and checked it out. The place was hit with heavy artillery."

Sanborn didn't believe in coincidence. Willow needed a passport, and a forger's place was hit the same day Gideon would've tried to procure one.

"How heavy was the artillery?"

"MP5A3 submachine guns. Armor-piercing rounds punched holes through the walls. Traces of C-4, concussion and incendiary grenades."

He hoped those two weren't bleeding out somewhere. *No.* Gideon was too talented to let that happen.

"This reeks of bounty killers." Making the situation far more dangerous for Gideon and Willow. "Could you track the assailants from nearby CCTV footage?"

"No. They were very careful."

Or very good. Hopefully, not as good as Gideon. "Find out who contracted those hitmen. Ballistics might lead somewhere."

She nodded.

He pushed into the conference room, ignoring Sybil, and sat at the head of the table, meeting the weary gaze of the DNI now flicking onto the live video feed.

Thanks to Sybil, updates had been endless, muddying the water, but Sanborn had managed to stop her from delivering any behind his back. With access to every network and system, she was finecombing through everything. No question in his head about what new information she intended to serve on a gilded platter to the DNI. If only his people would stop digging in places he said to leave alone. At least he'd beat her to the punch and color it with some common sense.

"Where do we stand, Bruce?" The DNI shielded a yawn with a hand.

"One of my analysts"—he refrained from saying *the incorrigible Daniel Cutter*—"found a villa in Deux-Sèvres, France, with the deed in Harper's name."

"Paid for in cash." Sybil sneered as if the less-than-accurate detail substantiated Harper's guilt.

He wanted to snap her bony neck. "Actually, paid for in Bitcoin. Untraceable." A fact that supported his suspicion Willow was being framed.

"The deed and the offshore account are both in her name, for goodness' sake." Sybil folded her arms, stiffening in her chair. "And one of *my* analysts checked the entry records to the server, where power to the observation room was disconnected the night Novak was murdered. Willow Harper was the only person to access it."

"You mean Willow's PIN was used to access it," Sanborn countered.

Sybil gave him a pointed look. "The evidence is damning. What do you need? A trail of breadcrumbs spelling it out? She's the mole. Why do you keep pussy-footing around the facts?"

"I'm inclined to agree with Sybil on this."

A smug smile hitched her mouth.

Sanborn's eye twitched and he wrestled the urge to slap the Cheshire-cat grin off her face. First time he'd ever wanted to hit a woman.

He softened his expression in opposition to his mounting annoyance. "The so-called evidence is circumstantial at best, too tidy and convenient. Just enough to point the finger at Harper and give the appearance of guilt, with nothing to substantiate it."

Glaring at her with daggers of disgust, he mentally stabbed the hell-raiser to death but refused to lower himself further.

"The bank in the Caymans," Sanborn said to the DNI, "has denied our request for copies of the documents used to open the offshore account. Attempts to hack into the system have been futile. The external firewalls are brutal."

Sanborn straightened, squaring his shoulders. "The deed to the villa is in Harper's name, in a country where we have extradition. Not the best place to hide. Also, she didn't use her offshore account to pay for it—instead, she supposedly used Bitcoin. Why would she go to the effort of using untraceable underground cryptocurrency to cover her tracks, then slip up by putting the property in her own name?"

He took a hit of coffee to strike the beat of a pause for effect, a casual show of confidence. "I may not be a forensic accountant, but this sure as hell doesn't add up."

"Doesn't she have a sister who's married to a Frenchwoman and living in Paris?" Sybil asked for the DNI's benefit.

"That true, Bruce?" The DNI pinched the bridge of his nose, looking in desperate need of a power nap.

"She has a sister there and a sister-in-law who could've provided a French stooge to list on the deed so we'd never know about the villa. Since the discovery of the offshore account, Willow Harper's house has been torched, and her father is now in a coma in ICU. Also, I was just informed that forensics confirmed the brakes on Harper's car were sabotaged. Traces of a rare and highly corrosive chemical called dedtrex were discovered. We're trying to track down where it came from."

Sybil rested her forearms on the table. "Sir, this only proves whoever Harper works for obviously wants her dead before she can be found and talks."

"The only thing *obvious* is the danger of someone with zero operational experience weighing in on matters beyond the scope of their comprehension."

"I have a dog in this fight." Sybil stabbed the glass table with a painted talon, throwing him a frosty glare. "More than Operations is at stake here if you continue to fail."

Sanborn cut his attention from her, looking to the DNI. He hated to tug at personal strings in a professional situation, but everything was about to be razed to ashes.

Careers, lives, the Gray Box. He'd sacrificed and risked too much to lose it all now.

"Lee, you and I go way back. My reputation—"

"Needs no reiteration with me. They don't make them like you anymore. Truth be told, if you weren't the one handling this, I would've insisted the president assign an interim director in your stead at the first piece of evidence pointing to Harper, regardless how shitty or shoddy. That should show how much I respect you."

The hollow declaration brought no comfort. Lee was a veritable politician and dished out what others wanted to hear.

"Give me seventy-two hours." Gideon and Willow needed time to do their job and find the real traitor. Neither would betray him, the Gray Box, or this country. "I'll run this to ground."

"Thus far, you've produced zero results." Lee raked a hand through silver hair that made him look ten years older than his true age of fifty. "Despite your previous assurances."

Sanborn folded his hands atop the cool glass. "With the budget cuts, I'm working with limited resources, a smaller staff, and one hand tied behind my back." Their black budget had been chopped in half with the change in the last administration. Meant he couldn't provide his operators the proper support or leverage resources to their full potential, forcing him to find other ways to remedy the situation. "I'm not a magician, Lee. You know well enough what it takes to run this type of operation."

"The Gray Box has proven its capability and worth time after time. Your team was just awarded another unofficial letter of appreciation from the president for preventing the worst terrorist attack in U.S. history and saving thousands from a nasty bioweapon. And that's with one hand tied behind your back. You're doing fine with limited resources."

Fine was bullshit. They needed the resources to operate at the top of their game. "Too much is at stake to dismiss mitigating factors."

"Don't preach to me about the stakes. The intel community can't handle another blow like Tice or Manning or, God forbid, Snowden." Lee flipped open a bottle of Tums and popped some in his mouth, washing them down with the whiskey sitting in a tumbler in front of him.

No doubt a twenty-five-year-old Glenmorangie Grand Vintage Malt that cost more than some folks' car payment.

Lee rubbed his forehead. Deep circles under his eyes looked heavier and darker than the baggage Sanborn lugged around every day. "One more movie about our dirty laundry and I'm going to rip someone's throat out and vomit in the cavity. What if Harper decides to talk to foreign press about the Gray Box? Use what she knows to protect herself from us? Can you imagine? Jeeeeee-sus! The president will burn it all to the ground before I'm called to stand in front of a Senate Select Intelligence hearing and he's impeached."

Tension knotted in Sanborn's chest at the rash look of dread on Lee's face. Frightened men made poor choices. "It won't come to that. Trust me on this."

"I'm sorry, but I'm not the one calling the shots. You have forty-eight hours to fix this problem." His old friend sighed, and Sanborn knew in his bones what words would follow. "Otherwise, the president has authorized two whitewash teams to be dispatched. One to find Harper and her accomplice, Gideon Stone. In the event they can't find her, the other will clean the Gray Box, make it look as if it never existed."

A shrill gasp flew from Sybil's wretched mouth.

Sanborn stood, a reflexive fist clenching at his side. The president intended to screw over the Gray Box to cover his own ass, the lives of innocent officers be damned. And Lee wasn't going to lift a finger to help. Sanborn wasn't going to take it sitting down like a paper pusher. He might work behind a desk these days, but he would always be first and foremost an operator.

To this day, you'd never catch him unarmed or out of ammo. In a bind, he could shit bullets if necessary.

"The Gray Box is an unprecedented organization. We do what the other agencies can't. We plug the hole in the shield that safeguards this nation."

Not that he had to sell Lee on the merits of the Gray Box. His old friend had recruited Sanborn. More like coerced. The choice had been simple: stand up the Gray Box and run it for at least five years—to the detriment of his marriage—and in return, Sanborn's CIA team, who had gotten themselves into trouble overseas, would be spared. His history with Lee was long and sticky. Ironic that Lee had been the catalyst to bring the Gray Box into existence and would be the one to oversee its demise.

If it came to that.

"Killing the Gray Box would be a major blow to national security in the long run," Sanborn said. "I need sufficient time to send a team to France." Not that he'd waste resources or precious time following a dirty lead meant to divert them from the truth. "Give me seventy-two hours and—"

"Not like you to make excuses." Lee drained his glass of whiskey. "Hope it's not an indication that the one man I know with a spine of steel and brass balls is feeling that four-letter word."

Fear. To Sanborn, those four letters meant *Face everything and (motherfucking) rise*. "You know me better."

The DNI poured himself another round. "Good. You have forty-eight hours."

The videoconference screen went dark.

"Shit!" Sybil slammed her palms on the table, springing to her feet. "You're going to get us killed."

Well, *he* sure as hell wasn't going to end up in a body bag. This wouldn't be the first whitewash Sanborn had survived, but he'd staked everything he was on the Gray Box. He'd be damned if he abandoned them.

"I'll handle this."

His every move was being watched and he couldn't play his hand too soon. He needed to wait until the last possible minute, then time for a Hail Mary. Gideon wouldn't like it if he'd gone to such lengths to protect Willow, but his star quarterback, turned into the finest assassin still breathing, better follow the damn play.

"Well, la-di-fucking-da. I guess I'm supposed to feel better. But I don't!" She stalked around the room, heels stabbing the carpet.

"Oh, come on. You have to have a heart to feel."

Sybil froze, glaring at him with feigned offense.

It took everything in him not to roll his eyes. "Your conniving"—he pointed an indignant finger her

way—"placed our necks in this guillotine, getting the
DNI fired up to run to the president after I already had
him managed."

"How was I supposed to know you were besties with
the DNI?"

And therein lay the problem. The vanity. The hubris.
For her to think she would ever know more than him,
much less know everything.

"You'll shut your mouth and stay out of my lane."
Sanborn crossed the room, drawing so close to her, the
fury in his eyes made her cower. "Don't do anything else
to jeopardize this mission. For your sake, I hope this is
sinking in. If you don't do exactly as I've said, so help me,
Sybil, you won't have to worry about a whitewash. Because
I'll bury you myself."

36

GRAND CAYMAN ISLAND
MONDAY, JULY 8, 1:45 A.M. EST/2:45 A.M. EDT

The waves crashed on the shoreline in a soothing rhythm, the relaxing sound rolling in through the two open windows. Gideon spooned Willow with his face pressed to her hair, inhaling the heady scent mixed with light florals from the shampoo. They'd cleaned up together in the shower, and she'd let him wash her from her scalp to the soles of her feet.

Hands down, it had been the most intimate thing—without having sex—he'd ever done with a woman. And the sex last night had been different. Still off the charts, but more intense. Although he'd described it as fucking, they'd gone from screwing to something deeper, as if every touch and kiss was an investment of his heart and soul. He'd *made love*.

With Kelli, he'd had amazing sex, but it'd been just a physical act for pleasure. By the end, screwing had become a chore. She'd never known who he was, and when she'd seen a glimpse of the real him, she'd bailed on their marriage and run straight to another man.

Willow saw him, but the truth hadn't scared her off. She wanted more of him. *Crazy.*

The way she touched him, looked at him, said his name, spoon-fed him affection and adoration, told him *this* was what he'd always craved. What really threw his world spinning off its axis was how he found nourishment in the sight of her, simply holding her.

This was happiness.

He curled his arms tighter around her.

"Tell me why you joined the CIA." Her gentle voice sent his heart skittering in surprise. She'd been so still, her heartbeat so slow, he would've sworn she was asleep.

"The *why* is tied to unpleasant history." Bloody. Painful. Edgy tension trickled through him, but there was no knee-jerk reaction to close off and shut down. Not from her. She had a lovely way of robbing him of his defenses.

"You said to ask another time." She stroked his forearm, nuzzling close. "Well, it's another time and I'm asking." Her voice was light and lazy.

A cool breeze swept in, rustling the curtains. Kissing the back of her head, he buried his face in her hair.

"Tell me, how does a star football player end up working for the CIA?"

"You're really curious," he teased, tickling her ribs.

She squirmed against him. "I can't figure it out. With your all-star looks and talent to match, you could've done so many other things."

Then I never would've met you. Every ugly act and dirty deed was worth it to know her.

"Tell me." She tugged on his fingers with impatience.

Whenever she touched him, he softened, stilled. This casual intimacy with her was anything but casual. And it terrified him.

She was so much more courageous, pouring herself out to him. He couldn't give her a future, but here, safe with her curled around him like a second skin, he could bare his soul. The one true thing he had to offer.

"My dad left when I was four and never looked back. It broke my mother."

"A husband deserting his wife and young child is enough to break a heart."

"No, not just her heart, something deeper. His leaving broke her spirit. She wouldn't get out of bed, didn't go to work, stayed up all night crying. I had to fend for myself for a bit, making do with the food in the fridge, ready-made prepackaged stuff in the cabinets. I'd leave dry cereal or cookies and water on her nightstand, hoping she'd snap out of it."

"Goodness, Gideon." Willow kissed the back of his hand. "How long did it go on?"

"Weeks." To the best of his recollection. "When she managed to pull herself together, boyfriends rotated through the house. Dirtbags who drank, did drugs. Some liked to hit."

"Did they hit you?" She turned, resting her head under his chin, pressing satin curves to his chest, her breath caressing his throat.

He rubbed his knuckles over her spine in tender brush-stokes, grounded by her softness, keeping the rage and sorrow of the past from boiling up. "One night, Clint—he was the worst—kicked me out of the living room because he wanted to watch television. I didn't grab my toys fast enough. These silly Matchbox cars. He knocked me around for being too slow."

Willow pulled back and caressed his face. He glanced at her eyes. Warmth and kindness shone. No poor-you pity.

"How old were you?"

"Eight." The year his life changed course. "But I fought back as best I could against a grown man. By the time my mom got in between us, one of my eyes was swollen shut."

She pressed her head to his chest and hugged him, tight and firm, as if afraid he might slip away.

Sharing his story for the first time, he expected the impulse to detach to take hold of him. It didn't. He relished the intimate threads drawing him to Willow. Despite the torment of anger and pain roiling inside at dredging up the past, letting her in was giving him something he'd never had but always needed.

"I ran from the house. Had no idea where to go. Ended up sneaking into my neighbor's garage. A friendly couple with no kids. The husband, Benjamin, found me. Asked questions I refused to answer. He brought me inside, and Hannah, his wife, tended to me.

"She was a nurse. The sweetest lady. Pretty good cook too. Somehow Ben got me to finally answer his questions with a nod or shake of the head. He walked me home and had a chat with Clint. First time I saw a man kick the ass of another without throwing a punch. Ben deflected, turning everything Clint dished out back on him. It was like watching a superhero."

"What did your mom do?"

"Nothing. I think she was in shock. Clint was so embarrassed, he got on his bike and took off for days."

"Must've been a relief."

"Should've been, but my mom blamed me for driving him off. Told me I was a little shit, like my dad. A spitting image of him, and every day it was harder to stomach the sight of me."

You're not enough, Gideon. I need more than just being your mother. I need a kind of love you can't give me. Don't ruin this one for me, you little shit! Know how hard it is for a woman with a kid?

Recalling his mother's cruel words set his heart drumming. He hadn't expected such acute pain in his chest. Willow caressed his torso and he remembered to breathe.

"Clint eventually came back. When I went to Ben and Hannah the next time with a busted jaw, the cops hit the house a few days later while my mom was at work. Found a bunch of drugs in one of Clint's bags. My mother swore it wasn't his, but he was sent to prison. Afterward, my mom wanted nothing to do with me."

"Losing one parent is hard. I can't imagine two turning their back on their own child."

Willow had the biggest heart. Even though she was suffering, not knowing if her father might live or die, she made room for his pain. He was grateful for her tenderness.

"Once my jaw healed, Ben taught me how to defend myself. I had this wild, crazy energy and couldn't focus. So he used a metronome. Had me concentrate on the beat instead of the movements at first."

She gazed up at him. "I can see the practicality of a metronome. I overheard you sparring in the gym once with Castle and he couldn't understand how you beat him. You'd said fighting was all about rhythm and tempo, moving at the proper beat." Petal-smooth lips brushed his jaw. "For the record, so is dancing."

Grinning, he held her tighter. "Why am I not surprised

you were eavesdropping?" But he was surprised she'd been close enough to overhear a conversation and he hadn't noticed her. His senses always trained on her if she was in the room.

Willow covered her face with her hands. "More like spellbound by you than eavesdropping. I couldn't help it."

He pried her fingers away and looked into her eyes. "I never want you to feel embarrassed around me about anything. Okay?"

A smile lifted her mouth, and it was like the sun rose in his heart. He was the one awestruck.

"Well, if a metronome can increase a musician's awareness and focus, I imagine it works in regard to fighting," she said.

"Centered me like nothing else."

Focus will carry you all the way, Gideon. All the way. Ben's words were ingrained. His tutelage enabled Gideon to survive, taught him to cauterize pain and overcome anything.

"Ben and Hannah used to take camping trips and would bring me along."

"Your mom didn't mind?"

He kissed her forehead, wondering what kind of mother she'd make. Loving, patient, fiercely protective most likely. "I think my mom was secretly thrilled to have the house to herself and her latest boyfriend."

"Did you learn to fish and hunt?"

"Ben showed me a bold new world. At nine, I thought it was normal to use a SIG Sauer SSG 3000 tactical sniper rifle to kill a deer. Normal to use a 9mm with a silencer."

Willow stiffened in his arms, but he continued spilling the details he'd held secret for more than twenty years. "To break down a weapon, clean it, and put it back together blindfolded. Normal to learn how to defend myself with a fixed blade or fishing pole, take someone down with tackle line, or maneuver out of any hold. Skinning a deer always shifted into how to stop an attacker with a knife and practicing how to use a blade."

Sounded odd hearing it out loud, but his time with them had been the best days of his youth. The bowie knife he kept in his go bag had been a gift from Ben, and he cherished it.

Willow reeled in his arms, nose wrinkling, eyes narrowed. "What did Ben do?"

"He said he worked in insurance, traveled a lot for business." Gideon had simply soaked everything in and hadn't asked questions that might have messed up the one safe space he'd found. "Ben did a stint in the army when he was younger, where he picked up the Arabic, Farsi, and German, all of which he taught me. He was big into politics and foreign affairs. Talked about the importance of national security, the greater good, protecting one's family and home by eliminating any threats. No matter what was required."

"Did Hannah think that was normal?"

He shrugged. "Ben sprinkled his rhetoric like seeds when I'd tag along to run errands, helped with house repairs. Until one day, my belief system grew into an ideological garden of his making." He caressed Willow's head, running his fingers through her hair. "Hannah never went hunting. She hung out at the campsite and was never around for any training, except when we played CHAOS."

"What's chaos?"

Gideon chuckled. "Conscious honed awareness of surroundings—the CHAOS game. We'd go to a restaurant. Before we ordered, Ben had Hannah and me close our eyes and answer questions. How many waitresses were inside, if there were any white cars in the parking lot, the location of every exit, to describe the people at the tables around us. That sort of thing."

Snuggling into his body, she slipped her thigh in between his, tangling their legs. "How long were they a part of your life?"

"Years. When I started high school, Ben encouraged— more like ordered—me to pick a sport and stick with it. He said I had natural athleticism and could parlay it into a scholarship. He was right. About lots of things. In my junior year, Ben got transferred overseas and they moved."

"Overseas for an insurance job? Hmm. Did you stay in touch?"

"No." He heard the bitter upsurge of pain in his own voice, and Willow brushed her lips across his sternum. He wrestled between the gloriousness of the present and agonizing disappointment of the past.

Ben and Hannah had given him a home, shown him love, and he'd come to rely on them for support, for his abnormal sense of normalcy. Then they were gone.

"Losing them felt like abandonment."

The anger had burned him up for years, even though Hannah had reached out with emails he declined to answer out of childish spite.

"My senior year in college, agency recruiters approached me. Their spiel about duty and patriotism, safeguarding the greater good…it all hit home." Like a bullet to the heart.

There was no way he could've said no. He'd been called and he was ready to serve.

"After my time at the Farm, I was at headquarters, Langley. Found out I'd been selected for a deep black program." Where the CIA trained him to be an assassin. "In the hall, I ran into Ben."

She shot up, leaning on her forearm. "Were you shocked? Do you think running into him was an accident?"

"Yes and no. He'd just gotten transferred back stateside. When I saw him, everything made sense. Who I'd become, why, how. Pieces of my life, sort of an unsolved puzzle, fell into place. I was grateful to know the truth and for a second chance to have them in my life."

"Did you ask him if he'd trained you for this?"

"No." They'd smiled, shaken hands, and shot the breeze in their abnormal everything-was-normal way. "We never said a word about it."

"Do you still see them? Or your mom?"

"I haven't spoken to my mom since I left for college. She remarried and gave me the impression it'd be easier for her if I stayed gone."

The emptiness of how his mother had discarded him never waned, but he no longer wanted it to eat away at him, defining his value.

"I didn't waste time renewing my friendship with Ben and Hannah." Friendship was such a shallow word. Family was better, yet still wrong. "You're the only person I've ever told about my childhood or the truth about Ben."

"You never told your wife?"

"No." He hadn't told Kelli so many things, and the stockpile of omissions and lies had doomed their marriage.

"She didn't know how much they meant to me or how they'd saved me. She just saw them as friendly childhood neighbors. Right before I transferred to the Gray Box, I learned Ben died on a mission."

Shutting his eyes, Gideon wished he'd had more time with him after learning the truth. Not taken for granted that one day, they'd have *the* conversation instead of pretending there was nothing to discuss.

"I'm sorry, Gideon. Sounds as if he was the closest thing you had to a father."

Father. Mentor. Friend. The one man who'd taught him how to be strong, the meaning of courage, the importance of sacrifice for the greater good.

"I stay in touch with Hannah. She's always been a surrogate mom to me. We don't talk often, and she doesn't see me nearly as much as she'd like, but I don't know what I'd do without her."

"I'd love to meet her and hear stories about you as a child."

Stark wariness scraped him raw. The comment was premature. Contemplating the future while stuck in the thick of war was tempting fate. But it was a testament to her optimism and faith in him to get them through this alive.

"I can't think past tomorrow."

Willow sagged against him, arm slackening over his torso, hand slipping from his body. "I want this. Whatever *this* is between us."

He was the only man she'd ever really been with, and she was on the run for her life. Safe bet she didn't really know what she wanted. "You've come closer to death more times in the last four days than some operatives have in their whole careers. The need to hold on to something to keep from feeling lost is clouding things. In this heightened state, emotions become flawed and can't be trusted."

She lifted on an elbow and speared him with a hurt glance. "Don't dismiss what I feel. My judgment isn't clouded. I'm asking if you want *this* too."

If only the answer was simple and the question not premature.

"This"—he squeezed her tight against him, memorizing the feel of her in his arms—"is complicated. Keeping you alive and proving your innocence are all I can focus on."

"I'm not asking for anything." She lowered her head. "I never should have—"

He tilted her chin up with his forefinger and kissed her, hard and fierce. She was the kind of woman who should ask for everything she wanted, and she deserved a man who'd give it whenever she needed. Not when it was convenient.

She slipped her tongue into his mouth, opening to him. He clenched his fist in her hair, locking her lips to his.

His lifestyle came with sacrifices. A razor-sharp edge required emotional distance to keep from dulling. He couldn't shake the sense it'd be selfish to be in a relationship with her. It wasn't easy to be with a man like him. Kelli had reminded him of that often enough with agonizing clarity. He didn't want to disappoint Willow, fall short of her expectations.

Better for her to have the best life possible, loved by someone who had more to offer than the caged heart of a damaged survivor.

He kissed her, funneling his desire to communicate the

truth he couldn't speak—she was special, and he adored and loved her in a way he'd never experienced before or would again. He threw himself into the kiss, into the blistering connection, in a hard freefall. All the time knowing when *this* came to an end, he'd crash.

37

GRAND CAYMAN ISLAND
MONDAY, JULY 8, 8:55 A.M. EST/9:55 A.M. EDT

Willow strode beside Gideon, headed for the Nova World Bank.

Thirty minutes earlier, he'd left the hotel wearing the bulletproof vest under his clothes for a final sweep of the bank. Once he was sure it was safe, he came back for her.

Smoothing her dress from a tepid breeze as they walked, she gathered her wits and concentrated on the instructions Gideon had drilled into her. They'd practiced several conversational models and come up with prompts for him if she forgot anything.

"Remember, you're an important client. Speak to the account manager with authority and insist on the things we talked about. Cut him off if necessary, but just stay on task."

She nodded. "Okay."

He held open the bank door for her. Strolling inside, she adjusted the sunglasses on the bridge of her nose and lowered the brim of the sunhat he'd purchased this morning.

A zigzag of line dividers snaked up to a row of tellers sitting behind glass on the right. She panned one hundred eighty degrees, glancing over a staircase running up the center of the far back wall. Three spacious offices stretched across the left side.

Gideon stopped near the entrance and scoped out the interior while she approached one of the two security guards as he'd instructed.

"Good morning." She mustered a tentative smile. "Where do I go for concerns with my offshore account?"

The guard pointed to a woman with gray-streaked hair twisted in a chignon sitting at an desk in front of the three offices.

Giving a nod of thanks, Willow took a calming breath and strode to the left. Gideon was at her side, clutching the strap of the backpack slung over his shoulder.

"Hello, I'd like to transfer funds from my offshore account."

"Please sign in." The woman handed her an electronic clipboard.

Willow typed her real name and returned the digital notepad.

"An offshore-account representative will be with you shortly. Would you like coffee or tea?"

"No, thank you."

The woman indicated chairs to the side in front of a large window where they should wait. Once seated, Willow kept her head lowered and shades on.

Gideon remained standing, back to a wall, gaze sweeping the bank and the street.

She fiddled with her late mother's pearls, running through the list of everything she had to remember. *Make occasional eye contact. No fidgeting.* Willow lowered her hand.

Give a soft smile, before or after speaking. Comment with "uh-huh" or a head nod. Ask reciprocal questions. Speak slowly and firmly.

She didn't want to do or say the wrong thing. This was their only shot to get evidence to clear her. Everything was riding on this. She had to give the social performance of her life.

"Ms. Harper." A middle-aged gentleman with dark-brown eyes and bronzed skin approached. "I'm Mr. Walters. Please, come into my office." He extended an arm of invitation to enter.

Willow forced a grin, heart thudding in her throat. "Good morning." She stood and walked past him as she crossed the threshold.

Gideon followed close enough for his body heat to send a tingle down her spine. They each took one of the twin chairs in front of the desk.

Mr. Walters took his seat. "How are you today?"

"I'm fine." Willow swallowed past the lump forming in her throat. *Ask reciprocal questions.* "How are you?"

"Very well. Thank you for asking. How may I be of service to you today?"

"My name is Willow Harper." *He already knows your name.* Her face heated. She removed her sunglasses, chiding herself, and took a deep breath. "Did you receive the urgent email I sent yesterday regarding my account?"

"No, madam. I'm afraid not." He glanced between her and Gideon. "We just opened."

She nodded and waited for Mr. Walters to find the email, but he simply sat there staring at her. Gideon nudged her knee with his.

"The manner in which you can be of service is outlined in the email," she said. "I took the time to write it. Please, do me the courtesy of reading it."

He cleared his throat. "All right. Passport, please."

Gideon withdrew Willow's passport from the backpack and gave it to her. She passed it to Mr. Walters and folded her hands, fighting every fidgety impulse beating through her. Following all these new rules had the thick knot in her stomach twisting, but she'd written down the behavioral cues Gideon had outlined and pulled up the list clearly in her mind as if on a teleprompter while he sat languid in his chair, ankle propped on his knee. The only thing to betray the intent behind his relaxed appearance was the unblinking sweep of his cold eyes.

After eyeing the passport, Mr. Walters typed on his computer. "Here it is." He began reading and frowned. "I'm sorry you're unhappy with our service and would like to withdraw the full amount from the account. Ms. Harper, you're a valued client and we'd hate to lose you. Surely, we can find some way to fix whatever—"

"No. I've made up my mind." She and Gideon had gone over many versions of this sidetrack tactic. "As I've stated in the email, I'd like to wire transfer five hundred thousand."

"I'll need your current account number and the bank information for the new—"

"In the email, I included a temporary SharePoint link to my financial information, both for my account with you as well as the one for the wire transfer." She added a smile, not too broad, tight-lipped, reminding herself to maintain eye contact.

"SharePoint?" He considered her, his eyes narrowed, and dread churned in her gut. "Efficient way to stay organized and have everything you need at your fingertips."

Mr. Walters moved the mouse, his index finger lifted, hovering in the air a second, and left-clicked.

They were in. She released a long, subtle breath.

"Address, account and routing numbers. Excellent. You seem to have more than I need, really. I wish all our clients were as prepared as you. I do wish you'd reconsider—"

"Also, I want to withdraw the remainder of my balance in cash."

Mr. Walters's eyes grew wide. "Excuse me, madam. Did you say in cash?"

"Yes, and I'd like it immediately."

He adjusted his tie and straightened. "Ms. Harper, your request is quite irregular. Clients always prefer to wire their money. It's safer and easier. Why would you want to risk carrying so much cash?"

Willow swallowed thickly, hoping there was no hint of alarm on her face. She sorted through the choice of responses wallpapered on her mind and said, "That's none of your business."

Mr. Walters blinked rapidly and took a long sip of coffee, then folded his hands atop the desk. "Madam, I mean no disrespect, but won't you be concerned about your safety?"

"No. That's why I have him." She gestured to Gideon, who gave a tight smile.

"I'm afraid it's our policy that we need twenty-four hours to fulfill such a request," Mr. Walters said. "At the very least, we'd need until the end of the business day."

"And you wonder why I'm unhappy with your service? I have several important associates who use this bank. Perhaps I should recommend that they transfer their accounts as well." She was aiming for nonchalant but feared she might've overshot toward desperate.

Mr. Walters cleared his throat. Sweat beaded his forehead. "Let me speak with my boss."

He pressed a combination of two buttons on the keyboard at the same time—most likely locking his screen—grabbed her passport, and headed for the door.

"A moment of your patience, please, while I see how we can best accommodate you."

Mr. Walters taking her passport hadn't been part of the plan or the models they'd rehearsed. She shot a look at Gideon and began drumming her thigh.

He rested a hand on top of hers, stilling her fingers. "Everything will be fine."

Willow clasped her hands in her lap.

"Make yourselves comfortable. I apologize for the delay." Mr. Walters hightailed it out of the office, shutting the door behind him.

Glancing over her shoulder, she watched him skedaddle upstairs. A panicky unease bubbled inside her. "What do we do?"

Willow turned to find Gideon behind the desk in front of the computer. She'd never heard him move.

"Come on. Use your back door to get in and save the files." He waved the thumb drive at her.

They'd spent three days waiting for this, and now things were moving at high speed.

She flew to her feet, zipping around to the other side of the desk. At the blinking password prompt, she entered her preestablished rootkit code, which the operating system recognized as an administrator log-in.

"We're in." She accessed the offshore account files and typed in her name.

Gideon kept an eye on the lobby from the door, waiting for a sign of Mr. Walters. "Hurry, Willow. Once he comes back, we may not get another opportunity."

Scrolling through the fake data in her staged account as quickly as her fingers would allow, she searched for anything that might be useful.

None of the signatures on the first five documents matched hers. Helpful, but far from concrete evidence. A folder labeled *verification documents* was at the bottom of the list. A copy of the passport would be in there.

Please, don't let it be my picture.

She scrolled to the icon, her stomach turning over, and opened the folder. Four documents. One was a pdf of the passport.

This had to be the proof they needed. It had to be. Holding her breath, she clicked the file.

Her heart shriveled to the size of a dried prune as she looked at the image and the photo stared back. Comprehension rushed through her like a violent tide, hope draining from her.

"It's my picture." She fought not to throw up. "It's me."

Tension cut grooves on Gideon's face. He hustled to the desk and glanced at the screen. "That's your indoc picture from the day you in-processed."

"How can you tell?"

"Sapphire dress. The lanyard around your neck from your temporary badge."

She stared at him, wind-knocked-out-of-her shocked the traitor had the foresight to use a work photo and that

Gideon remembered what she'd been wearing on her first day, three years ago. "How could the bank let someone else open an account using my picture?"

"If the woman was wearing a hat and sunglasses like you are now and had a million dollars to deposit, I'm sure they didn't scrutinize the photo too closely." He clasped her shoulder. "There has to be something to exonerate you. Keep looking."

She sucked in a shaky breath and scanned the other documents. All of them were littered with her personal information, further cementing her guilt. She scoured every file name under the account, stopping on the beneficiary form. She opened the document and scrolled to the bottom.

A cold pit opened inside her like a grave. "Oh no."

―――――――――――

Gideon glanced at the beneficiary listed on the screen. "Judas Iscariot, LLC?"

"The disciple who betrayed Jesus for thirty pieces of silver."

The traitor had a sick sense of humor. They needed ironclad proof to clear Willow and keep her safe, and this wasn't even in the circumstantial zone.

Willow shot him a frantic glance. "The limited liability company is probably a shell corporation, designed to hide the identity of the owner to allow movement of money without it being traced back to them."

Gideon did a cursory sweep for anyone headed to the office. "This can't be a dead end."

They didn't come all this way and kill two days for nothing.

"Maybe not. Once we leave the bank, I can dig into the LLC."

"We're running out of time. The account manager will be back soon to tell you that you'll have to wait several hours to get the money in cash." Gideon shoved the backpack into Willow's arms. "Go to the hotel. Wait for me in the room. I'll get copies of the files and your passport back from Walters."

Reaching over her, he inserted the thumb drive and started closing files so he could drag the entire folder to copy.

"I can help, Gideon."

"Please, don't argue." This wasn't the time for her ballsy spunk. This was the time for her to follow orders. He guided her out of the chair and sat behind the desk.

"It'll be easier if I help you," she said, her voice insistent.

A bad feeling wormed in his gut. "I don't want you here if I have to deal with security. They're armed. I'm wearing a vest. You're vulnerable."

The guards were out of shape and looked slow, but he wasn't taking any chances with Willow's safety.

Gideon searched for the removeable media icon on the screen where he'd drop the folder, but there wasn't one.

"I can't copy anything. The thumb drive isn't showing up. Why isn't it working?"

She looked at the screen. "The USB port has probably been disabled."

"Shit." They didn't need Murphy's law today. "Is there a way to reenable it?"

"Yes. We have administrator privileges."

"Tell me how to do it and then go."

"You have to use the command-line interface to edit the registry key."

His heart pounded as time grew short. "The what?"

She swatted his hands away, and her fingers danced across the keyboard in mind-blowing defiance, making his blood pressure skyrocket.

The woman was going to give him an aneurysm.

A black box popped up on the screen. She typed several lines of letters and symbols.

Whatever command she'd entered worked. Seconds later, the account started copying to the flash drive. Her expertise saved them precious minutes, but she needed to fall in line from here.

A digital bar on the screen showed only twenty percent of the files had transferred. It would take time to complete, which they didn't have.

"I still need to get your passport. Walters will be inbound any minute. Worrying about you will distract me." Too easy for a nervous guard to let his finger slip on an easy target like Willow. Not a risk he was willing to take.

She opened the backpack and handed him the gun. "Take it. You might need it."

"Better not to use deadly force on the local security guards." They still had to get off the island. He shoved the Maxim 9 back in the bag and grabbed the hammer and screwdriver. "Go to the hotel, out of harm's way. And wait for me. Now."

Flinching at his clipped tone, she rushed from the office, slinging the backpack on her shoulder. He hated snapping at her, but there was no time to debate.

Gideon stuffed the tools in his pockets, covering them with his shirt, and stepped into the doorway. He tracked Mr. Walters accompanied by another suit headed downstairs, pointing in his direction.

As Willow pressed through the front doors, stepping outside, his chest loosened.

Then two men in dark gear strode in past her. They sported military high-and-tights and had a dangerous swagger.

Mercenaries. There'd be more than two.

A terrible fear seized Gideon.

He'd sent Willow to the hotel alone. Panic would handicap him if he let it bloom. He snuffed it out with reason—the two stalking in hadn't recognized her, and maybe the others wouldn't either.

It was possible to reach her before anyone else did. But he had to hurry.

Gideon ducked down in the crouched position and eased up next to the receptionist's desk. The older lady recoiled, but before the question on her face slipped from her lips, he flicked on his quarterback smile. She giggled, clutching her chest, cheeks flushing.

Walters and another suit strolled in front of him, peering down with perplexed expressions. One man opened his mouth to speak, but something on the other side of the receptionist's desk snatched the words from his lips as the older woman turned to stare in the same direction.

No guess required as to who stood on the other side.

Gideon whipped out the hammer from the back of his pants and the flathead screwdriver from his pocket, ignoring the slack-jawed faces of the bankers. Better suited to playing offense, he leapt up and slid across the side of the desk, swinging.

The hammer nailed one merc in the side of the face, shattering a cheekbone as the guy's neck wrenched with an unnatural whip. Gideon's feet hit the floor as the other merc reached into his jacket to draw a gun.

Gideon stabbed the man's forearm with the screwdriver and smashed the hammer across the clavicle in a sharp one-two. Bone cracked, a guttural cry rent the air, and the man dropped to his knees. A boot heel to the face crushed the guy's nose, knocking him out.

Not even winded, Gideon stood steady as a blade, two bloody bodies at his feet.

The bank alarm sounded.

Both security guards approached, weapons drawn. Making eye contact with Gideon, the guards faltered. Everyone else rushed back. A wave of palpable tension crested.

"Put your hands up," one guard said. Trepidation flashed in his eyes.

Gideon waited for his opportunity, blood-stained weapons in his raised hands.

The guards eased in on him, exchanging apprehensive glances. The guns shook in their hands, and they took measured paces, each step more hesitant than the last. He was tempted to strike, but the steady ticking in his mind tempered his reflexes. The optimal window would open.

Closer.

Almost.

A little more.

He forced himself not to move, his stillness reeling them in.

"On your knees." They closed ranks, side by side, as if there was safety in numbers.

Gideon tossed the hammer to one guard. The natural inclination was, of course, to catch it. A simple ploy wouldn't work on a well-trained guard with honed vigilance, but he was banking these guards had dull senses.

The fool dropped his gun to catch the hammer, and Gideon smothered a laugh. Flipping the screwdriver in his hand to hold it by the metal rod, he swooped in on the other, fluid and swift as a blink.

"Stop. Stop!" The security guard aimed at Gideon's chest, but he'd sidestepped before a bullet was fired.

A dead click. The safety was on.

How much were these guards getting paid?

Gideon popped the guy's wrist with the handle of the screwdriver, and his fingers opened, releasing the gun. It fell into Gideon's palm. He caught the terrified gaze of the second security guard as he went for the weapon on the floor.

"Tsk-tsk." Gideon shook his head in warning.

Raising their hands, both guards backed away, and he picked up the second gun. Not injuring the security might go a long way with the local authorities if he had to face them.

Tucking one gun against the small of his back and holding the other, he swiped his tools from the floor. He hustled to retrieve the thumb drive, vectoring his gaze to the entrance.

No other mercs rushed inside the bank. But there were

most certainly more of them. The only question was how many were outside after Willow.

He snatched her passport from a stunned Mr. Walters and plucked an earpiece from a downed merc. The sound of his pounding footsteps filled the lobby as he cleared the twenty feet to the door and bolted outside.

38

GRAND CAYMAN
MONDAY, JULY 8, 9:37 A.M. EST/10:37 A.M. EDT

Willow darted down the street, weaving in between people. She risked a quick glance over her shoulder.

The tough-looking guy who'd been lurking in front of the bank still followed her. She couldn't outrun him. If she put enough distance between them, maybe she'd lose him in the hotel. But could she make it to the room before he caught her?

Abject fear prickled along every nerve ending. She snapped another peek back and met the eyes of a stone-cold killer.

She whipped her face forward and gathered her courage. Hustling to the corner, her sneakers slapping on the hot pavement, she prayed for a break in traffic to cross the main street to the hotel.

Three more men stalked out of her hotel lobby, dressed in clothing dark as death. One was huge and familiar. The same husky monster shaped like a powerlifter from Ken's.

Gideon, where are you?

Their gazes zeroed in on her. The harsh glare of their mirrored sunglasses speared her in place. She fought to swallow past the lump choking her throat.

Balmy air pressed in, licking her skin. Street noises—car

radios, vehicles braking, rubber tires rolling across asphalt, pedestrians chattering—rose in an amplified crescendo, filling her ears.

Lowering her gaze, she went to turn as casually as possible, but the men leapt into action. They pounded through the traffic, tearing across the road. The other mercenary on her side of the street charged toward her.

Her pulse kicked into a wild streak. Mind spinning, she scrambled to escape. She was moving, with no sense of direction except away from the danger closing in.

Where to run? How would Gideon find her?

She needed to keep moving and to think.

Whirling left, she faced the gleaming glass doors of a mega resort on the other side of a small road. Gideon wouldn't know to look for her in there.

Oh, God. There wasn't time for other options. Her hand flew to her throat and she gripped her mother's pearls—the only heirloom Willow had left.

She yanked hard on her necklace as if it were the ripcord of a parachute.

The vintage choker popped. Pink pearls rained down, scattering like last-ditch breadcrumbs. She bolted across the side street, pushing through the gut-punch of grief.

She ran to the front doors of the resort, glancing over her shoulder.

The men were almost on her, their faces those of rabid jackals thirsting for blood.

Run. Run. RUN. She took off at a sprint and burst inside the resort. The sprawling lobby teemed with droves of tourists. Chatter buzzed around her.

She threaded past people, dropping the last pearls.

Three directions to choose from. She couldn't pick an option that'd leave her cornered.

No time to deliberate, she dashed left, ripping off her sunglasses, and ran past a line of shops.

Her nerves screamed, driving her faster.

But not fast enough.

She was all alone, her lungs stalling, her legs heavy as lead when she needed to be light as a feather in a breeze.

The hat flew off her head. Her body thrummed with desperation.

To hide.

To escape.

To live.

Shouts and curses rose behind her. She dared a glance back.

Four black-clad mercenaries barreled down the walkway in vicious pursuit. Shoving people from their path, they devoured the distance between them and her.

Oh God. God. Please.

Two ladies strolled out of a clothing store, and she ducked inside. She spotted a bank of changing rooms in the rear beyond racks of dresses and beelined for one with an open door. A salesperson slid out of the way, eyes wide.

"Call the police!" Willow scurried into the stall and locked the door.

She pressed against a full-length mirror, heart crashing against her rib cage. She struggled to hold herself together.

There was no space between the bottom of the door and the floor to see if the men were homing in on the fitting rooms. A gap at the top was large enough to peek out. But if she stood on the bench in the stall, they'd spot her.

A woman screamed. *Bam. Bam.* Gunfire echoed in her bones.

She slapped a hand over her mouth and swallowed a convulsive sob.

They were in the store. They'd find her. And it wouldn't take them long.

Her knees softened as if her legs might buckle, but pressure built in her chest. Pursing her lips to keep quiet, she pulled the backpack off so it wouldn't scrape against the stall.

"Willow," said a deep male voice outside the dressing room. "We have your sister Laurel. You called her last night. Touching conversation."

Her insides shuddered in a backwash of nausea.

No, no, no, no…

"I'd hate to ruin her pretty face. Hate even more to kill her. Come out. Cooperate."

She pinched the back of her hand, frothing with defensive anger. Cooperate? With them framing her? Killing her? Maybe they had plans for something worse.

But they had Laurel. Willow's nieces weren't even seven yet. Too young to lose a mother.

"Make it easy. Come out."

She'd die to protect Laurel, who had a husband and kids, a family who needed her, but men like this couldn't be trusted. No guarantee they wouldn't hurt or kill her sister anyway.

If there was a way to be sure…

Boom! A loud thud followed by a splintering bang made her jump. Trepidation clogged her throat, and her lungs held air hostage.

Boom! Another crashing clunk.

They were kicking in the dressing room doors. Only five stalls. Heavy boots struck the carpet, drawing closer.

Her mind raced in circles at a frantic speed. What to do? What *could* she do?

Tension bubbled in her head, putting pressure on her entire skull. It was impossible to think, to breathe, with the bombardment of loud noises. Panic threatened to swamp her, and she smelled the musty stench of her own fear.

She fished her earbuds out of the bag and put them in. Forcing herself to take a slow breath, she gathered her wits like armor.

Her gaze landed on Gideon's gun. She grabbed the weapon and dropped the bag.

She locked her sights on the door, hands trembling. The impulse to fight was a live wire running through her, overriding the anxiety.

Another whack—softer to her ears this time—was followed by the splintering thump of a door slammed open in the room next to hers.

She drew in a breath and started a controlled exhale. *Focus. Aim. Fire.*

Thwack! She recoiled, heart thrashing in her chest like a caged wild bird. The lock gave way. Her door swung in, smashing against the wall.

An imposing body dominated the doorway, and a savage face glared at her.

Willow pulled the trigger and—with a soft pop—blasted a hole in his skull in a flash of blood and brain matter.

A shocked cry snagged in her throat. The man keeled backward, hitting the floor.

The other three ducked out of sight.

The throbbing tension in her head eased in the unnatural silence that fell and thickened. What if they tried to sneak up on her and she couldn't hear them moving?

She took out one earbud and tucked it in her bra.

A cold numbness bled through her, but her mind churned like a piston. If she didn't find a way out, they were going to kill her.

The glass storefront stretched so far off, it might as well have been miles away. She aimed the gun and fired, missing her target but taking the head clean off a mannequin.

She heaved a breath, refocused, and pulled the trigger. The safety glass shattered.

If the commotion didn't bring security or police, nothing would. But she was out of ideas.

9:49 A.M. EST/10:49 A.M. EDT

Gideon flew down the street. Adrenaline flooded his bloodstream, tingling beneath the skin. Scouring the streets, he followed the path she would've taken to the hotel unless forced to deviate. He fought the raging pulse in his throat. A cold sweat broke out on his brow.

There'd been five mercenaries at Ken's. To come looking for her here, there'd be more than two. His comms equipment was in the backpack with Willow. It would've been too conspicuous to wear an earpiece while talking to a bank manager about an offshore account.

He put on the ear mic he'd swiped off a dead merc. Silence. He double-checked it was live. Why wasn't there chatter? Where were those fuckers?

His gut pinched with sickening dread. He should've kept her pinned to his side.

If they found her, hurt her…

An unholy tangle of emotion made his heart squeeze to the point of physical pain. His rib cage throbbed and his pulse pounded at his temples.

Gideon raced toward the hotel, scanning for indicators of trouble. A lady with a stroller surrounded by a gaggle of kids slowed him for a heartbeat to avoid knocking a child down. He reached the last corner before crossing to the hotel.

Pearls strewn on the ground, rolling into the side street, caught his eye. He scooped up a handful. Faint iridescent pink. *Willow's.*

Did they pop the necklace snatching her, shoving her into a car?

Bracing for every dreadful possibility, he did a hasty visual sweep of the road, burning precious seconds. There were pearls scattered in a path that led to the doors of the glitzy resort.

He charged across the street, ignoring the blaring horn from a braking car, and stormed inside the resort. People meandered throughout the lobby, strolling in three different directions.

More pearls rolled on the polished floor.

Wherever Willow was, she was in dire trouble, and it

was tearing him apart. His muscles tightened to a throb, feet carrying him on instinct.

The path straight ahead led to elevators, most likely to hotel rooms. To the right, a bubbling fountain and break-fast rush at eateries. To the left, a row of boutique shops.

Sunglasses lay on the floor. Dark tint, feline flair, like the ones he'd purchased this morning. He bolted down the walkway, dodging murmuring men and women, his head on a one-eighty swivel. His blood was a roaring current of rage, but he grappled to hold tight to his sanity.

To save Willow, his professional cylinders needed to fire hot.

Gunfire shattered a storefront window ahead of him. A chorus of screams broke out from the crowd. He blasted toward the fray.

Broken glass crunched beneath his feet as he raised the bank security guard's gun.

"Flush the bitch out," someone said in Gideon's earpiece. "Keep cool. No sloppy bullets in her. Needs to look like an accident or suicide."

Gideon paused at the edge of the adjacent storefront and peeked inside.

Three mercs were in the back of the store. Looking over the top of clothing racks, he watched one kick and punch the side of a dressing room wall from within an adjacent stall. Another crept around, flanking in. Willow must be cornered.

He strained to keep his fury in check and reached for the icy calm he was accustomed to.

"Your sister is counting on you to save her life, Willow." The big one spoke in a deep baritone, not staying in sight.

"I could send someone to snatch those twins, bring them to mommy. Save your nieces. Come out."

They were holding her sister hostage? Threatening children? Bastards were good at finding the right bait. He hoped Willow wouldn't fall for it.

Crouching, he slipped inside the store. He silenced a groan at the sharp sound of glass breaking under his feet. Bye-bye advantage of surprise.

The pounding sounds stopped.

"Not cops. Omega, think it's Stone?" another asked over the comms.

"Count on it," the same baritone said. The one they called Omega. "Pincer."

A maneuver to trap him. Maybe hit his flank, close in like a claw. Whichever direction the attack came from, he needed to be ready on the opposite front as well.

He crouched and wove in between the displays and racks. Maintaining cover, he duck-walked to stay low. A dark flash of clothing darted by on his right.

Halting, he listened for movement. A set of muffled footsteps shifted across the carpet, coming in an arc to cut him off. He doubled back to a clothing display and regained his bearings.

One shuffled. Quick. Quiet. Toward his eleven o'clock.

Gideon cut left past a row of mannequins. Coming up at a forty-five-degree angle behind a merc—the only one making sound—he leaned against a solid particleboard display. It limited his field of view but provided better cover.

Something heavy landed atop the display table. A shadow loomed above him. Gideon rolled out of the way as bullets popped into the patch of real estate he'd just occupied.

Drawing up on a knee, he pumped two bullets dead center in the man's chest, one in the head.

A mass of muscle charged, tackling Gideon to the floor, and the gun slipped from his grip. He let the momentum carry him, flowing into the fall and driving his knees into the merc's torso, flipping him overhead.

Before the merc with a Magnum PI mustache fully recovered, Gideon spun and sprang upright, kicking the weapon out of his hands. Gideon drew the second bank guard's gun from his back, readying to shoot Mustachio, but the stealthy bruiser from Ken's—the one called Omega— landed a blow to his forearm, throwing off his aim.

Two bullets nailed a mannequin. Gideon whirled to redirect fire, but Omega expected it and dodged, knocking the weapon loose.

Pain flared in Gideon, but no bones were broken. He disconnected from it and pushed on.

Fast. You need to be faster than you've ever been.

Gideon pulled out the hammer and let the ticking beat in his head propel him.

In a round-robin smackdown, he alternated walloping each guy. He delivered lightning blows and kicks, striking any flesh within reach. The mercs were fast and organized, and each threw hard, well-timed punches and knees in turn.

Gideon headbutted Mustachio's face, crushing his nose, and punched his exposed throat, sending him sprawling to the floor, out cold.

But taking down one man had left Gideon vulnerable to the other.

Omega launched himself, lowering his shoulder, and slammed it into Gideon's chest like a battering ram, lifting him off the ground. The hit was worse than anything he'd endured in college football, bringing them both to the floor with enough force to dislocate Gideon's spine. Only the angle or luck had saved him that misery.

Without thinking, without feeling, Gideon drove his elbow into Omega's head, knocking the bruiser off him. It was muscle memory. Pure survival instinct.

Omega scrambled from the floor, grabbing a knife along the way, and reached his feet at the same time as Gideon. Thank God he could stand.

But if Omega charged with that weapon right now, Gideon wasn't sure he had the strength to take him. His blood chilled at the split-second thought—at the idea of failing Willow.

Blinking it away, he dug deep and braced himself.

Movement grabbed both of their attention. Willow stood in front of a dressing room, holding the Maxim 9.

A low, distinct pop whispered in the air. The hot slug would've hit Omega in the forehead, but he threw a mannequin between them. Willow's bullet struck the figurine's chest.

Omega didn't give her a chance to fire a second round. He ran, barreling through a door in the corner of the shop. Gideon swiped the gun from Willow and pursued.

Putting an end to that man now if possible was best. Gideon followed him into a back office that led to a small storeroom filled with neatly stacked boxes.

Omega flicked the lock off an exterior door and charged into an alley. By the time Gideon made it to the doorway, Omega was hopping over a six-foot brick wall.

Every instinct and years of training tempted Gideon

to track the threat and eliminate him, but leaving Willow alone, unprotected, wasn't a mistake he'd repeat.

He hustled back into the main shop.

A rush surged through him at the sight of her. She ran to him, wrapping him in a desperate hug, whispering his name over and over again. Her trembling body was crushed to his as he held her back. The hard knot in his chest loosened.

"I thought I was going to lose you," she said in a frantic voice.

He didn't want to entertain what might've happened if she hadn't fired the gun. "I'd die before I let anything happen to you, but I told you, I'm hard to kill."

Stroking her hair, he soaked in the smell of her—the unique scent that was all Willow—her warmth, her tenderness filling him with a deep rush of gratitude that he'd never known before. Exhilaration welled until he thought his heart might burst from joy. Nothing in the world had ever felt better, and everything else fell to the wayside.

They were nowhere near out of the woods. They still had to prove her innocence, and that bastard Omega had gotten away.

Ben's old warning came back to him: *Better to put a bullet in a threat than give it another chance to put you in the grave.*

There were no truer words. And they had a monumental task ahead of them.

But for a few precious seconds, having Willow in his arms was all that mattered.

39

GRAND CAYMAN
MONDAY, JULY 8, 10:31 A.M. EST/11:31 A.M. EDT

A familiar heated prickle of warning raced across
Gideon's forearms like fire ants crawling under his skin
as he sensed them closing in. He whirled, gun at the ready,
shielding Willow behind his body.

Maddox was on point, leading the way. The rest of the
Gray Box's black ops team hurried inside the store behind
her. Relief dripped through him—a conditioned response
to familiar faces—but he stayed wired tight in case he had
to fight friendlies.

"I knew if we followed the mayhem, we'd find you."
Maddox smiled, and the tension abated in his shoulders.
A little.

"I had my doubts." Ares holstered a gun. "The Reaper
is always quiet as a wraith when he works."

Gideon lowered his weapon at the nonaggressive
gestures but kept his guard up, finger on the trigger. Why
had they come here?

"Maybe this is how he rolls on vacation." Reece knelt,
checking the pulse of Mustachio.

The banter and unguarded body language enticed
Gideon to relax, but his spine tingled. Something
wasn't right. He surveyed their faces, every nuance of

movement, waiting for the red flag he knew in his gut was coming.

"If you guys are here to help, you're an hour late." His voice was hard, unyielding to the pleasantries.

"Perfect timing." Castle's gaze swept the trashed store. "You did all the heavy lifting."

Alistair scooped a decapitated mannequin head from the floor, closing the semicircle they'd formed around them, blocking off the obvious point of egress. "I feel a bit cheated. You had a knees-up party without us."

Willow came up beside Gideon, slipping under his arm. Instinctively, he tucked her close against his body.

Silence dropped like a nuclear bomb. Every set of eyes zeroed in on the pair of them. Gideon clenched his jaw at the abrasive awareness, longing for chewing gum. But his nerves and neurons were alert to the possibility of this situation turning on a dime.

"Wonders never do cease to amaze." Reece's low voice carried.

"Hello, luv." Alistair smirked, a mischievous gleam in his eyes. "You look ravishing. Positively glowing." Damn British accent rolled smoother than butter. "Odd, considering the circumstances. Must have something to do with the *island air*."

Willow lowered her head.

"Fuck off, Allie. What are you all doing here?"

Maddox stared at Willow with a deadpan face, then cut her narrowing, accusatory eyes to him. His stomach churned.

"The chief has some kind of gun to his head." Maddox's tone was frosty. "Sanborn is worried, and he never worries."

There must be a countdown to the whitewash. Based on the expressions of the others, none of them knew how dire things really were.

"Forensics confirmed Harper's brakes were sabotaged," Maddox continued. "We know her house burned down—arson. And her father is in the ICU."

Willow's hand dug into his shirt. "Is he still in a coma?"

Maddox nodded.

Willow pressed her face to Gideon's chest, sucking in a ragged breath. He wanted to reassure her somehow, but he only tightened his arm around her shivering body.

"We found your passport maker's place by the trail of dead bodies." Reece checked the last merc. "Got a live one here."

"What are your orders?" Gideon didn't have a clear bead on their intentions, keeping him on the razor's edge. No one had yet mentioned a word about *how* they planned to help.

Maddox shuttered her eyes, mouth setting in a grim line.

Whatever their orders, she'd just tipped him off that he wouldn't be onboard.

Shielding Willow behind him, Gideon raised his gun.

"Whoa." Ares strode forward, empty hands lifted, but those dark eyes trained on Gideon like a double-barreled shotgun.

If anyone else had moved, Gideon would've taken it as a sign they wanted to play nice, defuse the situation. But Sean fucking "Ares" Whitlock advanced before clarifying their orders.

Sanborn sent Gideon on missions to eliminate threats. Ares was sent to level battlefields. He was the best one-man wrecking ball out there.

Until someone clarified the situation, in terms clearer than crystal, the only way to view Ares closing in was as an act of war. "Stop moving. We're friends, but I'll put a bullet in you."

Ares halted, flashing a calculated grin laden with eerie friendliness.

Willow grabbed one of the mercs' guns from the floor, covering the forty-five-degree angle to Gideon's left.

"Someone's been getting private tutelage from a very good teacher." A smart-aleck smirk lifted on Alistair's face. "Bet you've learned all sorts of naughty things from him." He winked. "Ladies say he's a real corker in the sack, but I bet he's more of a damp squib with that pretty face. Care to weigh in?"

Gideon quashed his instinct to shoot the cheeky Brit. Allie was doing his job, trying to rattle Willow, perhaps enough to take the gun from her.

"We're here to cover your back," Castle said, scrubbing a hand over his shaved head. "Sanborn thinks Harper's innocent, despite a deed for a villa in France in her name and the fact that her PIN was used to access the server room the night Novak was killed."

Willow turned ashen. Shaking her head, she looked ready to hurl.

"Sanborn figured bounty killers were after her." Castle tapped Ares on the shoulder, nodding for him to stand down. "We're here to help."

But that still didn't answer the fucking question.

Ares moved, and so did Gideon, closer toward the blown-out storefront with Willow at his side. If he was on his own, he'd try for the alley, but he wouldn't be able to get Willow over the brick wall and follow before the team caught them. Heading toward the crowd and busy lobby was the better option.

"What are your orders?" Gideon asked again, his gun hand steady as ice.

Maddox said nothing, her head bowed. Not a good sign.

Tension thickened, growing darker and more toxic with each second, like exhaust fumes.

"Hopefully, you found a solid lead at the bank," Reece said.

"Otherwise?" Gideon crept away, keeping them in his sights with crushing focus. They had nothing to exonerate Willow, much less to stop a whitewash.

"We use her as bait to flush out the traitor." Castle's defensive-tackle body drew taut. "The mole wants her dead. Whoever it is won't stop trying."

Their plan was to let the traitor try to kill her? That was never going to happen.

Willow clutched his forearm, urging him to lower the gun. "Gideon."

He met her warm eyes. The gentleness reflected in her beautiful face had him softening. The others blanked out for a second, fading into the background. "Our lead might be a dead end." His gaze flickered to the team, ensuring no one took advantage of his divided attention.

They all stood riveted, a restless energy buzzing in the room. His pulse beat in time to the metronome ticking in his ears.

"It's okay," Willow said, drawing his gaze.

He'd give her anything but this. Running was better

than letting Sanborn use her as bait. He wouldn't risk her life. Not to catch the traitor. Not to save the Gray Box.

Not for anything in the world.

Willow stepped in front of him, putting herself between him and the team. "The real traitor is hiding behind a shell corporation. Give me time to dig, and I'll find tangible evidence."

The others exchanged questioning glances.

"We're short on time," Castle said. "We've got a Gulfstream requisitioned from Homeland Security on the tarmac, encrypted system onboard. We can give you the duration of the flight."

"No." Gideon roped an arm around her waist, hauling her toward the exit.

His teammates' hands flew to their holstered weapons, but no one drew.

She pushed at Gideon's arm, trying to pry him loose. "I'll find something we can use."

"Hell fucking no," he bit through gritted teeth, carrying her, keeping the gun trained on the others. Pain twisted through his wounds, but he didn't stop.

"Trust me." Her bony elbow hit him in the injured side as she struggled, and agony ballooned in his rib cage. "Gideon. I need you to believe in me. Please."

The *please* stilled him. His gut burned, and he ached to fight.

But it was slim odds they'd make it with five Gray Box agents up their ass—especially Ares—and they needed off the island. Maybe the appearance of cooperation could recalibrate their chances to a favorable outcome. If she didn't find what they needed, he'd come up with a contingency plan, but under no circumstances was she walking into the Gray Box as bait.

"Okay." Gideon released Willow, hating every second of the movement.

Maddox canted her head, bewilderment stamped on her face, an expression that was mirrored in the faces of the others.

Willow put her hands to his chest, giving him a woeful smile. "It's impossible for a mole to hide for years without leaving a digital footprint. No matter how well hidden, I'll find it."

But could she find it in time? A Gulfstream meant a three-hour flight.

When he looked away from Willow, his gaze collided with Maddox's. Her steely eyes dissected him to the bone, transparent worry replacing the surprise on her face.

He washed his expression clean, tightening down his emotions. It was as if Willow sensed the change. She drew away, hands falling to her sides, doe eyes questioning him.

"Okey-dokey." Reece gave an enthusiastic clap. "Let's rock and roll before the cops arrive."

Local law enforcement would only delay them with questions. Surprising they weren't on the scene already, though it was possible they were hemmed up at the bank. Good thing the crime rate on the island was low.

"We need the merc," Gideon said. "They're holding Willow's sister hostage."

Ares flashed a wicked grin and elbowed Alistair. "Guess we might get to party after all."

40

Daedalus stared in the dingy bathroom mirror, running an electric razor over his cheeks. Nothing beat a hot towel shave with a straight razor, but his Braun was a close second. He swiped a hand along his jaw, the barest hint of stubble prickling his palm.

Unease dripped through him over how he'd left things with Omega.

Vincent.

Daedalus had been so fired up over Cobalt's insurance and Stone wiping out some of their best men, he'd blamed Omega for this catastrophe.

They were bound together in this, for better or worse, since the beginning. Not once, in all the years they'd hustled, strategized, manipulated to rise like conquerors had Daedalus dumped the entire shitload of responsibility on Omega's shoulders. Not until last night.

He raked his dark hair into place and clenched his hands, disgusted at himself for not having unleashed his venom at the proper target. Stone and Cobalt.

In this business, venting was a necessary evil. He relied on Vincent to be a sounding board, offering solid advice, even when it was unwanted. The man was more than his right hand. Vin was…his foundation, supporting him, holding their empire up with his dauntless backbone.

Sometimes Daedalus said things in anger—his hot-blooded Italian temperament flaring—but only behind closed doors. And only to Vin, who always brushed off harsh words in his usual steely fashion.

By the time he finished ranting last night, he'd seen the damage he'd inflicted in Vin's eyes, the burden that weighed on him. Daedalus was the sole reason Vincent had stepped back into this cesspool of a business after washing his hands clean. If anything happened to him…

Daedalus drew in a deep breath, maintaining a grip on his unraveling sanity. Inside him, a tinderbox was ready to ignite and incinerate the world.

This was the doomsday scenario they had shed blood, broken bones, and subjugated souls to avoid. If they didn't fix this, everything they'd worked for could be wiped out.

They had a sizeable nest egg, capable of providing comfort in hiding, but their empire wasn't solely about money. This came down to something far more satisfying.

Power.

They'd do anything to hold on to it.

There was another possible asset inside the Gray Box. Cobalt had done the research and given him a name last year. Reluctantly, but it meant less pressure on Cobalt to produce intel if the other person panned out. Vin had advised against digging around on the secondary. A tricky move at best, incendiary at worst. MI6, British Intelligence, supposedly thought Alistair Allen was dead.

Asking questions about a ghost would raise red flags, and Allen seemed equally as likely to cooperate as he did to go out guns blazing in defiance, but these were desperate times. Using desperate measures, Daedalus had thrown out feelers a few days ago to have his contacts in Britain verify the credibility of the leverage.

For now, he needed to shut down the assassin and the analyst and take care of Cobalt.

The rest of their men could be here within two hours, but it wouldn't help Vincent.

"Still no word." Rho hovered in the doorway of the dilapidated bathroom. "He should've made contact hours ago. No one has picked up comms."

Daedalus tightened his fingers around the electric razor. The hot rush of blood pounding his head blared like white noise.

Rho folded his arms. "Vincent wanted you to initiate the evacuation protocol."

He chuckled. "Cut and run?" *Never.* He was the master of his own destiny.

"We should kill the woman." Rho nodded toward the other room, where they had Willow Harper's sister. "Let Cobalt hang and leave. Vincent wanted—"

"Don't presume to tell *me* what *he* wanted." No one knew Vin better, understood the complicated layers, appreciated all he had to offer. The indomitable strength, inexhaustible passion, radiating an endless heat that burned Daedalus down to his soul.

Vincent was his Omega.

And there'd never be another.

"What are your orders?" An edge laced Rho's voice.

"Do whatever is necessary to find Cobalt's insurance. Start by grabbing the family." Daedalus squeezed the shaver in his hand, trying to keep the anxious fury contained. "Bring in the others to help."

"How many?"

"All of them." It should've been obvious.

"Sir." Rho crossed the threshold, brows knitted. "Cobalt is probably camped out at that impenetrable fortress, the Gray Box, and if so, unlikely to take the bait. It's my understanding the sub-facility can withstand a nuclear explosion. We should leave. This move isn't worth the risk."

This move was all he had left. He'd see it through to the end.

Rho let out a deep breath, like he didn't want to share what was on his mind but planned to anyway. "Vincent wouldn't want this. He'd tell you if he could. He'd never allow himself to be taken alive. If he hasn't checked in by now, he's probably dead."

Rage sparked hellfire in his blood. "I know."

If the tide didn't turn in his favor, he'd at least get payback for Omega and take out those Gray Box agents in a firestorm. They couldn't hide in their compound forever.

"We should cut our losses. Forget Cobalt. Bring in just enough men to help tie up the loose ends we can and escort you to safety. More can be here in an hour by helicopter."

Daedalus threw the electric razor against the wall, smashing it to bits. "I said to bring ALL OF THEM!"

SOMEWHERE OVER FLORIDA
MONDAY, JULY 8, 2:15 P.M. EDT

In the front cabin of the Gulfstream, Gideon stood, watching Willow run into one dead end after another. The Judas Iscariot company was managed by another shell company, which was managed by another.

He bit back frustration while plotting his contingency plan. Perched in a leather seat across the polished hardwood table, Maddox kept her shrewd gaze locked on both of them.

"The owner of the shell corporations is buried. Deep," Willow said.

A fist smacked flesh in the rear of the luxurious cabin, where Ares worked over the merc for information. Willow cringed at the sound and Gideon rubbed her back.

She pulled out her noise-reducing earbuds and put them in. "There are too many layers. Setting up an elaborate financial network for the sole purpose of adding a beneficiary on one offshore account is overkill." She grabbed a pen and started doodling on the notepad beside the keyboard.

"Do you think the shell companies are being used for something else?" Gideon asked.

"What if I'm looking at this wrong? What if the LLC wasn't created by the mole? Maybe Daedalus funnels money through these shell companies to our mole and perhaps to others, to hide the source," Willow mused, drawing a circular maze, a labyrinth, with the head of a bull at the center. "We don't need to know who owns it. We need to know where the money from the companies is going."

"Wouldn't the forensic accountants have caught payouts?" Maddox's gaze swung between them.

"Not necessarily. It wouldn't have been flagged if it was a stock distribution. Say dividends below ten thousand dollars and taxes were paid, making it look like it came from a *legal* source."

"How does this help?" Gideon asked.

Willow dropped the pen and opened a second secure laptop. Her fingers clicked across the first, bringing up a different screen on the system, and typed mind-numbing lines of symbols and text. "Those corporations have tax identification numbers. I just have to hack into the most antiquated system of the federal government. The IRS. They're at least two generations behind in the Windows operating system they use, making them vulnerable to a common hacker, much less someone with my skills."

"That's terrifying," Maddox said.

"Isn't it?" Willow nodded, her fingers tapping on the second computer. "I'll cross-reference those tax ID numbers with the tax returns for Gray Box personnel and personal associates from our records."

"How long will it take?" Gideon asked.

"It's a small, narrow query—shouldn't take too long."

Another wet smack of flesh came from the cabin. Willow didn't flinch this time, absorbed in her work.

Hopefully, Ares would get the intel needed to find her sister, and Gideon wouldn't have to step in. Willow might know what he had done in theory, but he didn't want her to see what he was truly capable of.

One laptop dinged. "I got a hit." Willow eyed the screen with a frown. "But it's not someone who works for the

Gray Box. I don't recognize the name. I'll have to go back into the Gray Box records. It must be a family member."

Gideon peered over her shoulder. The name didn't ring a bell with him either. "Who is Mary Johnson?"

The blood drained from Maddox's face. "That has to be a mistake. Run the query again."

"There's nothing wrong with the query," Willow said. "Mary L. Johnson has two tax returns—married filing separately—showing dividends from the shell companies."

"Who is Mary Johnson?" Gideon asked.

"It's a mistake," Maddox repeated, her tone and posture turning defensive.

Gideon stepped closer to her, and their eyes locked. "Who is she?"

A genuine look of confusion washed over Maddox. She just sat there, blinking, waiting so long to answer Gideon thought he'd have to ask her again.

"Amanda's mother," Maddox said. "Johnson is her maiden name."

The response hit him like a sucker punch.

Maddox was right, this was some mistake. Amanda was one of them, part of the black ops inner circle. Not a traitor.

"Amanda is the mole," Willow said softly.

"Don't accuse her of that," Maddox snapped, leaning forward. "This could be another decoy. A plot within a plot conspiracy to frame someone else in case the plan with you failed."

"The money doesn't lie," Willow said.

"You have a million dollars sitting in a bank account. Are you saying that's not a lie?"

"Calm down." Gideon put his hand on Maddox's shoulder, but she flinched away from him. "I don't want to believe it either. We all care about Amanda."

"I never touched the money in that bank account," Willow said. "How do you explain regular payments to her mother over two years? Possibly longer? And why under her maiden name if not to hide it?"

Maddox's gaze fell and she shook her head. "It can't be her. It can't."

Maybe there was another explanation. Something they were overlooking. Gideon trusted Amanda. Maddox trusted her, *everyone* had…for years. How could she be guilty of conspiracy, espionage? How could she be the type of person they were trained to hunt? The enemy who had manipulated them all?

"Damn," Maddox said in a defeated whisper, forehead creased.

"What is it?" Gideon asked.

Pressing her lips tight together as if the words were too terrible to utter, Maddox looked stricken. Almost heartbroken. "I overhead Amanda ask Nicole Tully how the power was shut off to the observation room the night Novak was killed. When Nicole mentioned the server room, Amanda asked if the entry records had been checked."

"She baited Nicole to find that evidence against Willow," Gideon said.

Maddox nodded and dropped her head back against the seat.

The stab of betrayal went deep and twisted. Amanda was a field operative—or at least she had been before switching to analysis—and understood the magnitude of this. She'd jeopardized national security, but this was also personal. Amanda had endangered the lives of every operative and had burned one of their own.

Besides that, she had more to lose than anyone. More than her career or her future behind bars. Her son, Jackson, meant everything to her.

No way she'd risk not being there for him, watching him grow up—not for money, and she was no ideological nutjob on a crusade.

"Daedalus must've compromised her somehow," Gideon said.

Maddox sat silent, now expressionless, staring out the window, but a pang of sympathy still went through him for her. She'd recruited Amanda from the DEA. They were best friends, and she was Jackson's godmother.

"How could she have fooled everyone for so long?" Willow asked.

Maddox drew in a strained breath. "You mean, how could she have fooled me? Lied to me every single day without my knowing? Pretend to be my friend without me suspecting?"

"No, I didn't. I meant all of us. I admire her…admired. How she managed to juggle so much as a single mother. She was always patient and nice to me." Willow stroked her throat as if searching for her pearls. "But she planted trackers on me, framed me. She tried to kill me."

Had Amanda also been responsible for the brake failure on Gideon's truck that killed his wife? He thought he'd be relieved to learn the truth, like finally scratching an itch that plagued you. Instead, his stomach churned with disgust.

He didn't want to believe it. That Amanda was capable of such things.

But Amanda had done a lot of deep undercover work, pretending to be someone she wasn't for years. Her first day out of the DEA academy, she'd said she was making a buy as part of a sting to bring down a drug lab. And Sanborn had thrown her into the deep end the moment she signed on the dotted line to work for him. It wasn't until she got pregnant with Jackson and wanted something less hazardous that she'd ever pushed papers.

"She fooled all of us," Gideon said.

Ares tapped him on the shoulder. "That guy won't crack. So tightlipped, you'd think he didn't have a tongue. I can't get him to break, but I'm sure you can get him to crack like an egg."

A watery sensation sloshed through Gideon's gut. He looked at Willow, dreading the words forming on his tongue. What would she think of him, once she saw who he really was? How ruthless, how pitiless he had to be sometimes?

The horror she would witness, the terrible things she'd see him do in the next hour would forever define him and color the way she looked at him. This moment was inevitable. Sooner or later, whatever they shared had to come to an end.

Willow glanced up at him with tenderness radiating from her, and the sick feeling inside him intensified.

If she didn't consider him a monster now, she would by the time he was finished.

"Ares, lay down plastic so we don't ruin the carpet. I'll break him."

41

Omega took his first-class seat on the flight from Grand Cayman bound for Dulles International. He'd sent the helicopter back in lieu of the faster commercial option. He clutched the burner phone in his palm that he'd bought in the airport, dreading the call he had to make like a coward.

Defeat was a corrosive burn in his blood, leaving a bitter taste in his mouth. Shame was the only thing keeping the killing edge of his temper in check. He'd be dead if not for instinct and sharp reflexes that had saved his ass.

Would Daedalus be happy to know he was alive even though he'd failed?

There were many days when their empire seemed more important to him than anything else. As though he were willing to sacrifice Omega, all they shared, and all they could have in the future if it meant that Daedalus would get to keep his crown.

Omega hated the ache in his chest. It wasn't so much that he'd fucked up the mission as it was that he was about to break Daedalus's heart with disappointment.

The flight attendant asked everyone to *please turn off and stow electronic devices.*

He needed them to know his status and decided to text Rho.

Stone and Harper are alive. Proceed with exit plan. I'm flying commercial to Dulles. O.

"Sir, I'm going to have to ask you to power down your phone now," the flight attendant said.

He needed to wait for acknowledgement first. "In a minute. It'll be off before we taxi." He threw in a glare for good measure.

Her smile fell, and she took the hint, moving on to nag another passenger.

The phone rang. He didn't need to look at the number. It was Daedalus. Rho would've texted in return.

After the things Daedalus had said to him the last time they'd spoken—conveyed the imperative to kill Stone and Harper—he wasn't up for going another round with him. Not yet.

The ringing stopped. A text chimed.

Quitting is beneath you. This can be salvaged. We need to go to war, or we'll lose everything.

They wouldn't lose each other, but Daedalus wanted to have it all.

Omega ground his molars.

Another text came through.

Will send helicopter to Dulles for you.

Walking away from everything they'd built would be like chopping off a limb. Neither of them *wanted* to do it, but this was triage. Daedalus was going to get them both killed.

A third chime on the phone.

None of this means anything without you. Come back to me. D.

The viselike tightness in Omega's chest eased, and the heated sting in his blood lessened.

Love was a fool's game, but it was the only one he wanted to play with Daedalus. He was the only person Omega had ever hit all six cylinders with. They'd been together many years, were a part of each other, and Omega knew Daedalus would never accept retreat. Not when they could still win, no matter how slim the odds.

And Omega would risk everything for him, time and time again. The strategy wheel in his mind started spinning.

He sent one last text before powering off the phone.

I can't seem to deny you. Bring more men. Arm up heavy gear. We go to war.

SOMEWHERE OVER NORTH CAROLINA
MONDAY, JULY 8, 3:33 P.M. EDT

Soul-shredding screams filled the cabin of the plane. The sound was filtered through Willow's earplugs but not muted.

She should've listened to Gideon and Maddox and not looked, but without work to focus on, how could she not?

The situation was surreal. She sat in a plush leather chair, thick carpet beneath her feet, polished surfaces of the cabin glinting with soft light, but her stomach churned as she watched, horrified, while Gideon did one of the things he did best.

Interrogation.

A mechanics tool chest was open beside him. Ordinary devices turned into instruments of pain were spread out on one of the plastic-lined seats. Gideon asked the mercenary a question. If he didn't get an answer, he used one of those tools. With shocking precision and gut-wrenching imagination.

The rest of the team didn't appear fazed. Alistair slept, stretched across a leather sofa. Reece read a comic, *The Walking Dead*, sipping a prepackaged protein shake.

As Gideon ripped out a man's teeth with pliers—an evil man who'd tried to kill her—Maddox filed her fingernails, rounding each tip into a perfect oval, rubbing a peachy-smelling oil into her cuticles. Giving herself a freaking manicure!

Oh my God. Willow would never be able to stomach the scent of peaches again.

With earbuds also tucked in, Sean—or rather, Ares—nodded to the beat of whatever music played from his iPod, but like Castle, he never took his eyes off what Gideon did.

They acted like torturing a man for information was normal, another day in the field, protecting and serving the country. But this was…

Extreme.

Violent.

Nauseating, yet necessary. This craziness was their baseline.

The last few days had shown her the true depths of danger that came as a package deal with Gideon's job. She'd been inches from death today and shot a man in the head in self-defense. A terrifying man trying to kill her, yes, but she'd taken a life. Acid roiled in her gut.

Gideon wasn't just trained as an interrogator. He had done *this*, exclusively, for months with the CIA. She understood the ugly nature of what transpired at black sites where prisoners were grilled, where he'd done his work.

But knowing a thing and bearing witness to it were worlds apart.

The information they needed was vital. Her sister's life depended on the answers this mercenary provided. Yet no amount of rationalization stopped bile from burning her throat. The man wailed, handcuffed to a seat. Blood-chilling screams broadcast through the cabin, and the agonized sounds twisted her insides.

"Daedalus!" The merc spat out a gob of blood. "Daedalus has her."

Gideon stood motionless, but Willow reared back, taking the blow of surprise for him.

If Daedalus was alive, then Gideon killed the wrong man three years ago. Amanda must have tampered with mission details somehow to protect his identity.

"Is he on-site with her?" Gideon's voice was tight as a whip.

"Yes. He wanted to handle things in person."

"Where are they?"

The battered man shook his head, sniveling. "He'll kill me. I-I can't tell you."

Gideon held out his latex-gloved hand, smeared red with blood. Eyes ice-cold, body taut with a honed hardness.

Castle slapped a power drill into his palm.

Squeezing her eyes closed, she couldn't take anymore, but she also couldn't sit fifteen feet away and not look. She pried her eyes open.

Gideon pressed the spinning drill bit to the mercenary's kneecap.

Her gut convulsed, slushing up the breakfast in her stomach. She flipped the buckle of the lap seatbelt and dashed to the bathroom, legs quaking like toothpicks. Inside, she slammed the door shut and retched into the toilet.

42

GRAY BOX HEADQUARTERS, NORTHERN VIRGINIA
MONDAY, JULY 8, 4:56 P.M. EDT

The sickened expression on Willow's face was tattooed on
Gideon's mind. How she'd rushed to the bathroom—no
doubt puking up her guts—and stayed inside until
Maddox told her the interrogation was done wouldn't
leave him.

Worse, he'd seen fear in her eyes. Fear of him and what
he was capable of when push came to shove.

Better for her to have seen firsthand the misery and
wretchedness permeating his job, his life. His soul.

The rest of the flight had been tense. He'd kept his
distance on the other end of the plane, with Castle and
Ares. Neither busted his balls about Willow, keeping the
conversation to straight-up shop talk about how to rescue
the sister and maximize their chance to capture Daedalus
for interrogation. Once they'd landed, they'd moved rapid-
fire into separate vehicles and headed to the Gray Box.

The cars screeched to a halt in front of the grand gray
building, and they all poured out onto the concrete under
the glare of the sun.

Willow ran around to the steps leading to the entrance.
"Gideon, I need to talk to you."

"Not now." If he had it his way, they'd bypass this

conversation and simply return to the way things were before they went on the run—as if that were possible. "I've got to gear up."

She threw herself in front of him and wrangled him to a standstill, her small hands fierce and tight on his arms. "It's important. Please."

Reece clasped his shoulder. "We'll get the gear. You can take ten minutes, man."

Ten? Hell, Gideon didn't want to take one. He was in no rush to tear out his own heart by having *the* conversation with her.

"I'll wait for you in the lobby," Maddox said to Willow. "You shouldn't be alone until we have Amanda in custody."

Gideon spun on his heel and stalked off to the far end of the parking lot, not stopping until he was under the canopy of trees and surrounded by hedges.

Willow hustled alongside him, and when he came to a halt, she faced him with a shaky smile. The warmth emanating from her hit him with the explosive force of shrapnel, but the look in her eyes nearly made him double over from the vicious weakness softening him.

"You're safe," he said with a reflexive coldness that startled even him. "My assignment is done. What do you want?"

She recoiled, the tentative smile slipping from her face. Everything inside him locked with regret. "I wanted to talk to you about what happened on the plane." Willow reached for him.

He struggled against the electric pull to be near her, like trying to fight gravity, and shuffled backward. His fingers flexed with a gut-wrenching ache to touch her, to be touched by her, but he had to be strong and do the right thing.

"What you saw," he said, "that's what I do. It's who I am. Sorry I sickened you. Frightened you."

"I've read about the things you've done, interrogating people at CIA black sites. But I got sick because I've never seen anything like that before. I wasn't prepared. Gideon, I wasn't afraid of you. I was afraid for you."

What the hell? He was the monster who served in the shadows, snuffing out lives in the darkness. Others feared him, not *for* him.

"I saw how taxing your job is, how much you sacrifice for it." Pure love poured off her. "It must be so hard not to lose yourself amid such horror. To remember that it's okay to relax, to let light in, to heal from the scars it must leave on the inside."

No one ever worried about him, but she did. Having a front-row seat to see exactly what he was capable of hadn't terrified her, hadn't sent her running to find normal.

Not only did he have to protect her from him, he had to protect her from herself. She wasn't thinking straight. No sane woman would choose him or still think of him as a hero after what he'd done on the plane.

If she did, her head needed to be examined. Kelli had been smart to want to bail.

"I can't do this," he said, his lungs constricting.

She wrapped her arms around herself. "I didn't want you to think my feelings have changed after what I saw. This isn't the time or place for this discussion. I just wanted you to know. Maybe I can stay with you for a few days while I figure out where I'm going to live, and we can sort through things."

"No." He rubbed the back of his neck to ease the discomfort crawling over him. "My place is a hot mess." *I'm a hot mess.* "You wouldn't be happy." Not in the long run. "I don't have the capacity...the room for your..." Softness. Tenderness. Love. "Stuff."

"Everything burned down. I don't have any stuff."

She was a real expert at painting him into corners. Why couldn't she make this easier?

"I know you have to go," she said. "Tonight, we can talk about us."

"There is no *us*." He strained to maintain his composure despite the battle raging inside. He was fighting for the selfless side to win. On the boat, he'd almost believed in happiness that endured, in a future where he wasn't alone. Almost.

But what he'd had to do on the plane made him face the bitter truth, reminded him of how ugly he had to be for good to triumph over evil, and his fragile illusion of hope burst like a soap bubble.

"Why can't there be an us?" Her voice was raw with emotion. "I need to hear you say it."

"Say what? That I'm only good at fucking and killing? That you'd be better off without me? Trust me, you don't want this."

Wasting the best years of her life worrying every time he went on assignment if he'd come back injured, in a body bag, or at all. Growing to resent him for the things he couldn't give.

"You don't have to be good at caring about someone.

Either you do, or you don't." She drummed her fingers against her thigh, the color rising in her cheeks. "Don't make excuses. I can handle the truth. Just tell me."

"What do you need to hear?"

"That we don't fit. That I'm not the right type of woman for you." Her chin angled up in a challenge, and something hard as steel ran through her. "That you could never be with someone like me in the real world."

Unbearable pressure roiled through him, deep beneath the cold-wash front he presented. "Go inside and clear your name, Willow."

"Don't be a coward." Ugly fury punched through her tone. "Say it."

The air shifted, tension distending between them. How long could ten minutes last?

"Say it." She shoved him.

He had to do it quickly, like ripping off a Band-Aid or slicing a jugular.

"We don't fit."

She flinched like he'd slapped her. Agony rippled across her face.

Liar. He was a liar, and uttering such a horrible untruth ate at his gut.

Fate was cruel to put this incredible person in his path, his starling. He didn't choose this life—it chose him. Sometimes, he hated that life. Right now, no question, it hated him right back.

"Go inside," he begged. "I need to clear my head so I can do my job."

In a blur, she fled from his field of sight.

A sinkhole opened in his chest. The pain rising in him

was worse than anything he'd ever endured physically. For a moment, he couldn't move.

For her own good. For the best.

Best for her.

He stormed toward the building. It was better to end it before things between them got any deeper. Turbulence inside him spun and swelled. Then it slammed against the wall of his chest and he couldn't breathe.

Staggering to a stop, he leaned against his Jeep. Kelli's Jeep. He pressed his fists on the hood, and their last argument before his Daedalus mission came roaring back to him.

"You can't keep making choices for me, Gideon!" Kelli said.

She'd complained about driving the old Toyota, even though the sedan would've lasted forever. Surprising her with a new car should've made her happy. Right? Wrong. Again.

"A tiny sports car isn't practical." He dropped onto the sofa. *"You'd get stuck in the snow and wouldn't stand a chance in a car accident. You'll thank me for the Jeep come winter."*

She threw the car keys at his head, and he ducked. "I'll never thank you for making decisions for me. For taking away the life I wanted to live."

"Are we talking about a car?"

"Yes! And no!" She marched around the living room like a crazy person. Mental diagnosis: perpetual infuriation. "You were a quarterback with a killer arm who could outrun receivers! You could've been a first-round draft pick instead of third, if you'd wanted it. You were supposed to go pro. Who turns down a multimillion-dollar contract to work for the CIA?"

This again? For years, it was always between them, like cancer. "You swore going pro didn't matter."

Her cheeks flamed red. "There were other options besides this." She flung her hands out. "You could've been an anchor. A coach at a big school. Something. You never even told me you applied to the Agency."

He stormed to the kitchen. The situation demanded a drink. Belgian or microbrew?

Of course, she followed him. The woman had to dig into every argument with fangs and talons until she drew blood. "You announced you were leaving for the academy. You informed me we'd live in the Beltway. In the same disrespectful manner you bought that Jeep."

How in the hell did she turn a gift into a sign of disrespect?

"Listen"—he pointed a finger—"I wasn't used to being in it with someone, discussing everything. I needed to go through my own process when I applied to the Agency."

She folded her arms. "You're still not used to it. You keep everything to yourself. Disappear for days at a time for work. Come home banged up, no explanation. And when you're here, you might as well not be. You don't share anything."

He took a hefty swill of beer. "Let's get counseling."

"Two years after I ask, you suddenly want to try counseling? So you can throw on your QB smile, charm your way through the sessions, and paint me as a nagging bitch?"

He set the beer on the counter since he couldn't enjoy it and sat in the dining room to ride out the latest wave of batshit insanity. "What do you want from me?" He threw his hands in the air. "I'll return the Jeep. Buy whatever you want."

"You don't get it." Fury gleamed in her eyes. "If you love someone, you don't make decisions for them. Even when you think it's best. Being with you is like living with a ghost—a damn dead person—who controls everything."

"I have an hour commute each way because you wanted to live in the city. I had no say in paint colors, furnishings, where my clothes are hung. I'm a visitor in your house, but I pay the mortgage. And the last time we fucked, you didn't complain about me acting like a dead guy."

Her upper lip curled in disdain. "Unreal."

"You said the same thing after your third climax."

"Ugh!" She snatched the beer bottle from the counter and launched it at his head.

With a deft swipe, he caught it, but frothy ale splashed on the floor.

Battening down his emotions with glacial ice, he leveled her with a glance. "Throwing my beer is crossing the line." The good stuff was his one luxury, and the shit was pricey.

"Your beer? That's crossing the line?" Sighing, she shook her head, disgust on her face.

He wished he could do or say the right thing to fix this.

Something dawned in her eyes, some aha moment that twisted her expression into a look of fear. "I don't know who you are at all, do I? I can't believe I married you."

The comment sliced through him. "But you did marry me. For better or worse. So let's put the past behind us. Start fresh. Get to know me better. Ask me anything nonwork-related."

"That's the crux of our problem, Gideon. Your work and whatever the hell it is you do for the CIA."

He was no longer with the Agency, but he couldn't tell her about the Gray Box.

"For some people, what you do is what you are. For you, it goes deeper. The CIA is like this mistress that you love more than me, the only one you share your secrets with. I'll never truly know you, never get in, unless you tell me everything."

Kelli had been right all along. Regret and anger and frustration boiled over inside him. Gideon slammed his fists on the hood, pounding the Jeep until his side ached, wanting to yell.

And to his shame, wanting to cry.

"Hey, Reaper!" Reece's voice cut through the blinding haze of raw emotion.

Gideon stopped beating the car and hauled in heavy breaths.

"You all right, man?" Reece asked.

Would he ever be all right again? "Fine. I'm fine."

Reece shook his head with a woeful look. "It's okay to hurt. It's okay to rage. I did a lot of both after my divorce. Still do. But right now, save your energy. You're going to need it."

Gideon nodded, needing to lock down all this messy stuff Willow brought spewing to the surface. This weakness. For Christ's sake, she'd brought Reaper to the cusp of blubbering like a baby. Not to mention had him thinking about himself in the third person.

Reece handed him a black duffel. "Gear up in the car. We'll sort through the rest later."

There was no sorting through how he'd demolished Willow. No sorting through how the miracle of her wanting to be with him felt like a mistake.

Gideon took the bag, resigned to his place in the world. Monsters didn't get happily-ever-after, even if they worked for the good guys. He hopped in the SUV. "Let's go do what we do best."

He stared at the Jeep as they pulled out of the lot, his heart crumbling to ashes. He'd been too dense to understand Kelli's perspective, to learn the lessons she'd tried to teach him.

Here he was, screwing up. Again. He loved Willow—and God, wasn't this the perfect way and time to figure it out—but hadn't given her the respect to let her choose, one way or the other, what she wanted for herself.

He didn't have time to fix it. Going out with his brain fuzzy and his heart conflicted was a surefire way to come back in a body bag, and right now, his only concern had to be saving Laurel and bagging Daedalus for real.

Squeezing his eyes shut, he cleared the zone—of Willow, mistakes, love—leaving nothing but the steady beat rapping away in his head.

43

This was Sanborn's Benedict Arnold?

Spotless personnel file. No red flags. The one person who knew the inner workings of black ops firsthand from experience and was the supervisor of analysis, privy to all current operations.

Through his suspended state of disbelief, the sting of betrayal still set his teeth on edge.

Desperate times called for him to do something unprecedented. In violation of protocol, he allowed topside security to enter the sub-facility. Sanborn didn't want Maddox or Daniel to be the ones to restrain Amanda. Too many messy emotional ties with those two.

Sanborn had ordered topside to haul Judas into Interrogation Room 1 with a Glock pointed at the back of her head and handcuff her. No explanation, not a word spoken to her.

He wanted her to squirm. He wanted her sweating bullets.

Now, thirty minutes later, he sat across the table from Amanda, studying her as she stared at the printouts of the damning evidence Willow had unearthed.

"Is it you?" Sanborn asked. "Are you Daedalus's insider?"

She didn't have a leg to stand on, and if she tried, there wasn't anything she could say to convince him that she wasn't guilty. But he was curious to see how she'd respond.

Amanda swallowed hard, her gaze staying lowered. "Yes, it's me."

Sanborn had expected feigned indignation, some smooth-tongued explanation. Not for her to take the high road of admission. Although she looked like a trapped animal eager to scurry into a deep, dark hole.

For the life of him, he didn't understand why. Amanda had been one of the good ones. An idealist with ironclad values willing to sacrifice for the sake of the country. She didn't have gambling debts, no high-end lifestyle that exceeded her means. She wasn't a greedy opportunist selling out her country for money and had been dedicated to the Gray Box—to him. Or so it'd seemed. It left him confused and rather vexed, his mind spinning with questions.

"How could you do it?" he asked. "You compromised Maddox on a mission. Endangered her life. I thought you two were as close as sisters. She's the godmother of your kid, for Christ's sake."

A pitiful tear slid down Amanda's cheek. She looked at the one-way glass, rightfully assuming Maddox was on the other side. "I swear on my life, I never wanted anything to happen to you. I knew someone dangerous was interested in the auction to buy a bioweapon. Once I leaked the information that a Gray Box operative would be there, I thought he'd back off. No sane person would've risked the heat and still gone to the auction."

"You gave that psychopath"—Sanborn stabbed the table with a finger—"Aleksander Novak, her home address."

"He wasn't supposed to hurt her." Amanda faced the glass again. "You're smart, Maddox. Always prepared. You never let your guard down, not even at home. Rather than him getting the drop on you, I thought for certain you would've killed him."

Did Amanda have any idea how much bigger this was? The magnitude of her actions? All that had been jeopardized?

"You nearly caused a whitewash," Sanborn said. "You risked the lives of a lot of good operatives. Not just Maddox. All of them trusted you. I trusted you."

Amanda's shoulders dropped, and she took a deep breath. "I'm sorry. If I could go back, do things differently, I would've…" She shook her head as if lost for words, tears falling down her cheeks. "I don't know. Everything I did was for my son. And I don't regret saving his life."

"Your son? What does Jackson have to do with this?"

"Daedalus got to me through Jaxi, shortly after he was diagnosed with leukemia." She whisked away tears, the restraints on her wrists jangling. "He approached me in the hospital after the doctor told me none of the treatments were working. Daedalus pretended to be a rep from a pharmaceutical company, running trials for an experimental drug that might help. He baited me. Reeled me in."

Sanborn recalled when her son had been diagnosed. The battery of treatments that had been tried and failed, little Jackson growing gaunt, losing his hair, the dark circles under his gentle eyes. Sanborn's heart had gone out to her. He'd encouraged her to take time off, but she'd said that work—the mission—kept her sane, and with help from her parents, she'd manage.

To think, he had admired her strength.

"Jackson responded to the drug therapy. He was eating again and had the strength to play. Weeks later, Daedalus said the drug was close to approval and we had to go through my insurance, but it wasn't covered. I couldn't afford it on my own, and the idea of losing my baby was unbearable. Daedalus befriended me, listened to my frustrations. Got me to trust him. One day, he asked me to tell him about where I worked, to give him a few harmless details to get my son back in the program."

More tears slipped and fell. She wiped them away, not once looking Sanborn in the eye—as if she couldn't bear to.

"I wrestled with telling you I'd been approached, but my son's life was on the line. His health started deteriorating again. I couldn't let him die." The waterworks went into high gear, turning into hiccupping sobs. She finally met his gaze. "Don't you understand?"

That was just it. Sanborn did understand, better than most. During his time with the CIA—long before the Gray Box had become his fate—he had lost his son, his only child, in an Agency mission gone wrong. There was no greater agony for a parent...other than being forced to watch that beautiful creature you loved more than anything in the world wither painfully at death's door first.

His eyes moistened at the memories. A swell of renewed grief washed away his anger, but he tamped down those murky emotions and stiffened to steel.

"How did Daedalus know you were vulnerable? How did he know to leverage your son against you?"

Amanda picked up the water from the table. The glass

shook in her hands, the clinking of the restraints like weird background music. "Daedalus built his network of spies—"

"Traitors," Sanborn corrected.

"He used a pyramid model. He recruited one, then had that person find one or two others who could be exploited. My ex—Todd, Jackson's father—gave Daedalus my name. He was my partner at the DEA. When I suspected Todd might be dirty, he ended our relationship, even though I was pregnant. Later, he apologized for compromising me with Daedalus but said it was the only way to possibly help Jackson."

Amanda kept talking, about how Daedalus had trained her at a facility in Montana. About how the bodies of those who refused to cooperate or who'd made mistakes were buried out there. About how Daedalus wanted to cement his foothold in the Gray Box by having a second spy.

"Did you give Daedalus any names?" Sanborn asked.

She squeezed her eyes shut as if ashamed, her face blotchy from crying. "One, but I knew it wouldn't pan out."

His gut tightened. "You gave him the name of someone from the Gray Box to leverage?"

Pursing her lips, she nodded.

His jaw hardened, nerves stretching thin. It wasn't enough that Amanda had compromised her best friend in the field—*dear God, how must Maddox feel?*—committed treason and murder and betrayed Sanborn's trust, but she had offered Daedalus a Gray Box name too? Someone else to be compromised and coerced and dragged into her mess?

"Who?"

"I'm sorry." Her voice cracked on a sob. "I never

wanted to put anyone else in the position that I was in. I'm so sorry."

The knot in his gut twisted. "Whose name did you give?" Sanborn pounded a fist on the table, rattling the glass of water.

A slow, sick misery pooled in Willow's stomach like raw sewage she wanted to expel as she listened to Sanborn's interrogation.

She pressed an unsteady hand to her forehead.

Nothing could be trusted. Not Amanda or the kindness she'd shown Willow. Not Gideon or the passion he made her feel. Willow couldn't even trust her own judgment.

Gideon had stared at her in the parking lot with cold, unfathomable eyes, his face hard-set, and had spoken to her as though she were a pest to be dismissed.

She hadn't meant for the conversation to take such a vicious turn. Talking to him seemed of the upmost importance after he avoided having any contact with her on the plane. She'd only wanted to reassure him that everything was still the same between them.

But it wasn't.

We don't fit.

She'd expected the words to leave his mouth, had braced to hear them. But she had been unprepared for the startling pain, the scathing embarrassment.

Her throat closed again, choking her as though someone had shoveled sand down her esophagus. She'd asked for the truth, and he'd given it to her. She pinched the back of her hand, chewing the inside of her lip—bit down hard on the sensitive flesh until copper hit her tongue.

Standing in the observation room with Maddox and Daniel behind the one-way glass was the only thing forcing Willow to hold herself together.

"I'm sorry." Amanda's voice cracked on a sob. "I never wanted to put anyone else in the position that I was in. I'm so sorry."

"Whose name did you give?" Sanborn pounded a fist on the table, rattling the glass of water.

Amanda raised her head slowly as though it weighed a hundred pounds. "Alistair Allen."

Sanborn's face contorted into a look of rage, and he hurled the water against the wall, shattering the glass. It sounded like a soul detonating.

The true nature of Alistair's circumstances was close-held. Everyone thought he'd been cast into exile from MI6, but in truth, British Intelligence presumed he was dead. The only reason Willow knew was because Sanborn had asked her to help clean up Alistair's digital footprint and discreetly move some of his assets. Any news that he was alive and well leaking out would spell big trouble in their little world of politics, espionage, and death.

"Amanda would've sold out any of us," Daniel said. "God, I can't believe she tried to kill you, Willow." He paced, shaking his head. "I'm sorry I gave you a hard time about your Pandora program. Amanda said if I pitched in, wrote an assessment, she'd give me additional responsibilities. She even encouraged me to follow *my gut*, to keep digging into your financials after Sanborn told me not to. Congratulated me on finding the deed to that villa in France. I'm such an idiot for letting her use me like that."

"It's not your fault," Willow said. "She used all of us."

Amanda was a ruthless manipulator who'd pulled everyone's strings.

"I hope Sanborn sends her to the Hole," Daniel said. "She deserves to be in a supermax and never see the light of day again."

The Hole was a classified supermax prison. Hell on earth in a cement box. The worst threats to national security went in and didn't come out.

"Everything Amanda did was to save Jackson," Maddox said in a low voice. "An innocent little boy."

"How can you defend her after what she did to you?" Daniel asked. "To Willow? To all of us?"

Sanborn shook his head in the other room, stark disappointment clear on his face. "Do you have any idea what you've done?"

"I didn't *want* to do any of it," Amanda said, her eyes swollen from crying, her voice brittle. "When I needed to leave the DEA to get a fresh start, you gave that to me. When Todd left me to have a baby by myself, all of you took me in and became my family. I care about every single person here. I'm so grateful for everything that you've done for me. And I love all of you. But I love my son more."

She wiped her face with the back of her hand.

"Willow?" Amanda stared at the glass, her entire body shaking as she sobbed. "I'm sorry for taking advantage of you and for sabotaging your car."

Willow turned her back to the one-way glass,

swallowing past the tightness in her throat. She wanted to believe Amanda, but this could all be an act.

"Maddox," Amanda said. "I understand if you hate me, but you're still Jaxi's godmother. Don't punish him for what I did wrong. Please. Let my parents know I'm in trouble. Give Jaxi a hug for me."

"Unbelievable!" Daniel threw his hands in the air. "She's still trying to manipulate you."

"We know about the next-generation locators you planted on Willow. Did you bring any other surveillance equipment inside the facility?" Sanborn asked.

"No," Amanda said.

Nonetheless, they'd have to research countermeasures for the stealth technology. No tech was unbeatable.

"You fool." Two low words from Sanborn leveled the room. "A person always has a choice. When Daedalus first approached you, if you'd come to me, I would've helped you. Instead, you spied on us. Committed murder. Sold out your country. Stabbed *me* in the back." His voice chilled Willow's heart. "You're going to rot in the Hole. I'm going to make sure you have a long, long life there."

"Yes!" Daniel cheered and clapped. "Justice."

"That's not justice," Maddox said.

Amanda crumbled into convulsive tears, hiding her face in her hands. Sanborn looked ready to spit fire and incinerate her, but a quick death was too good for her.

Sanborn stormed out of the room. Maddox threw open the door and darted into the hall after him. Willow stood on the threshold.

"If they bring Daedalus in alive," Maddox said, stopping Sanborn, "you'll need someone who can testify against him and turn state's evidence. And if they kill him, then Amanda might be the only one who could lead you to the other traitors in the government who worked for Daedalus. What she did was horrible. Unforgivable. But cut her a deal where she won't go to the Hole. That way, she can still see her son."

"You want to show her mercy after what she's done?"

"I want mercy for Jackson. Both of his parents are going to prison. And he can't visit her in the Hole. We could use her cooperation. Just consider it. Will you? Please."

Sanborn cut his gaze to Willow. "You're free to get out of here. Don't worry about doing any reports. I'm sure you want to see your father."

"Thank you, sir."

Sanborn stormed away and disappeared around the corner in the direction of his office.

"Would you mind giving me a ride to the hospital?" Willow asked Maddox.

"Of course. You must be dying to see him. I can break the bad news to Amanda's parents later."

The weight of the last few days pressed down on Willow, everything she'd been through, everything she'd done to survive. She'd killed a man. A fact she hadn't had time to deal with yet. Right now, she just wanted to get out of here and to the hospital. To see her dad, hold his hand.

Doc rushed down the corridor. "Is Sanborn still in the interrogation room?"

"No. Amanda confessed," Willow said. "He just went back to his office."

"One good thing from today." But Doc didn't sound or look relieved.

"What's wrong?" Maddox asked.

Doc pushed her long hair back behind an ear with a trembling hand. "I need to get into Fort Detrick and talk to someone in charge, but they won't let me on base."

Daniel came into the hall. "Why Fort Detrick?"

"The weaponized smallpox was made by us. Our government."

Willow shook her head. "President Nixon outlawed our biological weapons program."

"It shouldn't be possible." Doc pressed fingers to her temple like she was trying to keep her head from exploding. "But my source at CDC headquarters swears otherwise. A government contractor has been making bioweapons and shipping them to Fort Detrick. A shipment was hijacked, and a lot more than smallpox-M was stolen."

As if a mutated strain of smallpox wasn't enough.

"Any idea what else was taken?" Willow asked in a low voice.

"Not for certain. That's why I need to talk to someone at Fort Detrick. My source said there were whispers of souped-up anthrax and something called Z-1984."

"Anything starting with a *z* and ending with numbers sounds bad," Daniel said. "Not just epidemic bad but end-of-civilization bad."

"Once Sanborn gets you access," Maddox said, "you shouldn't go alone. Take Ares with you."

"Why does everyone keep trying to partner me up with *Whitlock*?" Doc spat his surname. "I don't need a partner, and if I did, he's the last person I'd choose."

Maddox raised her eyebrows. "Okay, but going alone isn't smart. Take someone with you. If I'm around, I'll go."

"Thanks." Doc nodded. "I need to update Sanborn." She rushed off down the hall.

Once Sanborn found out the American government was responsible for creating smallpox-M, he'd make this business with Amanda look like a Category 1 storm with a catastrophic 5 on the horizon. He'd once told Willow that he'd seen a lot of ugly things perpetrated by the government. It usually started under the umbrella of goodness, then something or someone took a vile turn. He was glad he no longer worked for the CIA and appreciated the freedom of heading up the Gray Box, where he could accept or reject any mission. There was going to be hell to pay for someone over those bioweapons.

But Willow was trapped in her own sort of tempest, and she couldn't afford to break down. Not while her father's and sister's lives hung in the balance.

44

NEAR THE POTOMAC RIVER, NORTHERN VIRGINIA
MONDAY, JULY 8, 6:22 P.M. EDT

Geared for war, Gideon and the rest of the team stormed the side of the hill overlooking the abandoned warehouse where Daedalus was holding Willow's sister captive. Adjacent to the Potomac River, the grassy ridge was steep and the earth muddy, but they ate up the terrain in steady strides.

Gideon flattened against the strategic crest of the hill, below the actual peak, where they had maximum visibility without advertising their position. The building was four stories high but appeared to have only two floors. The ground level had three-story-high windows and probably a thirty-foot ceiling. Two tactical helos sat on the roof. No fire escape was visible. That meant there was either one on the far north side or direct access to the roof from inside.

Peering through the Eagle Eye scope, he swept the two floors of the warehouse. Mercenaries in tactical gear crawled throughout the place. The top level was a wide-open space, similar to the bottom floor, but had office space in the far back. Gideon glimpsed a familiar face.

Omega was talking to a man in a suit who had his back to the window.

Fucking perfect. Gideon was a highly trained killing

machine who persevered through pain and never hesitated to take out a target. In hand-to-hand combat, he was not only formidable but also powerful. But he'd rather have his prostate checked than go another round with Omega.

Gideon went back to scoping out the place. There were open cases of weapons laid out on the first floor—they had an arsenal—and a fleet of black SUVs was parked outside.

He noted the tail numbers of the helos and relayed them back to Janet along with the team's status. "Also tell the chief we're going to need eyes in the sky."

Despite the abundance of satellites, not every swath of land was always covered, and it was easier to part the Red Sea than redirect one of those suckers. That garbage they showed in the movies—a click of a few buttons and a satellite zooms in on any location—was just that, a crock of shit.

Sanborn would tap and reposition one of the many federal surveillance drones spying on Americans every day.

"Got it," Janet said. "He just walked in. I'll let him know."

Gideon disconnected.

"Damn army down there," Castle said, lying in a prone position.

"Pishposh." Alistair's cavalier tone was too light for the circumstances, but that was him, all the time. "We've got this in the bag. SEALs knock out stuff like this for breakfast."

Castle nodded. Once a SEAL, always a SEAL.

"Reece, don't you Delta Force boys live for this shit?"

"Hooah," Reece replied, staying low to the ground.

Alistair nudged Ares with an elbow. "I know you're a little intimidated by the vast numbers down there. Don't worry. We'll protect you."

Ares chuckled—the sound sharp-edged, damn near homicidal—and flipped off Alistair.

Popping cinnamon gum in his mouth, Gideon said, "Remind me again what you're going to do?"

"Nice to see Reaper has recovered the power of speech since we landed." Alistair winked, then sighted through the scope of the crippler—a tympanic disruptor.

The weapon was patterned after a multiround grenade launcher, fitted with long-range scope but loaded with sonic charges that incapacitated anyone within hearing range.

A special toy courtesy of their weapons designer.

"I'm going to get this party started." Alistair fired, launching the tympanic disruptors around the north and east sides of the building, debilitating the armed men out front. Then he targeted each level, shooting devices onto every floor.

Everyone put in soundproof earplugs. Gideon flicked off his Maxim 9's safety. The last traces of distraction dissolved in a jolt of adrenaline. His pulse quickened, his muscles tightening in readiness.

They swept down the hill in a V formation, wearing sleek tac helmets, bulletproof vests, and gas masks in preparation to breach the entrance and pop smoke.

Within seconds, they were in position at the front of the building, facing south.

Men around the perimeter had dropped to their knees, covering their ears. Some rolled on the pavement, shaking as if on the verge of having a seizure. Gideon hated that Laurel was inside suffering along with these scumbags, but the sooner they got to her, the better.

Off his left flank, Castle and Reece took out the mercs

on the west side of the building in a controlled sweep of muzzle-suppressed fire.

Alistair and Ares planted trackers on the vehicles parked around the building as a contingency in case anyone slipped through their fingers. They prepared for everything.

A guy staggered out the main door, hands clamped to his ears, stumbling toward an SUV. Gideon put him down with a single shot to the head.

The team flattened up against the brick facade of the building on either side of the doors, and Reece whipped out stun grenades. A tap on Gideon's shoulder drew his attention to Ares pointing at three dead bodies—mercs who'd snuck up from the northeast side. Ares had clipped them, despite not being able to hear them close in.

Razor-sharp instincts made the team the best and helped keep them alive.

But how had the mercs managed to get that far with tympanic disruptors active?

Ares yanked out his earplugs with no side effects and signaled for them to do the same.

"What happened to the crippler?" Gideon asked.

Ares shook his head. "The devices wouldn't malfunction. Signal must be jammed."

Putting a communications earpiece in, Gideon checked one of the channels. No static. No pulses. But no chirp in response to the ping he'd sent through either, as though all signals had been swallowed into a perfect void.

The hairs on the back of his neck prickled. "A *smart* jammer."

He took out the security device that'd monitor the

mobile trackers. Bright red dots were lit up on the screen. It had GPS antijam tech, but he wanted to make sure it hadn't been affected.

"Something next-gen like that isn't easy to come by," Castle said. "It must be big and powerful if the radius can cover the entire warehouse."

Gideon backed up, testing the perimeter of the jammer. Fifteen feet out from the building, the next ping he sent through comms squawked in return.

He marked the zone with a hand signal for the others and hustled back.

"We're outmanned five to one," Castle said. "They're well-armed, and we just knocked."

"But I bet we're better-looking." Alistair's face was deadpan.

Gideon heaved a breath. "What's on the other side of the building? Is there a fire escape?" he asked Ares.

"There are a couple of parked cars and a fire escape from the roof down two stories with a pull-down ladder. It's old, rickety as shit, and not hanging on by much. I don't think it'll support any body weight."

"Okay. No way Laurel is on the ground floor. A sure bet the jammer is upstairs along with her and Daedalus. Ares and Reece, breach the rear doors on the north side." Reece was the best with demolition and could get them in quickly. "We'll enter here. It's going to be a combat zone. They're armed to the teeth. If we disable the jammer, we can end this cleaner and faster."

Everyone agreed and holstered their 9mms in their thigh rigs, opting to use their SIG MCX Rattlers instead. Since this was no longer going to be a simple walk-in and cleanup, they needed something with a greater kick. The suppressed compact submachine guns strapped across their backs were chambered in .300 Blackout rounds—hollow-point and subsonic with pretty sweet knockdown power.

"Let's do this," Castle said.

Ares and Reece went around to the other side.

It was rare for the team to work in such a large group, but when they did, they functioned like a well-oiled machine. Hardcore synergy.

Castle pulled the pins on two stun grenades from his pack and pitched both inside the building through broken windows. A barrage of bullets fired outside and sprayed the steel door. In five seconds, a devastating bang of 185 decibels and eleven million candelas of flash, followed by white smoke, would go off. Anyone standing close to it would have ruptured eardrums and temporary blindness, and everyone else would be distracted.

Try to jam that, motherfuckers. Gideon counted down with his hand. Five. Four.

The front doors to the warehouse blew off and a glowing projectile shot past them, hitting a tree. The trunk exploded into cinders.

Holy hell. They had RPGs.

The stun grenades inside detonated with a concussive boom.

They had to move now.

Gideon gave the go signal. He, Castle, and Alistair flowed inside, peeling off in different directions.

Dense smoke wafted throughout the entry of the industrial space, not reaching the high ceiling where metal ductwork ran in heavy rows. Dark figures skated in between concrete pillars and rectangular cases, digging in for the fight.

Gideon knew how his team would maneuver across the wide warehouse floor based on their special operations training and his years working alongside them.

He eased to the far wall, looking for a different angle to exploit.

There wasn't much to take cover behind. Risking exposure was necessary if he was going to find an avenue to gain the upper hand. He followed the path of the ductwork along the ceiling to a wall and series of pipes.

Gunfire came from the far side of the space. Controlled bursts, teams sweeping in toward the entrance where the rest of his team were no doubt picking off targets.

With signals jammed, they were operating in the dark from one another, but everyone was capable enough to pull off this op lacking comms without hitting a friendly. Even Alistair.

The one equalizer—the mercs were functioning blind too.

An explosion came from the north, followed by more automatic fire. Reece and Ares were in.

Gideon skirted the wall, scanning for hostiles, until he hit a barrier. A half wall, maybe an office or, from the heavy industrial look of the space, an old clean air room used to house special AC equipment.

He shook a pipe connected to the wall, testing the stability. Solid. He holstered his gun and scrabbled up, using the bolted brackets for footholds and handles. Sweat dripped from his forehead under the gas mask, rolling down his temples, pooling under his chin.

There was a four-foot gap between the pipe and office-type structure. He pushed off the pipe, grabbing onto the top of the self-contained space. Hoisting himself onto the roof, he didn't make a sound. Plenty of clearance to the ceiling, and the position was well above the cloud of smoke obscuring the front half of the space. The rest of the floor he could see clearly.

Gideon stood but stayed low and ripped off his mask to better survey things below.

Reece and Ares were quickly turning the foes in their vicinity into mincemeat.

Six dark-clad figures carrying tactical armored shields circled closer to Alistair and Castle, who'd already taken out five. Gideon locked sights on the two closest tangos. A couple of soft squeezes on the trigger and he took them out from behind. By the time he eliminated the rest, the team had moved toward the staircase.

Gideon jumped from the high structure, landing on the balls of his feet. Pain torpedoed his body and fatigue punched in, but he bottled it up and buried it for later. Hustling to catch up, he passed several open cases. Most were empty, but a few had heavy artillery, RPGs, and short-barreled shotguns. The shortest illegal barrel he'd ever seen. The decreased length made it more powerful and deadlier because the ammunition was propelled faster. He grabbed one, slinging it over his shoulder, and took an armored shield that had a triangular viewport.

Catching these guys by surprise came with unexpected benefits.

The corridor leading to the stairwell was free of smoke, and the others had lost their gas masks. Castle and Ares each had a Gray Box massive six-shot, revolver-style grenade launcher at the ready, both loaded with nonlethal pepper-spray projectiles.

Those mercs would be heavily dug in upstairs behind cover. The pepper-ball rounds didn't have to hit them, only go off close enough to fuck with them. Alistair had also swiped a tactical shield, probably from one of the dead guys.

Gideon took point, with the shield at the ready, and rounded the corner to the staircase with Reece on his six.

A wave of bullets rang out in a striking clang. Suppressive fire swept over the metal staircase to keep them from ascending.

Their team ducked back, taking cover. Reece pointed to his own eyes, then to the stairwell. Pulling out a telescoping-wand camera that allowed viewing without getting your head blown off, he ventured to the edge of the staircase to determine the location of the gunmen. Reece shifted the wand around the corner for a complete picture. He slipped back beside Gideon and used hand signals to communicate.

Two shooters. One at the top of the stairs. The second leaned over the railing. Taking turns with bursts of fire.

After the report, he slid out of the way, taking Gideon's shield.

Reece was a good shot. Decisive. Sharp. Gideon was faster, more precise.

Now that he knew the setup of the shooters, he listened for the pattern and the rate of fire. The man at the top had the best vantage point of the steps, making him the most dangerous. He needed to be eliminated first.

Waiting for his blink-of-an-eye window to open, Gideon

removed his helmet. He couldn't chance the gear getting in his way, throwing him off the slightest centimeter.

The bottom stairs cleared of gunfire for a breath, the shooters prepping to alternate bursts of shots. Gideon dove, sensing where to aim as much as sighting the targets. He fired and rolled, readjusting, and shot again. The first man slumped over the staircase with a slug in the forehead. The second took a bullet to the throat.

Gideon sprang to his feet and let Reece slip ahead of him, leading the way with the ballistic shield. They bounded up the stairs. Quick. Quiet.

The landing was a short hall, and the stairs faced the wide-open room beyond it, where every other merc was dug in. There was minimal space for their team to maneuver and hide. Whatever was waiting could hit them full force as they came up the stairs before they had a chance to take cover on either side of the double-wide doorway.

If only they didn't have an innocent civilian that they needed to get out alive, then Reece, their demolition guy, could've wired the place with explosives. *Kaboom.* End of Daedalus and Omega. End of story.

Bracing against the railing, Gideon put his helmet back on. "I didn't see Laurel when I scoped out the place. She must be in the far back office with Daedalus. Don't get crazy. We don't need her taking a stray bullet."

A round of acknowledging head nods.

Castle and Ares got into position near the top of the stairs. Both fired pepper-ball shells into the room, popped smoke, and ducked back.

A riot of gunfire kicked off. Copper-jacketed lead poured through the doorway, raining hot bullets on the stairwell.

Reece raised the ballistic shield. Gideon and Castle lined up behind him.

A tap on Reece's shoulder signaled *go*. They moved single file, crouched as one unit to the right of the doorway.

Alistair led the rest of the team behind his shield to the left.

They each took turns, exchanging fire with the mercs. Shots whistled overhead, pinging the railing and biting into the concrete wall on the other side. Gideon pumped three shells into the room, taking out one man and leaving him with two in the shotgun. Daedalus's men were dug in and picking them off like this would take forever. While Gideon's team continued their assault, he looked for a different angle of attack.

At the end of the short hall, he spotted a door. It was a tiny storage closet—mop, bucket, old cleaning supplies, rusty sink. Nothing useful.

Damn it. As he was about to rejoin the firefight, he spotted the vent on the wall near the ceiling. It was one of those eighteen-by-eighteen-inch industrial covers. He turned the mop bucket upside down and stood on it. Something inside the lockpicking kits they carried should work. He found a tool to fit in the grooves of the screws and removed them.

Taking off the slatted cover, he set it to the side. Gideon went back to update Reece.

"I found a vent," he said over the raucous hail of gunfire. "If I'm able to turn off the jammer, I'll let you know over comms. Then use the tympanic disruptors to shut these assholes down and end this shit."

"Roger that."

Gideon returned to the supply closet, adjusting the submachine gun on his back, and hoisted himself up into the darkness of the metal air duct. He belly-crawled through the square tunnel, going slowly, partly due to the constricted area but also so that his thigh rig, the tip of the Rattler on his back, and the shotgun in his hands didn't make any noise.

Not that it was easy to hear over the deafening staccato of the automatic-fire storm.

Gideon crept past two vents off the room with the bulk of Daedalus's men. Some were wiping their eyes and coughing. The pepper spray pellets were working, slowing them down and throwing them off their game. But their arsenal still presented a serious issue.

Someone was setting up an M2. The Ma Deuce was a .50-caliber heavy machine gun usually attached to vehicles and aircraft.

Gideon wished their comms were operational so he could warn the team.

Bypassing another duct that connected to the one he was in at a right angle, he finally made his way to the end of the air shaft and peered through the vent in the office. He couldn't see anyone or a device that looked like a jammer, but voices carried over the gunfire. A conversation, three men. It seemed to be coming from the right, back three feet down the cross vent. He squirmed and shimmied in reverse to the intersection and barely made the tight turn.

If he made any noise in the cramped space, not only would he lose the slight element of surprise, but he'd also draw gunfire.

Through the grate, he saw a filthy bathroom. A large window let in natural light.

A woman, bound and gagged with duct tape, sat in a chair. It had to be Laurel. She was alive. Other than a pink face puffy from crying and some smudges of dirt, she didn't appear hurt. But she was wearing a vest rigged with grenades.

Omega told one man to go wait by the chopper on the roof, and he sent the other guy, called Rho, back into the office. Then he spoke to the man in a dark suit responsible for all this violence. *Daedalus*. Same suave, upper-crust looks, slicked-back hair, and clean-shaven face from the photo that'd been in Gideon's digital case file two years ago. Only then he'd been identified as an asset, and another man—the wrong man—had been listed as Daedalus.

"I want you to go and take the woman with you," Omega said.

"I'm not leaving you." Daedalus put his hand on Omega's shoulder. "You don't know what it was like, wondering if you were alive or dead. It was torture. I won't go through that hell again."

"You've done it before. You can do it again."

"No. This time was different. The only way I leave is if you're with me."

"I won't leave my men to fight on our behalf while we slink off like cockroaches."

"Then it's settled. Neither of us will be a cockroach." He laughed, calm, self-assured, like this was any ordinary day. "We'll see this through together. Side by side."

"You can really be a stubborn dick sometimes."

Another caramel-smooth laugh. "That's what you love about me."

"No. It's not. Stay in here so I don't have to worry

about you taking a stray bullet." Omega left the bathroom, closing the door behind him.

Daedalus turned to Laurel, gun in his hand. "All that racket out there is over you."

Her glassy eyes went wide.

"And me, of course. I'm the star of this production. Do you want to know what'll happen if those men make it to you?"

Laurel shook her head like the answer was the last thing on earth she wanted to hear.

"I'm going to pull a pin on one of those grenades strapped to your vest. Then you're going to go pop!" He slammed his heel down on a bug crawling on the floor. "Just like that."

Laurel started crying.

There was no sign of the jammer in the bathroom from that angle. The only thing for certain was that he had to put down Omega first. If Gideon gave that bruiser the chance to get the drop on him, he wouldn't live long enough to regret it.

This small element of surprise was all he had, and he was going to make it count. He crept back to the main air duct rear first and reoriented himself at the T-juncture so that he had the advantage of seeing everyone's position in the room.

Rho stood behind a concrete column. "Our men are holding their own out there. The last car of guys will be here in five minutes. When they creep up behind those motherfuckers, this will be game over."

As if Gideon's team didn't have enough to contend with. Their attention would be focused on the ongoing assault, and the gunfire would mask the sound of anyone coming up on their six. He considered making the slug-slow crawl back to give them a heads-up, but it'd eat up precious time, and he might lose a possible window of opportunity to get into the office and finish this. Finding the jammer and disabling it would solve the problem.

Besides, the team had Ares. They'd manage.

"But I agree with you," Rho said. "The chopper is ready. It's better for Daedalus to wait this out someplace safe."

"He won't go without me, and before you say it, no. I agreed to this COA and I'm going to finish it. But I'll try to convince him to leave one last time."

Heavy footfalls headed back toward the bathroom.

"Hey," Rho said, moving a few feet away from the pillar, gifting Gideon with the right positioning for a shot. "Daedalus is the primary objective. We're supposed to do anything to protect him. Maybe that means setting your colossal ego to the side and getting the hell out of here with him."

"Fuck you." Omega's voice boomed underneath the intersecting ductway—four feet away. He would be to Gideon's five o'clock once he was out of the vent. "I'm not leaving you guys behind to fight our battle for us."

The heavy thud of boots hitting the floor resumed.

Gideon took the butt of the shotgun and popped out the vent. He shifted the angle of the weapon quickly and pulled the trigger, pumping a round of lead into Rho, up high near the throat. The force sent him sailing backward to the ground like a ragdoll.

Getting out of the air duct was part art, part math, and the rest was physics.

Moving with speed and agility that would make a ninja proud, Gideon dropped out of the vent, rolled, made it to his feet, and spun around with the shotgun raised.

Omega descended upon Gideon like the damn apocalypse.

There wasn't time to pump the shotgun, loading another shell, aim, and fire. Gideon flipped the short-barreled weapon in his hands and swung it like a baseball bat.

The metal butt connected with a steel chin. Omega stumbled but grabbed the gun with both hands, and Gideon found himself in the unfortunate position of being on the wrong end of the barrel.

Omega's finger slid to the trigger. Gideon moved his head out of the way just in time. The shotgun blasted a hole in the door instead of his skull.

The .50-cal in the other room was in full gear, taking out chunks of the cinder block wall Gideon's team was using as cover.

Adrenaline spiked. Gideon swung his right elbow up and around, thrusting it hard into Omega's head. The guy was strong and didn't release his grip on the weapon despite the blood that had been drawn.

Gideon twisted the barrel with his left hand and slammed his palm up into the bruiser's nose. Blood flowed, and the big guy's grip loosened on the shotgun, but then Omega threw a knee into Gideon's injured side again and again.

Skin tore around the staples, the wound reopening. Omega secured a hold on the shotgun and yanked it away. Gideon reeled back into a roundhouse kick, driving his foot forward and knocking the gun from Omega's hands.

But the maneuver cost him. A shockwave of scorching pain radiated along his wounded side.

Somehow Gideon drew his Maxim 9 from his holster thigh. Yet Omega was right on top of him, matching him move for move, and whipped his forearm up, jarring the Maxim loose from Gideon's grip. It went spinning to the right onto the floor.

Neither man stopped or slowed. Vicious blows volleyed back and forth. For a nanosecond, the inevitability of this moment registered. They were two high-speed trains locked on a collision course.

Gideon couldn't afford to lose, couldn't afford to give an inch.

Driven. All the way.

He hammered on the merc, but the big guy stayed with him. He hurled a blow at the bruiser's face, and his fist glanced off Omega's cheek. A solid knee to the groin only elicited a grunt. Gideon kicked and punched, threw elbow strikes and headbutts, every move designed to bring pain and break bones.

But none of it mattered.

He had met an immovable object.

45

NEAR THE POTOMAC RIVER, NORTHERN VIRGINIA
MONDAY, JULY 8, 7:06 P.M. EDT

Gideon took an almighty punch that should've rendered him unconscious.

His head spun, right along with his brain. The taste of metallic salt hit his tongue. It was like he'd been slugged by a two-by-four.

Omega picked up Gideon by the collar and groin, hoisting him in the air, and bulled him against the wall, shattering the window. He went down like a sack of cement, the brutal impact jarring his bones and teeth. Glass shards cascaded over him.

Dazed, Gideon scrambled to his feet, his vision blurry and instinct driving him to run. But Omega was faster and charged, power-driving Gideon into the stone pillar. A rib cracked. Liquid warmth seeped from the gash in his gut. Excruciating agony poured through him, weakening his entire body. He slid to the floor in a battered heap.

Heavy footfalls drew away from him in the ticktock rhythm of a countdown to the end. Gideon prayed it wasn't the end of him. Light winked off the glass covering the Maxim 9 four feet, maybe five, off to the side. Might as well have been fifty while he was waylaid by the full-body ache holding dominion over him.

Gideon dragged himself upright, and white light bloomed behind his eyes. He leaned against the column, the MCX Rattler strapped to him digging into his spine.

His vision cleared to the sight of Omega picking up and pumping the shotgun.

Gideon slipped the submachine gun off his back, fumbling to take aim. Omega turned, and the next shot blew the SIG from Gideon's hands and sent it skittering far out of reach.

A gleam brightened Omega's feral eyes as he pumped the shotgun once more.

But it was Gideon who smiled. He'd been counting, and he knew something Omega didn't. The shotgun was out of shells.

Gideon spied his gun beneath the shards of glass. He rolled for it.

Click! An empty sound followed by silence as Omega realized the gun was no longer loaded. Glass bit into Gideon's arms and hands, and he flipped over, leveling the gun at Omega.

Their gazes met. Gideon slid his finger to the trigger. There was a flicker of realization—a glint of *oh shit* in Omega's eyes. And Gideon fired, getting him in the face.

Omega's head snapped back and he dropped.

A quiver sliced through Gideon. He was alive, barely. His enormous relief collided with reality. This was far from over.

He climbed to his feet, steeling himself to finish this, and scanned the room. No sign of the jammer, but he spotted a ladder along the far wall leading to the roof.

WWIII was in full swing in the other room.

He walked toward the bathroom, wishing he had Reece at his side.

His brother-in-arms was not only an artist at blowing shit up and defusing bombs, but he also did hostage rescue.

It took Gideon several breaths to come down from the angry high of the fistfight.

New pain—deeper, soul-numbing agony—surfaced. He looked down. His side was bleeding, badly. He needed to hurry.

Gideon pushed down the handle of the bathroom door and opened it.

Daedalus stood, using his hostage as a human shield, the barrel of his Beretta Storm pressed to her head.

Laurel trembled. Up close, she was an older, washed-out version of Willow.

Gideon's gaze flickered for a second to the table that had been out of his view from the air duct. A metal box the size of a large suitcase was in the center next to bottles of water and extra ammo. The jammer.

"Omega!" Daedalus called out, staying behind Laurel.

"He's dead."

"Vincent!" Daedalus narrowed his eyes, jaw hardening, voice turning strident. "Vincent!"

"It's not pretty either. Right in the face. No open casket. Sorry about that."

Gideon sensed the tension shift—that deadly quiet before the storm. All expression fell from Daedalus's face, but seething anger burned in his eyes. Gideon expected an explosion of emotion, an outpouring of rage, some rash act of grief that he could take advantage of.

Instead, Daedalus stood with the gun steady in his hand, pointed at Laurel, nodding to himself in an eerie manner Gideon didn't quite understand. Then he said in the calmest voice, "Drop your gun, Agent Stone, or I'll put a bullet in her."

"If you do, I'll put a bullet in you. Somewhere painful. Not as quick as the face."

Daedalus didn't answer for a moment, a flash of anguish leaking through. "Do you think I care about dying now that Vincent is gone?"

"Yeah, I do. Everyone cares about dying. Prove me wrong and step away from the woman."

Daedalus jammed the muzzle into the back of Laurel's head, not leaving an inch of himself exposed. She whimpered, tears streaming down her face.

"Test me and you'll lose. I'll make sure she doesn't get an open casket either. Drop it."

Testing this man might be a mistake, and Gideon wasn't going to gamble with Laurel's life. He tossed the weapon to the floor only a foot away, within easy reach. Maybe Daedalus would be too bereft to pay attention.

"Kick it toward the door."

No such luck. Gideon did as instructed.

Daedalus moved with Laurel to the doorway. She shook so violently, she stumbled every step. He picked up the Maxim 9 and stuffed it in his waistband.

Gideon stepped back as if playing the cooperation game, but all the time, he was getting closer to the jammer.

Daedalus glanced at Omega's body, not long enough for Gideon to make a move, but it was plenty of time to light a fuse in a madman. When Daedalus stared back at Gideon, the guy looked like a junkyard dog, gnawing at the bit to tear something apart. He took aim at Gideon.

"Hold still." Daedalus's voice was measured, and the gun didn't waver a centimeter.

"Why?" Gideon braced, already knowing the answer, but the question had slipped out nonetheless.

"If you try to play dodge the bullet, I might hit you in a vital organ, and I'm not ready for you to bleed out."

Before Gideon responded, Daedalus fired.

Searing pain ripped through Gideon's flesh. "Son of a…" He snapped his jaw shut, not wanting to show that bastard how much it hurt.

The bullet only grazed his upper thigh, near his hip, thanks to quick reflexes. It simply wasn't in him to stand there and be shot.

Still, fire sang through his leg. He doubled over, and a line of sweat ran down his spine.

"I'm glad that hurts. Now you feel an inkling of my misery," Daedalus said. "I'm not going to kill you just yet. Do you want to know why?"

"I bet you ask a lot of questions that you're just going to answer yourself," Gideon said through clenched teeth.

Daedalus laughed, but it sounded bitter, savage. "I'm going to take away two things that you love first."

"What's that? My sanity and second amendment rights? So far, so good. This chitchat is driving me crazy." He swallowed a groan and leaned against the table.

"For starters, Hannah Davis."

Gideon's blood turned to slush. Anything he said, Daedalus would use against him, and there was no point in acting ridiculous by trying to deny his relationship with Hannah.

Daedalus knew full well who Hannah was and what she meant to him.

Amanda had overheard Gideon on the phone once, telling Hannah that he missed her and to take care. The traitor had joked how his wife would be jealous, and he'd let it slip that the person on the end of the line was like a mother to him. Amanda must've found her somehow.

"That's right. I know all about Hannah, down to where she is at this moment. Do you?"

Shit. He hadn't talked to Hannah in weeks. The last time they'd spoken, she'd said something about taking another cruise with her girlfriends.

Was she already on it? Had she gotten back? Had she left yet? He didn't even know what port she was using. Sometimes it was Norfolk, sometimes Tampa.

"I'm responsible for your wife's death. The brake failure on your truck," Daedalus said. "The handiwork of my Gray Box insider, Cobalt."

"You mean Amanda Woodrow. We found your mole. She's going to go to prison for a very long time, right along with you."

"Arrest me. I'll make one phone call and be released within twenty-four hours. You short-sighted fool. You have no idea how this is going to end."

Daedalus must have someone pretty high up and powerful on his payroll if he wasn't afraid of doing jail time. How deep did this go?

"Did you think Amanda was my ace in the hole? Speaking of which, she knows you very well. It seems you love your job at the Gray Box more than you ever did with the CIA. You found a home there, a place where you feel appreciated."

Dear God, Amanda. What have you done, letting this megalomaniac into the back doors of our heads? It was true. The Gray Box gave him a sense of belonging and fulfillment he'd never had at the CIA.

"Strip you of being an operative, a government-sanctioned killer, and what are you? *Nothing.* After I'm finished with Hannah—by the way, it'll be slow, and I plan to use my own two hands—I'm going to kill the Gray Box."

Gideon stilled.

"First, in the court of public opinion. I have a lovely dossier on missions stateside and overseas that the media will have a feeding frenzy over. That rabble will be like a pack of starved jackals tearing you all to pieces. Your faces and names are going to be splashed across every news outlet around the world. And this country that you love and fight for will turn on you."

If their covers were blown and true identities thrown out there, that would be the end of any clandestine work. No one would hire them—government or private security. What else were they good at? Not to mention every baddie with a grudge against them would come calling for payback.

They'd spend the rest of their lives looking over their shoulders and sleeping with one eye open.

"Then I'll squeeze the senator in my pocket to take action," Daedalus said. "And when I'm sure that you're truly suffering, with nothing left, not even your sanity, I'll pay you a visit."

Daedalus shoved Laurel into the bathroom, and she scurried next to Gideon.

"Time to catch my flight." Daedalus's gaze darted to the big, heavy box on the table that probably weighed a good sixty pounds.

He wasn't getting that sucker up the ladder to the roof on his own. Might tear his suit and break out in a sweat in the process.

"If you want to keep her alive," Daedalus said, gesturing to Laurel, "I suggest you don't touch the jammer." He pulled out a handheld remote detonator from his pocket. "I had a sophisticated explosive device implanted in her. *That* is the only thing blocking the signal and keeping me from blowing off her head. The grenade vest was a crude improvisation."

Gideon looked at Laurel. "Is that true?"

With frantic eyes, she nodded, mumbling something incomprehensible through her gag.

Damn. The whole plan just went to hell.

"I'll be sure to give Hannah your regards." Daedalus narrowed his eyes in a look that was pure evil. "No open casket. Then again, I'm not sure there'll be enough of her left to bury." He let the door swing closed.

Something rattled and clanked against it.

Gideon limped over and tugged at the door. The handle was stuck on something. Gideon tried again, this time hoping to shift whatever was blocking the lever.

On each furious yank, the handle only clanked against the object on the other side.

Gideon scrubbed his hands over his head, wanting to tear the door from its hinges.

Garbled noises came from Laurel. He staggered to her, unstrapped the explosive vest, and began cutting the tape binding her wrists.

The sound of rotor blades starting up overlapped with gunfire.

He glanced at the grate to the air duct and considered an agonizing belly crawl in the cramped space with a tight turn and his leg and side both bleeding. It'd take him five minutes of inching along, and then he'd still have to get downstairs. He needed to get out of that room fast. Right now.

Laurel's hands were finally free. She pulled the tape from her mouth. "W-w-who are you? SWAT?"

"I'm Gideon." He went to the window and jiggled it until layers of old paint and rust gave way and it opened. "I work with your sister."

"You? I thought Willow worked with a bunch of brainy analysts. She ran off with some decoder guy. Is she okay?"

"She ran off with me. She's fine."

Clearly, she was surprised by the news. "It was a work thing related to this? Not a romantic thing, right?"

A work thing that turned into a romantic thing. "It's complicated." He glanced down at the four-story drop and ten feet over at the dilapidated fire escape.

Laurel looked out the window. "You're not going to jump, are you? That fall will kill you."

"Not from this height." He climbed out the window onto the ledge, hissing from the sharp pang in his leg and his side and, well, just about everywhere. "Worst case, I'd break something."

She stared at him wide-eyed like he was insane. "You can't leave me here. What about the device he implanted in me?" She pointed to a bandaged area on the back of her neck.

"Demolition will take care of it. John Reece will help you." If they ever made it through the war zone. He dug into his pocket and handed her an extra set of earplugs.

"What are these for?" she asked.

He hopped to the next window ledge, landing on his good leg. "On my signal, I need you to flip the switch on the jammer. Then put those earplugs in."

"No, no!" She stuck her head out the window, waving her hands. "Daedalus will kill me."

"Not if I kill him first." He stared at the shaky fire escape, now six feet away. The metal staircase swayed in the breeze. That wasn't a good sign.

The telltale *thwopping* sound cranked to full speed. They were preparing to take off.

"There's no time to argue," he snapped. "When you hear a huge explosion, it means the chopper is down and he's dead."

Gideon poised to jump, took a deep a breath and—

"Wait! Wait! What if he parachutes out or something? Then I'll still go pop!"

Jeez. Her fears were legit, but they didn't have time for this.

"I'll come back to the window to confirm. But you have to shut off the jammer. If you don't, the rest of my team isn't going to make it, including the one man who can take that device out of your neck without your head exploding."

Laurel nodded like she understood that more than her own life was at stake.

He leaped to the fire escape, catching hold of the top railing and using the bottom metal bar to support his feet.

Pain burst through his body, but the metal platform gave a startling jerk, stealing his full focus. A metallic groan bled over the fading *thump, thump* of the rotor blades.

The helicopter was airborne. Daedalus was getting away.

The steel apparatus creaked and groaned, tottering as though it would collapse at any second. Rusty bolts connecting the staircase to the brick wall popped out, and the emergency stairs wobbled.

Gideon shifted his weight a hair of a fraction.

In a loud screech of old metal, the fire escape gave way. The joints folded in, the last of the bolts popped from the wall, and the staircase buckled.

Laurel screamed.

Gideon jumped just before the platform crashed, sending up a cloud of dirt. Landing with too much weight on his injured leg, his ankle twisted. He tucked into a roll away from the wreckage, but he couldn't take in enough air to make sound.

Laurel was still screaming. "Oh God. Oh God. Are you okay?"

He dragged himself upright, shifting his weight to his right leg with a grunt, and gave Laurel a weak thumbs-up. He hobbled inside the building through the rear doors Reece had blown open.

Pressing a hand to his leg, he ran as fast as his injuries allowed, more of a hurried limp really. Sheer determination and rage fueled him. Daedalus wanted to take away Hannah and destroy the Gray Box. Gideon was going to take his life.

He found one of the cases he'd passed earlier, swiped an RPG, and hustled outside.

Not pain, not fatigue, nothing would stand in his way. *Nothing.*

He pushed the gut-wrenching hurt in his body from his mind and ignored the warm, sticky blood seeping from his abdomen and leg.

Backing up from the building, he searched the sky. He used his ears as well as his eyes. His heart went from a furious pounding to a desperate throb in the hollow of his throat.

There! To the east, he spotted the helicopter. It was within range.

Taking Daedalus in alive and squeezing every dirty secret out of him before killing him would've been better for the Gray Box and the country. But that fucker had murdered his wife and threatened Willow and now Hannah. Daedalus had the resources and the motivation to keep coming after Gideon until he made good on his promise to take away what he loved.

Daedalus had to die.

Gideon opened the sights and the grips on the yard-long firing tube and removed the safety cap from the tip of the rocket.

Dropping to a knee in the grass and wincing from the agony, he put the antitank grenade launcher on his shoulder.

He had to get this right. If he missed and Daedalus lived…

No. That was not going to happen.

The target was almost out of range. Cocking the

hammer, he closed his left eye. He lined up the sight with his right. Sweat dripped from his forehead, stinging his cornea. His vision darkened, and he shook it off. He focused on the beat of his internal metronome.

He wiped his face with the back of his hand, then scrubbed his palm on his pants.

The slightest jerk, the tiniest slip of his finger would throw off the shot. For the kill, he had to be dead-on. No mistakes.

Panic bloomed as his window of opportunity narrowed. He reacquired the target in his sights and inhaled. The acquisition display beeped. A tiny red light flashed. The helicopter had just slipped out of range. If he fired now, he'd hit nothing.

His chest heaved. He set the RPG on the ground. This couldn't be over, not like this.

When you go into a fight, it isn't to lose. You don't stop. Go all the way. Ben's words were so loud in Gideon's head, it was as if he were beside him. He couldn't succumb to defeat.

Daedalus was due a comeuppance and Gideon was going to be the one to give it to him. Today.

The drone. Gideon had the chopper's tail number and hopefully the drone was overhead somewhere. They could track that slippery bastard and still end this.

Gideon estimated his position on the ground was about thirty feet from the building, far enough outside the range of the jammer, and got on comms to the Gray Box. "Do we have a drone on site?"

"Yes," Sanborn said.

Gideon didn't bother looking for the small UAV. "Patch me through to the operator. Now."

"Hold," Sanborn said, trusting him and not wasting time asking for an explanation.

Gideon loved him for that. His breath came in ragged pants. The pain and the sting of his mistake burned through him.

"This is Jeff Pratt with—"

"Do you have a visual on an EC155?" Gideon asked, adding in the tail number.

"Yes, sir," Jeff said over comms. "It's headed due east."

"Track it. Don't lose it. No matter what."

"Are you certain you want me to leave the area, sir?"

Was this dipshit listening? "Yes! Yes. Follow the helicopter. If it lands, the passenger is the priority. Don't lose the passenger."

"Sir, please be advised, there is no passenger."

Gideon's heart squeezed, the air in his lungs stalled. "What do you mean?"

There had to be a passenger. Daedalus went to the roof and got on that chopper. He must have. There was no other way out of the building for him besides going through the rest of Gideon's team.

Did Daedalus turn into fucking Houdini?

"A man wearing a suit boarded the helicopter on the roof, but the chopper set down in front of the building and let him out. He's in a car headed south. Do you still want me to track the helo? Over."

Daedalus had expected them to track the helicopter. The range on that detonator wasn't infinite. A few miles out, Daedalus must have anticipated Gideon would flip the switch on the jammer, their guys would end the firestorm, and they'd seek support to locate the helo.

Of course, Daedalus decided to do what wasn't obvious and not be on it, so their team would be chasing their own tail.

Only Gideon had the foresight to already have eyes in the sky.

He grabbed the RPG and raced around to the other side of the building in a running hop, dragging his leg. He spotted the SUV, tearing down a road, leaving a dust trail behind it.

Gideon lowered to a knee, propped the tube on his shoulder, and lined up the crosshairs on the vehicle. "I've got you now, slippery bastard."

"Sir, are you talking to me?" Jeff asked.

"No, but I'm sorry for calling you a dipshit in my head." Gideon tightened his grip on the tube and applied smooth pressure to the trigger.

A roaring *whoosh* erupted, and the projectile launched in a blaze of fiery light. The rocket streaked toward the SUV, ripping through the air with a whizzing sound.

He held his breath, every muscle clenched tight as a bowstring.

Direct contact. The car jumped into the air as it exploded into flames. The SUV went up in a fireball that flipped and dropped to the ground.

Nothing had survived that.

No open casket for you either, asshole.

46

NEAR THE POTOMAC RIVER, NORTHERN VIRGINIA
MONDAY, JULY 8, 7:25 P.M. EDT

Gideon got up from the ground. Dizziness waylaid him, and the world spun for a second. Once the ground stopped seesawing, he began hobbling back around the building.

"Thanks, Jeff. Track the helicopter. We want the pilot too." None of Daedalus's employees were going to escape scot-free.

"Roger that, sir."

Gideon switched comms channels and reached the bathroom window. "Laurel!"

She stuck her head outside. "Is he dead?"

"Yes," he said, winded.

"Are you sure? I want to go home to my kids, not get decapitated."

"Hundred percent certain." He bent over, bracing one hand on his knee and trying to slow the bleeding from his abdomen with the other. "Shut the jammer off. Please!"

"Okay." She ducked inside.

Seconds later, a crackle resounded over the airwaves. "We're a go. We're a go," he said into his throat mic, giving the team the signal.

"It's so much more fun being a winner," Alistair said over the earpiece.

"More of Daedalus's men were headed back your way. They should've hit you guys by now."

"Yeah. Ares took care of them. That show-off," Alistair said. "Let's finish this. On my count. Five seconds."

"Hey, Allie, do me a favor?" Gideon's voice was shaky, his limbs starting to tremble.

"What's that?"

"Don't let me bleed out, and don't tell Willow that I'm in the hospital."

"I knew you guys were shagging. And that'd be two favors. Can't you count? Speaking of which, three, two…"

Gideon stumbled away from the building, putting in his earplugs.

He was so tired, bone-weary from exhaustion and blood loss. Weakness threaded through his legs, and his knees buckled. The last thing he saw was Willow's face in the sky before everything hazed white.

SAINT MARGARET'S HOSPITAL, VIENNA, VIRGINIA
MONDAY, JULY 8, 9:20 P.M. EDT

Willow sat in a chair at her father's bedside, singing the Frank Sinatra version of "That's Life."

She held his hand, crooning the brave lyrics, desperate to soak up a fraction of the courage and strength in the words.

The doctors had found a high concentration of methyl iodide in her dad's bloodstream, which caused his coma. In order to treat him, they'd been forced to stop the medication for his Hodgkin's and wait for it to leave his system.

His condition improved, and he'd been moved from the ICU that afternoon. According to the doctor, he was no longer in the worst stage of a coma and was in what they considered a minimally conscious state. An encouraging sign that he'd eventually wake up and might make a full recovery from the poisoning, but they wouldn't know for certain until he opened his eyes.

Maddox had been great, bringing her coffee, convincing the nurses to let Willow stay past visiting hours, paying to have the television in his private room turned on so he could watch his favorite shows when he woke up, giving her uninterrupted time with her dad. Maddox was out in the hall like a vigilant sentinel alongside the police detail who were still assigned to watch Willow's dad.

Willow pressed her forehead to the back of her dad's hand. She was scraped bare, with nothing left. Not her wallet. None of her identification. Not even her mother's pearls.

Or Gideon.

Everything inside her ached. She shut her eyes, fighting the pain hemorrhaging through her. "You're going to be okay, Daddy. You have to be."

The door opened.

She didn't look over to square off with the nurse about having more time. "I know it's past visiting hours and I have to go. Can I just have five more minutes please?"

"Willow?"

She swiveled in her chair, facing the door. It was

Laurel. Her sister looked as if she'd been dragged through the streets by her hair.

"Oh my God, Laurel." Willow shot to her feet. "Are you okay?"

Her sister nodded. "The people you work with rescued me. I'm fine, now."

She didn't look fine, not in the least.

"Your hair color," Laurel said. "It's different, but nice."

"I had to change it."

"I like the red on you." Laurel looked at their father. "How's Dad?"

"Better. He's still unconscious, but he's responding to the medication and the doctor is hopeful that he'll make a full recovery." Willow wrung her hands. "I'm so sorry you were kidnapped. It's all my fault. This never would've happened to you if I hadn't called and forced you to come take care of Dad."

Laurel opened her arms and eased in slowly. In her mind, Willow comprehended what was happening, but when her sister gave her a solid, warm embrace, it left her shell-shocked.

"It's not your fault. Your...*team* explained everything. I'm the one who's sorry."

"For what?"

Laurel pulled back and met Willow's eyes. "For being such a selfish bitch. For underestimating you and not giving you near enough credit. You've taken care of Dad on your own all these years and I shouldn't have made you feel like you were imposing when you asked me for help."

That was the first time Laurel had apologized for anything. Her big sister always twisted reality into a pretzel so it was someone else's fault. "Did you hit your head? Were you checked for a concussion?"

Laurel gave a dry laugh. "I don't have a head injury. I've just had a wake-up call." She went over to their father and kissed him on the forehead. "The nurse said we have to leave."

Willow nodded. "Did Gideon bring you here?"

"Um, no." Laurel looked back at their father and rubbed his hand. "John Reece brought me."

"Why didn't Gideon come? Is he okay? I mean, is everyone on the team all right?"

Laurel stared at her in the most peculiar way—her lips parting but no sound coming out—Willow didn't know what to make of it.

Her heart pounded in her throat. What if something had happened to Gideon? He was already injured and had put his body through more than he should've.

"Everyone is safe," Laurel finally said.

Willow exhaled with relief. Thank goodness he was safe. He might not want her or love her, but she didn't know what she would do if something had happened to him.

"Come on," Laurel said.

Willow nodded and kissed her dad on the cheek. "I love you to the moon and back. I'll see you tomorrow morning."

A flutter of a smile whispered across her dad's face, but then it was gone.

"I think he just smiled," she said. "The nurse said hopefully we'll start getting consistent responses from him soon and that I should keep singing and talking to him. Hearing a familiar voice is good for him."

Laurel ushered Willow out of the room.

In the hall, Maddox was waiting and talking to Reece near the elevators.

"I have to go home to see the girls. And Richard." Laurel's mouth twisted like she was sucking on a lemon. "John kindly offered to drive me back to Connecticut."

John? No one called Reece by his first name. Willow didn't understand why. It was one of those former military-isms that she didn't get.

"He saved my life. Gideon too. The whole team. But John removed an explosive device from my neck." She winced and pointed to the bandage. "He made it seem so easy, talking to me the entire time, making sure I didn't freak out. I'll buy him a first-class ticket to DC in the morning. He's such a sweet man. They're all great." Laurel rubbed her arm. "Every single one of them, really. Listen, I want you and Dad to come up for Thanksgiving. I know the invitation might sound premature with Dad's current state, but I believe he's going to pull through this and I want you both to come for the holidays."

Once Dad recovered, that was the last suggestion he'd want to entertain. "I don't think that would be a good idea."

"The things I said to you on the phone, that I could've been a better sister—I meant it. Dad and Mom always gave you so much attention. I resented you. And I was jealous because you were Dad's favorite. Maybe it was that you were the baby, or you looked the most like Mom, or the way you doted on him like he was your personal hero. I know that was awful of me, petty. Sometimes I felt like they only noticed me if I acted out."

Her sister had been wretched at times, but Willow

hadn't realized Laurel had been hurting in her own way. "I'm sorry, Laurel. I could've been a better sister too."

"I was the oldest and I knew better. You did nothing wrong." Laurel cupped Willow's arm. "Come for the holidays. It'll be different this time. I promise. I'm going to invite Ivy and Delphine. And if there's anyone special you want to bring, they're more than welcome to come."

Willow's stomach knotted in degrees, thoughts spilling through her head. The caresses, the kisses, the sweet words. She'd had someone *special*…for two whole days. Two. Now, he wanted nothing to do with her. The mission was over and so was his interest in her.

Her muscles tensed in the stilted silence.

"Let's go." Laurel walked over to Reece and Maddox.

Willow followed, unable to shake the sense of displacement. She had no home to go to.

"Ready to get on the road?" Reece asked.

"Yes." Laurel kissed Willow on the cheek. "I'm a masterpiece in progress. Bear with me, okay?"

Willow nodded. "Have a safe drive. And Reece, thanks for taking my sister home."

"Of course. No problem," he said.

Reece and Laurel took the first elevator and went up to the top walkway connected to the garage. Maddox and Willow caught the next one going down.

"Have you talked to Gideon?" Willow asked, staring at the elevator display.

"After Reece arrived, I called him and we spoke briefly."

"He didn't want to talk to me," Willow said. "Did he?"

"Gideon wants you to focus on your father and putting your life back together." Maddox cleared her throat. "You need someplace to stay. My condo is vacant and partially furnished."

As soon as Maddox had reunited with Cole, they'd gotten engaged and she'd moved into his place. Maddox was the only one in Black Ops who had a partner and love in her life. She was like a unicorn.

"Why don't you stay there, as long as you need?"

Grateful, Willow nodded. "Thank you."

They left the hospital together. The air outside reeked of moisture, a dankness that smacked of a storm on the way.

"I appreciate how patient you've been," Willow said. "It's late. I'm sure you'd rather be home with Cole."

"It's no problem. Really." Maddox hit her key fob, unlocking the car doors. "We should swing by a store and pick up things you'll need. Toiletries. Clothes. My treat—well, it's on Black Ops. The others will chip in."

"What? It's too much. I can't let you guys pay for that stuff." Willow should've thought to ask Laurel for a loan.

"You can, and you will. You survived a trial by fire with Gideon, and that makes you one of us. We're here for you."

"That's incredibly generous. Thank you. I don't know what to say."

"No need to say anything."

They hopped inside the car. Strange how bad circumstances brought people together. Willow's mind careened back to Gideon and all they'd survived and shared. Emptiness gnawed at the pit of her stomach.

Lightning sliced the black sky. In the distance, thunder rumbled. The first drops of rain popped against the car, echoing in her chest. Tears stung her eyes. Maddox's generosity overwhelmed her, but the incoming tide of heartache made her want to cry.

How could she bear to look at Gideon in the office? Every time she passed him in the hall or worked with him on an assignment, the wound would fester and spread like gangrene.

She shivered.

"Are you cold?" Maddox asked. "I can turn on the heat."

"No. I'm not cold. Did Gideon say why he didn't want to talk to me?"

Maddox turned the radio on low. "I don't know what happened while you two were on the run, but I can guess. If he's distant now, don't take it personally. He just doesn't form attachments."

"But he did. We did." A mind-blowing, life-altering bond that had changed her forever. And it wasn't one-sided. Of that she was certain.

"Maybe you read into things." Maddox shrugged. "Took it for more than good sex."

Willow didn't know much about men or relationships, but she knew, down in her soul, what they'd shared had been an amazing connection. Over the last few days, she'd seen the many facets of Gideon—from Reaper, the hardened assassin, to the gentle lover who'd opened a new world of sensation. More than that, he was the one person she'd ever been herself around. No inhibitions. No limits. No pretense. The sense of belonging and intimacy had been real.

The rain picked up to a torrent. She pressed the heels of her palms into her eyes. What if the things he'd said, the way he'd touched her was all part of his charm and meant...

Everything to her, and *nothing* to him.

Was it possible that he'd felt nothing? That the bond she would've sworn they'd forged had only been in her head?

With no experience for comparison, she clenched her hands in her lap, turned to Maddox, and spewed the details of what had transpired between her and Gideon. The intimate conversations, the intense lovemaking. How he'd broken his pseudo Vegas *what happens on the boat stays on the boat* rule by sleeping with her in the hotel. The way he'd held her, the tender affection he'd showered on her.

When she finished talking, an awkward silence ensued.

Did she make a mistake by telling her? "What do you think?" Willow asked.

Maddox stiffened. "Gideon is my best friend. A brother in every sense besides blood. Not once in the nights he slept on my sofa after his wife died or when I helped him pack that bitch's stuff—sorry to speak ill of the dead—did he tell me she'd cheated for two years. And had filed for divorce."

A pang of guilt stabbed Willow for divulging the specifics, but the only way to test her theory was by sharing some of what they'd discussed to see if it held the sacred value she'd assigned to it.

She didn't need to get into the granular details of his other secrets, violating the trust he had put in her further, even though he was acting like the biggest jerk.

"Why would he share personal things with me if he didn't care? Why say all those sweet things to me in the hotel? Why call me his starling?" Why end it in a parking lot, like she was disposable? "Do you think it was just…good sex?"

"Hell no, I don't. Sounds like it was a lot more. For both of you."

Willow should've been relieved at Maddox's answer. Her instincts about Gideon were right. But she had to beat back tears. She refused to dissolve into a pitiful mess, not in front of hardcore, tough-as-nails Maddox. Willow could use an ounce of her strength.

Who was she kidding? She'd settle for a single gram.

"Should I go to his place and see him?" Willow asked.

"No, no. Absolutely not."

"But why?"

"Give this thing between you and him a chance to settle."

"For how long? A day? Should I go talk to him tomorrow night?"

"Tomorrow, Gideon and Castle are driving to Norfolk to pick up Hannah Davis. She gets back from a cruise, and he wants to make sure she gets home safely. Daedalus found out about her and threatened to harm her."

"Oh no."

"Hannah is fine, and Daedalus is dead. Gideon is taking precautions." Maddox glanced at Willow. "How would you feel if when you saw him again, you two tumbled into bed, had earth-shattering sex and a lovey-dovey moment, and the result was still the same?"

Willow winced, unable to digest that possibility.

"Exactly. Do *not* go see him."

"What am I supposed to do?"

"Take a few days off to spend with your dad. Try a little self-care. Pick up the pieces, one day at a time. I know how badly it can hurt, believe me. Cole and I put each other through the grinder. I understand how shitty you might feel. I'll help you through it any way I can." She flashed a sad smile. "We're also going to need a big bottle of wine."

47

MARTINSBURG, WEST VIRGINIA
TUESDAY, JULY 9, 1:10 PM EDT

Hannah's farmhouse looked exactly the way she'd described it to Gideon. Peaceful. Sweet air caressing the grass. Birds soaring across a bright, cloudless sky. A place you could take long walks through the thick woods, camp out in a chair on the porch and read a book. Hell, setting foot inside her cozy home tempted him to take a nap. And he never napped.

Then again, it was probably the painkillers, lack of sleep, running off the dredges of an adrenaline cocktail, and the blood loss that made him want some shut-eye. The doctor had also said dehydration. Good thing Castle was driving.

They got Hannah settled, helped her put away groceries, checked out the house to be on the safe side, and had been persuaded to stay for a homecooked lunch.

"Wow. Your fried chicken is better than my mother's," Castle said. "Just don't tell her I said that."

"Don't worry," Hannah said, giving that easy smile of hers. "I'm pretty good at keeping secrets."

"Thanks for cooking." Gideon put his hand on hers.

"It's been ages since you let me cook for you." She cupped his face with her other hand. "The pleasure was all mine."

"I'll do the dishes and clean up." Castle stood, collecting plates from the dining room table. "Please don't argue," he said when Hannah started to protest. "You'll only waste your breath, and in the end, I'll win."

Gideon raised his brows, giving her a look of warning.

Hannah smiled. "I can tell when I've been beaten. Thank you."

Castle went into the kitchen, leaving them alone. The water ran, and dishes clattered in the sink.

"How are you doing, Gideon?" Her tone was warm and soft. "And I don't mean your injuries. Are you okay?"

Just missing a heart. I ripped it out and threw it away because I'm an idiot. Otherwise, I'm fine. "I'm good. Everything's good. I was just worried about you."

"What's wrong, honey? Don't bother lying."

Hannah'd had a sixth sense about Gideon when he was little. She'd known when to leave him alone and give him space while he hid out in her house and when to get him talking over hot chocolate.

"What makes you think something's wrong?" Bluffing was second nature to him. It wasn't in him to confess outright.

"You said good twice." She smothered a laugh. "Once for me, and once to convince yourself. What's troubling you? The job?" She searched his face. "A woman? Please tell me there's a woman in your life." Hannah pressed her palms together in prayer.

"I messed up. Pushed her away, but..." Fixing it was easier said than done.

"But what?" She took his hand in both of hers.

"Did you ever regret marrying Ben? I mean, did you

ever want a guy with a normal job, who didn't force you to worry while he was out doing something dangerous?"

She sighed. "Honey, not marrying Ben would've been the biggest mistake of my life. I knew what he did, and his job was a part of him. I loved all of him, even the tough, scary bits I had to learn to accept."

"Hannah, she's young. She could find a decent guy to give her a normal life."

"First, you're better than a decent guy. You're a great one. Trust me." Hannah nodded for emphasis. "Second, do you really want her loving another man?"

Fresh anguish bled through him. He'd rather endure a slow, painful death. Actually, he'd rather strip the flesh from the other dude's bones.

"I didn't think so. Gideon, the heart wants what it wants. There's seldom a choice. And don't let others dictate what's normal for you. People thought something was wrong with Ben and me or our marriage because we didn't want kids, but we were happy, just the two of us. We created the life we wanted. But then you came along, and you redefined our lives and our sense of normal."

His abnormal-normal childhood had love in it and had been made safe because of Ben and Hannah. He wouldn't have traded it for a cookie-cutter one.

"Do you love her?" Hannah asked.

More than he'd ever loved anyone. Willow gave him a haven, where being seen, being *known*, wasn't terrifying but comforting. He'd die for her, kill for her, but most of all, he wanted to live for her and give her all of himself in the only dysfunctional way he knew how.

"Yeah, I love her." He missed her so much, it was a

physical ache. Pretty scary for a guy who thrived on solitude.

"Does she love you?"

He blew out a heavy breath. "If she did, she doesn't anymore. Pretty sure she hates me now."

A soothing chuckle rolled from Hannah. "You men are such idiots sometimes. There's a reason people say there's a fine line between love and hate. Want some advice?"

He was in no position to turn any down. "Sure."

"Swallow your pride. Release your fear. Grow a super-sized pair and go get her back. For once in your life, give real love a chance and go *all the way*."

VIENNA, VIRGINIA
FRIDAY, JULY 12, 9:00 P.M. EDT

Gideon parked his vehicle in front of Maddox's condo. Apparently growing a supersized pair and learning how not to be a dumbass was easier in theory than practice. Gideon had run on autopilot, numb, waiting for Willow to turn up at work. He hadn't eaten or slept, replenishing his system in the evenings with beer. At work, he'd lacked focus.

Nothing had steadied his mind. Not knowing those mercs were behind bars and being investigated. Not the fallout from Daedalus—evidence on fifty people, spies around the world who had worked for him was delivered to the media, including files on the attorney general and the vice chair of the Senate Intelligence Committee. Amanda had called it Daedalus's insurance policy—to burn his assets in the event something happened to him—when Maddox visited her in a maximum-security lockup. Not the Hole.

Nothing had been leaked about the Gray Box. Maybe that megalomaniac hadn't prearranged anything, and Gideon hadn't given him the chance to make good on the promise.

The chief failed to get Doc into Fort Detrick. Gideon had pitched in to help search for the government contractor responsible for weaponizing biological agents and those who hijacked the shipment from behind a desk, to no avail. He should've been worried about how nasty Z-1984 might be or the potential death toll. Or why the government repeatedly denied the bioweapon shipment had ever existed—and to Sanborn of all people.

Willow had commandeered his thoughts, had his head spinning. He snuck glimpses of her workstation once an hour, as if hoping she'd materialize.

Asking Maddox how long Willow would be out hadn't been an option. His best friend wouldn't speak to him, only meeting his eyes long enough to shoot him a disgusted glare.

"Willow put in for a couple of weeks off to spend time with her father," Sanborn had told him when he finally caved and asked. "She has a ton of leave saved and didn't sound like herself. I think she needs it."

Weeks off? Gideon had been so appalled with himself after the way he'd handled things with her that he couldn't look in the mirror. God, he wanted a life—a real one with her, even though he didn't deserve it. But he owed her the truth and the ability to choose what *she* wanted.

A life with him, gritty downside included, or one without him.

He sat in the new truck he'd traded the Jeep in for. He'd held onto the past for so long, unsure why, but it was time to let it go.

Telling Willow the truth about how he felt was the right thing to do. She'd always been honest with him, and she deserved no less in return. The idea that she might forgive what he'd done and still choose him elated and sickened him at the same time.

How could he not want her to have a perfect life? If he was a better man, he'd let her find happiness with someone else. *Selfish bastard.*

At least Gideon could be a smarter one, learn from his mistakes, and have a life worth living.

Cole's black Kawasaki Ninja superbike was in front of the building.

Gideon contemplated waiting until after Cole and Maddox left, but he needed to face the music. Ten minutes passed. Twenty.

He wiped his sweaty palms on his pants, grabbed the wrapped jewelry box, and got out of the truck, leaving the cane he needed for the next week behind. Pulse racing like he was on a mission, he limped inside the building, grabbing the door as someone came out, then hobbled up the stairs and to Maddox's front door.

He rang the bell and waited.

Cole opened the door. Shock blanketed his face. "Whoa." He closed the door to a crack and whispered, "He-who-should-not-be-named should not be here."

"I need to see her." For some reason, Gideon whispered back.

"Not happening. Maddox wants to shoot you. In the ass."

Gideon lowered his head in shame. "Yeah, I gathered."

"Who is it, hon?" Maddox asked from inside.

"Jehovah's Witness. Give me a sec." Cole stepped into the hall, closing the door.

"I fucked up." Better to cut straight to it.

"Big time, buddy." Cole dragged a hand through his long, inky hair and folded his arms across his sturdy chest. The guy was cut like a brawler, lethal as a scalpel, but he lit up Maddox's life like a football stadium.

"Just give Willow a message. Tell her—"

"Noooo." Cole shook his head. "You're not dragging me down with you."

The door swung open. Maddox stiffened at the sight of Gideon and cut her eyes to Cole. "What's he doing here?"

"He's leaving." Cole raised his hands, urging her to go back inside.

"I'm not leaving until I talk to Willow." Gideon stood his ground.

Maddox put her hands on her hips, avoiding his gaze. "Tell him to leave or I'm getting my gun. Better yet, hon, why not knock some sense into him with your fists?"

"I messed up," Gideon said. "I'm here to fix it. I need to talk to her."

Cole looked between him and Maddox like a referee poised to throw a flag.

"Tell this selfish moron this isn't about what he needs. Willow has lost everything. Her father is in the hospital. The last thing *she* needs right now is to see him."

"Willow is everything to me." Gideon took a step closer, but Cole waltzed in front of him, blocking his path. "With her, I want to go *all the way*."

Maddox recoiled, her gaze pinning him. "You? All the way?"

He nodded. His best friend didn't know how significant the phrase was but knew he meant serious business. "If she'll still have me. If not, I won't bother her again." He leaned around Cole and handed Maddox the jewelry box. "Tell her I want to talk. If she wants me to leave, I will."

She snatched the gift. "This isn't a ring box, Mr. All-The-Way."

"Please, give it to her."

"If she decides to see you, admit you're an idiot. A damn fool. And you need to be on your knees when you apologize."

"Understood." Swallowing his nerves, he stuffed his hands into his pockets.

Willow finished hanging up her new clothes from the shopping trip with Maddox and Cole. They'd both been amazing.

The devastation of losing all her possessions was still hard to believe, but the insurance company promised to work quickly to issue a check. She was grateful her father was out of the coma now and talking. The hospital wanted to hold him a little longer to monitor his Hodgkin's, but he was officially on the mend.

She was also thankful for the friendship she'd never expected. Maddox and Cole treated her like she fit in, belonged.

Maddox had loaned Willow her car. After she spent the day with her father at the hospital, she met with Maddox and Cole every night for dinner. Sometimes they went shopping, using a *sorry-your-house-burned-down* fund collected at the Gray Box, and Maddox even took her to a ritzy salon to get her hair dyed back to her normal color.

They never talked about Gideon, although he was always on her mind. No pressure. No questions. Just comfort. Space when she needed it. A patient ear when she was ready.

The evening she'd broken down, weeping uncontrollably, and had shared what her last night with Gideon in the hotel had been like, Maddox had been the best listener, crying too and plying Willow with wine.

A knock at the bedroom door pulled her from her thoughts. "Yep."

Maddox and Cole eased inside the room, their faces grave.

"Did the hospital call? Did something happen to my father?"

"No," Maddox said. "Gideon is here."

Willow's lungs tightened. She clutched her throat and sat on the bed, needing something solid beneath her before she hit the floor. "What does he want?"

"To talk to you." Maddox sat beside her and handed her a small, square box.

Willow took the present and stared at it, her chest aching with each breath.

"You don't have to open it." Cole leaned against the doorjamb. "I'm happy to throw it in his face and give him a beatdown for you. But what's inside might sway your thoughts."

"Why do men think they can buy us with jewelry?" Maddox asked.

"He's not trying to buy her. He's trying to apologize."

Maddox rolled her eyes as she huffed.

"I'm on your side." Cole glanced between them. "I'm on *Willow's* side. Not his. I'm only saying he probably put thought into it."

Taking a breath, Willow untied the white bow and peeled off the red wrapping. A velvet box tickled her fingers. She didn't want jewelry but did want to know what was inside, so she opened it.

A necklace with a delicate chain. The pendant was a black bird made of darkened sterling silver, the intricate wings covered with pavé diamonds and a large diamond—at least a carat—set as the eye. In the bird's breast, at the heart, was a single pearl.

It had a faint pink iridescence like her mother's vintage choker, but it couldn't possibly be the same.

"Wow," Maddox said in a whisper. "Looks vintage."

Cole peered over. "Looks expensive."

"It's a starling." Hope bloomed inside Willow, but she was terrified to let herself expect anything other than an apology.

"His pet name for you from the boat. Awww." Maddox put a hand to her chest. "Okay, he put thought into it. The pendant was probably tough to find, but it doesn't excuse how he hurt you."

Having Maddox and Cole in her corner warmed her with comfort she'd only known from her parents. And, for a moment, from Gideon.

"Why would he give me this?" *We don't fit.* The words were nailed to her bleeding heart.

"I think he'll tell you," Maddox said, "if you talk to him."

Willow pinched the back of her hand, debating. Gideon had hurt her like no one else. And he'd waited four days to see her. *The gall.*

What was she supposed to say? What was she supposed to do? Fall into his arms and pretend he hadn't stomped on her heart?

"You can keep the necklace. Doesn't mean you have to see him," Maddox said.

Oh no, she wanted to see him. Clutching the bird in her palm, Willow strode to the closed front door. She hesitated, gathering her choppy thoughts, and opened it.

Gideon turned and met her eyes. Heat suffused her at the sight of his clean-shaven face and trimmed hair. Just being near him made her calmer, had her softening. But she refused to collapse into his arms, regardless of what he said.

"You changed your hair back to chocolate brown." He smiled. "God, you're beautiful."

Her belly quivered like watery Jell-O. "The necklace is beautiful. But I don't want it." She extended her hand with the starling in her palm.

He edged closer. Awkward, hesitant, as if his guard was down. He cupped her trembling hand, wrapping her fingers around the bird. "Please, keep it."

"Haven't you hurt me enough?" She'd hit the crest of this roller coaster of suffering and had been on the downward slide to dark emptiness. Now this. "Why torture me?"

"The pearl is from your mom's necklace. I picked some up from the street and managed to hang on to three. I found the bird in this little jewelry shop, and the owner only had time to work one pearl into the body. Rush job after I explained I was trying to make amends and said money was no object. I thought it'd make you happy, not torture you."

The gesture left her speechless. No one had ever done anything so considerate. Or romantic. She didn't know what to say, what to do.

His eyes met hers, soft and warm. "I lied. In the parking lot, when you asked about us."

Her mind swam, her heart trapped in the heavy swell of hating him and loving him.

He lowered to his knees, slowly, wincing, and clutched her hips.

"What happened to you? Everyone told me you were okay. Are you badly hurt?"

"That doesn't matter. I get hurt and I heal. What's important is that I'm sorry I hurt you. I was an idiot and blinded by my past failures. I was afraid that you wanted me and terrified I'd disappoint you. You may never forgive me, but you need to know. It was all real for me too."

Disbelief slid through her, but it quickly gave way to relief. Profound relief that made her tingle.

"You and I are a perfect fit. I don't want to lose you, Willow."

It'd been real. She wasn't wrong; she hadn't misread him. Hadn't misconstrued what they'd shared. But she was pissed.

"Stand up, Gideon. I never wanted you on your knees. I wanted you at my side. Why wait four days to make it right?"

She helped him up from the floor, wanting to hug him, but held back, waiting for an explanation.

"I needed to be sure."

"Of your feelings?" They'd only been together a handful of days, yet she'd been sure of her heart.

He ran his hand over her hair. "I can't pinpoint the exact moment I fell in love with you, but I've been certain since the boat. I love you."

For a moment, she forgot to breathe. "Say that again."

"I love you, Willow Harper." He caressed her cheek, and it was as though her heart sprouted wings and fluttered in her chest. "I needed to be sure that if you felt the same and I asked you to build a life with me, it would be the right thing."

"How could it be wrong?" Build a life with him?

Dazed, she let the words sink in, petrified he might not mean what she thought.

"You know how hard and dangerous this job is. I didn't want you wasting your life worrying about me out in the field, fretting, unable to sleep at night."

Smiling, she pressed her hand to his smooth cheek and brought his lips to hers. "Loving you would never be a waste, no matter what happens. You think I'm fragile, but I'm not weak."

"You're strong and courageous. I just didn't want to put you through that. You deserve a sweet man who does sweet things. Works nine to five. Leaves lovey-dovey notes in secret places for you to find. Plans surprises. Brings you flowers."

"I'll worry less knowing the details of your missions. I don't work nine to five, and I'm sometimes on back-to-back assignments. Why hide notes? I'd rather you tell me to my face what you feel." She held up the necklace. "This is a surprise. And for the record, I'm allergic."

"To diamonds?"

"Flowers. Sneezing, watery eyes. Same with perfume."

He cupped her jaw. "You're missing the point."

"No, you are. I don't want a sweet man who does sweet things. I want a strong man who's sweet on me. I deserve honesty and passion and the freedom to be myself, at ease with the right guy. With you."

"You need to know upfront what you're getting with me. I don't have a good track record when it comes to making others happy."

She grinned, suppressing a laugh at how the man could be so smart yet so clueless. "The point of loving someone isn't to be made happy by it. The point is to be better because of it. It's not your job to make me happy—that's mine." She'd learned a lot about love watching and listening to her parents. "And I'm happier with you than without you."

"You make me want to be worthy of you." His breath caressed her mouth.

How bizarre to think that the most amazing, beautiful man was worried about not being good enough. He might look like a god and have the powers of one, but he was mortal and flawed. And she loved him. "Gideon, you already are worthy."

"If you're right, then one day, I hope you'll consider marrying me."

She tensed, but he pulled her flush against him. The heat from his powerful body comforted her, seeping into her skin, her bones. Deeper.

"You don't have to promise me anything," she said.

"Yes, I do." He brushed his lips across hers and kissed her with such raw tenderness that her belly somersaulted. "I can be disagreeable sometimes and a bit of a control freak."

She nodded. "I know. But we both have issues."

Pressing his forehead to hers, he stared in her eyes. "I swear to give all of myself. Not hold back. I'll never leave and never push you away again."

The solemn words thundered through her, sealing something precious between them. She knew he meant it. They belonged to each other.

"I don't do plants and pets," he said, "but if you want kids down the road, I'd like a family with you. No rush. I think I might have daddy issues to work through first."

Willow had never known if she'd ever have a real boyfriend, but she'd always wanted what her parents had. Love. Trust. Unconditional acceptance. A family.

"I love you, Gideon, but I'm a package deal with my dad."

"Goes without saying. I'm already hatching a plan to smuggle in cheeseburgers and sneak him whiskey."

She slapped his chest. "Don't you dare."

"How about we start with sorting out living arrangements? I can help you find a new place with your dad. Or you two could move into my townhouse. I can make it handicap accessible. Or we find something new together. Whatever you want. No pressure."

She melted against him. This was happening. Gideon Stone loved her and wanted to build a life with her. Living with him was worth braving her father's wrath.

"I want a fresh start. Let's find a house for the three of us, something close to work."

"Done."

"I want you to let go of the past. And the Jeep."

He pressed the alarm button on a remote key. A faint horn tooted. "Done."

She chuckled. Wow, he'd been busy. "And I want you to learn how to dance."

Sighing, he tightened his arms around her, squeezing. "You're a tough negotiator. But anything you want that's in my power to give is yours. Consider it done."

"Who is going to square this away with my dad? He's old-fashioned. He'll give us a hard time about living together." Her dad would go on a tirade. Every single day. Maybe twice a day.

"I'll handle your father. As long as he's not holding a baseball bat." Gideon laughed. The husky sound lit up her heart, and she smiled.

He kissed her, squeezing her body to his, lifting her feet from the floor. Her lungs burned from the lack of air, heart pounding, skin on fire from the sweet heat of his touch.

Side by side, they'd survived the worst—stronger together than apart.

This love was worth everything, and neither one of them would ever let go.

EPILOGUE

Willow flipped pancakes on the griddle and spooned scrambled eggs from a pan into a serving bowl. Every time she strolled into the lavish gourmet kitchen, she was reminded of Gideon's generosity and love. He'd found this house, venturing above their price range since nothing else they'd seen had been right for them.

It was bigger than they needed, but they'd both agreed they'd grow into it.

The wraparound porch led out to a picturesque fenced yard she could see from the large kitchen windows. There were five bedrooms, a finished basement, and a second master on the ground floor that was perfect for her dad. She'd fallen in love with the space, abundance of natural light, and proximity to work but fretted over the cost.

Gideon had pushed for a speedy close. He'd rallied the troops to help him install a ramp at the front of the house, make her father's bathroom handicap accessible, and knock out a wall to open the family room to the kitchen, working everyone to exhaustion to get things done quickly.

Hand in hand, they'd picked out the Carrara marble for the countertops, new appliances, furniture, and paint colors. The kitchen, like the rest of the house, was a symbol of the life they were building together. As partners.

Gideon came up behind her, swiping a piece of bacon, and nipped the junction between her neck and shoulder.

"Two minutes." She kissed him, enjoying the taste of his mouth. "Then we can eat."

"I'm starving," her dad said from the spacious family room off the kitchen. "And prepare yourself, Warden. I'm going to have three slices of bacon. Don't give me a hard time."

Shaking her head, Willow sighed. "One slice, if you agree to try the vegan sausage."

"I'm the senior citizen, but I'd swear you're the one hard of hearing. I said three."

Gideon roped his arms around Willow's waist, his broad hands teasing her stomach. "Two is a nice compromise. Plus one fake sausage."

Her dad grumbled. "Fine. And coffee. Supersized, with cream."

Gideon squeezed her, his head against her hair, then took an oversized mug from the glass-front cabinet and poured coffee.

"A splash of cream," Willow whispered, plating the pancakes.

Smiling, he nodded. They had an unspoken code of conduct. Gideon was her dad's ally, slipping him treats and the occasional sip of whiskey, negotiating deals, but he never crossed the line to excess.

Hannah, Gideon's surrogate mom, laughed, pouring the fresh-squeezed orange juice into a pitcher. It had been nice having female company in the new house for the past week and hearing pleasant stories about Gideon as a child. Hannah lived less than two hours away, but when Willow had suggested she stay over for a few days to spare her the drive, Hannah had eagerly agreed.

Her dad took to Hannah immediately, the two bonding over music and movies.

"After getting to know your dad," Hannah said, "I'm surprised he hasn't griped about you two living together."

"Oh, at first, he did." Willow took out the waffles from the built-in warmer drawer. It was extra work making both pancakes and waffles, but Gideon preferred the former, her father the latter, and she didn't mind. Besides, Gideon was on dirty dishes duty and would grill dinner later.

"Every day." Her dad wheeled into the kitchen. "I reminded that boy of three things: be good to my daughter, I want a ring on her hand, and I'm not too old to use my baseball bat."

Hannah's laugh deepened. "Well, Gideon, you did an outstanding job with the engagement ring. Absolutely gorgeous."

Willow held up her left hand, admiring it. A rose-gold band sat on her finger with two pearls surrounded by an infinity loop of diamonds. Perfection. "The pearls are from my mother's necklace. I used to wear it all the time. The only thing of hers I had left, but it broke." She put a hand to her throat, touching the jeweled starling, and refused to dwell on the bitter memory. "But Gideon found three."

The pearls gave the ring a special meaning, as though her mother was part of everything.

"Incredibly sweet, Gideon." Hannah patted his shoulder.

"I had to ask the jeweler to rush the custom order," he

said. "Her dad made me sleep in the guest room in the basement and demanded Willow promise—"

"No boys in her room until the engagement was official," her dad finished.

Willow cringed from embarrassment. With her dad camped out in the bedroom on the main floor and her in the upstairs master, he had patrolled throughout the night and slept during the day, like a vampire, to ensure Gideon didn't get past him.

Little had her dad realized that Gideon could've gone upstairs at any time, stealthy as a grim reaper, but he hadn't, out of respect.

They'd still found creative ways to be together outside the house. A loophole, Gideon had called it, and sneaking around had been fun.

"I'm glad you two found happiness together." Hannah grabbed the eggs and veggie sausage from the gleaming counter and helped Willow set breakfast on the table. "And I'm grateful you're letting me share in it."

Willow was the grateful one. With Hannah being a retired nurse an easy drive away, she agreed to help with her father whenever needed, pitched in cooking, and showed her fantastic healthy recipes. Even her dad thrived from Hannah's jovial presence, complaining less and laughing more.

Gideon and her dad exchanged a weird look and nod. Hannah sat, smiling brightly, as Willow's dad hit a button on the universal remote.

Frankie Valli's "Can't Take My Eyes Off You" played on the surround speakers. Willow still missed the things that had been destroyed in the fire, like her dad's records, but the loss hurt less and less each day.

"Dad, what are you doing? You only listen to this when you cook, and you haven't cooked in years."

"Sometimes a song needs to be passed on."

Gideon whisked Willow into his arms. "I have a surprise before we eat."

He took her right hand, curling an arm around her waist, and swayed to the beat. His feet shuffled around the kitchen in seamless strides, his eyes locked on hers.

Love radiated in the scorching intensity of that look. Penetrated and suffused her, burning so hot, it was as though she'd swallowed the sun. "You learned to dance?"

Smiling, he threw his hips into a rock backward, bringing her with him, leading every step of the way. "Anything for you. My one and only."

Happiness flooded her, like millions of champagne bubbles in her veins. This beautiful man was hers. Loved her. Saw her. Accepted her. Would do anything for her.

He spun her out to the side, brought her back into his body, and in a simple underarm turn, twirled her again with the polish of a pro.

"Show-off," she said, smiling.

Holding her close, he mouthed her favorite part, *I love you, baby*. He stared at her as if nothing else existed, and she was equally enthralled by him. His touch. His piercing blue eyes. His devastating smile. The sound of his laughter.

The house phone rang, shattering their bliss.

They both glanced at it. Only the Gray Box had the house number.

"We don't answer until after our song," he said, spinning her again.

Work had always come first, and she never complained,

but at that moment, she wanted to rip the phone from the wall.

The ringing stopped.

Both their cell phones buzzed, vibrating in tandem across the slick countertop.

She tensed in his arms. Couldn't the world not fall apart long enough for them to enjoy their happiness?

As the song ended, he brushed his thumb across her furrowed brow and kissed her.

Their cellphones went off again.

Gideon answered his. "What?"

"Must be important," her dad said. "It's Saturday."

Hannah eyed Willow and smiled but looked sad, as if she understood.

"Fine. We'll be there in twenty minutes." Gideon hung up. "There was a hit on your keyword search."

After Doc had finally gotten useless answers at Fort Detrick, Willow had created a program that searched for specific keywords in any online communication. Figuring out which keywords to use that would get them closer to the stolen bioweapons without pinging millions of irrelevant messages had been painstaking.

"Something legitimate this time?"

He brought her back into his arms, pressing his mouth to her ear. "Z-1984."

Didn't get more legitimate than that.

"First," he said, "I want a do-over on my dance. Uninterrupted."

This was their first credible hit in nine weeks and he wanted to dance? "We should leave. It's important."

"There's always something important. Urgent. Dire.

We don't get any other kind of mission. But you're more important to me. So is what we have. We have to grab moments like these when we can. One more song, then we go. What do you say?"

Losing her mother at an early age, coming close to death herself more than once, and almost losing Gideon had taught her not to take one second for granted. The Gray Box could wait an extra three minutes and fourteen seconds. "Play it again, Dad."

Gideon scooped her up in a bear hug, twirling her in the kitchen. "I can't wait to marry you."

"Now, that's music to my ears!" Her dad chuckled, his body shaking with laughter, and reached for the bacon.

Hannah smiled, pulling the plate from his grasp.

They swayed in the kitchen to their new song, in their new house, singing the lyrics to each other, and glorying in every precious second.

AUTHOR'S NOTE

I love the Washington metropolitan area, which I currently call home. If you are familiar with the Capital Beltway, you might notice I altered some locations and took a few liberties with minor details to suit the flow of the story. I did my best to retain as much authenticity as possible to depict the richness, diversity, and energy of the DMV (DC, Maryland, Virginia).

ACKNOWLEDGMENTS

Thank you to the men and women who fight to protect our freedom. Your sacrifices are appreciated.

Without the support and love of my biggest cheerleaders, my husband and two kiddos, I wouldn't have been able to write this book. I'm so grateful for your belief in me.

Publishing a book is a collaborative effort. Thank you to Mary Altman for backing this series and for giving such insightful editorial guidance. It's a blessing to have an editor who gets your voice and shares your vision. You have been an amazing, protective partner on this series, and I appreciate you more than you know.

Thanks to my agent, Sara Megibow, who is always an incredible source of support, encouragement, and advice, all of which I would be lost without.

To the entire team at Sourcebooks, you really do make dreams come true. Thank you for all the hard work you put into publishing books.

Finally, thanks to the readers for picking up this book and opening your hearts to my characters. Your support is everything.

ALSO BY JUNO RUSHDAN

Final Hour
Every Last Breath
Nothing to Fear

Turn the Tide romantic suspense anthology